D1176741

T R U S T

BOOKS BY MARY FLANAGAN:

Bad Girls

Trust

MARY FLANAGAN

TRUST

PANTHEON BOOKS   NEW YORK

First Pantheon Paperback Edition

Copyright © 1987 by Mary Flanagan

All rights reserved under International and Pan-American Copyright
Conventions. Published in the United States by Pantheon Books, a division of Random House, Inc., New York. Originally published in Great
Britain in 1987 by Bloomsbury Publishing Ltd., and in the United States
by Atheneum in 1988.

Library of Congress Cataloging-in-Publication Data

Flanagan, Mary.
Trust.
(Pantheon modern writers)
I. Title.   II. Series.
PS3556.L32T7   1989   813'.54   88-43124
ISBN 0-679-72281-5

Manufactured in the United States of America

FOR MY FATHER

'One of us simply has to have faith in the other.'

'Very well; I will answer you with all the frankness you have just been representing as a duty: why should it be my lot to *have* faith?'

'Because the nature of things will have it so.'

Stendhal, *Lucien Leuwen*

I

·························

ELEANOR

one

Eleanor Linnane arrived fifteen minutes late for her appointment at Lincoln's Inn Fields. Charles Bevan had expected her to be even later. She threw aside her coat and collapsed into a leather armchair. She took him in. 'Getting fat,' she thought, 'damned classy layout, though,' then bolted ahead with her business.

'I don't see that this need concern anyone but you and me.'

The Anglicized tone didn't quite suit. Never had, really, in Charles's opinion. As with the new clothes, Eleanor and the language had not yet found each other's natural contours. The accent was something she threw over herself like this veneer of questionable chic – Isis beneath the Veil. Was she aware of how he would have liked to lift that Veil; even, with her delighted permission of course, rend the thing asunder?

'Naturally,' he replied from behind a veil of his own. 'But Jason – he's not to know? Not anything?' He tested her, although he was certain of her determination to stick to the principles of the document which now lay between them on his desk.

'Never.' She leaned towards him, that seldom-absent note of tension in her voice. 'Besides, you said only two trustees are necessary for a minor.'

'I said two trustees are necessary for a minor. Quite different. At any rate, dear Eleanor, please don't distress yourself. I understand your wishes and I must comply with them. Secrecy is absolutely binding between lawyer and client. He may disclose nothing of the client's affairs. It is called privileged information, the privilege being that of the client not the lawyer.' He spoke slowly, imparting a roll to the r's in distress and privilege. The sound reminded Eleanor of her favourite cat, long since run down and consigned to the frozen earth.

'What if you die?'

The question startled him. Obviously they were not going to adopt the usual procedure which was now so natural to him as to be automatic.

'Then the executor of my estate would become a trustee in my place. "By Representation." But we're rather jumping ahead.'

'I know, I know. I'm sorry.' She ran a hand through her hectic hair, the colour of which, over the past year, had turned from vibrant red to an auburn fading as fast as the leaves outside the window. The gesture sent a dozen silver bangles clanking over her bare, freckled arm.

'How thin she is,' thought Charles. 'Surely she wasn't always this thin.' He remembered her in Sussex where she had lived with Jason until four months ago. Never out of jeans and wellies. Charming. Slender, yes. But not this teetering on the edge of anorexia nervosa.

Down came the bangles with a clatter as she pushed forward the sleeve of her pink jumper and leaned both elbows aggressively on his desk. She was always twitching and shifting. One could never get hold of her, force her for a moment to take note of one, actually to focus on another human being long enough to perceive the warm appreciation with which that human being was regarding her.

She beamed him the smile she beamed for all. But her green eyes, he could see over the top of his half-lenses, were full of pain.

'Charles, I trust you. Nothing to do with privileged information,' she waved the bracelets about. 'Everyone believes in you and wants your advice. You're an honourable man – and an honoured one. It's all very rare and old-fashioned. Even at the age of – how old are you, Charles?'

'Eleanor, please . . .'

'Well, I happen to know you're barely forty. Anyway, what I'm saying is that I did not come to you because you're the Blacks' lawyer or the Facers' lawyer or the van Zuptens's lawyer. I've asked you to do this for me because I know you're a worthy man. I knew the second I met you.'

Heavens, how she ran on. Still, Charles Bevan, worthy man, was also a mildly conceited man. It was one of his few little failings. He basked in the woman's approval while censuring her lack of restraint.

'Right away I was aware of your delicacy . . .'

Still at it. Aware as she supposedly was, could she not see, damn her, what was, at the moment, the most obvious of his attributes? At any rate, they must commence a definite forward movement, make a few firm decisions. Simon was due at five.

'Charles, I swear to you' – Lord, the melodrama – 'I wouldn't have asked anyone else to make this thing for me – this pact!' She flung out a hand, at the end of which dangled a glove, in the direction of the document and sent eight pieces of legal paper fluttering on to the floor. Charles rose and stooped to pick them up. He was getting slow, eating too well and too often, making too much money. Apologizing, Eleanor rushed to assist him. There they were, both of them, down on their knees on the Turkish carpet.

'What does this mean – "accumulated?" ' She pointed to clause eight. Why would she not allow him to steer her gently through it with him worthily at the helm? But he was too good-natured not to answer her question immediately.

'Until Clover is eighteen, the money must be looked after. Obviously it will have to be invested, and the investment will produce income. With the income one of two things can be done. It can be what we call accumulated, which I think is what you want, but if necessary it would be possible to pay out the income to help her in any way while she's at school. You see. Hmmm?'

'Then with accumulation the money is just kept quiet.'

'Yes. Accumulation means that the income is simply added to the main fund and reinvested as it is received. The result would be that the final amount she would get would be the value of the investments originally made plus the value of all the incomes reinvested. Is that all right?'

'That's the general idea, I guess.' The American accent slipped through.

Charles found it wonderfully amusing to be nestled haunch by haunch with the lovely if loony Eleanor on the £2,000 rug Anthea had bought him for his birthday. (It was one of his outstanding qualities that his amusement could run a parallel course with his longings and frustrations.) The rug was not to his taste. And it was nowhere near as old as Anthea supposed it to be. She had been seduced into the transaction by the blandishments of Felix Koning. Snake Koning notwithstanding, Charles had warmly approved his wife's gift. In his quiet way he made the most of what merits it did possess, and passed over its obvious flaws. Anthea was easily hurt.

The heel of his shoe rubbed briefly against the soft leather of Eleanor's boot. Why did she not come to him, naturally and simply like a cat, and let him stroke her? It was all he wanted and it was what she needed, badly. She sat down on the carpet and pulled her long legs up under her woollen skirt. She was looking at him, actually looking at him, instead of talking at him. Calmly, he returned her gaze. Her wide-apart eyes, her face, the outline of her graceful, wasted frame showed him a psychic damage that could never be repaired.

'This is all for Clover,' she snapped, as though he were plotting to contradict her. 'Only for Clover.'

'Poor love,' he wanted to say. Instead he remarked gravely, 'You've been through a frightful ordeal.'

She required, he knew, the satisfaction of having that ordeal verified. She required it over and over. No, darling, no one has suffered as you have. For a minute he appeased her anger and her hunger and her hate. But they erupted again.

'Why the hell do you keep asking me about Jason? How do you think I could ever change my mind?'

He was tempted to submit that people had been known to do so, and after the most violent and prolonged attestations to the contrary, especially people of her own delightful sex. But he kept quiet and let her burn herself out.

'You think I'm a vacillating female.' She had read his thoughts. He was afraid she was going to spit. (Oh you irksome Irishwoman. Fractious, fabulous creature you are.)

'So Jason is to know nothing of our arrangement until Clover has come of age and the money is in fact hers.'

'Yes godammit, for the hundredth time! Jason's to know nothing,' she used her fingers, pushing back one digit with another to stress the vehement enumeration, 'Clover's to know nothing, no one's to know nothing.' She stopped. 'I mean no one but you.'

Charles scrambled, with difficulty, to his feet, offering her his hand. 'My dear,' he said, 'it's only that I want to be clear.'

'Clear!' she snorted. 'Bloody simple-minded, I call it.'

(And you, my precious, deserve a good spanking. Well.)

'Sorry, Charles.' She covered her face with hands, then looked up. She was definitely on something. Anti-depressants, perhaps? Apart from Anthea's sleeping tablets, Charles was unacquainted with such substances, his mild good humour being founded on a mild good health.

Eleanor jumped up and returned to her chair. Her eyes were very bright, and her long hands, too work-worn to match the newly acquired façade, trembled as she lit cigarette after cigarette.

'Shall we proceed?' He fingered the document with intent. 'In a systematic way?'

'Tell me, Charles.' She leaned back. 'Tell me everything.'

He told her, reasonably and automatically in the practised sequence: precise value, investment in dated government stock, gilt-edged –

'*Guilt*-edged?' She smiled.

Dear God, she was being plain silly.

Note for £50,000, today's prices, suitable gilt-edged maturing one week before Clover's eighteenth birthday, guaranteed capital appreciation of 26·5 per cent, guaranteed income on principal fund £5,000 per annum less income tax, current rates (can't speak for the future), net income tax £3,000 assuming no other income, approximately £1,500 every six months to reinvest, £100 in lieu of stamp duty.

Was she paying attention, he wondered. There she sat with her cheque for £50,000 and her broken heart. Reconciliation was impossible, Charles could see that now. Jason would never have her back, in spite of the money; no *because* of the money. That was the whole maddening point. Then there was her own well-grounded fear of progressive isolation which she would, he supposed, attempt to stave off with the remainder of that very money. Or would she? He watched her search her handbag for a lighter, also new, but thank heavens not monogrammed. Eleanor looked up and he shifted his gaze coolly to Jason Englefield's study for *The Three Virtues*. The drawing had adorned his office for the past two years – a reminder to his clients, he liked to think, of the possibilities held out by both Art and the Law for better things.

Or would she? He sensed in her a tough fibre which he had first noticed on that visit to Sussex. She had a sullen obstinacy. Oh it was there all right, in the contours of her intriguing face. How could something that soft and volatile be at once so adamantine? Hmmmm. Not much doubt of it: here was a ruinous woman made so bloody-minded by grief and predisposition that she might decide to meet the horror straight on; might embrace loneliness not out of masochism or bitterness but out of a conviction that there was nothing else to do. She might even believe that sort of heroism to be now required of her. And he knew Londoners. Damned few people would come to her assistance, unless she spread the money around. And her attitude to the money veered recklessly towards the nihilistic.

When he had finished his worthy steering she smiled at him.

'You're a real winner, aren't you, Charles? A conqueror too in your plum-pudding way.'

He allowed the smile to thrill him mildly. That was the trouble with charm, he thought. Had to be dragged out and exercised at least twice a day like a damned Pekingese. Well, well, do your worst, madam. I'll not prevent and you know it.

'What's all this about income tax?'

'Don't fret. On her eighteenth birthday Clover will be able to reclaim all the tax we've had to pay, and this will, of course, be an additional bonus. Now, have a look at clause ten.'

Why, he wondered, couldn't they just pop into bed together as people do. Most natural thing in the world. Happens all the time like slipping on an icy patch of pavement. Leaves you stunned for a moment, but one scrambles to one's feet and limps more or less cheerfully home. Oh why the hell not? Obviously she was intelligent. Couldn't she see the advantages for both of them? He didn't need her money, in fact he could help her there. But he was forgetting. She didn't want his help; only his conspiracy, only his worthiness. The money she seemed determined to throw away. Correction. She was not squandering it on Clover. That, of all her flailings about in broken-hearted irrationalism, was a calculated blow, meant to strike home in the most drastic way. Such was her intention, he felt sure.

'You think it's monstrous.' She may not give much of a damn about capital appreciation, but she was alarmingly accurate at divining his thoughts.

'On the contrary. I find it generous and loving to an almost inconceivable degree.'

'You don't believe in my love for Clover. No one does. Just because she's not mine.'

He felt himself about to be fastened upon by that indiscriminate anger.

'I believe very much in your love for Clover. I'm convinced of it. It's your wish for revenge that I question, not morally speaking, you understand, but its ultimate effects on all three of you.'

'That's not fair.' (Nothing was fair anymore.) 'You know I hate deception. I tried to be straightforward. I put the proposal to Jason ages ago, as tactfully as possible. He said it would make him feel "peculiar". Wait a while, I said. Think about it and tell me. But nothing. No response. Nothing. Not a letter or a phone call or a thanks it was a nice thought, but . . . Then I realized there never would be a response. And all because of a pride so grotesque that it would deprive his only daughter of financial security. Look, he may want to prevent Clover's having even the most basic advantages. God knows he wants to prevent everything! But am I to permit this criminal negligence simply because Jason in his cherished pride would feel peculiar? I tell you, Charles, it is my duty to Clover to trick him this way. I cannot love her as I do and do otherwise.'

'Well put. Very eloquent. But what about Clover? How do you think she'll react when, on her eighteenth birthday, she is told she is a wealthy woman? What do you think she'll do?'

'Buy her freedom.'

'Ah, you don't believe in her love for her father.'

'Her love for her father,' Eleanor slumped back into the large chair that exaggerated her fragility, 'is something with which I am all too familiar.'

She looked, Charles thought, wholly defeated. That was why she must win. He must help her to win. For a moment he loathed Jason Englefield. Yet he persisted in his subdued argument, aware that the effect of his reason was nil.

'How do you know she won't give all the money to him?'

8

'That's a risk. She's generous by nature. But he'd never take it. It would damage his idea of himself.'

'Then perhaps you don't believe enough in *her* sweet self. You doubt her ability to make her own place – without your money and in spite of her father.'

'She's honest. That means trouble in this horrible world. And she's been caught in the cross-fire of perverse relationships.'

'She appears not to have suffered any mortal wounds.'

'Who can tell, until it's too late? That's why – ' She stopped, tears in her eyes.

'Shall we go on?' He prodded her gently as he would an injured bird.

'OK. How much will all this maturing and appreciating and accumulating come to in the end?'

'Nearly £100,000.'

'Oh God,' she moaned to his surprise, 'who would have believed that I, Eleanor Linnane, reared as a socialist, bred in contempt for the capitalist system, would suddenly, at the age of thirty-five, be worth a disgusting £200,000?'

'All things considered, it is not too vulgarly large a sum.'

She ignored him. 'And be confabulating about unit trusts and reinvestments with a smart London lawyer who guards the interests of the ruling classes.' She was very excited. 'I hate the money. I hate it. All money is tainted.'

'That is true.'

'The minute one has any, one becomes tainted too. That's why there's only one solution: get rid of it. Give it to the most deserving person you know. Save someone.'

Ah, thought Charles, then she is also assuaging her guilt.

'Perhaps your father was thinking similarly when he decided to leave his money to you.' (And perhaps he was assuaging *his* guilt.) 'He trusted you to make the best possible use of it.'

'You can't think I'm betraying that trust. Certainly not because of Clover.' She closed her eyes.

'Won't Jason allow you to see her at all?'

'With cruel infrequency.'

'But he promised you.'

'His promises are worthless. He's a tyrant, never doubt it. He arranges everything to suit himself. He doesn't care how I miss her. He has no idea how awful it is to be alone after – '

Charles produced a clean, white handkerchief from a drawerful maintained for such occasions.

'What the hell good is the money, I ask you?' She blew her nose.

'To go from nothing to everything is so dangerous,' he said quietly. 'The shock can kill one quite as much as the reverse predicament. And the price is very high.'

She glared at him, all misunderstanding. 'What do you mean, everything? Are you really implying that I'm fortunate because I have £200,000 to squander as I please? Look here, smart lawyer, I have no home, no country, no family, no love, no possessions, no rights. All I have is fucking capital! And what have I paid for this capital? My father, my brother, my children, Jason, the one place on earth where I ever felt safe, my peace of mind, my future, my hope. All these are the cost of my capital. I'd give it back in a minute if that would restore even one of my losses. Capital!' She leaned back, lit another cigarette and smouldered and dripped and ran her hand through her hair.

'The price is very high. Dear girl, you have what you have. Try to make the best of it.'

'He kept her to himself for her eleventh birthday. God knows when I'll see her again. I suppose I could go away. I can't bear looking at flats anymore. Who wants a fucking flat? I have to go away. What can I do? I suppose I'll go away a lot.'

Charles burned to ask with whom. He happened to know she didn't spend all her nights in solitude. But instead he said, 'Which brings us back to clause ten, subclause two. The question of reinvestment.'

'The £1,500 every six months.'

She *had* been listening.

'Yes. If you'll be away so frequently, who is to decide – ?'

'Oh you do it, Charles. You do it all.' She sent the bangles jingling and clanking once more. 'How do we arrange it?'

'You can give me what is known as trustee power of attorney, and in fact I've drawn up a document for that as well.'

'No one like you for foresight, Charles.'

She had recovered herself. She was almost flirting with him again, legs crossed, beaming that smile. Truly a mendacious female. He rang for Mrs Plumber.

'I don't want any part in these sordid affairs. I hate the money, I tell you. It makes me sick. If one gives ten seconds' thought to how it's made and where it all comes from – the corruption, the infliction of unspeakable suffering, the crime of politics, the crime of economics, the crime of possession, the crime of culture, the crime of war. Ach! But I have to forget it. I want to forget it. What good does my indignation do, or my feeling sorry?'

10

'Quite. Ah, here is our dear witness.'

'All I can do is protect the person I love most. I am allowed that – with my capital.'

'Money can be a great liberating influence. Please sign here and here.'

She did so, for better or worse.

'November the twenty-ninth, 1976,' whispered Mrs Plumber.

'Thank you so much, Mrs Plumber.' Charles smiled at his secretary who nodded and withdrew.

The moment had come. Eleanor was stubbing out her last cigarette, picking up her coat, pulling on her gloves.

'The Blacks' party is on Wednesday. You're invited, I'm sure you know.' She wasn't, but an invitation could be arranged. He tested to see if there were any possibility, any at all.

'Oh, the Blacks . . .'

A mild desperation took hold of him. Then Eleanor herself was taking hold of him. Suddenly, he could feel her spare vibrating warmth, her slender thighs, the inch and a half more of her than him. Unused as he was to spontaneous gestures, he was too slow to return the embrace with anything but a flicker of the ardour he felt. He cursed himself as she drew back and smiled. Nothing, nothing of his emotions could have been transferred to her via that pathetic response.

'Charles, my eternal gratitude. We are partners in lovely, legal crime.'

'You must keep me informed of your whereabouts, you know, and of Clover's. That is one of the terms of our – um – crime. It is binding upon you.' Was this the only way he could hold her to him?

'Promise. I want everything to be quite correct too, you know. Oh and Charles.' Dear God, she was nearly at the door. He, a very clever man of great charm and powers of persuasion, stood mute before this woman on the run. 'She's not to have to wait a day past eighteen.'

'Of course not. I am bound – '

'Hand and foot,' she laughed.

'Dear Eleanor – ' The world was collapsing.

She opened the door and waved at him the bangled arm encased in an expensive green leather glove.

'Right, Charles. See you in seven years. Or see you Wednesday.'

Wednesday? Wednesday? She could have jetted to Hong Kong by Wednesday, taken an overdose by Wednesday, eloped with the Snake by Wednesday.

'I adore you,' he said quietly as the office door slammed behind her. He hadn't even seen her out.

two

Charles returned to his desk to still his momentary panic and gather his forces for Simon. He studied Eleanor Linnane's signature. (He was something of an expert on signatures.) It was bold for a woman's, if temporarily unsteady. Will, intelligence and dissipation were all apparent. Dear Eleanor, mad Eleanor. He must begin to forget her immediately.

In her case, though, forgetting might prove difficult. Normally, he could forget with alacrity. He knew all the prescriptions for shifting depression and disappointment: films, ballet, dinners, company, drink, Tacitus, Stendhal. They worked every time, tried and true, no matter how beguiling the client or the woman who sat next to him at supper or who served him his tea or his whisky, and whom he invariably, transitorily worshipped. He loved them all, made love to them all in his genteel, erotic fantasies. And then he forgot them. He had to. It was not completely his choice; it simply would have been inconvenient to remember so many. He loved women. He was on their side. In every divorce case he secretly took their part. Oh, if everyone only knew how partial the disinterested Charles Bevan really was.

This accomplished forgetting was one of a number of safety devices by which he upheld the structure of his life and advanced its progress. It was not, he thought, all that interesting a life. Yet it was calmly comfortable, calmly successful, certainly not unpleasant. And he supposed he was lazy. Lazy and lucky and well-liked and well-looked-after. For such a life and such a success, forgetting was indispensable. But Eleanor came looming at him out of that crazy signature like a red-headed lamia. He longed to hold her and soothe her and shield her from all pain. The longing of order for chaos – weren't the two meant to require each other? But no, no, no. Besides, he had banished her once before from his lascivious imaginings and ought to be able to do so again. He had forgotten relatively soon after their first meeting: two years, two months and five days ago on the occasion of Jason's first one-man show at what was then Facer Galleries. There she was reeling around the room on Jason's arm. They were a shabby pair amidst all that London chic, but wonderfully *with* each other, somehow flourishing in their poverty. (How could it have happened? How could such poisonous recrimination have grown up like a carnivorous plant in that garden of love?) Vivienne Facer, an old Cambridge girl-friend, had introduced them. Charles Bevan, Eleanor Linnane. Vivi had pronounced it Linnahn, which made the other lady curl her lip.

She chattered away at him, green eyes glinting and roving around the room, fastening only on Jason. She likes me, Charles thought; she is also a little drunk. Anthea, he could tell, was jealous but pretended, when they were alone later that evening, to have taken a liking to her and to have found her vivacity a refreshing contrast to Jason's surly personality. Eleanor had insisted he and Anthea pay them a visit in Sussex. He had tasted the invitation deeply, turning it over and over in his brain like some hard and delicious sweet, letting it warm him as it melted into its sugary components and dissolved into his blood to stimulate and briefly feed a physical ardour.

Still, he forgot her. Until the opportunity to remember presented itself in the form of a wedding invitation. The wedding involved a journey; the journey would require that they pass not far from a certain road which in turn was not far from a certain lane, a bumpy pot-holed affair which led to a hastily reconstituted labourer's cottage alongside one of the reedy dykes that criss-cross the fields between Pevensey and Hailsham. Charles had rung, surprised to find Englefield in the book, astonished at the existence of any link with the outside world, so self-sufficient a unit did the three of them seem.

Jason had taken the isolated house as an escape from London rents and creditors and as a retreat for him to paint and for Eleanor to look after his and Clover's well-being. Open fires, vegetable garden, howling winds, ornithological paradise, views of the greeny-purple Downs. Interior primitive and spare, but plenty to drink.

Charles and Anthea had rolled up in the midst of Clover's ninth birthday party and a gathering storm. A dozen children in impromptu fancy dress were chasing each other in and out of a nearby beech copse – flashes of patchy colour and piercing screams among whirling snow which was beginning to obliterate the minimal landscape. Charles stepped from the Citroën and stood for a moment by a rusting piece of sculpture, a swap Jason had done with Dillon Butterworth. Jason, Charles thought, had come off the better. Shouts and laughter assailed his ears. He watched the children, fascinated, while Anthea pleaded with him to make for the shelter of the house. He helped her to the weatherbeaten front door, she wobbling and complaining as her three-inch heels sank into the congealing mud.

The Bevans were eagerly expected by Eleanor who sometimes required society. But they had been given no advance warning that there was to be a party. Again the Englefield pride. The Bevans were not to be

13

made to feel they must bring a gift. But Jason did not know Charles, whose car-boot was stuffed with games, sweets, a four-foot Steiff giraffe, two bottles of Glenfiddich, three of Dom Perignon and five partridges, grey-legs, although late in the season. Nowhere did Charles arrive empty-handed.

They were greeted by a harassed but enthusiastic Eleanor dressed in muddy jeans and an old black jumper of Jason's. Through its holes Charles caught glimpses of her woolly vest, yellow-grey from many washings. She hugged them both hard and led them into the kitchen, the only warm room in the house thanks to an ancient Aga, around which seven cats jockeyed for proximity. Above it was a wooden rack, operated by a pulley, where a fantastic array of laundry was drying and filling the place with the smell of damp wool. The wobbly oak table and chairs and the battered lino were littered with crackers, paper hats, prizes, wrapping paper, and the sticky, half-eaten remains of the birthday tea. Charles helped himself to an unfinished piece of cake.

'Clover insisted on mauve roses and a puce inscription,' said Eleanor who had been up all night baking for the occasion. 'What can you do? I suppose good taste will eventually out, but God only knows when. Too bad you missed the spectacle of Jason marshalling them all for Pin the Tail on the Donkey. Donkey's still on the wall, though. I'm sure the genius would be only too happy to put his John Hancock to it and flog it to you for a small fortune. Not interested? Oh well. Anyway betcha there's something in the studio Anthea will discover she just can't live without.'

Eleanor provided them with two chairs and two cups of tea and proceeded to clear away the mess, talking, laughing and being, Charles could tell, just a bit naughty and just a bit drunk. She suggested a shot of indifferent whisky as an accompaniment to their tea, but Charles proposed instead the Dom Perignon, now sufficiently chilled by its sojourn in the boot, and certainly appropriate to the occasion. Delighted, she pulled on a ragged plaid jacket and went out with him into the blizzard, leaving Anthea to fidget in the taciturn company of Jason who had come in from the studio.

The lawyer and the American lady had been reduced to some undignified shouting, chasing, cajoling and threatening in order to corral the unruly mob. Child-loving and childless, Charles was enthralled by the noisy freedom so seldom allowed him during the first twelve years of his existence. He didn't mind that his shoes were covered with mud and the cuffs of his trousers soaked through. Each of his hands gripped a cold, soft, dirty one of a raggle-taggle youngster whom he was meant to steer firmly back to the house. One of the hands was Clover's.

She smiled up at him. She clung to him and purposefully slipped in an attempt to make him fall over. Charles was very happy.

Automobile headlights lurched and bumped into the deeply rutted lane: anxious parents arriving early to collect their offspring and render accounts of hazardous road conditions, worsening by the minute. Charles felt a new surge of pleasure. The Bevans would have to stay the night.

They brought in the children and the Dom Perignon. They packed off the children and drank the Dom Perignon. Restraint slackened. They became as vociferous as the children. They began to feel as if they had known each other for eons and were in complete agreement on damned near everything. Charles was a brilliant lawyer, Jason a great painter, Anthea Her Serene Highness, and Eleanor just plain beautiful. Secretly, Charles slipped a pleading Clover a glass of champagne. In a minute she was ungovernable. Then the electricity went off.

'Godammit!'

'Shit, shit, shit, shit,' Clover chanted gaily.

'Does it all the time. Jason, where are the candles?'

'Eleanor, I've told you and told you. The candles ought to be there, *ready*, always in the *same place*.'

'Yes I know they ought to be,' said Eleanor sweetly, 'but too bad they're not, so stick it, darling. Charles or Anthea, do you have a lighter so I can find the torch so I can find the candles?'

(That's right. She didn't smoke then. She had given it up. She was living in the country, expecting a baby, et cetera.)

They removed to the sitting-room, each of them carrying a candle and a glass, and disposed themselves before the huge fire Jason had so skilfully and patiently constructed. Whatever Jason did, he did his best.

Charles presented Clover with the giraffe and with her first backgammon set. He taught her the game while Eleanor returned to the kitchen to cook the partridges wrapped in the leaves of a Savoy cabbage she had plucked from the garden, brushing the snow off it on her way back to the house. The birds were to be accompanied by bread sauce. Charles would show her his own method of preparation if darling, sweet Clover would please allow him a moment's respite from the backgammon. Then some pears and the last of a nice cheese. There wasn't much else.

Charles marvelled at the child's quickness. Having little besides resistible nieces and nephews to remind him, he had forgotten how readily he, at the same age, had grasped the most complex of procedures, designs, constructions, manipulations. For the right nine year old, nothing is impossible.

The storm continued. Charles and Clover, one arm clutching the giraffe, played game after game by the fire. How little attention he had paid to the conversation in which he would normally have been the liveliest participant. Quite happily he left it to Jason to declaim, opine and enlighten. Anthea was drunk and bored. Eleanor was drunker and getting bored. Jason was deriving huge satisfaction from the sound of his own not unpersuasive voice. Charles was experiencing a profound content. He watched Clover in the warm, mutating light, letting her take three games in a row before realizing she already had learned to cheat. After supper, she was dragged away to be bathed, scrubbed and represented to him in a red woolly dressing-gown and bright-green slippers with mice heads on the toes. She was allowed to stay up until her long hair had dried by the heat of the fire. Another game, then another. All right, all right. He watched the wispy strands as they unfurled; rising up and out around her forehead and cheeks. They were not curls, not frizz, bore no resemblance to any hair he had ever seen. Each strand, so delicate – how could it exist? *En masse*, they made a transparent golden cloud about her face, an ectoplasmic frame, a magnetic field, the emanation of her being, the stuff of her thoughts. With such hair, he told her, she could send out magic rays into the world. She laughed and said she thought she had funny hair and that his hair was nice but not nearly so nice as Jason's.

In a state of exhausted glut she was, nevertheless, resisting bedtime, inventing new excuses whenever the subject came up, as it began to do more frequently. Then came the inevitable post-party psychodrama: threats from the adults, then promises, followed by more threats, first Eleanor then Jason nearly losing their tempers, then a proper tantrum from Clover and a horrified silence from Anthea.

Charles thought he might or should try to help, as behaviour was deteriorating rapidly. Yet he did not wish this Mustardseed, this Mopsa to be whisked out of sight, did not at all wish to be deprived of her company, perhaps for ever, and left to make do with fifth-rate mortals. Like all adults unused to children, he was not aware of the quantities of free energy he had been imbibing from her, a subliminal but definitely physical transfer. She simply had so much to spare. And really he had no idea how one coped with the mania of a nine year old. Still, he felt he must make a stab at it, for the sake of exhausted Eleanor, and to prevent Jason taking matters into his own brutal hands.

'If you go to bed now, I promise to take you to Constantinople.' Charles produced a postcard of the Blue Mosque tinted in improbable pastels against the blazing background of the Sea of Marmara. A friend, Simon in fact, had recently visited the city and sent him a picture of the building. Charles had kept it in his suit pocket, finding the pre-war quality of the artwork endearing. Clover seized it.

'And there's the most marvellous restaurant down by the Bosporus. A fair drive out, mind you, but we can easily hire a taxi for the evening, and they serve the best lobster I've ever tasted.'

He told her about the bazaars, the softness of the air, and the strange, kind eyes of the people. She listened, enthralled.

'When can we leave? Could we go on Wednesday? We'd have to be back for Christmas though, because Eleanor needs me to help and also I want my presents. Will you spend Christmas with us? Can I go, Daddy, pleeeze can I go?'

Charles was amazed. He had not expected such an ardent response. Was his renowned worthiness perceptible even to a nine year old? Or did she simply trust him? What a miracle Jason and Eleanor had produced. He experienced an unfamiliar sensation – envy. Then he recalled that, biologically at least, Eleanor had had nothing to do with Clover. The child had been the issue of Jason's previous liaison with an unknown and seemingly unloved factor. Clover was a charming little mistake.

That small person was now being dragged off by one arm to her freezing bedroom, Jason having become thoroughly fed up with Charles Bevan and his eastern promise. She clutched the postcard of the Blue Mosque and, between screams and protestations, extracted from Charles guarantees of Concorde flights, Orient Expresses, scarves, slippers, sweets and more backgammon in the morning. Never in his life had bad behaviour so charmed him. He wanted to shower her with everything Harrods' toy department could provide, cover her with lilies, drape her in pearls, fling rubies and emeralds at her feet. Stupid, he chided himself, when no doubt all she really wanted was a packet of Huba-Buba.

In the morning, of course, she was gone, off in what remained of the snow, off in the winter light with the goats and the horses long before he and Anthea tumbled out of bed at quarter to eleven, late for the wedding and gravely overhung. But there was a quick tour of the studio where Charles, out of charity and a flicker of admiration, had purchased *The Three Virtues*.

The drawing was one – the best one – of a series of ten pen and ink studies for what would be a large and complicated painting. The culturally rich title surprised Charles. Jason never gave his pictures any but the strictest and least resonant names – Yellow Square, Blue Painting, Number 41. His work was untainted by hints of representation, liberated, so he claimed, from the prison of narrative context. Allusion he disdained as too lush. Expressionism, symbolism, surrealism he eschewed. But perhaps a virtue was pure enough.

The drawings were modules for the rhythmic organization of the painting: three panels with myriad subdivisions nearly obscuring the triptych. Jason explained how he intended to step up the beat, heighten the syncopation, by the addition of colours which in the drawings were indicated only by their names. He was still experimenting with juxtapositions within the field, and more studies would be forthcoming. They told, Charles thought, the story of a struggle to exercise absolute control right up to the moment of paint application. Jason was a hater of the happy accident. Rigorist or constructivist were the terms Charles would have used had Jason not been in the room. Jason resisted labels even more than allusions. No school claimed him and he identified with no school. He struggled alone against the influence of Influences.

Charles had liked the drawing, and Jason, he presumed although it was hard to tell, had liked the cheque. When the lawyer later appraised his new acquisition, he found it elegant, cold, neurotic, having less to do with faith, hope and love than with Jason Englefield's obsession with visual problem-solving. Still, it was not too bad.

The Bevans went on to the wedding. Charles set about forgetting. Yet he was aware of a slender but indestructible thread that bound him to Eleanor and Clover. He was aware also, on that morning, of a rift between Jason and Eleanor. A poison had crept in, stealthily, murderously. He sensed a poison constantly being recycled between them, gaining by the minute an awful potency. Mrs Plumber buzzed him. Simon had arrived. Blast. Well, he might stew while Charles indulged his last futile fantasies about Eleanor. Just one moment before he must forget her entirely. Where was the red-headed lamia now? Keeping a tryst, probably. He had heard things. She had been in London four months and already he had heard things.

'I adore you,' he said again, just audibly. 'And you, you are alighting from a taxi, somewhere near the Gloucester Road, no doubt. You are stopping at a chemist to renew your prescription for your abominable Ativan or whatever you are ingesting. You take two immediately outside the shop, so agitated are you by your coming encounter. You walk through the fog, rapidly, stumbling over an uneven paving stone, shivering in your coat which you pull tighter about you with a bare hand because you have left your expensive gloves in the taxi. You walk on, your heart leaping because yet again it is about to be broken. Oh it's the Snake, the Snake. I suspect you, madam, and my instincts are never wrong. You are turning right into Harrington Gardens, number thirty-seven if memory serves. You search your bag for a key you cannot find and, in exasperation, ring the bell. The door opens and you move nervously towards the smart, chilly lift. You run a hand through your sweet mop. Ah, the rustle of your nice new skirt, the click of your heels on the tiles, the strain, the terrible strain in your eyes. Oh my dear . . .'

three

The key, the bloody fucking key. The key to life and death. Eleanor rifled the handbag she held open against her raised thigh. Her knee was pressed against the door, and she rested unsteadily on one leg. She found what she sought just as the timer on the overhead light switched off.

In the darkness her hand went straight to the familiar lock and she let herself in. Charles had been wrong on only one point. Felix Koning was not at home.

She called his name to make sure. She was partly disappointed, partly relieved. As always, the prelude to their meeting had consisted in her winding herself up to a fantastic pitch, fretting over her appearance, terrified there would be nothing to talk about. A fifteen year old would have had more poise. That was part of Felix's power. He generated anxiety, made one suffer in advance, even though one knew he would behave beautifully when the time came. He would be unconstrained and affectionate. His proximity would calm all fears, and one would ignite in his presence, astonishing oneself by being the best one could possibly be. Eleanor was afraid of Felix.

She stood in the middle of the high-ceilinged room, diamond-white, immaculate and bare to expose fully the Victorian plasterwork, the high multi-paned window, the polished hardwood floor, the white azalea, the furniture reverently spare, the marble fireplace where cherry-wood logs were scenting the flat like incense in a temple. But what was really on exhibition were the paintings.

She used to dream of such rooms. They had filled her with envy and awe during her years of London poverty. Of all cities, she used to say, London has the best domestic sets. And even in Sussex, in the hectic happiness of family life, she had thought of them occasionally. She had imagined such rooms as she carried in the coal which had blackened every line in her hard, dry hands. She examined her hands. They were ugly. They were ruined. They would never again be as they were. They had forgotten how to draw, to write, to embroider, to play the viola. They were almost not her hands. She had spoiled them for good in the vegetable garden and the kitchen and the wood pile, by hanging out damp sheets on January days, and by working as a chambermaid in the Manor House Hotel down the road. She, Eleanor, who had a Masters in History of Art, read French, German and Italian, could make up a

Haiku or an Alexandrine and was an expert on Matisse and seventeenth-century Flemish painting.

This room might now be hers. Not *this* room (Felix hadn't lived with a woman for years, and it was unlikely she would be the one to break the pattern), but a room like this, an even better room in an even better flat in an even better building, upon which she might impose her cultivated but untried taste. A room made to bear witness to a superior eye, *such* a room . . . But she did not want it. Not anymore.

She wanted Felix to return, yet hoped he wouldn't. She was sick and restless. She dropped into a chair by the fire which Felix had lit for her. He did things like that – sweet, personal things of which Jason could not conceive. When Felix came back he would embrace her, give her a drink, enquire about herself and what she had been doing since he had last seen her. He would stroke her like a beloved animal, her hair, her temples, her cheeks. After going to bed, he would hold her for a long time and talk more about those trivial, consoling things that tricked her into believing they were the only balm for her wound. One must be kind to be cruel.

Felix did not come. Something had called him out, some manoeuvre or offer, some chance of a deal to which he would refer in an offhand manner and about which she would not question him further. His absence was bad, not that it implied he might break their date – where arrangements were concerned he was reliable to the point of morbidity – but because it left a vacuum which demanded to be filled by memory. She looked at her watch. In fact, she was early. Early for Felix, late for Charles.

Oh this vacuum! Even a few minutes supplied too much time to think, to review and renew the past two years as they played across the screen of her mind, flashed there by some diabolical projectionist who forced her, like a prisoner being brainwashed, to witness over and over the events which were the cause of her bereavement. That old-fashioned word. She *was* bereaved, beyond anyone else she had known. In times of war, thousands of women must have gone about in her present state, but they had a social and a governmental support. They had, above all, each other. They were a bona fide association. She was the isolated instance, deprived within eighteen months of father, brother, husband, child and unborn baby. Quite a record. But no one seemed impressed. Perhaps because her losses had not been incurred in the name of a good cause, no one took any notice. (She made a mental exception of Charles Bevan's watery-blue eyes.) She was tired of trying to attract others' attention, of telling them in a thousand perfectly obvious ways how much help she needed to recover from all this. It did no good. She was tired of wasting her efforts on them. From now on she was determined to shut up about her grief and simply do whatever was necessary to stop that movie. But if she ran out of substances to stop it, or distractions or changes of ambiance, if all three from time to time failed, she would just have to let it run on, keep very still, and watch in agony.

Over and over she watched it. Over and over the car turned, three, four, five times, mangled by the jagged outcroppings of granite peculiar to that part of the Adirondack range. The foot and a half of ice which covered the Kankamangus river split under the impact, parted, and swallowed the car. All so quickly that there would have been no time to open a door and escape, that is, if either of the two men inside the car were still alive after their descent into the abyss. (Oh God, let them have been dead already, let them have had no split-second recognition of their doom.) And even if they were alive, the shock to a human body plunged into twenty-degree water would kill immediately, wouldn't it? There would not have been time to feel what it is like to drown. Perhaps they were unconscious – blows to the head, et cetera. She had tried a thousand times to work it out. But however she recombined the figures, there was no equation. Her calculations rendered up no total either painful or consoling. They only bred more calculations.

She saw herself arriving barely in time for the funeral, with a plane ticket paid for by Charles Bevan; standing at the graveside with priest and extended family, taking it in that she was now an orphan, without siblings and without offspring, taking it in that the golden thread which had passed from her father to her and from her to her own child, who now floated like some rootless water plant upon the ether where unborn babes are set adrift, had snapped for ever, so delicate that repair was unthinkable. That last miscarriage had been indeed the last. Immortality was now out of the question.

She saw Jason, just for a moment real tears in his eyes, carrying away in a plastic pan the lifeless foetus her body had rejected, to do with it – what? She did not know. To take it where? She never asked him. He never mentioned it. And then the dreary wind-down to the end of their love, his ill-concealed annoyance at her mourning and finally her taking up with Felix.

She had deceived Jason for months, going on the train two or three times a week to meet Felix in London, returning to Sussex in the evening, describing flats she had not seen. Now there was her greater deception of this afternoon. And Jason had driven her to it. She deceived him both with Felix and with money because deceit was her only weapon, the single verification of her identity, proof that she existed at all. Since he would not listen to what she said, she had made a statement he could not hear. *He* was the real criminal. Jason Englefield: found guilty, for ever guilty of withholding love.

To Eleanor there was no longer anything extraordinary in Greek tragedy. The sufferings of an Alceste or an Antigone seemed an everyday affair. The gods did fix certain of their creatures for destruction. She was one of those creatures. There was no escaping the role. Proof of the futility of struggle could not be clearer. She who needed a place to hide, to lie down for a while in safety, found herself in the one spot that would give her no shelter.

The door opened. Eleanor heard a soft step at the end of the room. She did not turn. She was wiping away tears in the protective darkness.

'Beauty, hello. You're not letting the fire go out?'

Felix's voice always seemed to suppress a weary laughter. Sometimes the laughter infused the voice and gave it a pleasing crackle. He spoke quietly. There was an accent, slight, unplaceable, that came and went. He claimed Austro–Polish–Czech descent with a few South German ancillary ancestors. He was one-quarter secret Jew (obscure Kraków scholar) but educated by Jesuits (his Viennese mother had given birth to him no one knew where or under what circumstances). Somehow he had become thoroughly Anglicized. But to Eleanor he was all of Middle Europe. He was two thousand years old, although he appeared forty, his birth certificate had it that he was forty-three, his Dutch passport that he was thirty-eight, and his British passport thirty-six. No wonder his laughter was weary.

He passed her. His walk had a grace just verging on the conscious. The tread of the genteel predator. He kissed her forehead and adroitly threw two more logs on the fire. Felix was at once pragmatic and affectionate. In a moment he would fix on her his complete attention. Meanwhile it would be silly to let the fire go out. He sat beside Eleanor, took her hand and smiled. He did not remark on the tears it was costing her such an effort to restrain. Pleasure not pity was what he'd come for.

'Green eyes,' he whispered and stroked her tangled hair, still damp from her walk in the fog. She pushed against his hand with her head, her neck, her whole body, responding to every caress like the worn-out lovesick animal she was.

'But you're wet. Your coat is wet, you silly girl. Take it off and I'll hang it over a chair to dry. What have you been doing in this weather, so uncovered and exposed?' His eyes shone with the pleasure of seeing her. She gave him much pleasure, she knew. He raised her up and began

23

unbuttoning her coat with a practised tendresse. He drew her on to the long, black sofa and then on to his knees. She let him do everything – pull her coat back from her shoulders, extract one arm carefully from its sleeve, then the other, remove one boot – without tugging or twisting – then the other, and stand them side by side on the floor near the fire, but not so close as to damage the leather. Eleanor couldn't help laughing, partly at the way he fussed and partly at the way he was now manipulating her feet, toes and ankles.

'Darling,' (it was almost, not quite, dahlink), 'what?'

'The boots – they're so expressive silhouetted like that.' She stopped laughing. 'I don't know – touching.'

'Such a lovely creature you are. Such a funny little girl.'

She knew how well he liked the little girl in her, the rebel child tamed and trained by him. He turned her face towards his, forcing her to look into the only eyes in the cosmos capable of capturing her gaze and keeping it.

His long hands with the fair hair on the fingers moved slowly along Eleanor's leg, tracing over and over the shape of the calves he professed to adore. He lifted her jumper, studied the bare breasts, a little too large for his taste, and bit her nipples with a special ferocity. He *did* have a passion for her, she was certain of that, one he could express fully and with great artistry. Otherwise a deceiver, in bed he held nothing back. For the moment he meant it, like an actor who lives and believes his role as long as he is on the stage. But she had not been made so stupid by love as to imagine she was his only passion. He'd had many, was no doubt having them still and would go on having them. The passions, plus the two thousand years, she thought, must add greatly to his weariness.

'Come,' he said, 'we'll go to the kitchen and find a bottle of something and two glasses and our little tray and then go to the bedroom. I can't wait to have you in my arms.' Yet he waited.

She followed him obediently, liking the way he prolonged it all while complaining of the delay, making each episode in their encounter beautiful in itself, drawing out its special essence, making her feel it through and through. As though there were not and never could be any winged chariot hurrying near.

She leaned against the kitchen table, watching everything he did. He was incapable of an awkward move. There was much of the female in Felix.

'And what have you been doing, beauty? Hmmm? I never know. I have always to guess. It could be anything. I'm always surprised. I like that.

Perhaps it's the way you tell me. You're very witty – ' he kissed her cheek, 'sometimes.'

They got on so well. They never argued. There was nothing over which to contend, he tacitly having been declared the winner at the outset.

She had no intention of rendering him an account of the afternoon's events. Felix was very interested in money and, given the opportunity, would discourse endlessly on financial matters. (Money was the fourth area in which he presumed to wield his expertise, the third being drink – he had been a wine broker in the early days – the first paintings, and the second, which was really the first, women.) She did not want him to get on to the topic, and she certainly did not want to reveal anything of her pact with Charles. And so she lied to him.

'I went to look at some flats. One in South Ken and another in Campden Hill. The one in Campden Hill was charming. It had a little garden – lovely, with two gigantic camellias, one an "Adolphe Audusson", I'm told.' (Fifth area of expertise, plants.) 'But the place is a bit dark and the kitchen is minuscule. I don't know. Perhaps you'd come and have a look at it with me.' That was daring, since the flat did not exist. But then, it was unlikely that the flat would ever again be a topic of conversation between them.

'Darling, of course, I'd adore to.' He seized her hand. 'Tell you what. You must meet my old friend Willem Walberg.' (Sixth area: real estate.) 'He knows of places that never come on the market. He'll find the perfect flat for you, I know it. We'll invite him to supper.'

Eleanor held down and successfully smothered the anxiety she felt whenever Felix waxed enthusiastic over her projected life alone. Why did he not say simply Stay Here, Stay With Me. Oh those words. She must stop herself for ever from wanting to hear them. His even sensing she wanted to hear them would be calamitous. As a dog smells one's fear of it, the certainty of his advantage would make him turn on her. The process of alienation she so dreaded would commence. It would be the end of passion. And the end of passion would be the end of everything.

'And then I thought, I've had enough of this wretched, boring flat-hunting, I'm going to Bond Street. So off I went and found these marvellous gloves which were *so* expensive – well, I bought them of course and they really were beautiful, I was longing to show them to you, a kind of grey-green leather and very long, like gauntlets, but wouldn't you know I left them in the taxi.' She giggled. The champagne, on her empty stomach (she had eaten nothing in the past twenty-four hours), had taken immediate effect.

'Oh, darling, you are crazy.' She knew he found her taste in clothes questionable. They hinted at an anarchistic streak he did not care for. On that point, he and Charles Bevan were unknowingly in accord.

'And what have you been up to, my wily Felix?'

He smiled. 'I was late, wasn't I?' He wasn't going to tell her, or he would tell her only half and that distorted.

'About twenty-five minutes before you were due, I had a telephone call from Jeremy Black. Mumbled something about a painting, Flemish landscape, recently purchased by his wife. He was suffering a sudden attack of misgivings about its origin and value and wanted my opinion. What a bore, I thought. Still I'd better go. They are not too far away, and I could easily be back before you arrived.'

Eleanor happened to know that Jeremy Black was out of town. Mrs Black, however, was at home. As for the painting, both husband and wife were too knowledgeable on such matters to make the sort of stupid mistake implied by Felix. Besides, they usually bought contemporary art. Monica, though, was fond of the Flemish school.

'And is it a fake?' she asked him.

He shrugged. 'Oh no.'

'Where did they buy it?'

'They weren't wanting to say. They were making a fantastic story about Italians.'

She let him run on. His inventive capacities were excellent, especially when self-defence or self-esteem were the motivations. He strayed just far enough from the truth. He enjoyed his fabrications without allowing them to carry him away. He drank in the same fashion, that is, he never got drunk. Eleanor listened and laughed and did not believe a word, except that Monica Black was definitely involved. As usual she was impressed by his spontaneously clever mendacity. Felix rose to occasions.

They took the champagne on a tray into the bedroom, which was vast and white. A curtainless window looked on to the communal garden. The bed was also vast and white, and its linen was changed every other day. Felix's laundry bills must have been astronomical. He had turned back the counterpane to expose an abundance of pillows and the pristine sheets, their surface like a Zurbarán altar cloth. Passively, they pleaded to be creased, soiled, rumpled, dampened, stained, their gorgeous purity sacrificed to the chemical exudations of human sex. Felix placed the tray on the bedside table. Eleanor sensed his rising impatience brought on by the dimly lit vision of the sheets. He embraced her. Together they fell on to the bed.

Their bodies were alike, slender and greedy. Erotically twinned, each could anticipate, initiate, respond. Nothing need be named. They only said over and over, because they were unable not to, how divine, how perfect, how beautiful, how maddening and how they loved each other. There, there, yes, there. He proceeded as he liked, knowing that by pleasing himself he could please her. Consequently, and without intent, he freed her from the need to guard his ego. Oh he was rare all right. Eleanor wondered if her father might have sent her Felix the way he had sent her the money.

In the end, though, she could not come. She was too tired and too nervous, made anxious again by invading thoughts of time and the taking back of Felix's affections into himself. She saw her feigned cheerful goodbye, their separation, the cold night, then two or three days of misery until he called her again. Fear found its way in despite ardour and tendresse and expertise. Even the best pleasures were not an adequate barrier.

Eleanor held Felix as he lay quietly asleep inside her. She listened to the rumblings of her stomach. She synchronized her breathing with his, wanting to be even nearer his unconscious physical being. They respired as one. It was the closest she would ever come to possessing him. But she could not still her mind. She counted the weeks she had been with Felix. She had capitulated straightaway. She wondered if she should have held out longer, if she would now be more secure if she had made herself less readily available then. But she was too impatient for that sort of manipulation. If she liked someone, she liked him. Childishly, she went for instant gratification. She was incapable of sacrificing her immediate desires to gain a greater, later advantage. She refused to make deals, she refused to be a bunch of carrots. Oh she knew. She'd never get anywhere.

Felix was on top of her, slightly to one side. Their limbs were arrayed in curious formation, his face resting on her neck, her arm thrown backward over her head. Somewhere between them, she could not tell where, their fingers intertwined. She imagined looking down at their naked bodies. She saw how beautiful they were, long-stemmed water plants, the branch of a tree fallen in the forest.

She rubbed gently against him.

'Beauty,' he said at last. 'You didn't come.'

'Uh-uh.'

They moved together, not shifting position, their lips touching, sometimes finding each other's tongues.

'Darling, can you come now?'

For a moment there was no pain. She was a drowning woman, deaf to her own cries. When she opened her eyes she saw Felix watching her, smiling. His eyes were kind and cold, made vivid blue by the only thing that really interested him. Carefully, he loosened her grip on his shoulder.

'Hello,' he said. He could not have been more fiendishly wide-awake.

Anxiety came rushing back. She was tender as an abscess, and she had forgotten, fool that she was, to take two more tranquillizers. She pressed his hand to her beating heart.

'There's no one like you,' she said in spite of herself. It was the wrong remark, as unwise as the time she had told him about wishing she could offer him her virginity. It was uncomfortable, it was gauche, it was the truth. Felix preferred pretence of feeling to the real thing. Truth bodes ill for fun.

He kissed her and got out of bed, finishing his champagne as he did so. The moment had come and she must pretend it didn't matter. He was dressing. He was telling her he must be somewhere, a dinner party. He made no apologies for not inviting her. Prince of Liars, he could not now let drop the smallest consoling morsel of deceit? – what a bore, darling, so much rather stay with you, can't let old so-and-so down – nope. He seemed quite happy to abandon her for an evening with a lot of overdressed and overrated rat-bags.

She could never get used to his doing this. She longed to hold him in the night for all the night. Often she did stay, but he never allowed their behaviour to fall into a regular pattern. Thus he kept her safely his in her insecurity. It was such a Felix trick. It made her think of someone absently trailing a precious silk along a dirty floor. A beautiful, meaningless act.

She pulled on her skirt and jumper, her hands trembling. Best get this over with quickly. She lit a cigarette, something of which Felix disapproved, but she couldn't help it. She could never say what she really meant or ask for what she really wanted. He made her feel a child, afraid she had done or was about to do something wrong. Felix the warder, Felix the judge. If she were to displease him . . . the look in his eyes, the change in his voice . . . if she were to displease him . . .

'Darling, why must you smoke?' he asked sadly as she met up with him in the sitting-room.

'It's my little flaw, Felix. Even the most perfect objects have their little flaw, their little crack. That's what makes them exquisite.'

'Your only flaw, precious, is that you are losing too much weight.' He stroked her hips and bottom. 'Why aren't you eating? I'm very concerned. We will find you a doctor, the perfect one. We'll invite him to dinner.'

Eat? Weight? Didn't he know, no of course he didn't, that most of the time the sight of food revolted her, that her only proper meals were the ones with him in restaurants or those he cooked for her in his own kitchen? Even on these occasions she would eat only half of what was put before her. His presence drained off the appetite it had aroused, like an aperitif that failed to function. He obsessed her to the detriment of her most basic metabolic functions. Such food brings eternal hunger.

She shuddered at the idea of the force-feeding session she must undergo when she returned to her room. Felix mistook it for a shiver and wrapped her coat around her, murmuring endearments, saying he would ring her soon. (But when, oh when? Have mercy on me. Don't you see that my mind is unstrung, that I am ill, that I am in love and that I grow more and more ill because I cannot tell you? I must play by your rules or not at all. And what about that trip to Rome they had discussed so enthusiastically last week? Not a word of it today and she dared not bring it up.) She hung her head, saying nothing as he did up her coat buttons, punctuating each one with a kiss.

'Darling, shall I call you a cab?'

She said she would go alone. Sighing, he handed Eleanor her bag and scarf and escorted her to the door where he kissed her again before sending her out into the fog.

four

Eleanor lay on the bedroom floor. Before her were two halves of an avocado on a plastic plate. Beside the plate were a teaspoon and a bottle of Worcestershire sauce. For ten minutes she had been trying to eat the avocado. If she could manage to eat the avocado, her stomach might stop eating itself. The pains might cease. With the cessation of the pain she might be able to eat a boiled egg and a piece of buttered toast, the most perfect meal known to man. That's what Dillon had advised: eggs and avocados, dearie. They'll slide down when nothing else will. She had thought the Worcestershire sauce might lure out her old love of spice and tang, but it had failed. Nothing could tease her into believing she really wanted the bloody avocado. Its consumption must be an act of pure will.

Come on, Eleanor, dig in. Tsk, tsk, naughty girl, when you could be dining on lobsters or oysters or steak tartare. Close your eyes and think of Bangladesh.

She forced down three spoonfuls. The avocado tasted, mercifully, of nothing at all, but it clung to the roof of her mouth so that she had difficulty swallowing it. Nausea came and went. It was disgusting, revolting, this innocuous fruit which once she had consumed in great numbers and with great gusto. That had been when she liked life. It seemed a pretty straightforward proposition that if one does not want to eat one does not want to live. But starvation was proving unpleasant. She must eat, eat, eat before she could do anything else at all and before she disappeared without a trace.

Twenty-five minutes later Eleanor had eaten the avocado. She rolled on to her back and lay staring at the low ceiling of her basement room. She could be staying at the Ritz or in a serviced apartment, dining out, dining on the best. Instead here she was, a rat in a hole, poking about in the coid dark box which was the ground-floor flat of Deirdre Mallard's otherwise messily sumptuous house. The place had been kindly offered by Deirdre and, in her fear of hotels and isolation and anonymity and her need for the proximity of a family, Eleanor had taken the flat for six months. But it had been a mistake. It was not working out. The loneliness she'd hoped to assuage was exacerbated by the sounds of five people running up and downstairs, arguing, playing music, slamming doors, absorbed with their lives. They had lives. Lives were something other people had.

It was late afternoon of the day following her meetings with Charles Bevan and Felix Koning. She looked out through the French windows at the garden. A magnolia tree was anatomized against a rosy, winter sky in the process of decline, the pink seeping from it like a transfusion in reverse. The sky was dying above as she was dying below.

The flat had a view of the garden but no exit to it. The French windows opened on to a tiny yard and a four-foot concrete wall. To reach the garden she must go upstairs and pass through the busy Mallard kitchen with its family noises and its family smells and its family warmth that tore open every crack in her armouring. It was not worth going into the garden. She who loved gardens, who could now have or make any garden she wanted, could not go into the garden.

She would only be reminded of everything she missed. The garden, the country, the family: all three had seduced her. She was addicted to their pace and their sweetness. She had never thought she'd want them. She had been amazed at her readiness to receive them. To be locked away like this, shut off from fields, skies, flowers and wind, not to move freely in that world so fresh and safe – it was a death. Sussex had been difficult, but the days had been vivid, tangible – how could they have been lost? How could *they* be in the process of turning into memory?

Felix had not rung her. She had no hopes of his ringing that evening. She resolved to get up and eat a raspberry yoghurt. Then her hand encountered the envelope from British Telecom which Deirdre had slipped under the door that morning as Eleanor lay fully dressed and narcoleptic. Ah yes, the loneliness bill. Deirdre must have been shocked by its dramatic increase since Eleanor's arrival. When Eleanor got drunk she panicked and when she panicked she pounced on the telephone, seeking disembodied succour from the four corners of the globe. When she did not panic, the drink provoked fits of elation marked by a noisy medley of Cole Porter, Gershwin, Fats Waller and hits from her teenage years. The habit had annoyed Jason. As for Felix, she would not dream of subjecting him to such a performance, not after singing him 'Our Love is Here To Stay' and having him disappear for three weeks. Only Dillon liked her singing. Anyway, she had best stick to the telephone or there might be complaints from upstairs. The loneliness bill she could pay.

She was not getting up. The problem was not so much physical disability as lack of motivation. Get up for what? To whom does one run when no voice calls? Why hurry when there is no deadline for dinner, no crises, large or small, that require one's attention, no gardening chores, no laundry, no dental appointments, no practising of scales to oversee? It occurred to her that it might be for life itself that one could get up. The thought alternately bored and horrified her. She had grown too used to being needed and to thinking of herself as being needed. And being needed presupposed another, or others. All conspicuous by their absence. Get up? For what?

She remembered Charles Bevan's invitation. Now there was someone who appeared to be interested in saving her. She would call him and say she'd be delighted, blah, blah, blah. Might prove awkward with the Blacks, though. Oh, fuck the Blacks. It would be a start, a social straw at which she might grasp. She did get up, wrapped in her silk dressing-gown which was creased and stained (the only real money she had spent so far was on clothes) and searched the tiny room for her address book.

Once she had been organized. When you look after others, your self is looked after automatically. She ran three anarchistic lives with her own brand of executive skill. Now she lived in chaos. The bed was unmade, there was no reason to make it. Clothes, books and overflowing ashtrays littered the floor, the chairs, the top of the dresser. Why pick them up? Whose progress did they impede? Her own, she realized, since it took her several minutes to find the address book.

She rang Charles's office and spoke to Mrs Plumber. Mr Bevan was out, would she care to leave a message?

'Just tell him it was the red-headed nut.'

Silence. She was suddenly ashamed. Why be flippant with Mrs Plumber when there were so many others deserving of her asperity? The gods, for instance.

'I'm sorry. Please say that Eleanor Linnane called and that I'll be at home all evening. I'd like to speak to him. Thanks.'

Charles's absence was a shock. She had been thinking of him as permanently available. She squatted in consternation before the telephone, her appetite whetted by the connection. The lust to complain, to laugh, to gossip, to make arrangements overcame her. With trembling hands and the desperation of the true addict, she dialled the first number that came into her head.

'Hello, Caroline. It's Eleanor.'

The background was a tremendous racket: shouts, curses, Radio One, what sounded like toppling masonry.

'Who?'

'Eleanor Linnane.' Already she was edgy and upset.

'Eleanor! How lovely! I heard you were back in London and I've been meaning to ring you, but it's been absolutely – excuse me – no, no, no, not by the window, over *there*, and please mind the lamp. Sorry. We've got the builders in, I'm afraid, and you know what it's like.' (No, she did not know what *it* was like. She had never owned a home of her own, and Caroline knew that.) 'Pandemonium! They're installing a new boiler. Can you believe it? The entire central heating packed up, and in this awful weather. And the children have flu and I'm getting my period and Trevor has invited ten people to dinner, and I haven't even *thought* what I'm going to give them. Anyway,' she wound down with an exhausted sigh, 'how are you, darling?'

'Well, I suppose you know that Jason and I – '

'Oh no! They've knocked over the benjamina. Please, please *do* be careful. Look, Eleanor, this is obviously impossible. I'll have to ring you back. I'd really love to see you. Come and have dinner with us.'

'Fine. When?'

'Well, everything is mad until after Christmas, and then we're in Suffolk for a week. But in the New Year, by all means let's get together. It's been too long. Oh God, there they go again and the baby's crying. Darling, I *must* stop. I'll call you back and we'll make a firm arrangement. Lots and lots of love. Bye.'

Eleanor slammed down the receiver.

'You superficial, hypocritical fuckhead!'

Caroline hadn't even asked for her phone number. Clearly, loneliness was a disease others feared might be contagious. But the telephone fever was in her. She thought of trying Charles at home, but was put off by the idea of Anthea's polite drawl. She flipped through the address book, thinking it might be nice to have lunch with Sarah Debden, even though she was a melancholic and a bad poet and probably had had an affair with Felix. Eleanor was also beginning to want a drink.

Sarah's voice sounded as though it were coming from a sensory deprivation chamber.

'Hello, Eleanor,' she responded dully, as though it had not been more than six months since they had last spoken.

'How are you?' A dangerous question, but she knew for certain that Sarah hadn't the least interest in anyone else's condition.

'Well, I'm a bit shattered, really. I've only just come from my women's group and it was, I mean, it was terribly interesting. Really a lot came out, but two people broke down completely and the rest of us had to devote all our energies to bringing them round. I mean it was tremendously satisfying and everyone learned a lot, but I'm rather exhausted as a result. I've been terribly fragile lately, very up and down, the slightest thing unnerves me. I cry when I hear music. Oh and last week I saw an allergy specialist who told me that my diarrhoea is caused by a zinc deficiency and that I'm allergic to eighty different substances. I've been eating nothing but lamb and pears for five days. Do you think it's a bit extreme?'

'Yes.'

'Well, I don't know. I feel I must go on with it now I've begun. Anyway, Eleanor, I really don't think I can talk anymore. I think I should go and lie down.'

'You do that.'

Eleanor rang Dillon Butterworth.

'Flame! Hi, dearie. Listen, drop whoever you've got hold of and go to the telly immediately. *Roman Scandals* is on. Eddie Cantor and Ruth Etting. Do it now, sweetheart, and ring me later. We can't miss a minute of this.'

The English: the most selfish, the most neglectful race on earth. Eleanor reached for the bottle of Jameson's. Sarah's lamb and pears did not strike her as an amusing combination for lunch. By the time she had drunk three whiskies, nothing struck her as amusing. Aggression replaced loneliness and she did what she always did in this worst of all possible conditions. She rang Jason.

Clover answered.

'Oh my darling, my dumpling, it's Eleanor.' She was nearly in tears.

'Oh hel-lo!' Clover gave a characteristic squeak of pleasure. 'Guess what. You'll never guess.'

'No, I probably won't. Tell me everything.'

'Well, I came second in my maths exams. Can you imagine. Me! And it was all decimals. Jason says he's very proud of me.'

'So am I. *I'm* proud of you.'

'Thank you. I know you are. We went on a super hack on Saturday, way up on the Downs and took a picnic, and I ate with my best friend, Emma. You know Emma. And we stopped by that stream you like so much and I thought about the last time we went fishing there. It was a bit cold but the sun was shining and we got back home really, really late . . .'

Eleanor grabbed at the string of inconsequences. It was all she wanted to know – besides what Felix might be up to.

'Are you practising the piano?'

Clover hesitated. 'Eleanor, you might as well know that Jason is selling the piano. He says there's no sense in my learning two instruments and that I'm probably not good enough anyway – '

'What awful, awful rubbish!' He was at it again, removing every vestige of her influence, effacing her name as the Egyptians would do to

34

a queen fallen from favour, rubbing out her immortality. 'You're gifted, you're a musical child – '

'I'll live, I expect.'

'Jason doesn't give a damn about your education.'

'Oh Eleanor, please don't be upset. I'm fine, I really am. Anyway, Jason says I have to stop now. Have you seen Charles?'

'Charles Bevan?' Eleanor poured herself another whiskey.

'I have to go. Jason's taking the phone away. I miss you, miss you,' she added in sing-song.

'Clover, please don't hang up.' But Jason was already on the other end.

'Eleanor, what do you want?'

'I – I wanted to know – how you were. I wanted to know when I could see Clover.'

'We're fine.'

'Can I see Clover? Can I come down?'

'No.'

'Could you put her on a train and I'll meet her at Victoria?'

'I don't have the money for the fare.'

'Well I do, dammit, and you know I do.' Again she had torn open her own wound.

'You can't buy me, Eleanor.' Jason's tone was as bleak as the Berlin wall and his emotions as well patrolled.

'Buy you! You should be so lucky, who'd buy you? Who'd be paid to take you away? Apparently no one, as you haven't sold a painting in months.'

'Goodbye, Eleanor.'

'No, Jason,' she pleaded. 'Please no. I'm sorry, I really am. I just want to see Clover, just tell me when I can see her, whenever you like, whenever suits you, it doesn't matter when. Oh please, Jason, please understand.'

He gave a short, hard laugh. 'No one may buy me, but no one will understand you.'

'You don't want to understand me.'

'No I don't.'

'But why, Jason? What have I done?'

'You've irritated the hell out of me. Now leave me alone.'

'That's the point. You're not alone. You have Clover. You don't know or you won't admit what a support a child is. And you'll never know – until you're without it. That's what *you* don't understand.'

'I understand you're a neurotic nuisance who can't control herself and only damages her own cause. What I don't understand is why I'm talking to you. Piss off.'

'Why sell the piano? It's stupid and cruel. Let me buy her a spinet.'

'Don't you dare buy her anything.'

'Why do you hate the money? I can't help the money.'

'I don't hate the money. It was a relief. It meant you could leave.'

'You hate me because I can't have children and the baby died. That was when you began to hate me, wasn't it?'

'You're the most negative person I've ever met.'

'You didn't want me to have children. You were glad I couldn't. You don't want me to have anything. You want me to die alone, that's what you want.'

'No. But that's what you'll do.'

'You hate me because I helped you. That's the reason, isn't it? You can't bear help, yet you're always forced to accept it. You accepted Monica's – '

He laughed. 'What makes you think you ever helped me?'

'I worked for us. I got money for us. I raised your child. I believed in you!'

'Ha!'

'I did, I did. And you want to kill all that. You want to forget and you want Clover to forget. You want to pretend it never existed because it's so damaging to your idea of yourself.'

'At least I have an idea.'

'You certainly don't have a heart.' She was crying.

'And you have no idea how little you interest me.'

'Some people like me,' she sniffed. 'Some people think I'm beautiful.' Their conversation was nearing its usual bathetic climax.

'Well, ponce Felix may think you're the Madonna of the Rocks but to me you were never anything but funny-looking.'

'You hate me because of Felix. I don't love Felix.'

'What do I care who you love? Oh go play with your dilettantes.'

'First you say I'm too serious, then you say I'm too frivolous. How can you think I'm a dilettante?'

'They're the only people you see. Like attracts like.'

'I don't see anyone.'

Jason gave an exasperated sigh.

'Oh Jason, I'm only trying to find where the hate comes from. That's what's tearing me up. I can't understand, I don't know what I did that was so bad.'

'You irritated me. Oh this is so boring.'

'But you have a mind. You're human. You must want to find out too. You must want to know why.'

'I don't know what you mean and I'm not interested.'

Against Eleanor's protestations ran Jason's uninterrupted litany. 'I'm not interested, I'm not interested, I'm not interested, I'm not interested,' until, without warning, he put the phone down.

five

Eleanor hurled herself from corner to corner of the cold, dark box. She banged her head and beat her fists. She had one desire – to escape the confines of her room, her body and her mind. It seemed impossible that she did not blow up, turn to atoms and dissipate into the ether. Solidity was intolerable.

Then she saw the bottle of sleeping pills. She flew to the bathroom and swallowed four, returned to the bedroom and lay on her back on the floor. She stared at the plastic plate and at the skins of the avocado that were slowly shrivelling. The bottle of Worcestershire sauce had toppled over and its contents were seeping into the carpet. Beside the bottle lay the spoon, the telephone bill and the spilled contents of her handbag. In the corner opposite were the jumper, tights and boots that Felix had removed the previous afternoon. There it was strewn before her: her life. No, not quite her life. She recalled that somewhere in the dresser was a savings deposit book from the Barclays down the road. The book confirmed that she was in possession of £175,000. With that and the bottle of pills she still clutched in her hand, she supposed she could die a rich woman.

And what would her father say to that, after stuffing the money away for years and not telling her? What a mean, sordid joke it would make of all his efforts for her and James. Had James known how much there really was? Had Daddy confided in James, he being the male sibling, the sober, stable sibling? The will had been explicit about dividing the money equally between them. That was her father, scrupulously fair to his two children in the dispensation of both love and money. No, if he had not told her, he had not told James. For whatever reasons he had kept the amazing coup to himself and the lawyer.

How had he managed to accumulate his small fortune? How, when he had risen no higher than the rank of senior civil servant and, with his touching veneration for education, had struggled to put both Eleanor and James through universities – good ones – meanwhile supporting a semi-invalid wife who, even when in perfect health, had contributed little beyond housework and anxiety to the family's financial support? How? By the intelligent and bold manipulation of certain stocks which miraculously doubled and tripled their worth; and by some very good luck with interest rates on several certificates of deposit.

His covert, protective industry wrung her heart. He had lived first for his family. The interests of his fellow men came second in the end. He had been a selfless man, the only one she had ever known. Proof that such persons, rare as unicorns, could and did exist. It was so ironic: he was a product of the double ethos of his generation of Americans. Despite his social utopianism and gentle, well-documented lectures on the crime of ownership, he had put his children's material well-being above all and exploited the system he deplored. For them alone he burned out all his cleverness and all his quiet zeal.

Father and daughter had little in common. Eleanor thanked the gods for James who had taken a route more comprehensible to the old man. Dearest James, winning tangible rewards, doing the obvious things that Daddy could boast of to his cronies. Thank the gods for worthy James who stood reasonably and simply by when their mother took her terrible time over dying, keeping sane as they all drew nearer to dementia, watching her week after week, wasting away. The dreaded American hospital death (covered, of course, by their father's fabulous medical insurance; not a penny was to be drained off his children's legacy). Thank the gods for James who went to university nearby, worked nearby, lived nearby and, seemingly without effort, provided whatever was necessary to the old man's deserved emotional stability. No flying off to foreign capitals for James, no artist lovers, no divided loyalties which, without intention, always appeared to betray. No. Just application, thoughtfulness and pursuit of his comprehensible goal.

From the age of eighteen he had diligently proceeded to become exactly what his father would have been, could he have managed anything more than a High School education; exactly what he wished but did not ever say he wished for his son: a lawyer. A successful lawyer who visited his father once a week, rang him regularly, talked politics and baseball with him and took him, along with his serious, political student girl-friend, to dinner and to the movies. Took him for drives. (For drives on winter nights when the roads turn icy and the snow, to which everyone in New England imagines they are so used, comes suddenly and treacherously.) James was his pride and his recompense.

Capricious Eleanor delivered no such goods. She was his irresponsible and somewhat ungrateful daughter. She wore too much eye make-up; her skirts were too short. What could he do? She would pay him brief visits then flit away, impatient to be off, guilty at abandoning him. But the guilt was never strong enough to keep her. She knew he was sad, wanting her to stay, but never saying so. She saw the smile on his face and the longing in his eyes whenever she waved goodbye to him from the bus or the departure lounge. She would remember dancing with him when she was a young girl, gliding along with him, ever so gently steered. He was such a good dancer. He was so gracious whenever she fled from him. She was his volatile and beautiful little mystery, the mystery in himself which he dared not explore. He could not risk such inner disturbance. He let her go. He let her be.

No, she did not intend to insult him by suicide when all that accumulated love translated into capital was sitting down the road needing to be spent. Not according to his intention, possibly, but then he had been anything but tyrannical and she suspected that he took a secret pleasure in her misdemeanours.

What he could never enjoy or understand, although he came, after his fashion, to terms with it, was her love for and her living with Jason Englefield. Dashing away from him, she would stay with Jason. Of all her vagaries that one most roused the paternal indignation and with it hints of passion and jealousy, glimpses of vile taboos with which he was unacquainted and which he refused to acknowledge. He consigned them to the depths and, as a result, behaved peculiarly towards his daughter without wanting to. Strangely enough, James did understand and tried his quiet powers of persuasion to bring the old man gradually round. What the latter found hardest to bear was the fact of Jason's keeping her in Europe. Why could she not have taken up with a New Yorker or a Bostonian? If it were queer specimens she were after, those native towns seemed more than able to cater to her needs. Why rot abroad?

Patrick Linnane met Jason Englefield only once. The Englishman struck him as preoccupied and incapable of affection. He did not care for his manner and failed to see how Eleanor could love this inanimate creature, except perhaps for the obvious strength of character apparent in his veracious face and thick, brown hair. He could not see why she wished to hide away with this surly and impecunious painter of abstractions in a freezing house in the middle of a swamp and grow potatoes and wash sheets by hand when she had all the advantages of her fancy education and was a fine figure of an Irishwoman into the bargain. Why, as he put it to James, when she could have had anyone? If he had been capable of using a word like masochist, that's the one he would have used. He didn't want to appear a stuffed shirt, understood what James kept saying about art and everything but, hell, she seemed to him to be simply throwing herself away. All that and a good deal of benign, paternal grumpiness which James allowed him to vent, interjecting his spare but apt remarks whenever he spotted an opportunity.

What finally stilled the complaints and appeased the nagging bewilderment was Clover. Patrick met her in that one discomfiting visit to Sussex. He adored her. He loved her fairness and her frankness. She appealed directly. She knew what she wanted and said so. And she expressed affection without restraint. Nothing could be more guaranteed to win his uncomplicated heart. He wanted grandchildren and neither his son nor his daughter had obliged so far, although he knew James would marry, being a man who did what was expected of him. He was acquainted with a bit of Eleanor's gynaecological history, which swung between the sordid and the macabre. The rest he did not want to know. It distressed him far more than what he recognized as her meretricious tendencies. Clover soothed that particular ache. He saw and deeply approved the way she and Eleanor loved each other. He concluded that if Jason Englefield would not or could not make of Eleanor an honest woman, this eight year old somehow did, and in a way that was more restful to his heart. The dubious complexities of her origins, he determined to ignore. His nature was too generous to consider them of any importance. In the end he forgave Clover her father. Patrick Linnane and Jason Englefield were polite to each other for three days, exchanged a firm handshake on parting, and never saw or spoke to each other again.

Daddy and James had timed their one and only transatlantic journey (neither of them had previously been further abroad than Montreal) to coincide with Jason's first important London exhibition. In the six and a half years Eleanor had lived with him, they had never met. She went annually to New England with an air ticket paid for by her father, an air ticket for one.

Eleanor lay on the floor, quiet now, thinking that the night of that opening might qualify as the last happy night of her life. Two months later, Daddy and James were gone, and her relationship with Jason was moribund. But that evening it had undergone a remission, like a patient who seems suddenly and magically to make a joke of the medical prognostications, or an ageing beauty who, catching a glimpse of herself in the mirror with benign backlighting or in a rare moment of unselfconscious pleasure, witnesses the resurrection of her twenty-year-old radiance.

God, she had been happy. High and happy and complete. Jason was there, and in glory, however transitory; her father was there, James was there, Clover was there, all their friends were there. She loved London and she loved her life. Above all, she loved Jason.

The remission had come to nothing. Jason's show had come to – not much. The euphoric affair had been founded on an illusion. No one, no one who counted, liked Jason's paintings or was interested in the elaborate theory of aesthetics on which his oeuvre rested. George Facer had paid lip-service, but after the débâcle what everyone had known all along became clear; George did not like Jason. Jason in turn did not like Eleanor. So they went back to Sussex and bickering and poverty and unrequited work. The disease proved terminal. Inexorably, it took its course and they descended to the next level, the level of violence.

Still, that night had existed. Perhaps somewhere it existed still. At least, she thought, it cannot be cancelled. For little instants she could live in its glow. It too could be run off on that internal projector and she could watch herself laughing in Jason's arms as they danced alone, both so drunk they could barely stand, but not ungraceful or in the least ridiculous, clinging to each other, swaying to some music barely audible above the human noise, alone in the middle of a circle of amused but approving smiles. Turning themselves, they were the axis on which the world turned. They stopped and stood looking into each other's radiant faces. There was soft applause. How had all that come about? Who brought music into the gallery? She could not remember. But she remembered making love with Jason in Caroline's spare bedroom with Clover asleep on the floor in a heap of blankets. Success, resurgence of love, and lack of space – the single bed was very narrow – threw them again and again into each other's arms. She felt his true strength, his honest ardour. All he sought was an obliteration of consciousness and the restoration of a balanced libido. With Jason one might substitute almost anything female. What he experienced of her as Eleanor she never knew. His lust was blind, his tastes undeveloped. He liked two or three things. But honest ardour has its thrills. In place of tendresse there is long familiarity and lack of expectation. Spent desire brings dreamless sleep and the comfort of familiar respiration. Sex like that is not interesting sex. It is appeasement and security. It is a draught.

Who brought music into the gallery? She could not remember. Anyway, she had been, she guessed, a success. She had been exuberant without losing her self-control. She had talked well to everyone: pop, op and minimal artists, mainstream abstractionists, primary structurists, rejectivists, formalists and anti-formalists. Even the arrival of the Blacks hadn't fussed her, even George Facer's silly wife. Felix Koning had slithered past and she wondered who the interesting piece of continental cheesecake might be. She had met Charles Bevan who had praised Jason's work and taken an obvious fancy to her. In her happiness she had invited him and Anthea to Sussex.

The image of Charles brought her out of the movie theatre. She thought of his invitation, then of the telephone which had not rung. Charles had helped her tamper in a big way with fate. No doubt there would be repercussions. Who cared? As if anything else could happen to her now.

Eleanor longed to sleep. Dear God, let me feel nothing. Just for a moment. Please, I want to feel nothing.

Darkness had become her element. She was lunary. As of yesterday afternoon all striving in the light among real creatures had ceased. She would simply let things happen until nothing happened anymore. She would squander her existence as a substanceless shadow among other shadows, surrounded by night scents and night sounds, expecting only the worst. The allure was undeniable. She would leave the light to Jason and his ilk, except that in that sunshine world Clover existed too.

She heard Jason telling her, 'You are a totally negative person. I cannot live anymore with your negativity.' And she questioned him over and over. 'Why, Jason, why? I loved your art when no one loved it. I loved you when no one loved you. I loved your child. Nine years ago I met you and I did not like you, Jason. You were cold and English and all opinions. No one loved you. But you had this baby girl with the silliest name I ever heard and no mother. And you wanted her. That is your great mystery – the way you wanted her and would not give her up. The way you want her still.

'One evening you turned up in my old flat on Westbourne Terrace. There you were, alone in the big, bad world with your baby and your ideas. Clover could walk by then and be quite amusing. But I kept back a little because I was shy of her, sensing in advance that she would force me into unfamiliar feelings. You were sitting opposite me on a rather pretentious divan I had inherited from a friend. (*I* had friends.) You were holding Clover who was squirming like a fat little worm wanting to be off burrowing in her own element. You looked at me and your expression changed. You were asking me something with your eyes. You let go of Clover, encouraging her with little pats on the bottom to crawl towards me. You smiled. You even laughed. She was coming closer and I did not know what to do. A *baby*? I wanted to draw back but you kept holding me with your eyes, eyes that said take her, take her. How could I not? I let her crawl on to me. Tentatively, I held her. She was wet, sticky, hyperactive. You had not changed her nappy in hours. Still, her gurgling made me silly and I giggled. I complained that she stank and you chuckled. I had never thought much of you, but suddenly you evoked in me a very strong sensation. It was not unpleasant. I grew to like it along with your child. You had recognized me, all right. You chose carefully, although I think on the spur of the moment. A week later you and your daughter moved in.'

At eleven-thirty Charles Bevan rang Eleanor, but she was too barbiturated to answer the telephone. Charles had returned home late and consulted his answering service. Disappointed, he determined to call her again in the morning, allowing her ample time to creep home from wherever it was she had been trysting. His concern transcended ordinary speculations about her activities. The visit from Simon had been not at all what he expected.

His old friend and cousin was in a state of agitation over a family affair. His sister Monica had recently purchased, for £5,000, a painting attributed to Teniers. Was it a fake, Charles asked. Quite the reverse. In which case it was a bargain. Therefore the delicate problem must involve the original owner. Right, but worse. Ah, the police. Afraid so, and they had already impounded. Purchased in a Market Ouvert? Um, not exactly. Private sale? Sort of. (Why this hedging?) Cash or cheque? Don't be silly, who wants records? Well, proof of import is not required in Great Britain. Have her write an immediate disclaimer. Not so simple.

Simon was groping for advice without wanting to give too much away. He stressed that he relied on Charles's discretion, no one else the family felt they could trust and so on, Jeremy being out of town. Charles persisted. The name of Felix Koning finally came up.

At ten o'clock the next morning Eleanor was awakened by the telephone. She experienced a moment of stillness before the daemons of consciousness rushed in on her. For a split second there was no pain. She crawled to the telephone, her thoughts in confusion, aching in every limb after a night spent on the floor without blankets.

She answered, her voice barely audible.

'Beauty, hello.' Felix hesitated. 'Are you all right?'

'Oh yes, yes I'm fine. I just – had a late night.'

'Good. You should have more of them.'

She couldn't answer.

'Well, do you think you might collect your scattered wits and run away with me?' He laughed.

'What?'

'Say yes, darling. I've been missing you so. We'll go to Rome. We talked of it. Surely you're remembering.'

'I am. I am remembering. But golly . . . ' She touched her unwashed hair. She had no clean clothes. Oh hell, she could buy some.

'Yes,' she said, trying not to sound excited. 'Yes, I'd adore to. London is horrible. Oh let's go, Felix. Let's get out of here. Only when?'

'Tonight. Can you manage it?'

'I think so.'

'Listen, darling, I have a great many things to do. Could you be an angel and book the flight for us? And could you collect also the tickets? And be at my flat by seven? And hold the taxi?'

'I think so.'

'You're adorable.'

'Thank you.'

Eleanor surveyed the wreckage of the room and shrugged. She was too dazed to question the implications of Felix's proposition. She only wanted to see him. She bathed, washed her hair, and forced down two bananas. She wrote out a cheque for Charles Bevan and put fifty pounds in an envelope addressed to Clover Englefield. (Not even Jason could tear up ten-pound notes.) She dressed quickly in dirty clothes and hurried off to South Molton Street.

Five minutes after she left, the telephone rang. When it had rung twenty times, Charles Bevan put down the receiver. At six pm he tried again. No reply. And he had told the Blacks to expect her. Well. Rashness did not suit him. He should have known better. At midnight, upstairs in his beloved study with Anthea asleep two floors below, he made a last attempt to reach Eleanor. He was in a mild panic. His instincts told him she had gone and with whom. Something must be done. He began to contrive as he let the telephone go on ringing. It felt weirdly futile, like trying to contact the dead. The sound of the telephone bounced back and forth off the walls of Eleanor's cold, dark box. The bed was still unmade, dirty clothes lay in heaps and two avocado skins shrivelled in the night.

six

Unpacking in the flat above the Via Serpente was no joke. Eleanor was not pleased with the contents of her suitcases. She would have been almost relieved to have uncovered one of those pieces of porcelain which she knew Felix had tucked, securely padded, into his own luggage and about which he had said nothing. But on opening her bag she found what she had half-expected to find: suicidal thoughts.

She stood looking at them, reflecting on the notion that growing up, in the final, falling stages of the disease, means being used to having one's suicidal thoughts accompany one abroad; relinquishing the hope that they might just this once remain at home to be picked up and dealt with later. Nope, there they are among the belts and tights and shirts, staring you in the face, confirming the chilling platitude that it is impossible to escape oneself. This is culmination of the growing-up disease: the surety that nothing can soothe beyond the merest extempore, that love is a cheat and a trap and that God, if still alive, has, like a bad parent, abandoned one to fate and the devil.

'And now you know all these terrible things,' she said aloud, for Felix was at lunch and she was alone, 'congratulations, you are a grown-up. And that means you are almost dead.'

It was true. Even the past week at the hotel and the great illusion of love in luxury had failed to banish the constant thirst, the itching, the bouts of exhaustion and her alarming weight-loss. More disappointingly, it had failed to banish anxiety. Was the problem psychosomatic or was something really wrong? She knew she ought to consult a doctor, but she was too frightened. She preferred familiar doubts to new certainties. And she dared not tell Felix who was annoyed by illness and even minor disabilities. (Two thousand years of sex and weariness makes one impatient with the little complaints of others.) Already she could sense his restless boredom. For, repress them how she might, her anxieties were seeping from every pore. She could smell them. One could not accuse Felix of insensitivity of body, however cavalierly he might treat the mind, heart and spirit. So she had better bath before he returned.

The memory of the hotel made her lower regions go up and down like the rococo lift, and she smiled in spite of herself. She had so completely lived out a fantasy. It was as though New England had never existed. The week was so successful that it had almost, but not quite, cancelled her life. With the exception of Felix's three business appointments, they had spent six days in bed, everything flourishingly supplied with the best Italian grovel. Loving, sleeping, eating (Eleanor a little), drinking (Eleanor a lot), watching television, talking, unaware of the time, the date or whether it were day or night. She supposed it was what the old-fashioned honeymoon was meant to be, except for any trace of shyness, except for any inexperience, and except that when the bill was presented Felix solemnly paid his half. He was no husband but he was no gigolo either. Those six days would certainly help to compensate for the horrific reels in the projection booth.

Where was Felix? He'd said lunch but that could mean anything. Although she had had glimpses of the company he appeared to be keeping in Rome, she was strictly excluded from his business engagements. But he could not prevent her guessing that those Italians and the porcelain had a dubious link which, in turn was connected to Felix's share of the hotel bill, their abrupt removal to the flat on Via Serpente (recently vacated, so he said, by a dear friend of many years and mysterious movements), the 'lunch' to which she had not been invited, and a letter from Monica Black whose handwriting he could not have known that she recognized.

He was plotting something. He was arranging bogus letters and papers from a dealer who could no longer be reached because he lived in Beirut or some other war-torn city. An issue was being complicated, and Felix was deeply engaged in the process. He was throwing up smokescreens between himself and something in England. Between himself and Monica? Eleanor didn't pry. Felix and his Italians might be plotting to steal a nuclear warhead for all she cared. She had given up wishing to know anything beyond what passed, true or false, between the two of them. Where love was concerned she was without scruples. If only she could learn never to count on him when she really needed him.

She took two tranquillizers, poured herself a glass of wine and continued unpacking. The flat comprised one room plus a small kitchen and bath. It was on the first floor with an outside stairway for an entrance, overlooked a small courtyard and was very charming: one of those lovely hideaways peculiar to Rome – and she could not help the feeling of its being very much a hideaway. Except for its charm, it was not so different from her room in London. She was either alone with Felix or alone with herself. She hung some skirts and dresses in a closet alongside his immaculate shirts. His preoccupation with clean linen in all its varieties was approaching the pathological.

She was by now craving his presence and very much on edge. Mustn't let the anxiety accumulate, though. It would be all the more difficult to dispel once she heard his soft tread on the stairs. Oh yes, and better have a bath. She lay in the tub, counting the months, weeks and days she had been with Felix, turning them over and heaping them up like a miser his money. The accumulated time was a kind of insurance. Every day that passed was a day passion had *not* ended. She could console herself with it after he was gone. 'We were together that long, at least . . .'

When he returned at four-thirty he found her still immersed, and very nearly unconscious from the combination of pills, wine and warm water. Without hesitation he removed his outer and undergarments, carefully folded some and hung the rest over the back of a wicker chair. He climbed into the tub and embraced the passive body with the breasts rather too large for the boyish proportions of the rest of it. Her wet hair was a very dark red. Her sedated eyes told him how long his absence had seemed.

He wrapped her in a large towel and carried her to the bed. She guessed she was leading a decadent life. Well, what else should she do – volunteer her services to Mother Theresa? Just before falling asleep she told Felix that she loved him, and unfortunately he heard her.

Felix continued to go out a good deal on what he preferred not to describe as business. He did not do business, but rather assisted in the movement of objects from one point in space and time to another. With his 'assistance' the Italians were transferring small Roman statues to Holland, easily skirting the export ban. This plundering of a nation's artistic heritage she would normally have found repellent, but in Felix's case she passed no judgement. He might do as he pleased as long as he remained with her. But she knew what he was up to, all right. Felix, among his other accomplishments, was an international fence. And a good one. Not, she suspected, first division, but well up there; far enough up to be used to exercising great caution. Whatever had just happened in London constituted an unprecedented slip-up for which he would never forgive – someone.

His announcement that they must shortly quit the Via Serpente did not surprise Eleanor very much. The news came bare of any future plans. Naturally. There was nothing to plan for. There were no ties that bound; they were wonderfully at liberty. They had nothing in common, not even a cat.

She was writing a letter to Clover when he told her. He came in, having been out all day, looking neither pleased nor worried. He kissed her, stroked her temples and hair, informed her for the hundredth time that her green eyes were very beautiful. He showered and changed, slipping with distaste from the apparel he had worn for only six hours.

She smiled at what she would have liked to call his personal daintiness. He emerged in a dressing-gown and sat opposite her at the small table. She went on writing, paralysed by his presence.

She waited for him to say something, too wretched to open a conversation herself. There are four of us, she thought, always four people present: two who lie and two who tell the truth. The two who lie have made a gentlemen's agreement to keep the others quiet so that forms may continue to be observed and life go on unruffled. The two who tell the truth sit bound and gagged watching the liars play out their charade. No probing, no questions, no arguments, muzzled by this mutual consent for the sake of law and order. But the longer the two remain muzzled, the stronger their presence grows. It fills the room. It is insupportable. The liars carry on. They smile, just a little, and appear cool. They speak their lines.

'Darling, what have you been doing all day?' he asked as though he had not just torn out her heart and dined on it.

'Went to the Villa Julia to look at the Etruscan stuff. Came back. Waited for my mysterious Felix.'

'How nice. There are some lovely things at Villa Julia. Did you have lunch?'

The eternal question of the eternal city.

'Yes,' she lied, describing a place she had seen in a nearby street, inventing practically an entire menu.

'But you should have had the ossobuco, angel. It is excellent there on Thursdays. What are you writing?' Quizzical as always. God, to smile and smile and be a villain.

'A letter to go in Clover's Christmas card. It's Christmas next week.'

'Of course it is. I'll book us a table for lunch.'

Ah-ha, a reprieve. Perhaps she might not be condemned to spend the holidays alone.

'Oh Felix, can we?' In her excitement she knocked something small and hard and white on to the floor. Sharp-eyed Felix retrieved it.

'What's this, my precious? A little totem you hide away?'

She blushed at being discovered in her doting. 'It's one of Clover's milk teeth.' The tooth was one of a collection of tiny mementoes: a baby curl, severed at two from the adorable head, a drawing turned out at four and presented solemnly to her and her alone, some photographs documenting Clover's rosy evolution into early maidenhood, a mother's-day card, handmade and horrible, a mangled cat made of yarn. She carried the secret hoard in a bag which she took everywhere.

She thought Felix would make fun of her but he didn't. He took the tooth to the window and examined it in the late afternoon light.

'But it's so beautiful,' he declared with great seriousness. 'Hard and soft like a pearl. Like herself, no doubt. No wonder you keep it close to you. There,' he placed it beside the letter she had just finished. She felt like crying. He understood when she least expected him to. She opened the bag and handed him a photograph, the most recent, taken by Jason. Felix pronounced it as execrable as the artist's paintings. The poor girl was pretty, no doubt. He stared at the photograph for a long time. She wanted to tell him how dreadful it was to be deprived of the child of one's heart if not of one's womb.

'How like you to guard your little treasures. You're quite adorable.' He handed her the photograph, took up a newspaper and sat in the chair furthest away from her. 'But, darling, you shouldn't care so much,' he said from behind *Il Mondo*.

'That's very good advice.' And it was a death-knell.

'Sometimes you're very – mmm, *within*. It's a bit morbid. Gaiety suits you better.'

'Is that what you really think?'

'You say to yourself Felix doesn't know me. But Eleanor, I do know you. I know you, as the English say, terribly, terribly well.'

They spent Christmas together, but the day before New Year he announced that he must pay a visit to friends in the country and would return. He did not say when. He did not say who the friends were, he did not invite her, and made no apologies for not inviting her. He simply went away, leaving most of his belongings. Two days later when he opened the door and walked into the room on the Via Serpente, he looked like a light-bulb that had gone out. That interest which he had beamed on her and on which she was so dependent had been withdrawn. He had taken it back into himself until he should be excited enough to direct it at another. Perhaps there already was another. Yet he was, as always, a polite, elegant male with a hint of the female. A man who knew how the world worked and how inconvenient it was in that world to feel too much too long.

'Darling,' he said when he had kissed her, 'what will you do?' As though she were going shopping and it were a question of Bond Street or Knightsbridge. Simple curiosity.

She wanted to scream, smash glasses, kill him, kill herself. But she kept quiet. She kept still. That old fear of him – he was so damned efficient in maintaining law and order. She didn't cry. She acted almost as a reasonable person might act. She watched him watching her inner struggle. She imagined his thoughts: what did women want whenever this particular moment came? Why persevere, why even be hurt? Pleasure was pleasure, such a simple equation and one they wished eternally to complicate. No doubt he felt very tired of them all.

'Will you go back to London?' She answered his question with another.

'Eventually.' His surface was like sea sand when the waves withdraw, wiping away all imprints and leaving a beautiful, momentary sheen reflecting nothing but light and sky, awaiting, in its transient perfection, other imprints which also would be washed away.

'Why did you bring me here?' she asked him.

'Because you wanted it.'

She thought, I should have behaved badly as I would with anybody else. Behaving well doesn't get you anything and it doesn't make any difference.

'Where will you go now?'

'Stuttgart. This evening.'

'Why?'

'Eleanor, we will discuss this another time.'

She knew she must be the first to go. To quit the charming premises before he did would leave her with the only dignity she might salvage. Even now, the dignity counted not in her own view but in his. She cared so much how she appeared to him. There was an hour's silence as she packed two suitcases.

'Darling, shall I call you a car?'

'No thank you.'

Felix shrugged.

Her first impulse on reaching the street was to leave Rome immediately. She took a taxi to the airport and a plane to London. Her only wish was to see Clover.

Without sleep or food she took another taxi from Heathrow to Victoria and from there a train to Sussex. She did not know the day or the date, only that it was cold and that the countryside she loved was making no impression on her as she watched it through the rain-splattered window.

'I'll show up,' she kept telling herself. 'He can't stop me just showing up.'

Jason allowed her to spend the afternoon and early evening alone with Clover in her chaotic bedroom. They laughed and chattered nonsense and played backgammon. Eleanor could not stop hugging and kissing her. At six Jason announced that the London train left in twenty minutes and that he would drive her to the station, would she please collect her belongings. She was too tired to resist him. She would simply sneak back next week.

In silence Jason carried one of her bags to a first-class compartment.

'Eleanor,' he said as she collapsed into an empty seat, 'Eleanor,' his teeth clenched, 'don't you *ever* do this to me again.' He turned and left.

Eleanor opened the window and shouted after him as the train lurched out of the station.

'Fuck you, Jason, you son of a bitch, fuck you, you asshole creep. Just – Fuck You!'

People on the platform turned in astonishment. Jason disappeared down the stairway that led to the car park. Eleanor slammed shut the window, lit a cigarette between trembling fingers and burst into tears.

She arrived back at Victoria in a state of delirium. She had been travelling for twenty-four hours. Return to the Mallards' and a room full of dirty clothes seemed out of the question. But she did not know where to go. She could do anything she wanted and no one would care. That's what it meant to be completely free.

She stood outside platform nineteen, a suitcase in each hand, adrift in the world, a rootless being. She had no idea how long she stood there in semi-trance. She realized someone was offering, and had been offering, to help her with her luggage. A Frenchman. He was looking at her hard, and it occurred to her that the one thing she still might be was noticeable.

She had never had a Frenchman. With a pang she thought of Felix. This one was better looking than Felix, yet he was somehow lustreless and, despite the appraising Parisian stare, deeply unconfident. He radiated no light, absolutely none. From now on every other man would be fifth-rate. Eleanor thanked him, made a fatuous remark, and handed him her suitcases.

seven

Dearest Charles,

By now you must think I write to you only when I want you to do something for me. You're right. I make use of you. I'm sorry. But I think of you, Charles, I really do, more than any other man. And in a way I am fonder of you than any other man. You are the only one I trust.

I suppose I ought to feel guilty, especially now, asking you for help when you have had your own misfortunes, even disasters. You, of all people. But I have only heard things – rumours, gossip. I don't believe any of their twisted tales, those hypocrites of whom I am now, thank heaven, thoroughly rid. I shall withhold judgement until I have the truth from your own lips. Is it so bad? It can't be so bad.

I shouldn't be pestering you yet again to sort out my tangled affairs, but I still can and will pay you, Charles, if that is any consolation, and I suppose at this point it must be. If the rumours are true. But you know it is difficult for me to feign guilt, much less feel it. I want what I want, although I seldom get what I want – save for the practicalities you provide so cleverly and so graciously. Anyway, I call on you again.

This is what I want: first, to make my will. I know you have urged me to do this for years but the idea was distasteful to me. Besides, I never believed there would be any money left except for what belongs to Clover. You know it was my intention to squander the rest. That was before I got sick and scared.

Now I have neither the inclination nor the energy to squander. I've been forced to conserve. So I thank you once more for the arrangements last year. The income is not much but it has saved me from a fate not pleasant to contemplate. You are a good man, Charles. I have been perverse in not following your advice. I have alternately pestered and ignored you. Yet you save me at the eleventh hour. You are a good man. Here is another thing I want you to do: ensure that my corpse, when I become one, is returned to England for cremation. Raised a Catholic, I have always been repelled by the funeral pyre. Now I want obliteration. And as fast as possible. I want to be *off*. No slow rot. Instant conflagration with nothing remaining to be reminded or hurt. Do as you please with the ashes. I am tired of my body and I do not want it to be resurrected. Fuck the Last Judgement.

I don't know why I never told you, but I have been very ill. You would hardly recognize me, I have altered so. (Could you come and see me, do you think? Could we do all this in Paris? Really I am too ill to travel. I would pay your fare. You are the only one, besides Clover, whom I could bear to see and who could bear to see me and not mind too much that I don't look the way I used to. I was beautiful, wasn't I, in a funny way?) But I am improving slowly as long as I stay put and follow the routine I have set for myself. The injections make it imperative that I do so. And Paris is somehow kinder than London. The English with their feigned concern, ugh! It seems more appropriate that, since I am a stranger everywhere, I speak in a foreign tongue.

So you see my wanderings have come to an end along with my squandering. Somehow the disease has given me back the concentration and discipline I have not had since I was an adolescent hungry for knowledge. You will be pleased to learn that I have returned to the viola. It is a crazy struggle with this most difficult instrument and I am not sure what the object of the exercise may be. It will lead probably nowhere. It is absurd except that it keeps me living. It and Clover keep me living.

And another thing. I want Jason to be notified of the whereabouts of my funeral. I want him to bring Clover, I want him to witness his accomplishment. And also – please don't be annoyed and please don't tell anyone this – I want Felix Koning and Monica Black to be there as well, if possible. (Felix must now be 2004 and Monica at least four and a half.) And remember – no boring, phoney memorial service. A real funeral. I want them to *see* me go out. I know. You think I'm vengeful and melodramatic. Well, I am.

Having begged your assistance yet again I suppose I should apologize for failing to keep our appointment last October. You must, however, be pretty inured to my *méchanceté*. I promise you I've changed – a little. I shall definitely be here. There is nowhere for me to go. In the atlas I bought for the purpose I have blacked out all of America and Europe, Chile, Brazil, Peru, Japan, Egypt and half the Middle East. I regret missing the Hermitage, but one cannot black out everything. Excuse me if I also say I have tried every man I wished to try – at least I think so.

But my apology, darling Charles, back to my apology. Let me explain. I was paying one of my flying visits to England, as you know. In between Prague and Toledo (God, I've seen so much art, so many churches, hotels, cafés, restaurants, they were like a drug, I couldn't stop), in between Claus and Luis, I came back as I always come back. Compelled by my need to see Clover and to confront Jason and do battle with him all over again. Because nothing has ever been resolved between us. I know now that it never will be. So my eristical spirit requires that he see me dead. You're thinking how morbid she is. She's come completely unhinged. I have, but I'm all right in my funny way.

I came back. I had not seen Clover for nearly six months, although I had telephoned her from all over the world. Jason can't always pick up the receiver first. I came back. I took the train from Victoria and a taxi from the station as I always do, intending to catch Clover as school let out, to walk home with her through the Sussex lanes before Jason arrived to pour poison on our happiness. But wouldn't you know, just my luck, it was sports day or jolly hockey day or whatever these athletic Bacchanals are called in the land of the euphemism.

I stepped out of the taxi to find 400 people, mainly Mums, seated on obdurate benches at the edge of a bleak and windy field under an ominous sky. I was dressed, well, as I dress, noticeably, I suppose, at least in relation to all that crimplene. I had also touched up my hair. (I have stopped that now. It is a dreary brown.) It was very red and very long and very blown. Everyone stared at me as if I were an apparition, though some of them recognized me. Nevertheless I smiled, thinking I have as much right to be here as all you tight-kneed, buttoned-up Christian fascists who think you still have to wipe your children's bottoms for them, whose only joy may lie in alternately wiping those bottoms and slapping them. I strode towards the benches, my heels sinking into the turf, feeling as though a sniper might pick me off at any moment. (Imagine mentalities so sick that they take umbrage at a little honest vulgarity.) Suddenly, I saw Jason, virtually the only man amidst that sea of Mums, scowling at me like the Grand Inquisitor. I waved at him and took a seat at the end of the lowest bench. Every head turned in his direction.

I sat there shivering. I had forgotten how chilling the Sussex wind can be. I watched the field hockey or whatever it is – God I hate sports – frozen and bored, waiting only for Clover's appearance and growing more and more frightened of Jason's wrath which would certainly descend on me the minute all this was over. I had given my solemn oath never again to show up unannounced. I always promise the same thing and I always break my word. Fuck him.

Finally the girls' netball team took the field with Clover as captain. She must have been three inches taller than when I last saw her. She was thirteen and nearly my height. (She should have been borrowing my clothes, stealing my make-up and my birth-control pills. What's a mother for?) They seemed to be playing brilliantly, as everyone was shouting approval. I wanted to cheer, to yell and clap my hands and jump up and down when she scored a goal. Do you call them goals? Even I could appreciate her obvious superiority. She is a little heroine, she really is. But I sat there paralysed with cold, aware of the first drops of rain and Jason's frigid gaze on the back of my head, afraid to make a move other than furtively swallowing tranquillizers. Afraid even to smoke a cigarette.

When the game was over, a decisive victory for the home team, Clover suddenly saw me and, after a glance at Jason, ran across the pitch to embrace me. I cried, she cried. Then there was Jason looming over us like the imminent deluge. He ordered her to collect her things from the locker, which she obediently did. I was aware that the Mums were having a field-day of their own observing the little drama which Jason was doing his utmost to defuse. I can scare him as much as he can scare me. I can make him tremble.

'You broke your promise,' he hissed.

'Does that surprise you? Can't we go to the car? I'm freezing.'

'*We* are not going anywhere. *You* are going home.'

'I don't have a home.'

'That's your problem.'

I stood my ground, my heels sinking deeper into the damp earth, my head and Jason's bare to the rain. He was determined I should not have a minute alone with Clover. He is the most determined bastard I ever met.

Clover joined us, smiling but clearly distressed. Her tie was undone and her shirt, with two baby tits pushing against the stained white cotton, was unironed. The zipper of her school skirt was closer to her navel than her hip, and half the buttons were missing from her cardigan. Hesitantly, she took both our hands. With my free one I straightened her skirt. Despite her dishevellment she was so beautiful that I nearly fell over: blue eyes turning to black, Jason's abundant hair, white forehead, little nose, full lower lip.

'You're worse than I am.' I laughed.

She shrugged. Then she laughed too. I kissed her cheek. Jason maintained his frozen frown. Clover asked if we could all go for an ice-cream. Simultaneously I said yes and Jason said no. It was raining, he said. It was time to go home. He'd make her a sandwich, *goodbye* Eleanor.

'Aren't you coming? Isn't she coming?' Clover turned from one of us to the other, bewildered by the irresponsibility of grown-ups. We're so irresponsible it's obscene.

Jason marched her towards the car, grasping her hand while I clung to the other, trailing behind them. Pig eyes and poultry faces followed our exit; faces set like jelly moulds in anticipation of something about to go horribly wrong.

Resolutely, I positioned myself by the driver's side of the car.

'I'm coming too. I won't stay long, but I'm coming.'

'No you're not.'

Then I saw the sacred rage which I am so wonderful at provoking. I had pushed things too far and I was afraid. Jason is very strong. Before I could say or do anything he had shoved me aside and thrust a weeping Clover into the back seat. He confronted me with the car door half-open.

'Piss off,' he shouted.

'I have nowhere to go,' I shouted back.

'Then go nowhere.'

I called him some name, I can't remember what, and he came at me like a meteor. Trying to escape the palm of his hand, I stepped backwards into the road just as one of the Mums with a car full of ghastly children rolled towards me, travelling slowly in the downpour. The car hit me. I was lifted on to the bonnet over which I toppled, landing on the wet pavement. Clover was beside me, then a lot of people I did not know and never want to see again, then I woke up in Eastbourne Hospital with one side of my face twice the size of the other. I had fractured my cheekbone, that was all. But Jason had abandoned me with no message and no ensuing communication.

There you have the major trauma of that week in October. But three days later in London I had an encounter in a restaurant which unnerved me terribly; someone I could not bear to see, still, after all this time, and the irony of his being with her, although I can guess why . . .

My face was so swollen and discoloured that I thought at first the two of them might not recognize me, but they did and came and kissed me, the vile hypocrites with their feigned concern.

'Dear me, what a nuisance,' was his comment on my misfortune. Imagine.

'Never mind,' I snapped, 'I'll win the next round,' and winked at that serpent with my one good eye. I knew I could not stay another night in London.

After that things really began to go wrong.

I've been a mad fool, that's what you're thinking, I know. All the men and the tearing about and the squandering. That was how I wanted it all the time. Non-stop, screw and scram. I didn't know or I didn't want to know what was really happening to me. I ignored the weight-loss, the weight-gain, the thirst, the sores, the dizziness, even the blackouts – all the clues that should have warned me. I've left it too long, maybe too late. But you can put some of it right, Charles. You can put right what remains. You can put everything right.

Come to Paris, please. I ask you for the third time, as in a fairy-tale. And could you bring Clover? You could persuade Jason to submit, just this once. Disarm him with your rationalism, Charles, and your goodness. Plead my case. Say that at least he will be spared the sight of me. Please, please. I must see Clover. She misses me. All her letters say so. But I suppose it will be too much trouble to bring her. Too much trouble for everyone.

How much is the trust worth now? I always ask you this, don't I, but I need to know. I'm worried about interest rates and the effects of inflation. I subscribe to *The Economist*. I, Eleanor Linnane, lapsed Marxist. Send me the most recent figures, dear Charles, and please, please come to Paris. Come for tea, I promise not to play the viola. We can listen to Haydn quartets. I have a vast record collection. That should cheer you up. Even you must be depressed at this moment. I am sorry for you. Almost as sorry as I am for myself.

Eleanor folded the letter, the first she had written to anyone but Clover in weeks, and put it in an envelope addressed to Charles Bevan, Lincoln's Inn Fields.

'Where are the stamps, where are the stamps?' She rose from the desk with difficulty and shuffled across the room. She dreaded having to hobble down to the *tabac*, dragging her swollen foot in its slipper, the toe and the outside of which she had cut open with a pair of scissors. The ulcers had been quiescent for the past two weeks, but now her foot was again inflated like a hideous balloon with five fat appendages. Only the mutilated slipper could contain it. To walk was agony. Once more she would have to ask the concierge to do the shopping for her. It was so humiliating.

After a temperamental search she found the stamps on one of the bookshelves which lined half the sitting-room. She had acquired a flat, she had acquired possessions, few and too late, but she had acquired them. All at once in a burst of panic spending, knowing she must stay put at last and that staying put meant having *things*, things to touch, to refer to, to lend her the support withheld by humans. Books, records, some furniture, a few pictures she liked.

It was not the flat of which she used to dream, not the one she had conjured and rejected standing alone by Felix's fire. It was not high and elegant and clean like Felix's. But it was beautiful in its cluttered way, its third-storey windows opening, eyrie-like, on to all of Paris cinquième. She could no longer afford the flat of her dreams. But she could look down from her little height upon the world. Now that it was too late.

The three other rooms off the narrow corridor were small and dark, but she liked them that way. In one she slept, fitfully, whenever she did not pass out listening to music on the chaise-longue in the sitting-room; in one she cooked simple meals which she ate alone at a table with one chair; the third she used as a store-room, letting cartons and old clothes pile up higgledy-piggledy next to the laundry and the ironing board. She thought that one day she might turn the place into a bedroom for Clover. One day in four years and eight months when Clover had purchased her freedom.

Eleanor spent most of her days in the sitting-room where she at last had exercised her cultivated but untried taste. It was not entirely satisfactory; much of what she would have liked was now beyond her means. But the colours were good – deep rose, pale cool yellow, opaque black. Diamond-white Felix would not have approved the intimate clutter: pictures of father, brother, Clover, cards and drawings by Clover, three small Englefields, sprays of dried flowers, rustic pots, antique toys, lace curtains, shells, small pieces of aboriginal art, gifts and remembrances from friends who no longer were. She had gathered them together in an attempt to surround herself only with what had been kind and not hurtful. Jason would have said it was a woman's room. It was true. She was a woman alone in a woman's room.

Three o'clock. Time to drink a jasmine tea and practise the viola until the foot refused to bear her weight. She had gained weight, a little too much. She wore glasses. One of her eyes was chronically inflamed and gave her a good deal of discomfort.

She took up the precious instrument she never had been, could not and never would be able to play. She scratched and scraped away at Kreutzer, muttering blasphemies. No one in the building complained, the viola was such an unobtrusive instrument, not shrill and exciting like the fiddle, but warm, dark and difficult, difficult, difficult. No, the neighbours had nothing to complain of. The late suppers, the laughter and the arguments had ceased as had the waking at midday. She was a quiet, regulated person who had structured her life in order to save it. She maintained a rigid schedule, rising at nine, neither before nor after, eating small amounts every two hours, giving herself the injections at eleven-thirty and four-thirty, reading, practising, sleeping.

Eleanor played until she could no longer stand, and her fingers, worn down at right angles, were bent with fatigue. The spring light was fading from the big window. The pattern of the lace curtains shadowed across the floor grew indistinct. It was nearly five and time to rest on the chaise-longue, to recharge before cooking her supper at seven. She lay down, too tired to mind about her deep frustration with the instrument. Like everything she wanted, it maddened and eluded her.

She gazed out at the blur of Paris. She imagined Clover coming to see her here, to stay with her in her flat. She would tell this grown-up Clover what it had been like to be Eleanor, to lead Eleanor's mistake-ridden life and to have come to Eleanor's just deserts. And she would tell Clover how her life would be different and how she would be the little heroine she was and had to be.

She took a letter from the stack which she kept on a table next to the couch and reread it. 'I love you with all my heart and you know that,' was the closing line written in a large hand which rose optimistically if unsteadily to the right, reaching towards some fuller expression but still anxious about spelling mistakes. A hand that showed candour, health, disorder, faith.

Eleanor read the letter again then let it slide to her breast as she began to fall asleep, something which, a year ago, she could never have done at this time of day and which two years ago she could not have accomplished at all without the aid of drugs. In her near-somnolence she heard a female voice singing faintly but distinctly. It tore at her heart in a kindly way. The voice was accompanied by an orchestra and seemed to find its way through her half-open window. It came from the streets, the parks, the clouds, the buildings, seeking her sweetly out, wanting to carry her off to the exotic regions of which the lyrics spoke so sensuously. She thought she recognized the music. Was it *Nuits d'Été*? And the voice – it was Regine Crespin's. Or perhaps it was her own. She might be singing or listening or dreaming or all three. She was happy. The music was all she craved: the excitement of imagined love, the consolation of imagined beauty.

She was seated opposite a man. The man held out to her a baby. The man's eyes fixed on hers and she could not look away. Take her, the eyes said, 'Take her.' A hand with long fingers and fair hair stroked her temples and cheeks, touched her face and tilted it, compelling her to look into eyes that were both kind and cold. But she turned away. She wanted to listen to the music, not look into the eyes. The music extinguished memory. It died away and left her, the room and Paris in silence.

II

....

JASON

eight

Jason Englefield was not successful. He told himself and everyone he knew that success signalled the demise of thought, the personal vision and the creative capacities. It meant that ossification had set in and that spiritual death was only a matter of time. He despised success and all it implied. This ascetic stance, adopted in his mid-teens, had alarmed his mother who feared he might join a mendicant order of monks. His father, an executive in an automobile manufacturing company, assured her that the phase would pass. With a little time and the right sort of deprivation, Jason would come to love money and possessions like any normal moral person. Secretly, he wondered if his son might be a homosexual, but calm consideration of the matter left him convinced that, among Englefields, aberrations of this sort were not possible. Still, Jason remained a stranger to pleasure and did not lose his virginity until the age of twenty. At twenty-one he became a self-taught artist and stayed adamantly so for the rest of his life. He did not want to be influenced.

After public school he refused university and curtly informed his father that he need not bother to leave him anything in his will. His two sisters might carve up the spoils.

Jason's strength of character both attracted and repelled others, mainly repelled them. He regarded himself as a superior being and set about amassing evidence to support the illusion. Yet he also reckoned that he was an honest man. He valued himself for what he refused to do, and cultivated a brutal directness which matched his natural indisposition to enjoyment. What notoriety he did attain was founded as much on his offensive behaviour as on his talent as a painter.

At a group show in Oxford in 1963 he took umbrage at a critic's remark about the work of Dillon Butterworth, his friend. His only friend. After a brief exchange, the critic lay on the floor with a fractured jaw. Jason was served with a writ for Grievous Bodily Harm. Nothing came of the writ. In 1968 when he was included in one of the Whitechapel New Generation Exhibitions, he caused keen embarrassment to the gallery which had acceded to Princess Margaret's demands that a vibrating black box be switched off. The opening's royal guest of honour said the buzzing had given her a headache. She was accosted by Jason Englefield who pointed out, loudly and at some length, that her title did not include the right to dictate upon matters of art. He spluttered about freedom, repression and the *divina artista* but the black box remained quiescent.

As a matter of principle he provoked arguments with anyone who wore a uniform.

Jason's goal was not to imitate appearances or illustrate ideas, but to make a reality of painting itself. He had first appeared on the scene in 1960 when he set up in London, and by 1962 had attracted some unsolicited attention. It was a time of confidence for artists and of acceptance for their work before the recession of the late Seventies brought reduced art investment as well as widespread resentment at government spending on art. The acquisition of bricks and dirty nappies for posterity provoked public outcry and a major scandal.

Mathematical abstraction was still in flower – just. It suited Jason's rabid individualism, but he made no compromise with expediency. Convinced as he was that 'art cannot win the world without losing its soul', he was impatient neither to show nor to sell. He relished the observation of his own development and the process of making each of his many paintings and drawings. He was in no hurry to accommodate the art market or the dealers who functioned as manipulators according to the bourgeois conception of property, turning paintings into consumer objects. He struggled to remain free of the business world. He was not going to allow his art to become an investment opportunity. He was not going to be possessed.

He needn't have worried because his work proved, in the main, unmarketable. It was as though his own negative will precluded its acceptance. There were group shows in Düsseldorf, Leicester and Oxford and the Serpentine, and at last in 1972 a one-man show at the Facer Gallery. But Jason's relationships with museums, collectors and dealers – especially George Facer – were strained and infertile. In 1965 he did not receive a Harkness Fellowship. In 1967 he was not awarded the Peter Stuyvesant Travel Bursary.

In the Whitechapel shows of 1964 and 1968 he refused to offer any comment on his two pieces. His space in the catalogue was a blank. He kept quiet, worked hard and did not advertise himself. His attitude was incomprehensible to everyone. He savoured his own slow maturation and spent years trying to solve the same formal problems. In his desire for purity he sought to control all aspects of his paintings. He despised the random, the gestural, the automatic, and remained eternally in love with the idea of repeating and perfecting a style.

He was contemptuous of the artistic eclecticism of the Seventies and declined to exhibit in the Royal Academy's 'British Painting 1952–

1977'. As a constructivist he scorned *laissez-faire* expressionism and what he regarded as the chauvinistic neo-romanticism of British art. It was whimsical, literary, definitely not pure. The efflorescence of representation was the last straw. He buried himself in Sussex, hiding from the world and an art market that did not care where or whether he hid. In 1980 he was not included in the Hayward Annual.

In his pride, which could assume majestic proportions, he stubbornly maintained that he neither wanted nor needed help from anyone. 'Help' he defined as, above all, money. Then came encouragement, which he equated with flattery; constructive criticism, which he deemed superfluous; and love, which made him feel peculiar.

So much the worse for Eleanor. He was permanently furious with her after her unexpected and ill-fated appearance on Sports Day. She had reminded him yet again of her former efforts in that broad category labelled Help. Why had she tried, why did she want to try, and for God's sake why bother to go on trying? Above all, why torment him with visits?

'It's only to see me, Jason,' Clover assured him as she scrubbed potatoes for the supper they always cooked and ate together in the isolated cottage, the rent for which Jason could not afford. 'Eleanor doesn't want you back, you know. She said so.' She deposited the peelings in the piggy bucket collected daily by an emissary from a farmer down the road.

'That would be a great relief if I could believe it.'

'Why not believe it? It's me who's telling you.'

'Look, princess – '

'Don't call me princess.'

'All right, twit – '

'I prefer twit.' Her father seemed to her most strange when he thought he was being affectionate.

'I'm not stupid. I'm not a monster. I know that you and Eleanor are fond of each other.' Clover said nothing. Jason placed six sausages beneath an unsalubrious grill. It had not been cleaned since his brief affair with a student. 'But allow me to speak up for myself and register my complaints against these sudden visits. They embarrass me and upset you. She's completely irresponsible.'

'But if she asked in advance to come you wouldn't let her.' Clover began to make some pastry. She had learned this skill from Eleanor and, partly out of the boredom of her solitude and partly to please her father, she was in the process of raising it to a high art.

'True.'

'But why?' They had had this discussion many times. She never tired of it and never gave it up. She had her father's persistence.

'Princess – uh – Clover,' Jason was becoming exasperated. 'Again I ask you to believe me when I tell you I know the woman much better than you do. She isn't honest. One can't believe what she says even if she means it when she says it. That's because she's controlled by her emotions which are completely unstable. They make her an untrustworthy person, incapable of honour or self-discipline. All her talk about belief in art and belief in me – '

'She does believe in you. She told me so. If *you* were ill she'd – '

'If I were ill, she's the last person I'd want to see. I'd take an immediate turn for the worse. Anyway, she's a dilettante and she can't be trusted.'

He didn't mention his suspicions about Eleanor and Felix Koning. Did she think he was such an idiot as not to have grasped that straightaway? He felt he ought to mention it to Clover, but he could not. His brutal honesty extended almost, but not quite, to his only daughter. He told himself he would disillusion her another time. Then the scales would fall from her eyes and the blossom would bruise at last. And *she*, *she* with the nerve to ask over and over, vexing him to distraction, what went wrong between them . . . mentally, he rendered Monica a grudging thanks for having the decency to suffer in silence. Not that he liked her any better for it.

'I know Eleanor's a bit mad. But at least she's not unkind. She wouldn't have left you alone in Eastbourne Hospital with no one to talk to and feeling all miserable.'

'It was her fault. She asked for it. The whole episode was her own damned fault.'

'That doesn't matter. It was a mean thing to do, Jason, what you did. And also it wasn't fair.'

'Fair! Huh! Your notion of justice is, as always, a bit naïve. You're very idealistic.'

'I'm not. I'm very practical. I can darn socks and make pastry and groom a horse and – '

'Well, I can paint.'

'So what. I can paint as well. And some day I'll be as good as you are.'

He was touched by the last remark, especially since he knew how angry, for a sweet-natured girl, she really was.

'That reminds me, did you post the card I made for her?'

'Of course I posted it. Do you think I'm not honourable? How could you think I wouldn't post it? But I'm sure she'd been discharged by the time it arrived. There was nothing really wrong with her.'

Clover made no reply.

'You're very irrational, you know. You think it's all my fault. You may not say so, but that's what you think. Well *it is not my fault.*'

They ate in silence. Two days later Clover began to menstruate.

nine

'I read one of your notebooks yesterday.'

Clover had been upstairs practising the cello. Jason was half aware of the patchy little tune she was dutifully scraping out and felt a pang at the image of her alone with her music and her new condition. But he did not realize, absorbed as he was, that she had put down her bow suddenly, come into the studio, and was now standing behind him. At her announcement he stopped painting.

'I couldn't not. You know how curious I am.'

He turned. She flushed and smiled a little. 'You leave them all over the place. I just picked one up. I knew that it wasn't one of your – um – essays. I knew it was personal.'

He took a deep breath and wiped his hands on a rag. Her disclosure left him annoyed, amused, afraid. He was unnerved by her candour. She had a genius for indiscretion, and to this trait had been added the fact that she was now technically a woman. She would be fourteen in a month. Within a year she could theoretically make him a grandfather. Talk about unsettling. And now this.

'I read this one.' She held up a dark-red notebook and walked towards him, keeping it at the level of his face. 'All of it.'

Like many misunderstood heroes of art, Jason kept copious journals in which he told himself all that he really thought and lectured into nowhere about everything others ought to think. They had begun as commentaries on works in progress and continued as attempts to synthesize and validate his theories of colour and painting. What Eleanor called his Ascetic Aesthetics. They contained sketches and studies, many of them interesting, some more interesting than his paintings. But they also veered into commentaries on his personal life, becoming compendiums of observations, daily events, gossip, malice, resentment, inspiration, anger and pain – all generated by a longing for human contact which he would have been loathe to admit. He preferred to regard himself as lacking peers.

He took the notebook from Clover and opened it. The first page bore the inscription, 'Art's reward is its own virtue.' He looked at the date on the spine: 1962–3. Ironically, unerringly, she had found *that* one. He told himself there was nothing for it but to be as blunt as she. She was a woman now, after all. She was asking for it. It was not his fault.

'Who is Monica?'

'Monica is your biological mother, as you know. I've made no secret of that.'

'But who is Monica *Black*?'

'Sweetheart, I – '

'You don't want to tell me, do you?' She glared at him. 'You promised me, Jason. You said when I was old enough, when the time was right. Well, look what's happened to me. I don't know why it's happening or why God made me this way – '

'I explained all that to you – '

'But you never explained why I feel the way I do. I feel alone and confused and I want to know about my mother. This must be the right time. It must be. Anyway, I say it's the right time.'

'Yes, yes, I agree with you, but will you let me finish what I was going to say?'

'No.'

'Then will you let me finish this bit of the painting?'

'No.'

'Clover . . .' Jason's voice deepened as his back straightened and his chin came forward, 'if you think you're such a grown-up young lady – '

'I cannot be grown-up *and* young. And I am not and never will be a lady.'

Her words made him wince. Their form and content were taken wholesale from Eleanor. At that moment she even looked like Eleanor.

'Can we at least sit down, daughter?' He capitulated as far as a strong, straight man can capitulate. 'I daren't call you anything else in this hair-splitting mood.'

They cleared a space on Jason's paint-splattered table and pulled up two wobbly chairs. Clover snatched Jason's pad and produced her own watercolours.

'I'm going to paint,' she said. She liked to and could do two things at once.

The early winter dark had come, and they could see nothing but black through the French windows at the other end of the studio. Jason switched on the green metal light fixture – also paint-splattered – which hung over the table and gave the scene the aspect of a police interrogation. Outside, bare shrubs huddled by the house against the Sussex wind. Jason and Clover heard the fog-horn in the Channel. The sound made them both hesitate. Clover broke the silence.

'Go on then,' she said.

'You might ask nicely.' Jason leaned back in his chair, appearing relaxed and feeling sick.

'Pleeeze begin.' She was working away with the brush.

'It all started with my bad teeth,' he said, thinking it might make her laugh even though it was also the truth. Her concentrating features did not change.

'Who is Monica Black?' she sighed with the air of being quietly at the end of her tether.

'The wife of Jeremy Sutcliffe Black, DDS and middle-brow art collector.'

'That means he's a dentist.'

'Correct. And that's why I began with – '

'Your bad teeth. Get on with it, then.'

'Will you stop interrupting?' Jason banged the table.

Clover looked up at him with blue-black eyes, eyes of a little girl. 'Sorry, Jay.'

'It's all right,' he said, ashamed. 'It's just difficult. Difficult.' He drummed his fingers. 'Well, anyway that's how I met her.'

'How?'

'My *teeth*! Because of my bad teeth, twit! Her husband is a dentist and I needed my teeth fixed. Now do you understand?'

'But that was before I was born.' Occasionally she could be as opaque as she was transparent, dense as she was fine. A child, he thought, she's a child.

'It had to be. Before you were born. Didn't it?'

'I suppose so,' she replied meekly and went on with her painting.

'I had no money, and my National Health dentist was an Aussie psycho on the Earls Court Road. I was in agony. I knew it was serious this time.'

'Your teeth are pretty horrible, Jason.'

'Not my most alluring feature.'

'You must have been really, really scared.'

'I was. That's why when Dillon Butterworth – used to be quite thick with Eleanor – anyway, when he told me about a genius dentist who was mad on art and would look after painters' and sculptors' teeth in return for some of their work, I rang him immediately. He didn't know me, of course. I had no reputation then – not that I have what might seriously be called a reputation now . . . '

Clover thought her father did not sound as proud of the fact as he usually did. She felt sorry for him and added softly, so as not to appear to be interrupting, 'Is that when your studio was in the little funny room behind the pub?'

He smiled grimly. 'That time, yes.'

JASON

Funny was not quite the word. Arctic, grubby, dank would have suited better. The room, over which he had come to terms with the sympathetic publican, was a post-war addition to the rear of the White Lion on Ripplevale Grove. Although the establishment itself was warm and endearing in its faded Edwardian way and at that time very popular with artists of no to moderate success, Jason's room was damp and bare with inadequate lighting. But Jason, who borrowed money for canvas and paint and could not afford to stretch his pictures, who wore third-hand clothes and smoked other people's cigarettes, was pressed not only for space but for any dwelling at all, and two pounds a week could just be managed. He needed a place to live and work and, like it or not, he desperately needed to sell some of that work. Even self-styled outcasts require asylum and, occasionally, money.

He gritted his very bad teeth and made the ultimate sacrifice: he borrowed fifty pounds from his recently married sister. With this sum he equipped himself and the room with the bare necessities and commenced a year of febrile creative effort. He made thirteen paintings and forty-two drawings. He filled a dark-red notebook – 1962–3 – with aphorisms, short essays, and autobiographical snatches. (This chronicle of his quest for underlying primal structure later evolved into Jason Englefield's *Postulates of Vision and Painting*.) He made no sculpture, not because materials were so expensive, but because he had no interest in the three-dimensional.

He was twenty-four years old. He was waiting and working, not running after dealers or shows. He despised those anxious to show and despised even more those who showed prematurely. He saw no one and half-starved himself. What food he did eat was consumed mainly in the White Lion where, after a beer or two at Mr Skeller's expense, he would turn to whoever stood next to him (he ate always at the bar, never at a table) and regale the dumbfounded customer with a detailed and florid account of his life's work. He was as hungry for human contact as he was for a decent meal. To neither of these basic needs would he admit.

He kept a cat. Cats were one of the few acceptable creatures. He slept on a single mattress on the floor. During the winter he could never get warm enough and was driven more often to the pub's open fire and the proximity of his own kind. It was on one of these occasions that he met Dillon Butterworth for the first time in several weeks. Dillon was accompanied by a red-haired American girl who was very drunk. She had a penchant for bursting into song – tunes from the Thirties and Forties to which she knew all the words but whose changes of key she found difficult to negotiate. In between these entertainments she consumed more whisky, told absurd stories and seemed unable to stop giggling. Jason found her irritating. He hated artists' molls, especially faggot artists' molls. Moreover, his head was racked by a toothache for which he denied himself the consolation of codeine. When he finally told Dillon of his wretched state, Dillon gave him Jeremy Black's telephone number.

Jeremy Black's patients were rendered horizontal by the automatic reclining mechanism of what was reputedly the most advanced hydraulic chair in Western Europe. In this marvel of humane technology the nervous, the suffering, the plain-terrified, floated ceiling-ward at the imperceptible pressure of Jeremy Black's left foot. They were addressed in anaesthetic tones by his long-haired and very pretty assistant who wore jeans, a plaid shirt and red high heels. (Jeremy seldom spoke and, when he did, was barely audible.) Metal instruments probed sensitive oral areas without so much as a clink. Enormous syringes were inserted and an assortment of the most advanced drilling attachments deployed against an aural background of Mozart and Vivaldi. Patients were returned, again imperceptibly, to terra firma and departed, scarcely aware of having undergone minor or indeed major surgery. Back on the street, they instantly forgot what might otherwise have been a traumatic experience; forgot it, that is, until one month from that very day they received a small white envelope. Mr Black presented with his compliments an astronomical bill.

The dentist's waiting-room was equipped with several large armchairs and a low, polished table on which were distributed copies of the *Guardian*, *The Times*, *Country Life*, *Apollo*, *Harper's*, *Studio International*, *Art Forum*, the *Times Literary Supplement*, *Private Eye* and catalogues from current London exhibitions. The literature reflected the status of the clientele. So Jason thought when, four days after meeting Dillon at the White Lion, he sat pale and in agony in one of those armchairs. He leafed through a copy of *Art Forum* which failed to rouse in him the usual reactions of contempt, envy and boredom, so acute was his discomfort. It was compounded by his being forced to look at the paintings and drawings which lined the walls, perfectly lit. He recognized a couple of styles. One drawing was inscribed to JB, another to Monica. What Dillon had told him about the man was true; Jeremy Black was a speculator in art. He trafficked in the talent of others who must have earned him a fortune. If this was how he decorated his office, what must the walls of his sitting-room be like?

Jason shuddered. Clearly this dentist, like all collectors, was an anally-retentive parasite of the Muse. The arrangement stank. How could painting remain pure when it played the tart to dentists, corporate accountants, real-estate agents and automobile executives? Better corrupt popes and arbitrary princes. And what was he, Jason, doing here, prepared to barter the fruits of his inspiration? A missile of pain was fired through his left jaw, reminding him what, exactly, he was doing here.

Twenty minutes later he could not suppress his grudging admiration for the artistry of the odd man with thick glasses and thinning black hair which curled, unattractively long, over his loose collar. He had a snubbed nose and a marsupial mouth and appeared never to have taken any exercise. Only his hands were beautiful. Delicate, immaculate, assured, they were soothing beyond expression. Despite his contempt, Jason, his pain alleviated for the moment and thinking that life was not necessarily the sewer he had been calling it lately, felt almost in Jeremy Black's debt.

'You mean he fixed your tooth before you gave him a painting or he even saw your work?' Clover asked, swirling her brush in a glass of purplish-brown water. 'He must be a very nice man to have trusted you that way.'

'Balls! He'd interrogated Dillon thoroughly about my future as a viable commodity.'

'What does that mean?'

'He asked Dillon if he thought my work would ever be worth any money.'

Clover shrugged. 'He might really have liked your work you know. It's not impossible that he did. Why do you think everyone is secretly nasty, Jason?'

'Because in most cases they are – well, more stupid and greedy really. But what do you mean? I don't think you're nasty.'

'I should hope not, Jason. I *am* your daughter.' She looked at him hard. 'How did you meet Monica?'

'She came to my studio with her slug husband. To see my work.' Jason lit a cigarette, although he had been trying for two weeks to stop smoking. Eleanor's visit plus the onset of Clover's womanhood had put him straight back on a pack a day. 'She shared his passion for Kunst, you see.'

'You're a very sarcastic person.'

'We can't all be Pollyannas like you.'

'I just don't hate anyone.'

'No you don't, do you?' He wanted to add, 'And it's beautiful.' Instead he said, 'It's the only way in which you're like your mother.'

73

'You mean she didn't even hate *you?*'

'She never said she did. If a woman hates me she usually tells me.'

'Oh?'

Because he had never loved Monica, Jason never asked himself whether she really loved him, or, later on, really hated him.

Clover carefully shaded in the wings of her butterfly while Jason told her about the Blacks' first visit to his studio. The place was, as usual, cold and stinking. He had not emptied the cat tray in ten days. He refused to make any special concessions to their arrival. He told himself he wanted them to hate the pictures and that their approval would signify a lurking decadence in his work.

They entered, she on his flabby arm – small, dark and pretty in her fur coat. There they are, he thought, as they inspected the pictures: rapacious in their highly-evolved greed, somnambulent in their luxury, but acquainted with everyone who matters – the Patrons of Art. Clearly they would do anything to get their hands on it. Still, he could sense a lack of warmth on the part of the dentist. He could see how it was his little wife who encouraged him in low tones, guiding him towards a painting that she must have known Jason wouldn't miss too much, then openly requesting that he purchase a drawing which she said she liked.

Jeremy wrote out a cheque for the latter, shook Jason's hand and said he would send round his packers next week. Now Jason Englefield too would hang in a dentist's waiting-room. Shyly, Monica held out her hand to Jason and he took it in his broad, flat one. It was like holding a bird, and it unnerved him as birds do. What could she want? Should he say something? What should he say? He was certainly not going to express his gratitude. As she preceded her husband through the creaking door that led to the public bar, he realized that he had not even offered them a cup of coffee.

For a moment he regretted his lack of hospitality, then remembered to pride himself on his lack of charm. Then he remembered what remained to be done to his bridgework. Further terms might have to be negotiated. One more painting would probably suffice. And after that, what? Jason experienced several novel sensations. He considered the future and panicked. He glanced at a painting and realized that he very much wanted Monica's husband to buy it. He thought of Monica and got an erection.

It amazed him that so passive and unspontaneous a creature should seek him out in his spartan lair, but she came back. She sent him a note which thanked him for being so kind as to allow her and her husband to see his most interesting and promising work and went on to say that she would come the following Wednesday afternoon if that suited because her husband wished to purchase another of his drawings. If the time was inconvenient would he please notify her at the above address. Otherwise she would be there at three and she assured him that she would take a minimum of his valuable time. He was unaccustomed to such formality. Only friends of his mother and father addressed each other like that. He would write to the little hypocrite immediately and tell her not to come – on Wednesday or any other day.

He did not mail his brusque reply. He needed money and apparently the drawing was not to be bartered for his dentist's bill. Then he recalled how her eyes had questioned him, asking him something he could not understand and could not possibly answer. Self-absorbed as he was, he missed even the most primal emotional signals. But he could not lie to himself. He could not tell himself that he did not want her to come.

She arrived, again in a fur coat which she did not remove, used as she was to centrally-heated houses in Knightsbridge. But her coat was open and Jason noticed how delicate she was and how simply she dressed. She wore no make-up. Her long dark hair was tied loosely back with a velvet ribbon. It seemed impossible that this child-like bird-like creature was the mother of three children whose father was that rich runt of a dentist. Jason hated him. Yet the conscience which had worked so hard to invent for himself pricked him at regular intervals as he watched Monica inspect the paintings she already had scrutinized so carefully. Why did it? Because he knew that whatever was taking place between him and the dentist's wife constituted a betrayal. What he was about to get from the man who appeared to be patronizing him in the best sense was a great deal more than something for nothing.

She took a leather-bound chequebook from her handbag.

'Would you like some coffee, Mrs Black?' he abruptly asked.

She removed a black glove. Diamond clusters flashed on her tiny fingers. He reminded himself that he didn't like small women. They made him think of toys and pets – gerbils, finches, music boxes that played 'Some Day My Love'. (Jason himself was exactly six feet and would have been considered a well-built man, even robust, had he remembered to eat regularly.)

'You're very kind. Please I would, yes.'

What a stupid reply, he thought as he lit the Baby Belling to boil water in his battered aluminium pot. What sort of an answer was that? Such hypocrisy could not be let pass without comment.

'I'm not kind, Mrs Black.'

'You are not unkind, Mr Englefield.'

He poured water into two dirty mugs with heaps of Nescafé in the bottom.

'I will not lie to be kind.'

'Of that you may be justly proud. Black please.' She spoke so quietly he could barely hear her. 'I should certainly lie to be kind. I've done so many times.'

He placed the coffee before her, hesitated, then sat down with her at his table – the same table at which Clover, opposite him, the light glinting off the wisps of hair Charles had found so mysterious, was putting the final wet touches to her gorgeous, if anatomically inexact, butterfly. He noticed that her hair had turned darker over the past few months.

'I think honesty can only be brutal. I'm irritated by social convention.'

'So I see. Yet you're not as offensive as you would like to be.' She smiled at him over the coffee which she sipped slowly. What gave her the right to smile at him like that? With her grey eyes. His father had told him that grey-eyed women were liars. Her teeth were, of course, exquisite. He could not help himself smiling back. She removed her other glove and warmed her hands on the grubby mug – hands that toyed with champagne glasses and Liberty upholstery fabrics and passed babies back to nannies after goodnight kisses and whispered endearments.

'Mr Englefield, I should like – and my husband would like – to help you. We believe your work is – '

'I don't want or need any help,' he said without expression. 'Why help me?'

'Because you are a good artist and a good man. It is my opinion that one day you will be a better artist and a better man.'

'That is very, very corny.'

'I don't express myself well.'

'You express yourself too well.'

'Therefore you mistrust me.'

'I mistrust you because you're rich.'

'For that sin I shall probably not go to heaven. But it is no reason for you to mistrust me. Here is my cheque – and my hand.'

Jason recoiled. Then he accepted the cheque.

'Thank you.' She continued to hold out her hand. Her eyes glistened. Good God, she was going to cry. Jason turned in his chair, his back deliberately towards her.

'How old are you?' It was the most ill-mannered question he could think of just then. He was very agitated by the tiny creature whose bones he would have liked to crack. In his mind he heard them cracking, one after another. He wondered if he were a dangerously disturbed person. He was twenty-four and had gone eight months without sex.

'I'll be thirty in a week.'

'On which occasion you will receive a handsome present from your ugly husband.'

'My husband is very generous.'

'How can you love something like that?'

'What makes you think I love him?'

Jason leapt up. He yanked the velvet ribbon from her hair. He tore back the fur coat. He was so angry with Monica Black that he could barely see.

'Do you want to go to bed with me?' he roared in her face. Her lower lip trembled. Tears fell. He had saved himself. He had frightened her.

'Well, do you, you godammed kind liar?'

She hung her head. Tears dropped on to Jason's hand. The hand flew to her head and caressed and tangled itself in her hair. Still she did not answer.

'That was an invitation not a question,' he said at last.

She tried to put her arms around him, but he pulled them away and dragged her to the single mattress on to which he threw her and then himself.

She was utterly submissive. Thunder cracked in his brain and he came immediately he was inside her. For ten minutes he was comatose. When he woke he saw that he had not even bothered to undress her. He rolled away from the creature he had so abused, curled up in a foetal position and cried.

'Go away,' he sobbed.

She rose unsteadily, pulling her skirt over her torn stockings.

'Is there a bathroom?' she whispered apologetically.

'No. You'll have to go into the pub as you are. You see,' he muttered, 'this is what it will be like. A single mattress on a freezing floor and dirty linen. But maybe you *like* that.'

'That is obvious,' she replied softly. She picked up her ribbon from the floor, took a brush from her handbag and tried to straighten her hair. Jason stopped crying, turned on his side and watched what seemed to him her pathetic efforts.

'Mrs Black,' he said uncertainly. 'Monica, will you come here, please. Please.'

She lay down beside him and took him in her arms.

'I love you,' she said. It was a statement to which he had never given and supposed he never would give the desperately required response.

'It won't do you any good,' was all he could say as he buried his face in the gentle neck, the bones of which he had wanted to crush.

The cheque she left was for £200.

ten

Jason felt obliged to give this part of the story a PG rating.

'And did you see her soon after that?' Clover began another painting. She was very serious and when she was very serious she looked like Monica.

'At first she'd just appear. Sometimes I'd be there, sometimes not. She'd leave a note. A long time would pass before I'd reply to her. I felt a bit guilty about Jeremy, even though I didn't like him. Two months later he bought another drawing of mine and by then he had finished my bridgework. His money was enabling me to live. I couldn't bear my false position. I thought of breaking off the relationship completely and asking my father for a loan, even going to the Arts Council or applying for a fellowship.'

'You mean Jeremy bought your work because Monica told him to because she loved you.'

'Probably. Yes.'

'I can see that might be a bit tricky for you. But you needed the money after all. And you didn't hate Monica.'

'No. I didn't hate her.'

He could not describe to Clover the initial sensations evoked in him by her biological mother. Jason, convinced he had never been loved, that there was no such thing as love, found himself nevertheless loved. For him a woman was risking ruin in the old-fashioned sense. A woman allowed him in his sensual and emotional ignorance selfishly to brutalize her and listened to him discourse at length about his art, his theories, his world view, his politics, his anger, his purity. Monica told him he was the only serious person she knew. She said she had longed for someone truly serious. That was why she had come to him. Ordinarily she never did such things.

He realized subliminally that the satisfaction she derived from their encounters on the dirty mattress was entirely emotional but very great. She loved to be loved, to love in return, to have children. It was a vital ingredient in his pleasure that she was unable to follow where he alone could go. Moreover she thought he was a genius. They did not laugh very much.

If life becomes too interesting, he wondered, will I want to paint anymore? He had stumbled upon the discovery that there is a deep gratification in exercising control over the psyche of another human being. It was too good to abandon in spite of cheques and husbands and purity. He had not realized it could be that much fun. Jason was addicted.

One day she again raised the matter of help. He needed a gallery, she said, and a lawyer and an accountant. He needed a small but faithful public who believed in him.

'You mean who can make money out of me,' he said.

'One has to have assistance,' she replied calmly. 'One can't be more than one is. And you need a critic or two.'

'I won't be tailed by cultural police agents. The work of art is more than they'll ever be able to find out.'

He accused her of trying to make him into an interior decorator for a production/consumption society. Her natural graciousness would be forever wasted on him.

She came naturally by everything. She had been born into a ready-made ambiance, carpeted, curtained and landscaped, which defined and upheld her: money, husband, schools, children, art, taste, comfort, society, friends, relations. Above all, relations. Monica's extended family seemed to include half the British Isles. She had been lifted by all these things, carried along by them to the preclusion of decision or will. She had never engaged in struggle. She accepted what was given. Why shouldn't she? Therefore, despite intelligence and sensitivity, she was severely and permanently limited. Jason constituted the one instance in which she had taken the initiative and grabbed what she wanted. He was her one and only choice.

She was motivated partly by maternalism, partly by sex and partly by a genuine pride in her lover. She was wholly irrational, assuming that all would somehow work together for the best. Why should it not? She did realize that Jason would fail to be grateful. But she allowed that thought simply to slide past her, to be dealt with later.

'Jeremy seemed unaware of Monica's motives in introducing me to the territory they'd staked out in the art world. I was surprised at his lack of surprise. I mean, why would such a timid woman launch herself on a collision course with a renegade like me? Besides, he didn't like my work. Said I had voice but no style and that I worked too hard to be hard. Ha! I guess he thought she was amusing herself by playing patroness. And she was, in her unassuming way, very good at it. God, she knew everyone. Drove me crazy.'

She gave dinners and parties. She offered him access to places where he would not otherwise have been invited. Sometimes he failed to show up. Always he resisted. But at the end of six months he had sold two paintings and four drawings, all to collectors other than Jeremy. This eased his conscience and lengthened the lifeline by which Monica held him to her.

'Is that how you met George Facer?'

'Yes. At one of those awful parties.'

'Why were they so awful? Wasn't there a lot of champagne? I remember my ninth birthday when Charles came. It was wonderful. Can we have another, please Jason?'

'Maybe.'

'You always say that. Sometimes I think you don't like to have fun.'

'That's what Eleanor said. At least it wasn't a stipulation of my arrangement with Monica that I have *fun*. Thank God that wasn't expected of me.'

'And did Monica introduce you to Charles?'

'Yes. But he didn't become my lawyer until later on. Now he's no one's lawyer, and no one's mine.'

'Tell me about Charles.'

'For a while I liked him. He'd read a lot. And he seemed to understand painting in a way the others didn't. Unlike the rest of those swankers he could listen. His remarks on what I said were intelligent.'

'I think Charles is a very personal person.'

'You mean personable. He's that.' Jason snorted. 'He's Monica's second cousin, you know.'

Clover brightened. 'Then he's mine too.'

'I guess. And just to cement the whole, sick, inbred, fascist arrangement, he went to Cambridge with her older brother, Simon. Like Monica going to school with Vivienne Facer. Most incestuous damned lot I've ever known. No wonder their class is so adept at closing ranks. Well, they'll be closing ranks on Charles soon.'

'Why?' Her eyes opened wide in concern.

'Not sure. I've just – heard things . . .'

'From Dillon?' Dillon was their only remaining London friend but they seldom saw him. Dillon was becoming famous. 'What things?'

'I said I'm not sure. And you are much too inquisitive, Pandora. Don't you think you've opened enough boxes for one day. Besides, I thought you wanted to hear this story. Monica's story.'

'I do, I do. But why don't you like Charles anymore?'

'Charles is privileged and so, no matter how nice a person he may be, or how intelligent, his view is warped. He'll always defend what bred him. He can't help it. He's been programmed.'

'I think Charles would defend anyone in trouble.'

'God, you're idealistic.'

'I'm not.'

But Charles had defended Jason. If he had not reminded George Facer of his obligations, the one-man show might never have materialized. George originally had promised Jason the show in 1968, but plans had fallen through. Jason suspected the subversive retaliation of Jeremy who understandably blamed Jason for the near-destruction of his marriage. Jeremy wielded some influence both with George and other dealers and might easily have destroyed the early recognition which Monica had engineered.

The last meeting between Jason Englefield and Jeremy Black took place in the very sitting-room that the former had imagined as he waited in the latter's office. Jason had no fear of meeting the dentist on his own ground. In fact he welcomed the opportunity, and said so, to dispense with the burden of hypocrisy. Jeremy had just been informed by his wife that she was pregnant with another man's child. There could be no doubt. She had severed physical connections with her husband for the past four months. She was a one-man woman.

Monica was not present at the meeting. She was upstairs crying like a teenager, being treated with homeopathic remedies for grief and shock and generally ministered to by her old nanny who had been summoned out of retirement to cope with this physical, emotional and moral crisis in the life of her little pigeon. Maisie had not been so happy in years. In two weeks' time she would accompany Monica to her sister's house in Wales. There Mrs Black would await her confinement in a private clinic. But on that afternoon Monica was unaware of the fate in store for her. Stronger personalities were bargaining over her future. Jeremy and Jason sat like Roosevelt and Stalin with the map of Middle Europe between them.

The previous morning a nearly catatonic Monica had broken the unhappy news to Jeremy. The announcement was most definitely not her idea. She had told Jason of her condition with some pathetic and undefined hope that he might not erupt, that he might be tender, concerned, even – fool that she was – delighted. She had dared to entertain the fantastic notion that he would ask her to leave her husband. (What she would have done had the notion become a reality she had not the faintest idea. For Monica the future was never more than a mild and pleasant fog. She was no Anna Karenina.)

Jason's first reaction was that of any hero of art, in his unassailable integrity, when faced with a similar predicament.

'Have an abortion,' he said.

'But I've never had one. I'm afraid. Oh Jason, how can I kill a child?'

'It is not a child, it is a foetus. Above all, it is a mistake – a mistake which, thank God, can be rectified. And don't think you're getting the money from Jeremy. *I* am paying for the operation.'

'Oh Jason, please don't talk about money.' She sat down at the table, laid her head on her arms and cried.

'You're a child,' he said not unkindly. 'You don't understand actions and consequences. Why didn't you take precautions?'

'I never do,' she blubbered.

'What!?'

'I love babies. I love them. How can I kill a baby – mine and yours, oh Jason, mine and yours . . .'

Her neat, quiet manner of expression was gone. Jason sighed and sat down next to her. He knew he could not make this demand of her, not so much because she had helped him or because they needed each other or because he felt genuinely sorry for her; but because he could not kill a baby any more than she could. He placed his hand on her heaving shoulders.

'Let me think about it. Come tomorrow and I'll have a solution.'

'You will?' She looked up at him like a four year old with absolute trust in his cleverness and his goodness. 'Oh, Jason,' she grabbed his hand and kissed it. 'When is there ever not a way out?' Providence just couldn't be, as she had been fearing for three whole days, that cruel.

Jason's 'solution' proved more devastating than any blow providence might have dealt her.

'Have it and I'll keep it.'

'You!' Monica collapsed on to a chair. 'How will you – '

'How the fuck do I know how I'll cope?'

'But what about me?'

'Oh for God's sake, Monica, you have three already. Isn't that enough? The rich are so damned irresponsible. At this point in history no one should be allowed more than one child.'

'But can't I stay with you?' The question seemed to Jason a *non sequitur*.

'Here? In this hole? You have standards, my dear. You can't live here. Besides, I don't think Jeremy would like it. And what about your precious darlings. Wouldn't they miss their Mummy?'

The truth, of course, was that he didn't want her – there or anywhere else. He could not say he had stopped loving her because he never had loved her. From now on they must be friends, full stop. He must convince her that friendship was higher than selfish, personal love. It was the highest form of love, the transcendent aspect of the social function. In other words, he must persuade her that his ideas were more important than her feelings. He had succeeded before, although, admittedly, not in such dramatic circumstances. She had already conceded the superiority of art to love, although she had found unconditional surrender to the proposition difficult.

The truth was that he wanted the child. He wanted to do what no other man would do; he needed the impossible task; it was part of his art. But more than anything he wanted the child. It would be hell. But at least it would be real. The only thing as real as a painting. Pure.

Monica was terrified by the prospect of telling Jeremy. And she was terrified that once she had had the baby she would cease to interest Jason. But she could not resist Jason. To offer a 'solution' of her own was beyond her imagination and beyond her will. She could fight neither him nor Jeremy. She did not know how to fight.

After the meeting she told Jason how she had lain on her bed while Maisie hovered over her with her cold flannels and hot drinks. She knew that arrangements were being made for the charade of her removal, her temporary disposal and permanent reinstatement. And she had no part in these arrangements. She was simply an object being moved from one place to another place. For the first time in her life, she said, she realized that she had surrendered responsibility for her life, and that her life was singular, discreet, unrepeatable. Therefore the question of her own reality was in serious doubt. She described how she had looked in the mirror to make certain she still existed. Yes, as long as she held the baby inside her she existed.

'Didn't she want me, then?' Clover asked the only question she had always wanted to ask and had not.

'Of course she wanted you, sweetheart.' Jason was moved and uncomfortable. He forced himself to say it, 'She wanted you very much. It's just that I wanted you more.' He hesitated. 'I wanted you so much I thought I'd die if I didn't have you.'

Clover came to him and sat in his lap and put her arms around him. He held her as she cried, rocking her gently. It was weeks since he had taken her in his arms. The way she clung to him, her warmth, her smell, the absolute genuineness of her feelings pushed him to the brink of tears himself. He had not wanted to cry since that moment of weakness when Eleanor had miscarried. He had taught himself to replace tears with sneers. Now he wanted to cry and he could not. He was like a newly reformed alcoholic: one drink and he would be straight back on the bottle. But he could allow Clover to cry and be physically there for her to cry on. He could not go to her, but she could come to him. Oh, Eleanor was right. He was not alone.

Clover's sobs subsided to sniffles. She made quick recoveries. 'What did you and Jeremy decide then?'

'That Monica would have you in secret. That none of us would ever say that she was your mother, that I was to expect not a penny for your support, ever; that Monica and Maisie would look after you for the first three months of your life at a hideout in Wales; that Monica was then to surrender you, without a fuss, as Jeremy put it; that you would be delivered to me by Maisie at a place to be determined later, that Jeremy and Monica would then go abroad for a while and that when they returned I would hopefully have left the country or at least left London. Monica and I were asked to give our word that we would never contact each other or see each other again unless by unhappy accident. I gave mine readily. I didn't want any interference on her part either in my life or yours. I think Jeremy toyed with the idea of having Charles draw up some kind of agreement that would bind us all legally – but that would have meant letting Charles in on the secret. Jeremy wouldn't even trust Charles. And from then on he certainly didn't trust his wife. Oh yes, Monica was not to leave you any money although she might see you after the age of ten if that was her wish, and provided she didn't see me. I agreed. Again, I felt as though Jeremy had almost done me a favour. But I'm neither grateful nor ungrateful.'

'And who named me?'

'Monica did. After Clover Adams. Wife of the art historian who, Monica claimed, had met her great-grandmother in Rome or Washington or some vortex of art and society in the 1870s. She had a big reputation, this Clover Adams, and was meant to be very charming.'

'Was she clever as well?'

'I guess so, yes. Clover was clever.'

'And then what happened?'

'You were delivered to me in Kensington Gardens at the age of three months. I was sitting on a bench. Maisie appeared with a pram and sat next to me. I couldn't help straining to have a look at you. You smiled at me.'

'Did I?' she laughed.

'I swear it's true. You were kicking your feet and looking very lively, but Maisie rocked the pram for a while and you fell asleep. She stared at you for a long time then got up and walked away. She never gave me a glance. I took you back to Islington in a taxi. Cost me all but the last few shillings I had, I can tell you. I sat and stared at you in the pram until it was dark. I was riveted. I couldn't even get up to turn on the light. There was nothing in the room but a bottle of milk and a book on baby care. Still, I just couldn't move. The same thought kept running through my mind: who are you little girl and what the hell do I do with you?

'Mr Skeller was very surprised, to say the least. But not as surprised as I was to discover £1,000 in cash under your lace pillow.'

eleven

During Clover's infancy and early childhood Monica sent secret petitions for news of her daughter. The first few Jason answered. Then he stopped answering. After all, he had made a bargain with Jeremy. He was an honourable man and must stick to his word. By the time Clover was six, letters from Monica had dwindled to one a year.

She rang Jason for the last time in December 1976. They had not seen or spoken to each other since the night of his opening.

'Monica, why are you telling me this? I can't possibly help you.'

'I must tell someone. You're not involved and so you have a kind of objectivity. Mine is non-existent.'

'Yes. So?'

'Jason, what shall I do? I could be charged. It's called handling and receiving stolen property. Who could have told the police? Felix won't answer the phone. I don't know where he is. What shall I do? What do you think I ought to do?'

'Tell Jeremy.'

'He already considers me emotionally unstable. He let me spend money on art because he thought it was a safe outlet. Oh God.'

'What the hell were you *doing* with Felix? Oh never mind.'

'It was business. I mean it *was* business. Jason, I shall go mad.'

She told him how she had been introduced to Felix by Anthea Bevan. Mrs Black and Herr Koning had come immediately to an agreement over a Chinese stem cup, then some Russian silver which they agreed was superior to anything in the V and A. Although, like most men, especially married men and homosexuals, Jeremy disliked Felix, he had not been able to overcome a grudging admiration for the man's taste, acumen and connections, dubious as some of them might be; and a certain pride in his wife's ability, utterly passive, to attract and capture treasures of such calibre.

Therefore, in the suppressed joy of his cupidity, he failed to subject to proper scrutiny the small Teniers which Monica purchased from the 2000-year-old dealer in the summer of 1976. Two days before her conversation with Jason, Monica was paid a discreet visit by Scotland Yard. Jeremy was not at home at the time. Monica replied to the inspector's questions with increasing confusion. His story had implications too distressing to contemplate. Fortunately for all concerned, she became hysterical, rang for the nanny and begged the police to excuse her until she might consult with a member of the male sex. They gave her to understand that they were gentlemen and not in a particular hurry. Moreover, she had nothing to be concerned about. She need only provide them with the name of the vendor. At this point she came completely apart, and the police withdrew taking the Teniers with them.

Jason listened impatiently to what seemed to him a very silly story.

'Tell Jeremy,' he said again.

'This is the second time that, in a moment of crisis, you have advised me to tell Jeremy.'

'Tell Jeremy and tell Charles.'

'My brother Simon is with Charles at this very moment. Perhaps it can all be saved. Surely Charles can save me. If he doesn't, if Jeremy – oh dear God. I'm on eternal probation, you know.'

'Monica, there are laws to prevent husbands dealing out that sort of summary punishment to their wives. You've committed no crime. You've only made a mistake.'

'But I may have committed a crime. Technically I may have. I am certainly one hundred per cent implicated.'

'Monica, I'm sorry you're in a fix. But what do you expect if you do "business" with someone like Felix?'

She did not reply. There was a long silence during which she began to cry. Jason sighed. He was weary of grown women. They were incapable of adopting a philosophical attitude.

'It will be all right, Monica, I'm sure. Just keep your nerve.'

'Jason, you know very well that I have no nerve to keep.'

'I suppose not. Well, goodbye.'

'Goodbye, Jason.'

Why had she called him? Obviously, in her dismay she had wanted to pluck at an old string in hopes of evoking a lost resonance. How useless. What a waste. Felix was a vampire and she was a fool.

The last time Jason had seen Clover's mother was at the opening of his one-man show in 1972. He had been aware of Monica's presence but he did not speak to her and was too drunk to notice her entrance or exit. His alcohol consumption had increased steadily during his years with Eleanor. From her he had learned the basics of pleasure. He suspected that as a result people had begun to respond to him. Sometimes he had thought they even liked him a little. Eleanor was fun, gaiety is contagious and not even Jason was immune.

Eleanor was also good to watch. He watched her that night distributing ebullience throughout the crowded gallery, waving it carelessly around like bubbles from a wand. She would catch his eye and laugh out loud and he would chuckle in spite of himself. She winked at him and he winked back. He, Jason, winked. He was experiencing all the emotions he told himself for years that he did not wish to feel: the enjoyment of approval, the pride of achievement, the anticipation of success, the desire for recognition, the pleasure of company, the security of family, the love of a woman. For a moment he saw that all this could belong to him and he wanted it. The possibility of happiness existed. Eleanor had brought him to this. He had worked hard to maintain his austerity, to keep his life uncontaminated by other people's flattery, blame and misguided sensibilities. But Eleanor had found the chink in his armour. Through it she had inserted the fine needle of her mind and injected the warmth of her personality. He had moved from dislike to fascination to something like domestic bliss. His guard was never dropped entirely. But she succeeded where everyone else had failed: she convinced him, for a time, that she believed in him, believed in him so much that she would take on physical deprivation, social ostracism and another woman's child. She offered the two strays the comparative comfort of her flat on Westbourne Terrace and the small salary she earned as an assistant to a carpet dealer. Jason kept the room behind the pub as a studio.

Eleanor was brave, loyal, amusing. She took risks. People liked Eleanor. People did not like Jason. She seemed willing to be disliked along with him if that was what was required to gain his confidence. Without giving up her friends entirely she focused more and more of her life on Jason and Clover. The first two years were difficult. There were nights when the two of them would pool their change, search drawers, pockets and cupboards for forgotten pound notes, and redeem for a pittance their empty cider and tamari bottles in order to scrape together enough money for supper. They borrowed to pay the electricity bill and the rent. The flat was hopelessly crowded, and Clover was an active, jolly, curious, messy child. They existed on the edge of chaos and for two years were as happy as people with natures like theirs can ever be. He called her Flame for obvious reasons. She called him Jay because he was as handsome and private as a jaybird. They had small successes and great reversals. Whenever Jason sold a painting they spent the profits immediately on dinners, toys for Clover, Covent Garden and booze. They were entirely generous with each other, never quarrelled about money, held nothing back for themselves. They didn't care how they looked and went about in old jeans and jumpers which belonged neither to one nor the other. Poverty made them inventive, hunger gave them an obsession with food. When they were flush they made huge and, under the circumstances, elaborate dinners for everyone they knew. On these occasions guests became very drunk and very loud and the evening ended with boisterous arguments. Few people returned their hospitality. When they were invited somewhere, no matter how smart and no matter how late, they always took Clover with them.

They talked endlessly about art. There was so much to say that often they would both speak at once, neither of them able or willing to yield the floor. It was as urgent, as much a necessity as eating, drinking and making love.

In his notebook for 1967 Jason wrote, 'The artist who wants to develop art beyond its painting possibilities is forced to theory and logic.' Jason was then preoccupied with number. Through number alone, all might be reduced to order, compelled to obey, made to submit to the superior intellect of the superior will. He read everything from the medieval scholastics to Max Plank. He worshipped structure and precision. Beauty lay in proportion. Exaggeration equalled ugliness. He regarded himself as a dispeller of effete symbolism, frivolous pop and flabby abstraction. 'Art is not excrement,' he copied into his 1970 notebook. The infinitude of ways in which the field might be divided and subdivided plagued and enthralled him. He continued to resist the labels minimalist, planned painting, hard edge. But Mondrian was his god.

He wanted to make an art of pure concept made tangible through line and colour. Line equalled measurement equalled intellect. Colour bound spirit and libido. His paintings were spaces both shallow and deep. Every colour straining from its tense linear boundary, every part of the field, divided by him through a process of conscious and painful decision-making, bore a specific and esoteric relationship to every other part of the field. Only he understood the spatial mystery of these relationships. He had developed and in 1974, when Charles bought the study for *The Three Virtues*, was still developing a colour code (strong, hard, pure) which he believed to be related to the atomic structure of the elements. Painting was more like chemistry, medicine and the natural sciences than anyone supposed. Leonardo had said it: painting *was* a science. An artist had first to study science then follow with a practice based on science. Jason went very far with all this. It was his dubious and utterly private discovery. Let the critics and public puzzle over his paintings. Let them reject his paintings. He wanted them to be rejected.

For a while he thought Eleanor understood, despite her limited, if vivid, imagination and her taste for frivolity. She could certainly talk.

She could certainly explain. In fact it was difficult to make her shut up and listen. She was under the illusion that she knew more than she really did know, even that she knew things *he* didn't know. Despite her amiability and her eagerness, she carried around her lovely neck the millstone of her misguided education and a Masters in the History of Art. All those influences! That American arrogance coupled with that insidious playfulness! Jason, uneducated by choice, overread, overworked and intellectually hyperventilated, found her information, coupled with her quirky, pungent logic, irritating beyond endurance.

'You think life is a dream,' he would say. 'Well, I want to come out of that dream.' Alternatively he accused her of having an academic and conservative mind.

'That's why you're always craving historical justification, as though the artist were on trial before history. You think it can all be *explained*. You're an influence junkie.'

He asked her why she loved museums. They were only full of dead things.

'What a rigorist you are.' She laughed at him.

'I just hate eclecticism.'

'You hate all intellect that isn't your own.'

'Well, you don't have an intellect. You only have enthusiasms. You were educated to be enthusiastic. All that energy – dissipated in enthusiasms.'

She talked about the irreconcilability of object and idea.

'You can't make theory and practice completely meet. Not possible, Jay.'

'Why the hell not?'

'The more dogmatic you become, the more purity eludes you. Life fights back. Still,' she tried smiling at him, 'I suppose the struggle isn't ignoble.'

'Don't patronize me. What would you know about struggle? You don't produce anything.'

'What am I, an automobile factory?'

'You like to think your life is your art.'

'Maybe. Why the hell not?'

'Let me tell you, life has nothing to do with art. Life and art are mutually exclusive.'

'That is an absurdly old-fashioned attitude.'

'Attitude replaces attitude. Out *there*', he pointed vehemently towards the window, 'where you'd like to be. Where I suppose you secretly are.'

'Jason – '

'Just remember this: there is no such thing as an honorary artist.'

After five years they found that what they had always regarded as discussions might more appropriately be called rows. The rows became heated and prolonged. Eleanor and Jason ceased to be objective. They were not shouting about ideas so much as feelings and personalities. They hurled quotations then insults. And they drank. They became competitive. They wanted to win. They did not care what they said so long as they scored off each other. They drank more. They became violent. Clover cried. The neighbours complained.

When they moved to Sussex in 1970 they still loved each other. In desolate, beautiful surroundings they found new ways of lending support to each other. At the same time, something perverse in both their natures had made them seek isolation in order to contend even more effectively. Life centred around Jason. After all, he was the genius. Eleanor was passionate in her caring for him and Clover. She became countrified and worked like a peasant. And he knew she sometimes missed London. Just what did she miss and why? She was confirming his suspicions that she was a frivolous person. Like everyone else she had failed to understand him. His return to inner isolation made his heart leap with an old, secret gladness.

Although they went on together for nearly three years until the money both enabled and compelled her to leave, he withdrew his affection little by little. Arguments no longer ended in sex. There was no sex. He began to loathe her ill-fated womb and dreaded another catastrophic pregnancy. He looked at the body he had so liked and shuddered at the potential for grief that it contained. All she could generate was disaster. In addition, he resented the way she had made life so insidiously agreeable, showing him how to have a good time and to take pleasure in simple, silly things. It had only served to distract him. He resented her novels, her poetry, her viola, her Cole Porter, her wanting to pay Sunday afternoon visits to gardens and churches. Her love for Clover vexed him. Her love for himself infuriated him. What gave her the right to have given her life away to him? How dare she imply that he had invited her to do so?

Eleanor guessed but would not fully admit that Jason thought and felt these things. She went on with her hard work and her stupid hope and only made matters worse. It was as though she were being ground down to nothing. She stopped singing, except when she was in the vegetable garden and certain that no one was near. She stopped laughing. Only when she kissed Clover goodnight or made her breakfast did she smile and sometimes giggle. Jason had defeated and frightened her. What good did it do to win discussions? She cried over his neglect and his frigidity, and he locked himself in the studio to shut out the sound of her crying. He worked and slept and hardly spoke to her except about art, long drunken conversations that went on until four in the morning and left them both in ruins. He hit her. Two weeks later he hit her again. Hitting her became a habit. Jason was unrepentant.

Vengeance was always the same. Their arguments became circular, repetitive, reducible to a formula. They threw overboard the excess baggage of reason and tolerance in order to speed their vessels towards the reefs of destruction. Each had their point to prove and set about proving it in their accustomed predictable ways.

Eleanor: 'Jason, you're a man torn between principles and necessity. You pose as an independent being. You spurn help yet you have relied on the emotional, physical, financial and social resources of Monica and myself. Because you despise money you regard yourself as a superior being, yet you are forced into deals with people you consider your inferiors.

'You hold emotions in contempt. You boast of having none or of having eliminated them, yet you cling to Clover more than she clings to you.

'You scorn success yet you crave recognition. You're suspicious of fame, yet you resent the fact that you have been ignored.

'You live apart from the world. You say this is what you want, that you prefer solitude to a corrupt society. And yet you are so lonely.

'You must rely on others, yet you trust no one. This is because you do not trust yourself. You are afraid that those who love you will undermine your resolve and catch you naked in your weakness.

'You feel threatened by anyone who does not demonstrate unquestioning belief in you. You think, mistakenly, that I do not believe in you. You feel threatened by me.

'You are a weak man who has brainwashed himself into being strong. You are a punitive and censorious person. You hate life.

'You have made a fortress of your art to protect the softness of your centre which is all chaotic feeling. You use art to escape the world. The world takes revenge and forces itself on you.

'You make me realize how dangerous deep conviction can be.

'Above all you want to perish. As a hero of art, a misunderstood genius, a pariah in his purity. You want the world to slay you because your martyrdom will mean it has recognized you at last. Do you know what that longing is, Jason? It is a dying god complex. It is cheap, mythological nostalgia. All you are doing after so many years and so much struggle is fighting your father. Isn't it pathetic?'

Jason: 'Eleanor, you are full of envy. You envy me because you've failed to make anything of your life. You've failed to make art. You have dissipated your energies in a stupid search for fun.

'You think it is enough to have sensibilities and be at liberty. You are not at liberty, you are at large. Like a maniac is at large. You cannot control your emotions. You think emotions are important. You think everything is personal. You are wrong; wrong and dangerous. Because you are dangerous I *do* feel threatened by you.

'Liberty comes through work. You can't work. You haven't the discipline or the patience or the inspiration. I won't comment on your abilities. Facile insults are your department.

'You say my work is cold and hard. But it comes from the most intense emotion of all.

'Because I'm an artist and because I have a point of view which is my own and which supports me when externals don't, you envy me. You want to *be* me. Because you want to be me you gave me your life. Now you blame me because I refuse to feel guilty about the sacrifice. You want me to tell you what a wonderful person you've been. Well, I won't.

'You think you influenced me. You think that somehow you made my paintings. Well, I made them. I, I, I.

'You moan because you can't have children. Why can't you accept your fate? I accept mine.

'Because you can't make anything you think you need love. Because you were Daddy's girl you think you deserve love. You accuse me of purposefully withholding this commodity. Yet you claim to be intelligent and perhaps you are. But if so, you must have seen years ago that I could not provide love. Why did you choose me? It is not my fault.

'You are not, repeat *not*, Clover's mother.'

Eleanor: 'And you are not God.'

Jason: 'I'm a creator, like God. I am the creator, I am God.'

Eleanor: 'God the Father as Artist.'

Jason: 'Why not?'

Eleanor: 'Well, Monica may have bought that crap but I don't.'

Jason: 'Offends your lapsed Catholicism. Anyway, you're jealous.'

Eleanor: 'Jason, you are not God.'

Jason: 'Well if I'm not, who the hell is? Certainly not you!'

Eleanor: 'I may not be God, but I sure know self-aggrandizing sophistry when I hear it.'

When Eleanor's father and brother died, Jason's sympathy was minimal. He locked himself in the studio to escape the negative atmosphere he was sure she was generating. Her loss verified his conviction that she was disaster-prone. This time Eleanor believed him. No discussion was necessary to prove his point.

Clover understood that nothing could be repaired between Eleanor and Jason. She was not surprised when Eleanor left. She was sad, but she was prepared. She knew that she must stay with her father and stand by him because their blood was the same. She told this to Eleanor who nodded silently. There was no question of abduction or seduction. Jason now had everything which he claimed he wanted: the pain of his solitude, the unshared love of his daughter, the frustration of his work.

twelve

Once again life was difficult in the way it had been during the first year of Clover's existence. Jason had to do everything himself since there was no helpmate to abandon her own pursuits and rush to his assistance. He told himself he was glad. He stayed on in the cottage at the end of the bumpy lane beside the reedy dyke. His job as a visiting lecturer at a nearby university enabled him to pay the rent and put enough petrol in the car to drive Clover to and from school. His acceptance of the post had been a capitulation of sorts. Financial straits had driven him to the only sustenance available to struggling artists: teaching.

He did the shopping, cooked the meals, with Clover's assistance, took their shabby clothes to the laundry, sat and watched the dryer go round while Clover did the *Puzzler*, fed the cats. He shut himself in the studio and made paintings no one wanted. He filled more dark-red notebooks with his reasons for making them and with self-assurances that both his lack of acceptance and his lack of money were blessings and not afflictions. He could be certain his work was still pure.

Winter came and the wind blew without stopping. The vegetable garden went to seed and then to weed. In the spring there was no Eleanor to dig the earth or prune the roses or harvest the sprouting broccoli. Clover watched it turn from purple spikes to pale-yellow clusters of flowers. She was too sad to cut it. She went to the dyke and lay down in her secret place among the reeds clutching Molly, her favourite cat, watching the clouds roll in from the sea and listening to the subdued clash and clatter of the reeds. She looked up at the enormous dome of sky. She sensed the width of the world and felt dizzy with insignificance.

In late February, if she stood very still in her gumboots, she could hear the saturated ground make squishing noises as it moved beneath her. Under her size-three feet the earth bubbled with life. The force of it seemed to travel from her feet through her legs and straight up her spinal column to her brain. She was full of its uplifting. Every part of her pushed heavenward. Nothing sagged, nothing ever would sag. She was rising out of the ground like a tulip or a lily, rising up from the bulb of herself. Every cell in her body felt it, every cell in her brain. Where did it come from, this pushing, this bubble in the mud? It was so important, so mysterious. She frowned and held tight to her cat.

Jason told her, as he always told her, not to go down to the dyke, but

96

she kept going and she kept falling in. When she came home and presented herself to him wet and muddy, she was always laughing. She would go to her room, cluttered now that Eleanor was not there to make her clean it, and paint watercolours and read novel after novel. Jason would not allow her a television. But she had a radio and, late at night when she was meant to be asleep, she would listen under the blankets to forbidden pirate stations and sing softly to herself.

Jason could not resist the temptation to equate himself and his daughter with Prospero and Miranda. They might as well be living on an island. They might as well be shipwrecked. Yet he treasured the certainty that she was his alone. He dreaded the inevitable day when a group of well-heeled Venetians would be washed by the storm of life on to their yellow sands and wreak havoc with his privacy. Meanwhile he could have done with an Ariel or even a Caliban. Oh for a spirit to whisk away the laundry, some witch's spawn to carry in the coal and do the washing up.

A sprite of sorts did come along. She was Jason's pupil, and she approached him one day in the university parking lot and announced that she wished to become his assistant. He had been teaching for over a year, hating it and having little contact with his students outside the classroom, although he was most conscientious about his duties and his role, particularly his role as critic. The girl was familiar and he knew her first name. Her work was pretentious and dull. But at least she listened to his advice and tried, in her way, to act upon it. She had shown some improvement. Otherwise he took no notice of her and never thought about her. Confronted in this way he at first failed to recognize her. She was gently persistent. He thought of the canvases to be stretched, the laundry, the state of the kitchen, the holes in Clover's tights.

'Tuesday at three,' he said and drove off, leaving Clarissa Welbeck standing in the empty parking lot, happier than she had ever been in her life.

She came on Tuesday and again on Thursday. She allowed Jason to go through the motions of chasing her around the studio before making love to her with nothing between them and the dirty, freezing floor but a scrap of canvas. Clover banged on the door then went away. Four days later the grill was clean and she found her tights, with all the holes mended, piled neatly on her bed.

Clarissa let herself be monopolized by eleven-year-old Clover, hungry for an audience and some maternal solicitude. She talked incessantly to Jason's new assistant whenever she could corner her alone. She recounted to her the plots of innumerable novels and every word that every one of her teachers had ever uttered. She told her the story of her life and the lives of all the cats, every litter, every injury, every visit to the vet. It was so mysterious, so important. She told her about Eleanor and how she and Jason used to argue. She made Clarissa come with her to the dyke, although she did not take her to the secret place, and to pick blackthorn and wild anemones. She promised that in the summer she would show her where the blue butterflies were. Clarissa barely spoke. There was little opportunity for response when one was dealing with an inherently social being, cut off from the world and uninitiated into the rites of siblings and friendships. Clover was anything but shy and Clarissa was a perfect victim.

Jason, on the other hand, hardly spoke to Clarissa except to issue orders and discourse upon art – his own. She kept the studio in order and cleaned from top to bottom the house which her mother would have described as being in disgraceful condition. Jason took little interest in her appearance and none in her mind. (Clarissa was not distinguished in either respect.) Although she spent an increasing amount of time in the isolated cottage, although she looked after Clover's mending and made sure her vests were clean, although she scrubbed behind the cooker and supplied the cats with Cat Loves – and all this for little or no money – although she spent an average of five nights a week in Jason's bed, his treatment of her had hardly altered since she had signed up for his painting course. All he thought about her was that she was *young*.

She was his pupil first and foremost. She had been his assistant for five months when he saw fit to pass the following judgement, in front of fourteen other students, upon her most recent effort.

'If I wanted to make a painting that had no meaning, no style, no form and no content, that is exactly how I would do it.'

Clarissa did not appear on Tuesday. The dishes remained unwashed and Clover's bed unmade. Jason could not find two of his brushes and he was very cross. There were no tins of cat food in the broom closet. When he met Clarissa in the parking lot he reminded her curtly of her hours and her duties.

'I quit,' said Clarissa Welbeck.

Jason shrugged, turned the key in the ignition and drove off. He supposed that even perfect victims have their limits. The next day he pinned a card to the bulletin board in the students' centre. On the card was an advertisement for an assistant to come to Lantern Cottage two afternoons a week. Thirteen students applied. Eleven of them were women. Jason was amazed and secretly pleased, although he grumbled that they must all be masochists. He determined in advance the sole criterion on which he would base his choice. Out of the eleven she would be, quite simply, the youngest.

Clarissa was replaced by Jane who was replaced by Fiona. They shared Jason's bed, cleaned his studio, mended Clover's tights, and were rewarded for their pains by a C minus. Clover and Jason, when they were alone, always called them by the names which Clover had given her dolls (now a sorry set of redundant amputees retired to the sanatorium beneath her desk), that is, Dolly One, Dolly Two, Dolly Three and so on. Over the years other Dollies came and shared the fate of their predecessors. Jason refused to feel guilty.

The only woman who really interested him was five feet two inches tall, twelve years old and often unobtainable because she was off on her bicycle or down among the reeds in her secret place. When the autumn evenings drew in, he would call her name from the back door with an aching in his solar plexus. When she at last appeared he would pretend to be angry. Then he would show her what he had been painting and they would discuss it. She would tell him everything she thought was wrong and provide elaborate reasons to uphold her judgements. These were the only times Jason really laughed.

A letter from Eleanor informed him that he loved Clover because she was 'part of his Idea of Himself'. He did not reply.

Meanwhile Clover was no longer alone in her secret place. Emma Tozer lived a mile and a half down the road – or a half-mile walk across the fields – in the hotel where her father was the chef and where Eleanor had once worked as a chambermaid. Emma had become Clover's best friend. Clover's new bicycle had opened up a world of freedom and independence. She cycled to and from school, explored by-paths and bumpy lanes which led out across the marshes and ended abruptly in beautiful, silent nowhere. Mainly she rode to Emma's and back. And Emma rode over to her.

Emma was a year older than Clover, not popular with her classmates, too tall for her age, physically awkward and spoke with a lisp. But she was good at maths, French skipping, Spit, and was highly knowledgeable about sex. (She had three older sisters.) Emma was a regular overnight visitor. When she stayed at the cottage she and Clover listened under the blankets to forbidden radio stations and played game after game of backgammon and Monopoly. She smuggled in sweets and taught Clover to play poker for money, meanwhile enthusiastically filling in the gaps in her friend's knowledge of intercourse, pregnancy, child-bearing and masturbation.

The relationship was a puzzle to Jason. It was so important, so mysterious. It made him feel an intruder, as indeed he was. Clover and Emma touched each other, whispered, giggled and ran up and down the stairs. They quarrelled and laughed for no reason at all that he could make out. They kissed each other goodnight and planned to be actresses and share a flat in London. They cycled miles, went riding on Saturdays, and gossiped for hours about the personalities and idiosyncrasies of the horses. Their friendship was not threatened by Clover's success in the netball team. Her popularity made as little sense to her as her former ostracism; already she suspected the transient nature of glory. She did not know how to interpret the behaviour of others. The athletics plus her devotion to the cello made her uncertain whether she were sensitive or strong. That was why she liked Emma. They were both indefinable. And they said what they thought. There was no mystification with Emma.

Clover could not bring herself to abandon anyone, although, like her father, she was short on pity except for animals. When after Sports Day she became a little heroine, she did her best to include Emma in the new group of friends who sought her out at lunchtime and breaks. She invited Emma to accompany them on their covert forays to the pizza parlour. Emma declined. Clover saw that she was shy with everyone but herself and that she loved her and wanted to be alone with her. When Clover got her period they went together to the secret place by the dyke. It was the last time Emma ever saw the place and the last time Clover visited it for over a year. The next time she was accompanied by a sixteen-year-old boy. After half an hour they left in confusion. For the following three days Clover considered herself in a very bad mood. Clearly she knew a good deal more than he did.

When she began to menstruate she also wrote to Eleanor, care of American Express in Paris. Two weeks later Eleanor sent her a poem which Clover liked but could not understand, especially as it was copied in Eleanor's scrawl. As she read the poem to Jason he turned his back.

> *What you are within your lone existence*
> *poets utter who have learnt to see;*
> *and they learn life through you from a distance,*
> *as the evenings, through the stars' persistence,*
> *grow accustomed to eternity.*

'Eleanor and her poetry.'

JASON

Never leave that distance to surrender,
should he seek the woman in the maid;
for his mind can only read or render
you as maids . . .

'Who is "he" Jason do you think?'
'I don't know. The poet probably.'
'Why does it say maid and then maids?'
'They're both collective. Oh I don't know.'
' "Leave him in his garden solitude". Jason? . . . Jason?'
He had shut himself in the studio.

Clover's precosity unnerved him. He watched himself being continually aware of it. It became a third presence in the house both emanating from her and drawing her on – on and on, past him and eventually away from him. He resisted it, although he knew resistance was both wrong and futile. He could not reverse the force which, even in their closeness, he sensed slowly eating away his security like the three-minute decrease in light each day after the summer solstice. He struggled against his growing need to guard and protect Clover, to keep her from the world and for himself. He disliked her peers, both boys and girls, and was suspicious of everyone. He tried to prise away these feelings that stuck to him. They were ignoble, he knew.

He recognized in his daughter a strength that could move people: not an innocence but an honesty, not a beauty but an attraction, not brilliance but acumen. She loved him but she would not cling to him. He feared the day she would cease to cling to him, and he feared his own feelings on that day. How could he hold her to him? She was lonely yet social. Unlike him, she needed friends and would find them. Loving her so, he drew back from her and became even less demonstrative. His behaviour both puzzled her and filled her with relief. She stopped wanting to sit in his lap. When she did long for affection, she thought of Eleanor and she thought of boys.

Isolation increased possessiveness. Still, Jason told himself that the work was everything, that the work lived on, and that when Clover grew up and went away he would simply continue as he was, staunch to the end of his days. ('He loves lone paths that stretch on far before,/and no white flitting under the dark beeches,/and most of all the dumb room and shut door.') When Clover left he would stoically bury his feelings and be as he always had been.

He saw no one except his students and other teachers. Since Eleanor had left, London acquaintances, with the exception of Dillon, had stopped paying visits. Dillon turned up every few months with never more than an hour or so to spare. Jason resented his fitting him in like that, but he missed his friend and was starved for a certain type of conversation. They smoked Dillon's Greek cigarettes and drank Dillon's Johnnie Walker as Jason silently paraded each new painting for his inspection. Dillon sat in the middle of the studio on one of the wobbly chairs, his long legs crossed. He nodded, cocked his head to one side, twisted his moustache, made some noises at the back of his throat, squinted and smoked.

Clover appeared with a plate of Jaffa cakes. Dillon winked at her and addressed her as Babyface. She smiled at him uncertainly and went away. She hated the smoke and she felt too sorry for Jason to sit down with them.

Dillon was kind. Jason tried not to be too bitter. They still liked each other. But Jason was secretly resentful as he observed Dillon cosily at home in his post-modernism, floating on the warm seas of fashion. His three-day growth and black jacket over faded jeans revealed rather than concealed his prosperity. He wore success lightly. He did not brood about purity or nurse his cherished vision. Alienation was *démodé*. He wanted his work to be accessible. (Did he really think it was doing everybody good? It was certainly doing *him* good.) He was not worried by what had been said or written about his video installation at the Venice Biennale. Thirteen thousand people had seen it, and that was all that mattered. Shows of his composite photographs were scheduled for Zurich and New York. He was a good-natured fellow.

After the most recent unsold Englefields had been viewed, Jason asked Dillon whether he wanted to paint anymore.

'Sometimes. For fun. I paint the cat, my lovers, the fridge.' He waved his cigarette around and smiled. 'I know, I know. You frown on representation.'

'At least it's still painting.'

'Tut tut, sweetheart. Art is wide open. Why confine yourself to canvas? You know there aren't restrictions anymore. Oh, I'm sorry.'

Jason had just written in his 1980–1 notebook: 'All wholly uncompromising conviction is religious.'

'You have a problem-solving nature, Jay. Only it's always the same problem.'

'You're thinking of *The Three Virtues*.'

'No. Well, yeah. It's been going on for – I mean, it's good, it's good.'

'It is. But no one will ever want it.'

'Well. I don't know. Abstraction is in hibernation.'

'Abstraction is and remains the most important breakthrough in the visual arts since the discovery of perspective.'

Dillon sighed. He looked at Jason standing so upright beside his painting, his expression resolute to fierce, and he started to chuckle.

'This,' said Jason, pointing at *The Three Virtues*, '*this* is not an abstraction. It's a *real thing.*' He leaned forward and glared at Dillon. 'More real than you are.'

Dillon crossed and uncrossed his legs and changed his tone. 'I understand,' he said placatingly. 'I agree. It's just that, my dear, abstraction is a dead end, it's too – um – individual. Too individual. You understand all that. Why not think about giving it up – for a while. Try something else. Try – '

'You're telling me the not very original news that painting is dead. Well, no one can tell me to stop painting!'

'You don't understand, Jay. It makes me *happy* to know there's someone like you out here in the middle of nowhere, working away, believing in art . . .'

It was the usual climax to their visits. And as usual Jason disdained to mention George Facer who was selling Dillon's work for handsome prices. His pride would not allow him to ask Dillon to intercede. Instead he repeated old formulas about not being interested in all that, and he could only presume that Dillon believed him.

Financial difficulties worsened. Without a gallery, selling his work was impossible. Two paintings appeared in a group show in Belfast but no one wanted to buy them. He thought of trying to sell his work to company collections, something his father might be able to help with. But he was not speaking to his father. In desperation he rang George Facer with the faint hope of arranging another show. George was in Düsseldorf, then in New York, then 'unobtainable'. Angry and humiliated, Jason left a message with the gallery secretary asking George to ring him when he returned. He even rang the van Zuptens, but they were in the Bahamas.

Clover's new school (she had passed her entrance exam) and new growth (she was five foot four now) would demand new clothes. Her cello needed repair and she had outgrown her riding boots. He had never doubted his ability to give her a happy childhood, but adolescence was another matter. Adolescence really did require money. If he took on more teaching he would do less painting and writing. But if he did not sell a painting or two there would be no alternative. The eternal teaching – how in this country where all visual sense had been channelled into bloody gardens was he ever to escape it? There were two answers: paint different pictures or go somewhere else.

His loneliness could be assuaged by Clover and, to an extent, by Dolly Five. But something inside him required a peer. Lecturing was not enough, whether in or out of classrooms. He realized, unwillingly, that he missed discussions, even when they did end in tears, locked doors and broken windows. He missed having someone around at whom he could get well and truly mad, in Eleanor's American sense of the word. How could he be expected to get mad at Dolly Five? She couldn't provoke the cat.

Eleanor had developed his taste for aggressive social intercourse. It was all her fault. He hated her the more and mixed with his odium his greedy love of his daughter, his anxiety about money, his obsession with his theories, his craving for solitude, his need for another, and his smothered hope that one day soon George Facer or Mrs van Zupten would ring him back.

thirteen

When the telephone did ring at the beginning of May 1980 Jason was annoyed to hear not the voice of a projected benefactor but Charles Bevan. Immediately he sensed something of Eleanor.

'Jason. Charles here.'

'Hello.'

'Are you well?'

'Yes.'

'And Clover?'

'Very well.' Even the scantiest preliminaries irritated him. At least Charles forbode to remark on the amount of time elapsed since their last meeting. Charles, in turn, did not wish to be subjected to Jason's persona for longer than was necessary. He simply could not help being polite.

'Dear boy, my reason for calling is very specific. I realize how valuable your time is, so let us come directly to the point.'

'I'd appreciate it.'

'Very well. I've received a letter from Eleanor.'

Jason groaned. 'I was afraid of that.' Naturally, the eight months of uneasy peace could not last. 'What is it now?'

'She's ill. Seriously ill and alone, although her spirits are good. She is settled and rational, not to say philosophical about her condition.'

'Which is?'

'Diabetes, from what I can make out. All the symptoms. She could live indefinitely or – '

Jason thought he detected a break in the lawyer's voice. His own heartbeats were for a moment uneven.

'She very much wants to see Clover.'

'No.'

Charles hung fire. He had geared himself to being very patient in this encounter.

'She has no intention of coming to you.'

'She's said that before. She can't be trusted. It's out of the question. Just tell her absolutely no.'

'Dear boy, please understand. She *cannot* come to you. She is much too ill.'

Jason was silent. All he could think was, 'It's not my fault.'

'What she has proposed,' continued Charles, gently putting his case, 'is that I take Clover to her. You may come or not as you please. She presumes not. At any rate, there are no conditions on her part.'

'I should think so. Who the hell is she to make conditions? She thinks that just because she's ill – if she is ill – her bargaining position is enhanced.'

'She is not bargaining with you. She is ill and alone. Clearly, she fears she may die – '

'She always had a vivid imagination.'

'Whether her fears are well-founded I can't tell. I must see her and see her doctor before commenting on the basis of her fears. The reality of those fears is indisputable. She wishes only to spend an afternoon with Clover. As her lawyer it is my duty to inform you of this. As her friend I beg you not to be so unkind as to give the matter no consideration at all. Perhaps you'd like time to – '

'There's nothing to consider. Listen to me, Charles. Eleanor has obviously succeeded in getting some kind of hold over you. She does that sort of thing to men. But I tell you that whatever her actions or her words, her motives are always suspect.'

Again Charles was silent. He was not buying what Jason was selling, and through his silence Jason felt what he never had felt before in the lawyer – a real strength, both of commitment and resistance.

'Besides,' he added hastily, 'I haven't the money to send Clover to Paris and from what I hear the trip might prove a straight gate for you too.'

'Eleanor will pay for the entire venture.'

'Oh indeed! It's financial blackmail again, is it? Well the matter's settled. Neither of us is going – absolutely not going!'

'I cannot compel you, Jason.' The voice lost none of its composure. 'I do urge you, though, to think the matter over, even for twenty-four hours, before making a final decision. The visit can do no harm to you – in her present condition the woman hardly poses a threat – and it would make both her and Clover very happy.'

'I'll speak for Clover's happiness,' Jason growled.

'Jason, why can't I go?' With a start, Jason realized that Clover had picked up the extension in the studio and probably had been listening to every word. How like her to be unable to keep silent.

'Hello, my dear.' He heard Charles's chuckle of pleasure. He felt sure a conspiracy was being hatched against him.

'Hel-*lo*!' came Clover's reply.

'Have you been playing backgammon?' Charles seemed to have forgotten Jason's existence.

'I have you know, but to tell the truth and I'm not really bragging, well there's just no one else as good as me, even Jason, and so I always win and everybody's a bit fed-up.'

'Clover, get off the phone.'

'Oh Daddy, pleeeze . . . '

'Put down the receiver,' said Jason in what was meant to be a calm and reasonable tone.

'Can't I say goodbye to Charles?'

'Yes,' he sighed.

'Goodbye, Charles. Goodbye!' Her words were like gay flags on a little ship disappearing over the horizon.

'Goodbye, darling girl.' There was a click. 'Heavens she must be – '

'Fourteen.'

Jason fumed inwardly, 'But you'll never see her.'

Charles said he would ring again in a few days. Jason replied that he could not prevent him, but advised him against wasting his time and his money. He supposed, with satisfaction, that Charles considered him a brute.

Jason felt anything but a brute as he sat at the kitchen table with his head in his hands, not even bothering to go to the studio to chastise Clover for her latest indiscretion. He was concerned only that Eleanor not be allowed to use her affliction to get the better of him and steal away the source of his life. He heard the back door bang. The source of his life was hurrying off on her bicycle to escape his wrath. He almost rose, then smiled to himself despite his agitation. What an imp she was. And how proud she had made him. She was his one great success, a success he need not worry would contaminate him.

As for Eleanor enlisting the services of Charles – how long, he wondered, had those two been in cahoots and what could have prompted such an unholy alliance. Trust Eleanor to choose a drunken dwarf like Charles to handle her so-called affairs. Trust her to latch on to him in what appeared to be his downward spiral. She likes backing a loser, Jason thought bitterly. Thinks it's democratic.

Both Monica and Dillon had mentioned the peculiar circumstances surrounding the Bevans. Something had gone very wrong with Charles, but he had said nothing about his rumoured misfortunes. He seemed as he always did – rational, good-humoured with a hint of irreverence. Arrogant bastard. Of course he was being appropriately British, not letting on he had hit the skids or was about to, pretending all was rosy in this best of all possible monarchic welfare states. Decline, that's what Charles represented, decline. Soon he and his kind would be dead, and there would be, Jason hoped, nothing similar to replace them.

Still, Jason could not forget his initial fondness for Charles in spite of what had been his success, his money, his comfortable, respected, protected life. It was only that Charles had made the fatal mistake of helping him and being good at helping him. Then there was the drawing. That was when his antipathy had begun to fester. *The Three Virtues* was good, very good. He had been working on the painting for over four years, unable to finish, unable to get it right. But it would be his best work and that drawing was the best thing he had done and one day it would be worth a small fucking fortune and he hated Charles for snatching away his little masterpiece. He hated being forced to part with it because he needed the money. He hated, quite simply, having to part with it. Of course Charles would choose the best. If only the transaction had been left to indecisive Anthea. She would have picked a less favoured piece, something he would not have missed so much, even though she would have paid less for it. Charles's generosity made Jason's loss all the more demeaning. And now Charles was about to be swept under the social carpet along with his nasally cosmeticized bladder of a wife. Whisk and away they went. Jason took grim pleasure in the imagined spectacle.

'Humph! No one is spared. Not even toffs like Charles.' Well, they had to go, all of them.

As for Eleanor, he refused to concede that she might 'go' in quite a different way. But there was no escaping Clover, now acquainted with what was billed as Eleanor's condition. It would be difficult to hold her back from Paris. He would be seen as a monster if he refused. Damn the woman, damn her! She'd go to any lengths to infiltrate his life and disrupt the peace and quiet which were all he valued. He must be tactful with Clover, and to that he was not accustomed. He must calm her enthusiasms and her fears. He would not be able to persuade her that this was simply a plot of Eleanor's, despite his own strong suspicions. Jason sat at the kitchen table until he heard Clover come in by the front door, remove her gumboots and kick them into opposite corners of the little entry hall.

'When do we leave then?' She was showing no remorse for her flagrant eavesdropping and had adopted a positively aggressive tone.

'Clover, you won't like hearing this, but I don't think it's a good idea to go to Paris.'

'What have ideas got to do with it? Cup of tea?' She plugged in the electric kettle. She intended to settle down and argue it out with him until she or he or both were in ruins. Christ, she was so like Eleanor.

'It will upset you.'

'It will not upset me, it will upset you.'

'Then think of me.'

'I do, but Eleanor is ill so I think of her too.'

'You're a good girl.' He tried another approach.

'Don't call me that. I don't know what it means and neither do you.'

'Well, I know you make a good cup of tea.'

'Stick to the point, Jason, and stop treating me like a child.'

'It's not very grown-up to eavesdrop.'

She shrugged. 'How else could I have found out about Eleanor?'

Jason covered his discomfort with righteous indignation. 'Do you think I'd hold something back from you, *lie* to you?'

'I think you might have. Now you can't can you?'

'Don't you trust me?'

'Most of the time. But my trusting you is not what we're discussing. Look, I really must see Eleanor. I haven't seen her since last October and she's ill. I know she needs me to – '

'To what?' Jason jumped in, unable to hold back his resentment.

'To cheer her up. To make her better. I can make her better, I know I can. Let me go, Daddy, oh pleeeze let me go.'

'Now you really are behaving like a child.'

'I'm asking you a favour, just like Charles was asking you a favour.'

'Don't talk to me about Charles.'

'Won't you do me a favour? Just this once. I won't be away long. Charles said – '

'Stop talking about Charles,' he shouted.

'Sor-*ry*.' She waited for his anger to subside and drank her tea.

'Whatever happens Charles will not be involved. He will not take you to Paris. What puts these lunatic ideas into Eleanor's head?'

'Well, *you* don't want to see her.'

'Too right.'

'Well, who'll take me then?'

Jason stood up, went to the studio and closed the door. Fifteen minutes later Clover stood behind him with a fresh cup of tea. He was working on a painting.

'There's only one person who can,' she said.

'Can what?'

'Take me.'

'Really? Who is that?'

'You know who. You.'

'Huh!'

'I put whisky in it.' She placed the cup on the floor beside him. Dolly Five had recently tendered her resignation and the room was in chaos. Clover touched Jason on the arm.

'Will you take me?'

Jason sighed and removed her hand.

'Yes. All right. Yes.'

'Thank you, Daddy.' She gave him a kiss, to which he did not respond, and went to her room. A few minutes later he heard her practising the cello.

fourteen

Nothing made Jason more angry with Eleanor than her death. His first reaction to the news was to wonder that he had not, years ago, despatched her himself. With her penchants for ridicule and the wrong man and with her addiction to emotional blitzkrieg, it was amazing that someone had not. He marvelled at the general level of restraint. It had been left to her own intent or misfortune to do the job.

Charles had been unclear about the intent. As to the means and results he had been quite specific. In a letter dated the 10 March 1981, and written with his usual irritating blend of discretion and sensitivity, he informed Jason and Clover that she appeared to have mishandled the injections, that was all. The concierge had discovered her within hours of the accident, and accident they must presume it to be. There was no note, no sign of desperation, no disarray. She had been taken to hospital where she died in a diabetic coma one month before her fortieth birthday. According to her instructions, Charles was arranging for the body to be returned to England for cremation. A small ceremony would be held on 21 March and he very much hoped that Jason and Clover would be able to attend since this was Eleanor's last wish. She had, it appeared, made Charles acquainted with all her wishes when he had paid that final visit to Paris. Oh, and there would be some things for Clover.

Jason was furious – with Eleanor, with Charles, with the incredible inconvenience of it all. And he had just begun a new painting. Trust the bitch to interrupt him like this and undermine his concentration. She was the most destructive female he had ever known. To top it all, he must break the news to Clover.

Clover was fifteen, tall for her age but fully-grown, a complete little human being with qualities both womanly and childish, straightforward and complex. Her candour was as embarrassing and disarming as it had been at nine. Her will and her ingenuousness remained intact. She said she wanted to be a biologist. She knew quite enough what she wanted. She quested beyond what girls of her age quested for. She was looking for something, Jason could tell.

If it had been simple ambition he could have understood; or just boys, since there seemed to be more than a few around. But it was neither, although it probably included both while reaching beyond both. Nature had dressed her up, decked her out for the party, leaving her to add the

111

finishing touches. But as yet she had nowhere to go. The party had not begun.

He knew her reaction to Eleanor's loss would be violent. He sympathized while remaining jealous and angry. (No one in his life ever could or would force him to mix his feelings like Those Two.) His announcement let loose the anticipated torrent. She had been late coming home from school that day and it was nearly dark. Jason could make no ceremony of telling her. He was unequipped for softening blows. And so he gave her the news full in the face as soon as she walked through the door. A slow wail wound its way up from below her stomach through her heart, breast, lungs and larynx, unstoppable, and, when it emerged at maximum pitch, came accompanied by immediate tears. Her grief, pain and frustration had expressed themselves this way since she was a child.

She flung herself on Jason who held her stiffly, saying nothing. Then she pulled away, not in anger at his lack of response but in plain distraction, made for the back door before he could stop her and ran out across the marshes without coat or boots. He had no hope of catching her, she could run like the wind. He knew she would run and run until she dropped. He would wait. It was better to let her run. But when night came he felt that old fear for her, the fear he and Eleanor had felt when they called her name from the back steps into the darkness. Clover, Clover, Clover!

(Oh why was he remembering that now? Eleanor, he thought, and was horrified to be thinking it, go and find her. It's getting dark. The fog is coming. I can hear the fog-horn in the Channel.)

Clover had run the marshes and jumped the dykes too many times to lose her way. At seven-thirty she was back with wet feet, freezing. She murmured an apology for worrying him, sat down at the kitchen table and laid her head on her arms, breathing heavily. Jason watched from a distance, afraid of her grief. Timidly, he touched her hair. She was fast asleep.

Clover nurtured dreams of high fashion, but was condemned to school uniform or jeans. For Eleanor's funeral she wore her only dress and her only pair of smart shoes, which had low heels (she was conscious of her height), pointed toes and clip-on bows. The dress was navy blue (cheap, the colour no one wanted). It was too short in the front and too long in the back. Its rectangular shape hid her figure, the proportions of which were further disguised by an old duffel coat that was a size too small and beneath which was visible the uneven hem of her dress. But between the hem and the pointed shoes were the unmistakable giveaways of her loveliness: her legs. She had put on black fishnet tights with a hole at the instep. This she covered with a pair of rolled-down, grey, school socks. She had pinned up her hair, but a thousand wisps were escaping by the moment. Her forehead was bare, white, prominent. Her dark eyes were full of doubt.

Jason wore his only tweed jacket, a bargain from a second-hand clothing store in Eastbourne. At Clover's insistence he had had his hair cut.

They were the first to arrive, too early for the service. But that had been Jason's intent. He wanted no encounters. He planned to go straight into the chapel and sit alone, silent and unapproachable. He would have taken a pew at the back, but Clover marched towards the altar before he could stop her. It was her habit to be as close as possible to the spectacle. On her rare visits to the cinema she invariably raced for the first row and everyone else followed. Clover insisted on the front row.

The chapel was cold, new and of cardboard quality. After all those medieval churches, thought Jason, for her to end here – against the express tenets of her faith and eschewing resurrection. Perhaps she couldn't afford anything better and was making a show of her poverty. Somewhere an organ played. 'Not a real one,' Clover whispered. There were, however, masses of flowers. From whom? Against Jason's will, she had ordered a large display and arranged to pay for it on credit. But the rest . . . The flowers could not all be from Charles. Clover strained to see a name or a message.

'There aren't any cards,' she exclaimed, forgetting where she was, unused to churches or ceremonies.

They heard footsteps, whispers. Someone else had come in. Then more whispers, more footsteps. Jason would not turn round and forcibly prevented his inquisitive daughter from doing so. Why did she care who came? Of what importance was it? Old Charles was sure to be there, but he couldn't imagine anyone else bothering. Eleanor had been out of the London social circuit for years, and no one forgot faster than dilettantes. Nevertheless, people were filling the chapel behind his back. Who were they? It didn't matter. All that mattered was that this charade pass off as quickly as possible. Then escape. Escape with Clover back to the safety of their yellow sands. Shyly, she took his hand. Hers felt cold and soft in his big, warm one. She had seen the coffin and the clergyman. She was aware of her father's taut nerves and was beginning to feel afraid.

She thought of Charles whom she had not met since Paris. She knew he was there and she wanted to speak to him. He would help her, she felt sure, to feel better. But she must not look round. Jason would be angry. That was because he was secretly upset. Jason could be so peculiar. She sighed and wondered if Charles had seen her.

Charles had seen her. In spite of his best efforts he was late, the last to arrive, and feeling a bit shaky for want of an eleven o'clock vodka. His eyes took a few moments to accustom themselves to the change from the bright light outside. He noticed the Blacks and made for their pew then thought better of it and sat by himself just behind them, in fact behind everyone. Despite his sadness, he experienced a certain satisfaction at seeing them all assembled, their backs to him, unaware of him, congregated for better or worse just as she had required. He had managed to grant her wish and, although it was a perverse wish, he was forced to concede to her, dead as she was, that he was beginning to see the point.

He strained for better glimpses of the company, failed to do so, except for the Blacks, and took out his spectacles. There she was in the front row. He recognized instantly the shape of the head. And he beside her, rigid as a barge-pole. The third critical head – where was it? Ah, there it was, and sprouting somewhat less of that fine, fair hair than when he had last set eyes on it. Charles derived a mild, unworthy gratification from the sight of that head, his own curls being so crisply intact. The rest of the assembly consisted of Dillon Butterworth who sat with George Facer and two other artists whom Charles recognized and had met once or twice. He had informed Dillon, according to Eleanor's instructions, and Dillon never went anywhere alone. As for George, he always did the appropriate thing, and Jason was, technically, still part of his stable. Or he was keeping Dillon company. Or perhaps he had even liked Eleanor. But his presence made Charles uncomfortable. The two artists were probably old loves of Eleanor. Then there were the three women, former confidantes, and two men he did not know, also, no doubt, old loves. Charles settled himself for the ordeal. He was aware of everyone trying not to squirm, all of them wishing it over and done, wanting to be somewhere else, awaited, anticipated, required. And he had thought that dull once, when he had been required, and by several of those now present. It mattered little to him how long the service went on. His office appointment book was nearly a blank. In fact he seldom went to the office. The firm had ceased to expect him. Only one in all the world expected him, and with an intensity he found difficult to endure. Nevertheless, he endured it.

The service began. As soon as the clergyman spoke, Charles's attention wandered. No point in listening to this, no point at all. Besides, concentration was impossible in such circumstances where every moment the past intruded upon the present. Perhaps that was Eleanor's intention – that the past might triumph. Well. He sat comfortably enough in his old, expensive suit. Should last him another ten years. Quality tells, all else is false economy. He watched everyone, able as always to derive amusement and satisfaction from the most unpromising circumstances. He observed them all. He put them together, took them apart, put them together again like a puzzle or a clock. He amused himself by endeavouring to read their thoughts, guess their feelings, divine their secret responses to each other. He tried being each one. It was an old game of his, originally developed for church and lectures, for exactly such occasions as this. Only the image of Eleanor made his eyes fill with tears and reminded him where, in the present, he was.

Charles studied the back of his second cousin's head and speculated about her reactions to what must be, for her, the very barbed presence of Felix Koning. Felix, he noted, was the only other really well-dressed man in attendance. Such a multitude of sins demanded immaculate cover. Clearly, Felix was prospering. Felix was legitimate. Meetings between him and Charles over the past five years had been rare and strained. They had never had much to say to each other anyway. Odd that their only common interest, aside from paintings, might be the cut of a cloth. He saw Monica give Felix a sidelong glance which he did not return.

What were they doing here, the Blacks? Why had Eleanor asked him to invite them? Yet Monica had been eager to come. She had assured him of that when, with some embarrassment, he had rung her a week ago. She was so sorry. She was so sad. It was she who had sent all the flowers.

That was his one conversation with her since the Blacks' account (the first of several) had been withdrawn. She seemed quite crazy and went on and on, telling him about the night in the restaurant when at first she had hardly been able to recognize Eleanor but had then kissed her out of a compassion she could not control. She had seen the look Eleanor had given Felix; she read the pain beneath the flippancy. She admired the defiance or the pretence of it. She herself, she admitted, could never have mustered such spirit. She herself had followed Felix like a spaniel, waiting for his attention when he cared to bestow it, letting him arrange everything since she could think of nothing better, since she was afraid to suggest.

She was so afraid. She was afraid even to move. And so she had waited too long and now it was too late and he was free. He had used her, Charles never doubted it, to keep his freedom. Against everyone's better judgement, Felix had been let off. And for that Monica had hoped he might love her. Did she realize the extent of her own naïvety? Probably not, or only partially, since she appeared to exist in a permanent muddle which prevented her functioning without the constant support of her husband. Jeremy certainly would not have allowed her to attend the funeral without him.

Charles watched Jeremy sit in apparently calm possession of his wife. Despite Felix and himself. How he must loathe them both. Felix had got the better of him without even trying. First the Teniers, then the wife. Jeremy would have divorced Monica on the spot if he could have borne the eyes and tongues of the world. To divorce her would have been to admit that on two calamitous occasions he had failed to guard her behaviour. Moreover divorce was unnecessary. With Monica threats were more powerful weapons than acts. To blame her was sufficient. To scold her was surfeit. She was more than willing to put her own head on the block. So he simply kept watch over her. Charles imagined the dentist reproaching his weeping wife. 'But darling, I can't really trust you, can I?' He allowed her to stray as far as the V and A, the Brompton Oratory, Harvey Nichols. Otherwise, he slipped on her lead and accompanied her everywhere. She would not misbehave again.

Charles wondered what Jeremy thought of the dead woman. No doubt he remembered her only as Jason's moll, some noisy creature at an opening who, years later, had failed to appear at a dinner party. Did he associate her, on the night of that dinner party, or even now, with the man who was responsible for the wounding of his pride, the loss of his £5,000 and the alienation of his wife's affections? Probably not. The memory of that dinner party, of Eleanor's absence then (her chair filled at the eleventh hour by a depressingly inadequate substitute), of her permanent absence now, made Charles ache for his forgone vodka. He sighed. He was on the women's side. He felt sorry for them all – the one in the coffin, the one who clung to her father's hand, the one so small and indistinct, caged bird, fettered to her husband. Never had he seen a lady so in need of the proverbial knight. He knew she thought he blamed her, but he did not. 'It's all right,' he wanted to tell her. 'Don't be guilty. Mad things are done for love.'

One thing was certain. Felix Koning was not feeling sorry for the women. Or for anyone. Maybe for himself, a little, Charles thought, since he exhibited all the signs of annoyance only tolerably veiled. His immaculate shirt, his silk tie, his tweeds, his nice new mackintosh were not contributing one jot to his physical or psychic comfort. He was clearly bored with this tedious service and this confluence of supremely uninteresting people, most of whom he had hoped never to see again. What bored him most, Charles expected, was the sight of Monica Black. She was a woman who shed a great many tears; she was an overflowing fount of them. How many times must Felix have sat and listened to her cry, trying his best to read or to muffle the sound with Chopin and Berg, bored nearly to tears himself? How had he endured it? Anthea had described his Monica liaison as gigoloing pure and simple. Self-preservation was the word Felix had used. What could he have meant? Anthea grilled Charles and drew a blank. Then Felix went to Germany where he remained for over a year, greatly improving his fortunes, and she forgot all about his remark.

Was Felix thinking of Eleanor as a means of distracting himself from his boredom? Charles felt sure he was thinking of Eleanor. Not the Eleanor decaying so unpleasantly in that coffin but the living Eleanor of long legs and flaming hair and the slightly sour smell of red-head. It must be a novel sensation to feel lust for the dead; the taste of sacrilege must be momentarily delicious. Perhaps that was also what she'd wanted. Perhaps it was part of her design for this bizarre gathering. She knew Felix well enough.

Charles admonished himself for carrying his perverse empathy too far. Felix would not be recalling anything. He would be thinking ahead. His mouth twitched. Then Charles saw him glance at his watch. Why had he come? Charles had been amazed when he said he would, although reluctantly. Maybe Felix was not entirely without gratitude to whatever provided him with unmixed pleasure, especially now that it was safe to be grateful. Maybe he was rendering a certain homage.

Charles envied Felix that unmixed pleasure and his envy hurt him. He switched his attention from the black of Felix's empty heart to the back of George Facer's empty head. But nothing moved him to venture inside that skull. It made him very uncomfortable and he was not sure why. He had not spoken to George Facer in two years and he had no desire to speak to him today. The silvery voice, the long face, the arrogant nose, the ecclesiastical smile would grate on his sensibilities. The mechanisms of polite distancing would sicken him. He could not say precisely why. He and George had been third-rate friends for more than a third of his life, until the dealer had cut him as the Blacks had cut him. Now the Blacks and George seemed not as thick as they had been, although Charles felt sure that George would still be happy to take their money.

With the possible exception of Felix, they all suddenly struck him as a sad lot on a downhill slope, more than a little afraid, himself certainly included. 'We've all had to stop for this, to stop and rethink.' He looked again at Clover. 'Even you, oh essence of spring, must stop and rethink.' He looked hard at her. His eyes flew to Monica, back again to Clover. 'Oh dear,' he said, almost out loud. Something had struck him, as definite and impalpable as a blast of hot wind in the face. But Eleanor had never said. Of course, like everyone present she had her confidences to keep. Still, it was very unsettling. He would have a closer look after the service. He would have a closer look at everyone.

He returned his attention to Herr Koning who no longer seemed distracted and bored. Charles sensed a ripple of interest across his detachment. Something had captured his attention, something in the front row. The focus of that attention was weeping audibly. Her sobs and the sound of the moving coffin brought Charles back to the present and put an end to his game.

This was Clover's first encounter with the rituals of death. She had never attended a funeral. No one close to her had died except a few cats. She watched in disbelief as the coffin rumbled slowly over the bumpy cogs and disappeared between red velveteen curtains which parted automatically to admit it. She suddenly realized that behind those curtains were real flames, that Eleanor was inside that departing coffin, and that the flames would burn up first the coffin and then Eleanor. Clover moaned out loud and threw her head forward, banging it on the front of the pew and feeling as though she were going to vomit. Jason yanked her upright. His face was set. Clover was aware of another woman's sobs.

Clover really had believed she could save Eleanor, at least make her better, at least cheer her up. She was convinced she had done so on that visit to Paris. But she could not, in the end, transfer her vigour to one so moribund. How could Eleanor not have recovered or at least lived to see her again?

Clover was a sunlight creature, and in the ignorance of her optimism, she failed to allow for the powers of darkness. She still imagined that Eleanor must be alive. Yet if she were alive, she was burning at this very moment, and that was impossible. That was unendurable. Therefore, thought Clover, death must be real. It was part of the world, the world was shot through with it.

She wanted to take Jason's hand again, but both were tucked securely under his arms.

'I love you, Jason,' she said to herself. 'I love you, Eleanor.'

Who was the woman who was crying?

Jason sat like a stone. He looked neither to the right nor the left. Although his eyes were open he did not see. Despite himself, he saw nothing but Eleanor. He saw her burn in death as she had burned in life – self-consuming and consuming all. He saw her striding across the marshes, red hair blowing; lying like a broken doll in the road outside Clover's school; naked, turning aside the sheets on a hot summer night, unaware of his watching her, so fragile and exposed. She took a cake out of the oven, smashed a bottle against the wall, rolled on her back and clutched her belly in uncontrollable laughter. He heard her awful singing, some missiles from her arsenal of smart remarks, her screaming 'Fuck you, Jason' from the window of a first-class compartment. He thought of the last time he had seen her – a shocking glimpse from a Paris doorway before he fled across the street: overweight, glasses, dingy brown hair pulled hastily back the better to squint at his retreating form, swollen foot in cutaway slipper, one eye clearly on the verge of sightlessness.

The next morning when he came to collect Clover, Eleanor did not appear. Clover stood alone, her battered suitcase in her right hand looking fragile against the high, baroque doors. She had tried to describe to him their meeting. But he had said no, do not mention it to me please. Let me off this time in return for the favour I have done you. Do not mention it to me ever again.

The awful rite was over and Jason was the first to rise. Gripping Clover by the arm (he suddenly felt the need to touch her), he moved crab-like from the pew, intent on making the fastest possible exit. On turning he became aware of the cast of this perversely engineered gathering. He saw what Eleanor, in collusion with Charles, had done. Escape was imperative but there was no possibility of escape. Because they had been the first in, they must of necessity be the last out. Once out, they must confront everyone. His arm went round his weeping daughter and he held her tightly against him. She did not resist, but pressed her face into his jacket. She could hear his heart beating hard. Yet he continued to look straight in front of them, cold and frowning. As they approached the light from the chapel door, he gripped Clover harder. They would all be out there in the bright March daylight, waiting. He knew what they wanted – to speak to her, to look her all over, to assess and appraise her, then to pass comment on her to themselves and each other.

He could not escape them. He must stand and bear their jaded scrutiny. Perhaps she would continue to hold him and hide in him. God, if only she would. But she had this way about her, of recovering through curiosity and simple love of attention. She was bound to look up. She would see them all and wonder about them all. And they would see her. They would look and look.

There were more of them than he would have imagined. Eleanor *did* have friends. Or they had come out of guilt or morbid interest. Charles must have told everyone. Charles, Charles, Charles. He was responsible for this. Like Eleanor, more than Eleanor, he knew things Jason did not know. Determined to remain unapproachable, he hesitated on the step, restraining Clover. When she walked through that door, she walked into the world.

Clover looked up. The bright light hurt her eyes and she pressed her face against Jason once more. Little groups stood on the grass, shaking off their brief sobriety. Everyone seemed slightly unnerved. No one said very much. And yet they stood there. For what, thought Jason. What are they waiting for? Why don't they go home? God knows they should want to go home. This place is insane, grotesque.

Jason and Clover descended the steps. People in the little groups began to talk. One of the three women, Caroline, was already hazarding a smile. She and Deirdre Mallard discussed their children. Dillon Butterworth was describing an exhibition at the Tate, puffing on his hastily-lit cigarette. George Facer listened politely while Felix Koning turned away to avoid the smoke. Jeremy Black was being civil to Charles Bevan who did not take offence at his civility but attempted to address Monica in a kindly way. She clung to her husband's flaccid arm, barely responding. The diamonds on her tiny fingers glistened in the sunlight.

Dillon called to Jason and motioned to him to join him, George and Felix. Reluctantly, Jason walked towards them, holding Clover by the hand and pressing it harder than he realized.

'Ouch, Jason!' She was recovering. She was looking around, suddenly curious about them all but still shy in her sorrow.

Dillon put an arm on Jason's shoulder and shook it gently. Jason allowed the familiarity. Dillon was the only one he might call a friend.

'Awful,' Dillon said, making no effort to lower his voice. 'Awful for you. Awful for you, Babyface.' He bent and kissed Jason's daughter who shrank from him although she knew he meant well.

'Why did she want this, do you think? Unlike her, unlike her. And she was a Catholic. Well, God knows what she thought in the end.'

'God knows,' Jason mumbled. (God and Charles.)

Dillon shook his head gravely. 'But I miss her, miss her. Most alive damned woman I ever knew. Barking mad sometimes. But so funny. Could make a knock-knock joke seem like Voltaire. We used to lie in bed together – strictly platonic, Jay, as you know – and read Maldoror out loud. Never laughed so hard. Never.' His voice broke and he shook his head again. Jason grew impatient, sensing that the artist was about to wax sentimental. 'The way she used to sing when she got – '

'Pissed. Quite. Could we not talk about it, please?'

'Sorry, old man. Must be hard on you.'

Jason shrugged. Dillon was genuinely sad. But he had not rung for weeks. Parties, no doubt. Trips to Basle.

George held out his hand. 'Jason,' he said, 'you're well,' as though precluding any information to the contrary. Jason took the hand. God, this was unpleasant.

'And you, my dear. Clover, isn't it?' He stood looking down at her like a vicar on a Sunday morning.

'We're well, George. Good of you to come.' How could he possibly have said that? Was hypocrisy so contagious? Did he really long for George to readopt him?

'You know Felix, I take it? Felix Koning – '

'We've met,' said Jason and briefly touched the slender hand with fair hair on the fingers. All of a sudden he was aware that George and Felix knew each other very well.

Felix smiled. Jason averted his eyes. Clover felt Felix look straight at her. Her courageous but impermanent hair-do was collapsing rapidly in the wind. Little strands blew in all directions. She did not smile at Felix because she was shy and because she had seen Charles. The only friendly face.

She waved, and he held out his arms in an avuncular way. Before Jason could stop her, she escaped, ran to the lawyer, threw her arms around him and kissed him quickly. She was nearly as tall as he was. Over her shoulder Charles saw George bend towards Felix and speak to him. (How familiar the two of them seemed. Felix and George? *Felix and George?*)

'Hel-lo,' she said, pleased to see him, yet pulling back from his obvious need to hold her longer. She sensed Jason's nervousness from across the grass.

He was nervous, and angry. How could she leave him? Yet to retrieve her would be undignified. So he remained with Dillon, George and Felix, not listening to what they were saying and catching snatches of Clover and Charles's conversation.

' – do so like what you've done with your hair.'

'What I tried to do, you mean. I suppose it's not much like the way it started out. Do you like my dress, Charles?'

He screwed up his eyes as though subjecting her to rigorous inspection. She was all wrong. But somewhere there slumbered a great natural, if eccentric, style. In his old-fashioned way, he determined that, poor sweet darling, she was only in need of a mother to wake it and bring it out.

'Something with a bit more line, perhaps . . . '

'The shops in Eastbourne are completely boring.'

'Then you must come to London.'

'I'd love to come to London. I'd love to go shopping in Harrods and Harvey Nichols, and Joseph and Charles Jourdan.'

'Then you *will* come. We'll have an extensive tour (on what, he wondered). Nothing will be missed. Tea at the Ritz, the Crown Jewels, the Post Office Tower, the Savoy Grill. And I shall beat you at backgammon.'

'No one can beat me at backgammon.' She hesitated. 'It's because you taught me.'

'I'm flattered.'

'But I can't leave Jason just now. Oh Charles, I'm very sad.' Her face clouded as suddenly as it had brightened.

'Darling, of course you are. I'm sad as well.' He wanted to embrace her but he too felt Jason's nervousness.

Standing between Charles and Monica Black, who was visibly distressed, Clover stared at the bows on her shoes. She could sense them all looking at her. Two pairs of light-blue eyes were looking especially hard and she wished they would stop. Charles glanced between her and Monica. He could not conceal it and was aware that Jeremy noticed it. Clearly, Jeremy wanted to get Monica away from that probing gaze, away from that brain that put pieces together, away from Snake Felix and surly Jason and this unkempt girl.

Jason also wished for escape. He must get Clover out of here, get her back to Sussex and Dolly Five's treacle tart as quickly as possible. How could she laugh and smile and flirt with Charles, then stand there staring at her shoes like Miss Muffet, letting them all take her in? Dillon said something to which he did not respond. He was thinking of some lines in Eleanor's hand, a poem she'd thought was about Clover:

> . . . *now your voices mingle from afar*
> *with the voices he would fain forget*
> *and his tender memories with regret*
> *that so many see you where you are.*

Clover turned to the woman in the fur coat who was smaller than she was and whose lower lip was trembling.

'Are you my mother?' she asked the woman.

'Mother? No, whatever gave you that idea?'

'Your mouth.'

Jeremy tried to draw Monica away from the dreadful daughter Jason Englefield could not control, obviously aware that Charles had heard yet hoping that he hadn't.

'You're mistaken,' Monica spoke automatically. 'Your mother is dead.'

'Eleanor wasn't my mother. And I didn't mean to embarrass you. But you are Monica, aren't you?'

'It is not uncommon. Time will cure you. You will get over your grief. I am so very, very sorry for you.'

'Thank you. I've been sorry for you all my life.'

Monica leaned forward. Charles feared a convulsion on the spot. Jeremy steered her away from Clover and Charles, bent on initiating some conventional exchange with George.

The three women had approached Jason and were taking their leave. Over their heads Jason could see Charles and Clover standing together, alone on the green expanse. Behind them a row of poplars was mauled by the wind. Clover's dress blew up over her knees. She wiped her eyes with the back of her hand. Charles touched her lightly on the head as though blessing her. They did not speak. He sighed. Now he knew.

Jason stepped back as Jeremy greeted George and nodded to Felix, at whom Monica stared as at a fetish. Jason thrust his hands in his pockets. How he despised them all.

'Monica, you're looking well. Lovely to see you.' Felix's eyes were kind and bright.

'Felix – ' she began.

He turned away to the Tate conversation. Jeremy gripped Monica's arm. The three women strolled towards the iron gates, talking and laughing.

'Clover!' Jason called. 'Clover, please come here.' He raised his voice above the wind. There was a surprised silence. Every head, every pair of eyes turned to Clover as she ran across the grass, her coat flying open, her hair now fallen down completely. She stood beside him, her cheeks flushed, her eyes still moist, her mascara smeared. Jason took her hand. He felt stronger.

Charles watched the group from a distance, an audience of one witnessing the emotional climax of some queer opera. End of Act Two.

Jason noticed George preparing to back off, no doubt anxious to avoid a private confrontation with the artist whose phone calls he persistently failed to return. From where he stood, Charles observed the commencement of George's ritual leave-taking. He and the dealer had not spoken but would probably nod and smile. Meanwhile, George was appeasing the Blacks who probably had bought nothing from him lately. They were not as social as they used to be and were seldom seen at galleries. Voices were carried to him on the wind.

'You must – '

'Come and see us.'

' – not so long this time.'

' – call you.'

' – Cologne.'

'Pity.'

'Rothko – '

' – so grown up.'

' – unfortunate circumstances.'

' – always remember.'

'Babyface – '

'Jay, old man – '

'George – '

'Georgia O'Keefe.'

'Dinner – '

' – never forget.'

'Lunch.'

' – New York.'

'Eleanor – hair – '

'Bye-bye – '

'Flame – '

'Jay – '

'Felix!'

Monica called to him as Jeremy pulled her towards the walk. Charles watched them coming to offer him a lift back to London, hoping to cover some tracks, hoping he'd refuse the offer.

Dillon and George preceded the Blacks on their way to the iron gates. Felix turned at the sound of his own name. He waved.

'Soon, very soon . . . Monica . . . Jeremy. And love to – ' Clearly, he had forgotten the names of their children. Without finishing his sentence, he veered round and confronted Jason.

'Look,' he said, switching from social to serious. 'I won't mince words. I know you are having – um – difficulties. I think I might be able

124

to help you. I have established a few excellent contacts in America – New York, Houston, Kansas City. In recent months I have been dealing successfully on behalf of several artists. England is a futile struggle and a failing economy. No one has an eye. You are aware of this. I understand your wish for obscurity, but obscurity can be made more, well, comfortable.'

Jason was stunned. He even laughed. 'I feel like Faust meeting Mephistopheles at the May Fair.'

'You would do, yes.' Felix smiled. He focused on Jason, not looking at Clover who was taking him in detail by detail. A confused memory, something out of the distant past, a room full of people, Jason's paintings, Eleanor laughing, so many grown-ups, a man – this one?

'But you haven't seen my new work.'

'Then I must come and see it. It's time I came. And it's time for you to open new horizons. London is a backwater for art. The effects of the recession have been devastating, you're not needing me to tell you. No more big important collectors. America is still good.'

'I don't like America particularly. Or Americans.'

'What does that matter? Surely you're not *fond* of the English.'

'I'm not fond of them. But I like the countryside.'

'As a piece of real estate it is not too bad. But there is countryside everywhere. England does not own the copyright.'

Jason shuffled, his hands in his pockets. 'Why back me? Don't you know painting is dead?'

'Corpses are saleable.'

'What's wrong with you?' He met Felix's eyes. 'Aren't you interested in Fun Art? Why don't you go and subsidize an earthworks?'

Felix smiled.

'You won't like what I do,' Jason mumbled.

'Perhaps not. My liking it is not what's at stake.'

'Oh. What is at stake?'

'Money.'

'Huh! At least you don't pretend.'

'I'm full of pretence. But not about money. I shall be brutally honest with you. I understand you have a taste for brutal honesty.'

'My reputation precedes me.'

'I would sooner say it follows you. But I can perhaps help it to precede a little. When can I come to your studio?'

'Next week. Thursday.'

'Here is my card. Call and leave travel instructions with my secretary.' Felix glanced at the gates where a car had just pulled up. Jason let go of

Clover's hand to take the card. As he read it, Felix turned to Clover and met her eyes.

'We haven't been introduced.' His smile revealed the spaces between his slightly yellow front teeth.

'Should I know you?' Clover asked, puzzled, pleased, uneasy.

'Yes, beauty, you should.' He brushed her fingers with his. 'And then you should know me better.' His attention reverted to Jason.

'I must go,' he said. 'Someone is waiting for me. But I look forward to our meeting. Goodbye.'

'Goodbye.' They shook hands.

Clover, her dazzling moment past, dropped again into depression.

'Oh let's go, Jason. Let's go.'

'Yes. Let's.'

When they reached the gates Clover turned and waved to Charles. He watched them walk slowly, hand in hand, to their car. He watched Felix get into a Mercedes. The woman at the wheel drove as though they could not get away fast enough. Felix had nodded as he passed.

'No thanks very much,' Charles said to Jeremy. 'I still do have transport. Anyway, I must stay behind to collect the ashes. I was her lawyer, as you know.'

The Blacks too passed through the iron gates. No one was left. No one was about. Somewhere a dog was barking. The wind tore at the trees. Charles pulled his overcoat closer and walked back to the chapel.

III

....

CHARLES

fifteen

Charles had promised to do the shopping on the way home. But by the time he had finished his sad business at the chapel it was late in the afternoon and the M4 traffic was inching back into London. Fortunately, the Europa on Fulham Road was open until nine. He filled his Big Snob Bag with slices of lamb's liver wrapped in cling-film, half a pound of mushrooms, endives browning at the edges, a bag of red kidney potatoes, a carton of long-life milk and half a bottle of Scotch and deposited it on the back seat of the Mini next to the ashes of Eleanor Linnane.

He smuggled his treasure into the basement flat on Halford Road, making two trips up and down the concrete steps with their sharp twist at the bottom and their unadorned iron rail. The food he brought first to lure Anthea into the kitchen and distract her from the ashes, to the presence of which she would be certain to object. Not only was she idle and morose, she had become superstitious as well.

Anthea tore herself from the television she had been watching and the gin she had been consuming since two o'clock and padded into the kitchen, dragging the heels of her furry slippers. She wore an old, green, silk dress, with matching scarf attached at the nape of the neck, and what remained of her jewellery. She peered into the bag and began to interrogate Charles. Who had been at the funeral, what did they wear, what did they say? Leaving her to inspect his purchases, Charles spirited the urn into the bedroom and hid it in his clothes cupboard among the shoes.

He returned to the kitchen via the long corridor, shabby despite the paintings which hung, cobweb-cornered, in the dingy light. Poor things, not much chance of making an impression here. One day, he thought, if matters went on as they were, this hallway, like others in his recent past, would also be bare of decor. Well. The odour of damp was worse than usual because the weather had turned wet and chilly that afternoon. Water dripped from a pipe on to a permanently sodden patch of carpet, but Charles didn't care. It was a dismal evening full of dismal prospects. Eliot had already described such evenings too succinctly and Dickens too lengthily for Charles to meditate further on their drab poignancy. He was simply grateful to the central heating which by some miracle continued to function.

'You didn't answer my question,' said Anthea, lighting a cigarette from the gas burner and leaning against the scarred formica worktop. She had not unpacked the groceries.

'Sorry, my love.' He removed the meat and vegetables from their plastic containers while feeding her news of the morning's encounters. Gossip starved and sustained her. He gleaned what he could and when he could to appease his wife's appetite – an appetite which seemed to grow more insatiable in proportion to her dwindling contact with the society she craved.

'Monica Black? But why should she go to Eleanor's cremation? Now that *is* interesting. What was she wearing?'

'The usual. Diamonds. Dark suit, splendidly cut.'

'Was she tanned? Had they been abroad?'

'Pale as ghosts. They didn't inform me of any recent travels.'

'But they did speak to you.'

'Yes, yes.'

'They were civil.'

'Apparently.'

'Apparently, what do you mean apparently? Oh Jeremy is foul, you know.' She puffed ferociously. 'I've always sensed that. Secretly, deeply foul.'

'Jeremy is – careful.'

'Which is why *he* is still rich.' She poured herself another gin. 'But explain what you mean by "apparently". You put things so queerly sometimes, Charles. You've stopped being direct with me.'

'On the contrary, my love, I'm relating circumstances to the best of my ability. I'm including all nuances of word and gesture. To generalize would be to distort the truth.'

'Always the lawyer – I mean the *ex*-lawyer. Now explain to me "apparently". I don't understand you lately. You're not yourself, do you know that? You talk about nuances – well I am still capable of grasping a few. No doubt you think I've lost the ability because I sit at home growing duller by the day. Well, I sit at home because I'll have no dealings with fair-weather friends. They may ring up as much as they please. Their efforts will go unrewarded. I shan't answer the phone.'

'That is your prerogative, darling.'

Of course the phone almost never rang. When the Bevans did receive one of their rare invitations Anthea was always too tired or too depressed or she had not been to the hairdresser's. She was still 'recovering'. She had been recovering for three years. She read newspapers and journals, watched television, chain-smoked, drank, picked at the food her husband cooked for her every evening, went to bed, could not sleep, did the crosswords, complained, cried, and asked Charles repeatedly how he thought such dreadful things could have happened to them.

'I suppose Jason Englefield was his usual surly self. Don't cook much for me, Charles. The stomach has been queasy all day. I hope to God it's not gastric enteritis again.'

'Darling, I am cooking nothing at the moment. I want a bath and a whisky, not in that order.'

'You drink too much, Charles. It's an expensive habit and you're reaching the critical age for heart conditions. You're forty-four, you know.'

'Forty-three.'

'Well, whatever you are, have a little consideration and for God's sake think of me!'

Think of her! He could not think of her as he could not think of a toothache, terminal cancer, a red telephone bill, the folly and mortality of the human race.

Charles sat on the unmade bed (she might at least see to the linen) and poured himself a large whisky. It was not her fault. She had been initiated early into the higher octaves of play, brought up to regard constant distraction as a right; she was by nature suited to it, she had had an abundance of it, she was addicted. Like any deprived *habitué* she was suffering withdrawal symptoms. He could no longer provide the string of dinner parties, ballet tickets, sojourns abroad at the villas of rich and grateful clients. Her distraction input had been so drastically reduced as to prove traumatic. It was not her fault.

Still, she might have made the bed or washed the dishes. Bad enough to live in a hovel, but a rotting hovel! Charles kicked off his shoes and leaned back on the pillows, sipping the whisky. The linen had gone unchanged for two weeks. Oh, he supposed he'd have to change it himself. He groaned at the prospect of a trip to the launderette.

Charles watched the movements of his toes, one of which protruded through an aperture in his sock. He sighed and thought how soothing it would be to listen to some Russian songs – a little Tchaikovsky ('At The Ball', 'None But the Lonely Heart', especially 'None But the Lonely Heart'), a little Rachmaninov, a little Mussorgsky. But the record player was broken. Too bad. That warm, sad language would have eased the effects of his surroundings and made food for his tired imagination. He was reduced to staring at the objects in the room: the lamp, non-functioning, with Chinese vase base; the bed they had bought second-hand from Anthea's sister; the mouldering Sehna kilim hung, as though crucified, on ghastly nails which were tearing its beautiful tendons and sinews slowly to pieces; the scratched and dusty chest of drawers; the books stacked and leaning dangerously in the corner – there must have been two hundred of them, all that remained of his estimable, his enviable, his beloved library. He held back the books as Anthea held back the jewellery. He couldn't blame her.

The furniture had been sold first, its departure signalling the beginning of their end. How he missed the 1810 table with its set of twelve chairs, missed the ormolu clock, the Mackmurdo screen, oh the accumulation was endless – endless and gone except for the few crippled survivors in the Halford Road flat. The paintings they were keeping. He told himself and Anthea they must be held in reserve, a hedge against the abject poverty which loomed large on the Bevan horizon. That poverty he imagined as an island where one day they would be forced to disembark and to remain for the rest of their lives in social, cultural and physical deprivation. The ship on which they had arrived would sail away. They would watch until it disappeared from sight. When it was no longer even a speck, they would turn and face each other and their eyes would meet. There would be nothing but a strange and desolate landscape and no eyes but each other's. Charles shuddered. Anything but that. Even if it meant the ultimate sacrifice, the Braque. But not yet, thank God, not yet. He poured another whisky.

The house on Chester Street had been the next to go. Because of its short lease, it had retrieved only half of what he had originally paid for it. With the proceeds they had escaped bankruptcy, just, and scuttled off to the borders of Fulham and the dismal flat with its tiny, redeeming garden. At first the Bevans pretended the place was a temporary temenos that would shelter them until finances improved, Anthea recovered her health, and they were invited, for an indefinite period, to house-sit a fifteenth-century Tuscan farm, refurbished with gardens and pool, close to the restaurants and paintings of Siena; or a flat overlooking the Bosporus or Lake Como. Three years later they conceded that the two-room basement with its minute kitchen and unsalubrious bath was likely to be their permanent abode. They even thanked the gods for it and hoped they could keep up the mortgage payments.

Charles had loved the house. Above all, he had loved his room on the top floor, his nest, where he might go on Sundays, or on those evenings when his presence was not required at dinners, drinks parties, embassy gatherings, gallery openings, new productions at Covent Garden, or by Anthea's lust for the latest foreign film, and shut himself away from the world which, at that time, he did not actively dislike, and from his wife for whom there was still some love left. There he might listen to Haydn quartets and Mozart operas and his 1938 Schnabel recordings. There he might collect his thoughts and sometimes put them down on paper. Oh he had loved his nest. He ached for his nest. In it he had possessed himself.

Now he must share not only his bed with Anthea, but his thoughts as well; thoughts not openly expressed but no less potently present. Small wonder his wife was an insomniac. Poor love. Nothing in her little life could have prepared her for this.

He had had glimmers, through his work, of what disaster might be like. And he had empathy and imagination which allowed him to put himself in the afflicted's place. Negative· capability he possessed in abundance. He had borne up better than Anthea, but he was not himself. He was not what he had been. Still, he could work his way through social and emotional mazes if need be or when inspired to do so. The bailiffs could not carry away his intellect in a van. With that intellect he reviewed the day. Now *there* was stimulation for his brain and a vehicle for his imagination. His nest need not necessarily be a requirement for setting all that in order. Could he not think as well in squalor as in consoling comfort? He looked at the wardrobe which was now the secret repository of Eleanor's ashes. He wanted to chuckle and cry simultaneously. He wanted to do something he had not done in a long time: he wanted to write, to give his thoughts a form and by so doing to put pieces together. It was, after all, his forte. He was meant to be a master of the summing-up.

Was there any paper? If he went into the sitting-room he would encounter Anthea and that would extinguish his sudden flare of enthusiasm. Where could it be, then? Why under the bed, of course. Wasn't everything except the Braque kicked eventually under the bed? Sure enough, he found an old Rymans memobook, part of which had been given over to his miserable accounts of their dwindling finances. The figures broke off abruptly. He had given up, despaired, could raise as little interest as his capital, raised a glass instead, ceased to give a damn.

He took his dear old Mont Blanc from his discarded jacket, hesitated, then hung the jacket in the wardrobe. One must make an effort, a human effort.

'This', he wrote, 'is a human effort.'

He settled himself on the bed, replenished his drink and studied the page. He turned the page and began a new one.

TRUST

My Thoughts This Day.

Everyone since the beginning of time and awareness has gone to fabulous lengths to rationalize misfortune. Religion, philosophy, politics and elaborate self-deception have been made to yield solutions to the overwhelming question: is it the gods or is it we who are responsible? The Law, on the other hand, assumes that it is always we who are responsible. That is what attracted me to the Law: we responsible and we correcting, we looking after ourselves without recourse to transcendental advisory bureaux. As a classicist I espoused moderation, tolerance, harmony, order, fidelity, honour. The Victorian view of classicism, I now realize. Classicism must include the pagan.

The problematical pagan, the primal, the unconscious, whatever it is, prevents me and everyone else from really knowing ourselves and each other in a rational, objective way. Only God or the gods could predict what any of us are capable of or what we may do next, given our arbitrary-fated set of circumstances. Still, we must behave – correction – *I* must behave as if I were responsible and as if I had only one chance to get the thing right and if I muff it I muff it and have no one to blame but myself; as if I have only one life and there is no such thing as reincarnation, although there might be.

Freud said that there is love and work. I maintain that there is, in addition, the way we treat each other. I believed in the Law because I believed it helps us to manage the ways we treat each other. True in theory, questionable in practice. The way we treat each other – yes, it is one of the three important things. What else have we? Science, religion, philosophy and politics are only fashion and are diverting, annoying, tiresome and compulsive like fashion. They are interesting games, but only games. It is we who count and we who must take responsibility. By taking responsibility we make ourselves count. (Perhaps this could be defined as negative culpability, i.e. the ability to assume many guilts without oneself being guilty.) We have recourse only to ourselves and each other, neither of which we can be sure of knowing.

All we have are our reactions as we encounter each other (I am thinking particularly of the social ballet I witnessed this morning); the holding over of these reactions, the keeping account of them and the reapplying of them to the next encounter; being forced to modify, adjust, correct them in the light of ever-changing and ever-predictable experience; incorporating the modifications on and on, over and over, ever and ever with each new encounter with every new and familiar person, our reality always in question, our identities always at stake. What can we know beyond these reactions? With everything and everyone so slippery what can we be sure of? We can only trust. Ideas are no help. They are fashion too. Like therapies. Conceptions and preconceptions are no use. We must take it all pretty much on faith or get out entirely.

The SOE defines trust as 'the expectation of safety without fear of consequences'. But how can we trust when there exists in the blood and bone and brain of all of us a treacherous and brutal animal who may at any moment escape and demolish our constructions for safety? How can we trust when none

134

of us can predict what we'll do? Well, we simply *have* to trust. Moreover we cannot hold on to our happiness if we are so fortunate as to find any. Trust is all that is left us. We can *only* trust, in spite of experienced betrayal and the obvious dangers of life. Trust or get out entirely.

Of all this I feel certain, and yet I am perplexed. I am the sanest person I know. When I am not a victim of my emotions I can see things very nearly the way they are. What good does this do me? I am a learned man. (Perhaps I'm not primal enough.) I love my learning and I treasure the treasures of this civilization. They are beautiful toys. They are fashions. They bolster my trust, console me in my self-doubt. I have been part of the process by which this civilization I love is maintained. What good does it do me or anyone? Love is betrayed, art is betrayed – and for much higher profits. I am perplexed.

All my life I have been interested in the way we treat each other. Contacts, relationships – they have been everything to me. But because of my recent calamities I am discouraged. And I wonder whether Proust wasn't right when he suggested that we must turn our backs on society where everything is so slippery and grow down into ourselves like the roots of a tree. I have decided (because I am perplexed and find it hard to trust as I know I ought to and must do) that I will try being the tree, at least for a while. I will write. I will draw. I will ignore the world's contumely. Meanwhile, Anthea must do the best she can with me. She will be acutely disappointed at my not hastening to re-establish our irredeemable prestige. She must learn to enjoy shabby gentility. It still has its charm. I shall not desert her.

Charles put down the pen and reread the words 'not desert her'. Anthea was forty-three and decaying rapidly. She was anxious, clinging, vain, nagging, bitter. She was well on her way to becoming a bona fide shrew unless he persisted in bolstering what was left of her belief in herself. He was her man and it seemed his function to provide her with an identity and protect her from the world. He was duty-bound to stick to her and not bolt. Yet every day he was tempted to bolt. In addition to the list of worries that plagued him – the money, the disgrace, the menacing inertia, the stack of unopened envelopes from the Inland Revenue accumulating steadily on the hall table – he must struggle against the daemon urge to bolt. It was an urge that daily increased in strength and demanded more and more of his energy to suppress and control.

Lord, what *had* happened? Wait, that was wrong, made it sound as if the gods were meddling again. Hadn't Homer made us see that divine intervention couldn't always be the case? Kindly rephrase the question. What had *he* done? He (plus the gods, maybe) had perpetrated his own ruin. What a shock it had been to find that what was supporting him was so flimsy. The edifice of his life had needed only the slightest nudge to topple it completely. It lay at his feet, a mass of plaster and papier mâché, a matchstick castle, a house of cards, a chain of diabolical dominoes. Mentally, he ticked off the list of catastrophes that, like metropolitan furies, had driven him to the borders of Fulham: the migration first of the Blacks then of George Facer's artists to Grievson, Gruber and Gruber, the decline of the dinner party circuit, the fuss over the Enderby estate (his fault entirely, a small error, he was unnerved), the disastrous investment. Again, not his fault – or was it? Then began the sale of the furniture, the arrival of removal vans, Anthea weeping openly on the front steps. Loss of money equals loss of friends and acquaintances equals loss of clients equals loss of trust equals loss of money. Of course, there was also loss of interest accompanied by too much drink and reading. Evenings at home then days at home in a house whose fixtures and fittings were being siphoned off at an alarming rate. It echoed. He spent more and more time in the nest.

His profession bored him. Although he went occasionally to the office, the compassionate looks from Mrs Plumber and the others only made matters worse. A few Cambridge friends stood by him but even their intermittent invitations dwindled. What omnipresent malicious whisper, audible to everyone but Anthea and himself, circulated in the London air, informing, insinuating, suggesting that Charles Bevan was no longer a worthy man? Crouch and Fielding still kept him on, tolerating him because of his one indispensable province: trusts and estates so complex and cunning that only he could have devised them and only he could unravel them. He now visited the office two or three times a month, did some unravelling, received a pittance for his trouble.

Part of the proceeds from the house sale had been put into an investment from which it seemed unlikely he would ever reap any of the promised dividends. Then came Eleanor's illness, his constant anxiety for her, the pulling up of stakes by his last important client. On the day of the withdrawal of the van Zuptens' account, Anthea announced that she was pregnant. For a while all else was dust and air. In spite of the sale of Chester Street, Charles was happy. He fantasized about moving to Norfolk, the love of the child, the life of the mind. But instead it had been Fulham and, in the eighth month, it had gone horribly wrong. To his list of woes was appended an inconsolable and utterly dependent wife.

It was eight o'clock and time to cook dinner. *The Paul Daniels' Magic Show* would be over. He had forgotten his bath but had hopes of an evening with Tacitus. He quickly read over what he had written. There seemed little sense in it. The crematorium had addled his brain. Better cook. Charles proceeded to the narrow, cluttered kitchen, and switched on the overhead fluorescent light that made him feel like an animal in a vivisection laboratory. Still, he enjoyed his culinary rites. Nothing could quite bury his natural invention or his capacity to take an interest in the ephemeral. He experimented with the mushrooms, adding soy to the stir-fried base of shallots and rosemary. Delicious. But his innovations went unapplauded by Anthea who only played with her food while remorselessly describing Monday's episode of *Coronation Street*.

'I do wish you'd watch with me, Charles. It's lonely in there with you in the bedroom scribbling and reading.'

'We did agree, my sweet, that post-prandial privacy was to be my compensation for doing the cooking and the washing-up.'

'You're a snob, Charles. You're probably not aware of this but there are many cultured and intelligent people who are devotees of not only *Coronation Street* but *Dallas*, *Minder* and *George and Mildred*. Wouldn't miss 'em.'

'I don't doubt it.'

'I know what your exalted brain is thinking. It's thinking let her just name one of these prominent personages. My erstwhile Cambridge friends would not be among them.'

'Nothing could be further from my exalted brain.' Charles pushed a puddle of wine around on the table which was covered with a white oilcloth splashed with big, red roses. Charles was especially depressed by the roses.

'Is the liver all right?' he asked.

'I suppose so. Nothing tastes the way it used to. Additives in the food. A person in Great Britain can consume ten to fifteen kilograms a year. Did I tell you about that terrifying article in the *Guardian*?'

'You told me.'

'Well, you must agree that the taste has simply gone right out of everything. *Right out*. Like life itself. Simultaneously bland and poisonous.'

'Well put, darling.'

'Do not patronize me, Charles. I may not be one of your lofty Cambridge friends, but I'm a well-informed woman. That you must concede.'

'I do. I do concede.' Charles put on a striped apron and began to do the washing-up. Anthea sat at the table drinking and talking. Whenever Charles looked at her it seemed that her chin had doubled then trebled and was at last merging with her neck, shoulders and back.

'Moreover, I am *here*. That is where I am. That is all I am. Where, I ask, are your lofty Cambridge friends? All swanning around imagining they're characters in an Anthony Powell novel. Where are they now the money's gone? What does your wit and your erudition and your generosity matter to them now? How much did they value them in the first place? I don't see a flood of invitations pouring through the letter-box, do you? We're not forced to take the receiver off the hook because of being driven mad by constant importunities for weekend visits and lavish lunches. They've abandoned you, Charles, that's what. But I have not abandoned you. I am a good wife and a good friend. Only I, and in weakened health, have stood by you through this terrible, this, this . . . '

Her voice broke. Charles kissed her on the forehead and patted the green silk shoulder.

'You have, my dear, you have. You've never given me any cause to doubt your presence.'

'Thank you, Charles,' she sniffed. 'A little appreciation is all one really wants. You see nice people *do* watch *Dallas*.' She banged the table. 'Nice, well-informed people.'

'Yes, yes. All right, all right.'

'Even though they may have their faults – too sensitive, a weeny-bit highly strung. But true bloody blue. Not like flitting fair-weather poofta Cambridge friends – '

'Anthea!'

'Faggot conspiracy. Misogynists. Control everything. Have since ancient Greece.'

'Enough!' It was over a week since he had used his courtroom voice with her. Immediately he was sorry. After all, she was very drunk.

'Isn't it nearly time for that film you wanted to watch, darling?'

'Film? Oh I've seen it three times. Some Trintignant thing. But – ' she suddenly sat bolt upright, 'what else is there to do? I've read all the newspapers and you forgot to bring the *Tatler*.'

'I'm sorry.'

'No matter. One gets used to going without and making do. Oh watch the film with me, Charles. Please watch with me.'

'When I've had a bath, darling.'

She stood, swaying slightly. 'How can you bear this?'

'Only with difficulty.'

'What happened, Charles? Where has everyone gone? And why have they gone? Something has been done to us, Charles, but what, what?'

'We're out of season, precious, like the oyster.'

'I refuse to be a mollusc.'

'But like the oyster *nous reviendrons* – as sure as death and September.'

'Charles, you've acquired a morbid turn of mind. Perhaps it's not your fault. You used to be nice too,' he heard her mutter as she staggered down the hall, 'before they started putting additives in the food.'

sixteen

The past infringed upon the present. The past would have its way and scored an easy victory over Charles as he lay holding Tacitus safely aloft, his head resting on the curved edge of the grimy tub, his eyes raised, reading from beneath. The telephone rang and a moment later he heard Anthea slam down the receiver. Another wrong number, poor love.

He read a paragraph, sipped his whisky, read the same paragraph again. Useless. He placed the book on the floor and sank back in the bath, conceding defeat to the past, soaking, drinking and remembering Eleanor Linnane as she had looked and behaved in his office on an afternoon that seemed like yesterday and fifty years ago. He had cursed himself for his congenital restraint, for his inability to grasp that queen of salamanders and make her, however briefly, his. He had asked himself over and over why he, unlike another, could not make love to her until she declared herself a beautiful rag.

After she left London, his lust had given way to depression which had given way to longing which had given way to tenderness, to concern and finally to respect underpinned by affection. He had come to know her. She had shown herself to him bit by bit over the years through quick meetings and long correspondence and finally given him just about the whole thing in that last Paris encounter. He liked her. She liked him. They were friends for ever.

Charles winked back his tears, but one escaped and spilled into the bath. He smiled. He blubbered. He was the mock turtle in a tub of tears.

He had been so touched by her room with its round windows opening on to light and sky. He had wanted never to leave. He examined the charming pictures, approved the canny, unobtrusive arrangement of the furniture, the treasures with which she surrounded herself and held herself up. So often the houses and flats of women who lived alone had engulfed him with the personality of the woman. It was like being trapped in her womb or, worse still, her brain. But Eleanor's place enclosed without encroaching, holding one with its warmth and interest, yet leaving the door quite open, anticipating without resentment any sudden urge for freedom. Only she was not free to go. And he was obliged to go.

Despite her altered appearance – a devastating blow for someone willing and able to trade on her looks – she had bouts of high spirits not unlike her old, flaming days. The difference was that she had steadied herself. She had resolved to live, he was certain. He had come away without the least anxiety that he would not see her again – and more than again. She had tricked him as he supposed he had tricked her, into believing that all was not as bad as it might be, that the future, in a way, still beckoned and was something to which one might occasionally look forward with childish enthusiasm. Oh they agreed – laughed and agreed. Most certainly they had tricked each other. She with Haydn quartets and with showing off to him the exemplary order of her life-style; he with his unremitting good humour and his stories that had never failed him or his audience.

They got through the will in the first half-hour. She knew exactly what she wanted and even supplied him with a detailed list of instructions.

'Now, Charlie,' she said, lowering her thick spectacles to the tip of her still adorable nose, and looking straight at him, 'we needn't ever bother with that again. How about some Haydn?'

She would not allow him to help her, but shuffled unassisted to the record player, leaning heavily on the cane she now required. Charles could not help staring at her swollen ankles and calves, so maddening in what had been their beautiful heyday.

'Disgusting aren't they?' she said, although her back was to him. 'Dragging my foot like Edie Puss. Who'd a thunk it? Know what they remind me of? Inflated prophylactics. The boys used to do that when I was in High School – blow up rubbers like balloons. We thought it was awfully wicked and funny. A hit at every party. Wouldn't be young again for anything, would you?'

He hesitated, deciding not to pay her what would have been the misplaced compliments about eternal youth which leapt instinctively to his practised tongue.

'I blush to confess that, unlike everyone else, I enjoyed my youth. I grew up surrounded by the most lovely women – my mother, grandmother, sister and, of course, Auntie Di. And school was very jolly. I loved the games, the reading, the companionship . . . '

'I forgot, Charles,' she laughed. 'You're a well-adjusted human being. The archetypal social animal.'

'Well . . . '

'How about *Tristan* instead, the Böhm recording with old Birgit. Let's blast off, Charles. True love is not of this earth.'

Slowly, Eleanor stretched herself on the chaise-longue. It hurt Charles to watch.

'Darling girl.' He leaned towards her, trying not to appear too serious.

'You're about to enquire after my health, Charles. Well, my body is still pumping around three grams of sugar to your zero point eight. But my body doesn't plague me too much provided I give it everything it wants and at the appointed hour. It's like feeding time at the zoo. Nothing roars or growls or gets dangerous unless I forget or fall a little behind – unless the keeper neglects her duties. That's the truth. Three bloody grams. Can we not talk about it anymore?'

'Of course.' He waited for her.

'My *puella eterna* is due here in a couple of hours.'

'Really? How marvellous!' So Jason had relented. He hadn't known. So he was to be treated to a glimpse of her after all. 'It's been nearly five years, although I spoke to her on the phone.'

'I know.' Eleanor smiled the smile that used to rend his heart. It was as though a veil were suddenly lifted, showing him the radiance that still throbbed and breathed behind her tired, bloated exterior. How sweet she was, gazing at him with so much confidence, her presence at last without thorns.

'Dear Eleanor.' He was afraid of crying. 'I'm so happy to be here. I'm so – ' he waved his hands about searching for something better then yielded to the simple, stupid word, '*happy*.'

'Charles,' she said after a pause, 'you're just the nicest, smartest person.' They listened in silence to the end of Act One.

Charles ran more hot water and tried to see again that smile, which existed only in the past, in his wonderful memory of it. The present infringed upon the past. Anthea rapped on the door. Bother the woman, he thought, then felt sorry, then was glad the bathroom had the only functioning lock in the flat.

'Charles,' she called, 'aren't you coming to watch the film? You'll have missed half of it if you don't come now.'

'To be honest, my love, I've seen it three times myself.'

No reply. He waited, hoping she would go away.

'Charles, you'll be all red and shrivelled if you sit in that damned bath any longer. Don't you know that water is a dehydrator?'

'Actually, no.'

'Charles, I must talk to you. I know you've locked the door. Please let me in.'

'Anthea, dear, I – '

'Come out. Come out and talk to me. Don't you want to talk to me?' Dear Lord, she was going to cry. He wondered how many gins she'd had.

'Of course I do. With you in a minute.'

'You won't be with me in a minute. You're hoping I'll go away and forget you. And you want to forget me and after I've stood by you all this time.'

Charles sighed. Suddenly he was very tired.

Anthea rapped again, harder this time.

'Charles, I want to talk to you. It's important, Charles.'

'Yes,' he drawled.

'Just one question. Will you open the door? I want to ask you a question.'

'Then ask me.'

'Not like this. I want to see you. I want to see your eyes, Charles.'

Bang, bang.

'In a moment.'

'Now! Now!' Bang, bang, bang. 'Open the door, you bastard!'

'Oh shut up – darling.'

Bang, bang, bang.

'*What is it you want to know?*' For the second time that evening he had been forced to resort to his courtroom voice. He could hear her sniffles through the door. He imagined the green dress and the matching mascara running down her face like pond scum. 'Well?'

'Why did you marry me, Charles?'

'Because you are such wonderful company, my dear.'

She started banging her head against the door. Charles jumped from the bath and reached for a towel, stepping on the Tacitus as he passed the mirror. How much thinner he'd grown. Perhaps, in one or two ways, deprivation wasn't such a bad thing. He unlocked the door. Anthea stood before him, looking as he had imagined.

'Oh Charles,' she threw her arms around his wet neck, sobbing. 'We had a bath together once, remember?'

'Of course I remember.'

'Was it fun? Did you like it, Charles?'

'I adored it.'

'You're not just saying that to placate me?'

'I wouldn't lie to you about anything so important.'

'It was in Florence in that wonderful hotel.'

'I thought it was Rome.'

She drew back. 'It was *Florence*, Charles.'

'Yes, yes, quite right. Florence it was.'

He put on a dressing-gown and helped his wife to the couch, the telly and the Trintignant. He sat, holding her hand until he was sure she had passed out, then he gently extricated his own, covered her with a rug and tiptoed to the bedroom, leaving the telly on and retrieving the Tacitus *en route*. He lay on the bed to have another go at the book. He opened to the paragraph at which he had become stuck like a broken record and smiled to find his damp footprint straddling the spine. Another cosy evening at home on the borders of Fulham.

'Sorry, old boy.' He put the book on the bedside table. 'It's just not on. Not tonight, dear.'

He wanted to get back to Paris, to be anywhere but here. Mostly he wanted to get back to Paris.

Clover was nearly an hour late. Eleanor insisted on going down to meet her at the door and Charles accompanied her, afraid she might lose her footing on the stairs. He stood back and let the two women embrace outside the spotlight of his admiring stare. He saw Jason Englefield skulking towards the Metro without a backward glance. The brute had no intention of seeing Eleanor. But he had delivered Clover, and Charles could only suppose that little else mattered.

While Clover and Eleanor chattered away on the chaise-longue, Charles adjourned to the kitchen to lay out the elaborate tea which Eleanor had bought. He took great pleasure in the ritual, slowly arranging the cups and saucers, plates, knives and spoons, giving The Two as much time as possible to be comfortable together again. He wished he could spend the rest of his life arranging the tea. He laid out the cakes and pastries, none of which Eleanor could eat. They would dine in the sitting-room, she had said, not in the tiny kitchen. There was an embroidered cloth to be spread on the floor. They would have a picnic.

It was both jolly and sad. Charles tried not to stare at Clover. He could sense her shyness with him, complicated by her obvious compassion and constraint with Eleanor. He missed the total ease with adults that she had demonstrated as a child. Her attitude towards them, he assumed, must now be mixed, half-grown as she was, yet not of them. Oh not of them at all. She was being cautious. But she still liked him, he could tell. She had kissed him without restraint and seemed eager for the backgammon he had proposed. But she kept very quiet at first, looking long and hard at Eleanor who, every so often, would reach out and take her hand and press it.

'You'll get used to it, sweetheart,' she said. 'Even I'm used to it. It doesn't take too terribly long.'

'Oh,' said Clover with a hint of her old, careless philosophy, 'I can get used to anything. Even when Bunchie died I got used to that.'

'I don't think I ever got used to that,' Eleanor replied.

'Are you still sad about Bunchie? You were ever so sad at the time, I remember.'

'I dream about Bunchie.'

'And Sussex – and me. Do you dream about us all?'

'All of you. All the time.'

'Sometimes I dream about you. But you look, you know, like you did – then.'

'I hope that in your dreams, Clover, I'll always look like I did then.'

'Oh don't worry, Eleanor, because I'll get used to it. It won't matter how you look. Does your eye hurt?'

'Sometimes. Funnily enough, it's not as big a nuisance as my foot.'

'Well,' Clover announced as though it were the only piece of information they had all been waiting for, 'I'm just fine!' Then, 'I can't imagine what it must be like not to run.'

'Ah, but you're an athlete and I never was. You're a little heroine.' Clover blinked.

'A heroine of our time,' Charles put in.

She smiled at him. 'Does that mean you think I'm a modern sort of person? I don't feel the least bit modern. I wish I were modern. We live in the country, you know. Sometimes I just feel far away from the world, like an alien, peculiar girl with no proper family and not understanding why other people act the way they do.'

'Darling, you understand more than anyone else in the world. And you're braver than anyone else in the world.' Eleanor was sweeping as always.

'What I think I meant,' said careful Charles, not wanting to embarrass the girl, 'is that you seem to me to be a modern daughter, knowing things daughters didn't used to know and coping with your knowledge in a way that I admire and that also mystifies me. Perhaps that's because I have no children.'

'I want to have lots of children. I feel sorry for people with no children.'

'So do I,' said Charles and Eleanor in unison.

'You know Charles had a child that died.'

'Did he?' Clover looked Charles straight in the face, serious, unperturbed, unpitying. 'Does that make you very unhappy?'

'Not too much, anymore.'

Clover asked if it had been a boy or a girl.

'A girl. I wanted a girl.'

'Why, do you like girls better?'

'Oh yes. They're much sweeter,' said Charles.

Eleanor groaned. 'Not to themselves. Not to each other. What do you think, Clover?'

'Except for Emma, I'm not sure girls like me. I'm not sure boys like me.'

'Of course they like you.' Eleanor rushed in.

'Perhaps', Charles mused, 'they're just uncertain of you. Boys can be awfully thick, you know. They can't work out how they should treat you.'

'Because I'm too young and too grown-up and too old-fashioned and too modern.'

'I'd say that was it.'

Clover laughed. Then she kept quiet while Eleanor and Charles gossiped about London.

'So Felix is legit.' Eleanor looked as though she would have liked to light a cigarette. 'Say no more, Charles. If Felix Koning is legitimate, which I cannot believe, the spice must truly have gone right out of life.'

'Don't fret. Many are groomed to take his place.'

Eleanor looked at Charles very hard. 'His is a place that can't be taken.' She yawned and stretched. 'And now, my angels, I must rest. The obligatory nap, heigh-ho. Who'd a-thunk it, eh pretty baby?'

'You, Eleanor! You never slept.'

'Well, now I must and now I do and I'm going to now. You two stay here and play backgammon. Oh, there's Monopoly on the bottom bookshelf. Bye.' She kissed Clover and limped off to the bedroom.

Clover won the first game which they played in silence. As she relaid the board she remarked a little longingly that Paris was very beautiful. Then she asked, 'Who is Felix Koning?'

'He was a friend of your mother's.'

She gave him an odd, quick look. He took the second game. Defeat fired her determination and she swept the board in their final encounter.

She lifted her arms in exultation, thumbs to the ceiling. 'I won!'

'You did, you did. Daughter takes all.'

Clover had puzzled and pleased him then as she had done this morning. Perhaps she *was* a little heroine.

He missed Eleanor terribly. How could she have simply slipped out of the world like that? How could such a thing have been allowed to happen? The gods were to blame. No, he took that back. He could not know, no one could know, who was to blame. He longed to creep to the wardrobe, take out the urn and cradle it in his arms. But if Anthea should suddenly stagger in . . . There was no lock on the bedroom door. So he picked up the discarded memobook and read again what he'd written. It seemed to make more sense, but he had no taste now for soft-core polemics. He was tired of trying to convince himself. He wanted to have an experience and not a lot of thoughts. Human contact was what he wanted, but there was only Eleanor really. All these years she had both sought him out and escaped him. Now her remains rested in the bottom of his wardrobe. Oh well, since he could never have her, since he could never even talk to her, he settled, sensible man, for what he could have. He wrote her a letter.

Darling girl, he began, excuse my interrupting you. I am sure you are just off, as you were always 'just off' on some adventure. But may I, as an old friend, detain you for a moment? (For I'm certain you have not yet quit the place entirely.) May I figuratively lay my hand on your arm? I need to speak to you before you go. I didn't know how much I should need to speak to you. Does one always feel this way about dead people, that they have the key and that they have gone and taken it with them and so we can never get back into the old place again, wherever that old place may be?

We told each other almost but not quite everything. We very nearly trusted each other completely. But it turns out that you held back and I held back. Isn't it funny? One cannot avoid conflicting loyalties. Maybe we'd have told each other eventually. But I'd better hurry on. Restless creature, no doubt you are champing at the bit, pawing the ground, wanting to be running loose. I hope you know, I'm sure you do know, that I have done what you asked. There they all were, and it was most bizarre. Did you laugh? Did you cry? Or does it not matter to you anymore? I laughed and cried – to myself.

Clover was sweet, Jason sour. I was surprised to see him confer with Felix who was – words fail me – well groomed, I suppose. Jason even took his card. (You see? Even now nothing escapes me, especially when I think it may interest you.) Jeremy was anxious, although wishing to appear benign. Monica was paralytic. George was vicarish, Dillon voluble, your three lady-friends absorbed in each other, your old loves, well, quiet. I was, except by Clover, barely tolerated and mainly ignored. But I saw and heard and I know now where Clover comes from. Are you surprised? And you never told me. And I was too dense to guess. Never mind.

Since I have just learned something vitally important which you chose to conceal from me, I feel I ought to reveal a thing or two to you. Seeing Felix reminded me of an incident you may or may not have got wind of. I cannot know what he told you. I assume you were mainly in the dark, perhaps guessing something, not caring much one way or another. The thing is, first, that I was in love with you. That afternoon when we devised Clover's trust – oh, you must have known, it was so ill-concealed and I was so wretched and feeble. I had guessed about you and Felix. I felt you wanting to go to him and it grieved me. My precarious state of balance when you left was almost toppled by my next client, Simon Delamere. What he told me made me sick with fear for you and prompted me to take an action that, although successful at the time, was irrational, short-sighted, questionable in its motives and destructive in its ultimate effects, some of them yet to be uncovered. Here is the scenario.

A woman, Monica, buys a painting, a Teniers to be exact, for £5,000 from a friend, Felix, who is an international fence. She is innocent, he is not. Felix is well aware that the painting is stolen, but tells Monica he acquired it from an Italian connection in return for some porcelain. Monica trusts Felix because she is in love with him. He offers to sell her the Teniers for £1,000 less than its true market value. The painting is charming and a bona fide Teniers. The fence is also charming but something less than bona. He asks that the transaction be made in cash. Nervous, Monica nevertheless agrees. After all, art deals are notorious for secrecy and everyone, including myself, wishes to mislead the Inland Revenue. Monica pays Felix in cash and hangs the painting in her husband's study. Her husband, Jeremy, is pleased with the present and with his little wife's good taste and business acumen. The fence is pleased with his profit and considers using it to take another charming woman, Eleanor, on holiday. But he has made a fatal and uncharacteristic error, or he was misinformed by the Italian whoever that was, it has never been established. The six-year statute of limitations on the painting has not, as he believed it had, run out. But then he may also simply have taken that risk. (Monica later confessed that Felix suggested she not hang the painting for a few months because it had a small crack in the corner, barely discernible, and needed restoration. And the woman supposedly knows about art. Love makes us all mad. Well.)

Four months later, in November 1976, while Jeremy is mercifully in Switzerland, the police arrive at Monica's house. They inform the horrified lady that she is in possession of a stolen picture and liable to prosecution under the Sale of Goods Act unless she can prove that she purchased the said picture either in a Market Ouvert or in good faith from a person who may or may not have sold it to her in good faith. If the former, documents will be required. If the latter, she must reveal the name of the seller. Appalled, Monica resorts to the simple but effective expedient of fainting. Sal volatile is produced. The police impound the Teniers.

Upon returning to her senses, Monica, fearing her husband's wrath and a courtroom drama, flies for assistance to her brother Simon, who in turn consults the trusted family lawyer, Charles. Charles, like any good lawyer, advises Simon and Monica to consider first the legal costs and the value of the painting and presses for a compromise with the original owner, a certain van Zupten, who is, naturally, well-known to Monica, Jeremy, Simon and Charles. To protect Monica, he tells her to write an immediate disclaimer, meanwhile allowing him to write to Mr van Zupten and put the seller, that is Felix, on notice. The astonished lawyer is then informed that, for various reasons both obscure and sound, Monica does not want the seller named. But her brother, being a bit of a bully and she an easy mark, has succeeded in extracting from Monica the name of the seller. And the lawyer, who is something more than a half-wit, extracts it in turn, although with difficulty, from the brother.

The lawyer masks his anxiety. Has Monica informed Felix of her predicament? Answer: Felix is unavailable. Charles feigns disgust. If Monica persists in disregarding the law she will be charged with handling and receiving stolen property. Monica asserts Felix's innocence. Everyone, it seems, is innocent. Then who stole the painting? And who reported it as stolen? Clearly, tracks want covering. And Charles is being asked, indirectly but definitely, to cover them.

The next day Charles consults with brother and sister. Charles has by this time spoken to the police and promised a disclaimer from his client. He has also learned the date the painting was stolen and that it was identified by a small crack in the upper right-hand corner. Charles hopes against hope that Felix will do the decent thing, whatever that, in such a muddle, may be. Tearfully, Monica reasserts Felix's innocence. Then where is Felix? Charles is now informed that Felix is in Rome. Felix is unobtainable for comment. Charles's heart stops. For Charles is in love with Eleanor. Being in love and being something more than a half-wit, he grasps the situation with alacrity. Felix has gone to Rome and taken the lovely Eleanor along as companion, leaving the entire business in the lap of Monica. Monica is distraught and for several good reasons. Husband Jeremy will return in three days and she must inform him not only of the loss of the picture but of his £5,000. (She has failed, you see, to insure the thing until restoration has been carried out or because she is plain stupid.) Despite her protestations, Felix's actions have led her to question his sincerity. Yet she loves the scoundrel. How can she protect Felix and save her own skin? How can she prevent her husband's understandable demands for the return of his money? How can she snatch Felix from Eleanor? How can the besotted client also hide her true motivations from the lawyer, her brother and her husband? How can the besotted lawyer hide *his* true motivations from the besotted client?

Monica begs Charles to help her and to be above all discreet. Charles promises that he will assist, they may leave the mess to him, all he requires is twenty-four hours to concoct a good story. Meanwhile, she must say nothing to the police and make no further attempts to contact Felix. That night, Charles rings Eleanor but, as expected, there is no reply. She has flown with Felix and his illgotten gains. Charles thinks. Clearly, Felix, anticipating Interpol, has left London in an effort to sever his connections with the thief and has gone abroad (Charles's conjecture) to arrange false papers, addresses, bills of sale or the like which will prove that the title of the painting was legally conveyed to him. Proof of import is not required in Great Britain. Continental law is a complex matter, the entangled Italian legal system is notorious, the English police are easily bored in such matters and want only a quick restoration or a quick conviction. After all, what do they know or care about art? The mix is to Felix's advantage and he knows it. Justice delayed is justice denied.

Charles, Monica, Felix and Simon are all tacitly aware that the stolen picture is not as dangerous an item as a further investigation prompted by the discovery of that picture – an investigation into the past and present transactions of Felix. Not one painting but a chain of paintings. Not just paintings but porcelain, silver, etc. What might the two fugitives be carrying into and out of Rome? How much does Eleanor really know? Investigation spells curtains for Felix, heartbreak for Monica, scandal for Jeremy, collusion for Eleanor – possibly – and acute anxiety for Charles, certainly.

Here is the picture, then, and the rub: Eleanor loves Felix. Felix may or may not love Eleanor. Monica loves Felix, *but* Charles loves Eleanor. Monica wants to protect Felix, Charles wants to protect Eleanor. Charles stifles his better judgement, buries his professional integrity, ignores his common sense and succumbs to his emotions. He forces ends to justify means. He paces his nest all night. Come dawn he has hit on a solution. It is, even if he says so himself, little less than brilliant.

The only ploy that can save all parties is to bring police investigation to an immediate and permanent halt. The lid must be clapped on and quickly. Charles could, of course, have Monica spin an elaborate yarn about foreign purchase, remote French farmhouses, false names, the usual. Such tactics might postpone and frustrate further enquiries, but there would be no guarantee that sooner or later some fluke might not explode this shaky scenario and land them all in an even worse one. But there is one fact with which Charles, being both relative and friend of the family, is well acquainted: the death of Monica and Simon's father from a heart attack two years previously. The deceased will provide them with an alibi although his reputation may be besmirched by the donation. Since their mother is also dead, she will be unlikely to protest, although she may trouble their sleep. This fortuitous set of circumstances allows Charles to devise a solution beautiful in its simplicity. He will create a false provenance.

The following afternoon Charles rehearses Monica. She is both nervous and relieved. He will do most of the talking but she must have her facts straight should she be questioned further. She is to claim that she discovered the painting some months ago among the belongings of her father, stored in her attic and not opened until after his death. She is to say that she thought the painting might be original but had not yet managed to find time to have it evaluated. Meanwhile, because she liked it and it had, so she thought, belonged to her father, she had hung it in an unfrequented room of her own house. Imagine her horror when, etc., etc. Since the picture was stolen five years ago in 1971, her father could easily have purchased it before he died, unaware, of course, that he was acquiring someone else's property. The picture could have changed hands many times before he bought it. It would be impossible to pick out any specific links in the chain since no papers relating to the sale had been found among her father's effects or, if they had been found, had been inadvertently destroyed or permanently misplaced. Her reluctance to come forward immediately with the story is explained by a fear of posthumous scandal, however slight. Understandable. After all, her father had never hung the painting. It was very worrying. But she has been persuaded by her brother and her lawyer to tell the truth. Naturally, she disclaims all over again any rights to the Teniers and is happy to see it returned to its original owner, poor dear Mr van Zupten. Neat. All that remains is to placate Jeremy.

By the time he has returned from Switzerland, the matter has been resolved to everyone's satisfaction, including the police and the van Zuptens who even go so far as to express their sympathy for the distress poor, dear Monica has undergone due to a series of unfortunate coincidences. Jeremy, however, is not amused. The conduct of his wife, his brother-in-law and his lawyer, not to mention that of the freebooting fence, has him smouldering with indignation. He even hints at a four-way collusion, having no idea of Eleanor's involvement. The three protest their own, and Felix's, innocence. Jeremy remains unconvinced, but there is little he can do to reverse the situation without throwing a very bad light on all concerned, himself included. Gossip would not encase his name in brackets as the injured party. He will therefore wait for an opportunity to make all four as uncomfortable as possible. Jeremy is a patient man. Charles is wary of Jeremy although he exults in Eleanor's timely rescue. One year later, Charles loses Jeremy's account.

That is the story, my dear love. How I should like to know what you think of it. Of course, there are gaps. Who, for instance, informed on Monica in the first place? It was not Mr and Mrs van Zupten who hadn't visited her house since Christmas 1973. The informer was acute enough to recognize the tell-tale crack in the corner of a missing Teniers. The informer was an expert.

The affair was a storm in a tea cup. But for some of us the wreckage was total. You know my passion for putting pieces together. I have my suspicions, although I am unable to run them to ground. And if I did, what good would it do me now? And yet, and yet. There is abundant proof that life turns on trifles – a hair, a fingernail, a crack in a corner. That tea-cup typhoon, if it did not perpetrate, certainly coincided with the beginning of my end. I did wrong for your sake. It was my love for you coupled with what I now recognize as the maternalism of my own nature. But why was the case not closed there and then? I cannot accept that my plague of misfortunes has been entirely a Job's affliction. God is not testing me. On the contrary, there is a reason for all this, a *human* reason. Within eighteen months of this affair friends' backs were being turned and clients were taking their business elsewhere. I grew nervous, made mistakes, lost money. The Inland Revenue rose like the Kraken. Anthea's anxiety over our financial straits, our furniture and our plunge in the popularity polls was responsible for the loss of our child. And so on until hounded to the borders of Fulham. And the cause, the cause. I can probably never be sure, but something in me links it to the movements of a small painting with a crack in the upper right-hand corner. Ach. I'm becoming a paranoic as well as a failure and a drunk. Even the passing of a white card from one hand to another bothers me. Why can't I not notice? Why can't I, like I used to, forget?

Still, I am a reasonable man. A reasonable man suspends judgement until all the facts are known and assembled. You may rely upon me, as always, to adhere to the terms of what remains of our agreement.

Sweet, goodbye. I'll keep you no longer to make you listen to this sad tale. You wish to be off. Go, salamander. The story began with my love for you, and so it will end, no doubt.

Charles

Charles was very drunk and very tired. Yet he experienced a certain satisfaction. He had held his final communication with Eleanor and had managed an overview of an incident which had plagued him for years. He folded the letter and placed it in the Tacitus. Anthea would never open his Tacitus. Some day he would destroy the letter. For now it was a consolation. Charles pulled the bedcovers over his head. He must leave the light on for Anthea who was frightened to enter a dark room. He fell asleep, resolved to be the tree.

At four in the morning he was awakened by his wife. She leaned over the bed and shook him.

'Charles,' she whispered urgently, 'what did you say Monica Black was wearing?'

'A hair shirt, my love, of immaculate cut. And diamond-studded manacles.'

seventeen

Grace Plumber rose from her desk, winking back tears.

'You're a rare sight, you are,' she said.

Charles grasped the outstretched hand and pressed it to his lips.

'Don't chide me, Mrs Plumber. I don't withhold myself from *you* out of choice.'

'But,' the lady flushed above her pink silk blouse and pearls, 'you do withhold yourself, Mr Bevan. All of us feel your absence most keenly.'

'Well, here I am and there you are, so let us make the most of my return engagement.'

'So long as it's not your farewell appearance.'

'Never that.'

Mrs Plumber frowned, knowing perfectly well that her former employer had just stopped in at the Goat for something horrid. And at eleven-thirty in the morning. Charles felt her watch him as he removed the overcoat he had worn for the past eight years and hung it in its old, accustomed place. She was marvelling, no doubt, that he rarely exhibited any of the tell-tale signs. Never a slurred sentence or a wavering footstep. She was concluding for the hundredth time that he knew how to conduct himself, that he was a gentleman, a good man, a *good* man. He was aware that she had supported him, even in the stink of scandal and a gale of accusations. No, she had said, it was most certainly not his fault, and placed the blame for his troubles squarely on his wife.

She sat down again, ready to do anything in the world for him.

'It's the Barret/Pleach account, isn't it?' She assumed her devotional attitude.

'You are, as ever, well ahead of me.'

'There', she produced a stack of papers and dropped them triumphantly on the desk, 'is everything you're likely to need.'

'Mrs Plumber, you're a pearl of great price, and you're the only one I trust.' He meant it.

Charles gathered up the documents and proceeded to the cubicle which served as his occasional office. To be so flagrantly demoted had been at first a blow to his pride. But he was a reasonable man. What else, after all, were they to do – reserve that sumptuous chamber for some very indistinct point in the future when he recovered his wits, his finances and his reputation? A better, and a younger, man now presided over his former sanctum, and rightly so. Charles had no complaints.

How could he when he himself had made significant contributions to the breach? If only the firm, if even Mrs Plumber knew what a relief it was to be rid of all that responsibility, all those confidences. He simply could not carry them around any longer. He had reached saturation point without being able to crystallize out. But he had, in the past three years, perfected the art of forgetting.

Mrs Plumber appeared with a cup of coffee and placed it on the desk with an air of a priestess bearing libations to a shrine. There was something she wanted to tell him, Charles was sure of it. But she was holding back, savouring her news, and – excellent secretary that she was – ensuring that he dealt with one problem at a time. He sniffed the coffee.

'Thank you, Mrs Plumber. Is it still – ?'

'Shocking, Mr Bevan.' She turned on the heel of her court shoe and left.

Wearily, Charles lifted each page as though it were made of lead. Raps at the door were welcome interruptions. There were still a couple of cautious supporters about the place who dared to press, quietly, for his return. Gratifying, but a return was the last thing for which he hoped. He had ceased to hope for anything, even to look forward to anything except the envelope containing his supplementary benefit.

The envelope was no longer addressed to Halford Road. Eight months previously, Charles had resorted to the desperate remedy – well, desperate enough. He had bolted, but not completely. It had taken all his inherent fluency plus the fruits of many mornings in court to persuade his wife that she would be better off and would stand a better chance without him. He still could not believe he had succeeded. Perhaps she had realized at last that they were too old to go on playing the Beautiful and the Damned. It was a miracle. She had acquiesced. She had let him go, although not completely.

'Look at it this way, my dear. I shall be away four nights a week. All right, three.'

The concessions involved were killing. Anthea kept the flat, the furniture and the paintings. The small profits on his South Sea Bubble went entirely to her. She had bought a new television and switched hairdressers. She had even, in his absence, struck up an acquaintance with the woman on the second floor who was, unlike Anthea, divorced (the question of a legal separation had never come up), and to whom in the past she had referred as a Vulgarian. They had discovered a wealth of common interests, paramount among them journals and gin. Anthea had even received an invitation to Bournemouth, over which she debated continually with herself and Charles when he came to cook dinner for her four nights a week.

'There, you see, darling. You're better off without me. I've been a millstone around your neck. It was unspeakably selfish of me.'

'Charles,' she sniffed, 'I shall always be here if you need me.'

It was a fifteen-minute walk from his bedsitter in Earls Court to Halford Road. He would do the shopping on the way, cook dinner, listen to his wife's laments, watch a film or *Panorama* with her, kiss her on the forehead and walk home, stopping *en route* for a last one at the Feathers. Why and how she had come to accept the arrangement he did not know. She must have considered that she *was* better off without him. He, on the other hand, found life a lonely business. There were days when he positively looked forward to Halford Road. At least he would be fed amusing and horrifying tit-bits from the big, bad world. He would be diverted. But he was always glad when the time came for his walk home through the back streets of Fulham, past the hospital and the coal yards and along the Old Brompton Road by the cemetery.

He would sleep until eleven am, wash, eat a banana and go to the Feathers. At around one he would return and climb three flights of stairs to the tiny room and a half which he made liveable with what remained of the books, a couple of paintings and his grandmother's kilim. He even had had Simon to supper, and once, on a very special occasion, Mr and Mrs Plumber who made no comment on his reduced circumstances. Otherwise he read, drew, wrote, drank, sat up until four and collected his supplementary benefit. Every few months he made his way to Christie's or to an old acquaintance in Mayfair and parted reluctantly with a painting or drawing in return for which he received a compensation never equal to his expectations and for the meagreness of which there were always incontrovertible reasons.

At three-thirty he had finished with the Barret/Pleach estate. The little Barret/Pleaches and their friends and relations would, he trusted, get everything that was coming to them. Oh why did he bother to disinter these mouldy confidences when all he got, all he would take, was a pittance for his pains? There was a knock at the door. Mrs Plumber stepped in and closed it softly behind her. He was about to be enlightened.

'I hope you don't think this is presumptuous of me,' she began.

'Dear Mrs Plumber, I – '

'No, no. Please hear me out. I don't mean to be impertinent. It's only that, well, Mr Bevan you once honoured me with a responsibility, one I take, I assure you, very, very seriously.'

'Yes?'

'I feel it my duty to remind you – of course you are no doubt aware – but I feel I would be remiss if I didn't, if I neglected to – oh please don't think I'm reproaching you in any way.'

'Dear lady, a reproach from you is worth a cornucopia of compliments from another.'

'Please, Mr Bevan, don't play the courtier. This is serious business.'

'I think I – '

'The date, sir. Surely you remember the date.'

'The date, the date, let me see. I know it's Tuesday.' He made a movement to consult the watch which had been pawned six months ago.

'It's the twenty-fifth, sir. The twenty-fifth of November.'

'Of course it is. Well, well.'

'The trust, sir,' her voice dropped to a stage whisper. 'Miss Englefield's birthday!'

'Clover?' He whispered too despite himself. Why did he feel they were suddenly conspirators? A chill ran down his spine. His scalp bristled.

'Mr Bevan, Clover Englefield is eighteen years old today.' He stared at the woman, mute. He burst out laughing.

'Mr Bevan, this is no joke.'

'No, no,' he wiped his eyes. 'Of course it isn't. Nevertheless, it *is* a happy occasion – for Miss Englefield.'

'Oh yes, certainly. Then you did – '

'Remember?' He laughed again. 'Mrs Plumber, darling, I had forgotten completely!'

She smiled at him. 'Then you're not offended?'

'On the contrary, I'm obliged and grateful. My faith in you has been more than justified. Not that I ever doubted I'd chosen the perfect accomplice.'

'Well,' she folded her hands, stood a bit straighter and addressed him in a normal voice, 'then everything is all right.'

'Everything is wonderful except for one little snag.'

'What's that, Mr Bevan?' Her eyes flashed. She was a conspirator again.

'I haven't the faintest idea where Miss Englefield is.'

'Oh but sir, under the terms of the trust – '

'I am meant to keep in constant contact or to know at least her continued whereabouts.'

'Oh yes, Mr Bevan. You mean you haven't done so?' Mrs Plumber's eyes were wide.

'In a word, no.'

'Oh Mr Bevan . . .'

'If you're thinking that I have not been a model of conscientious devotion to duty, Mrs Plumber, you are right as always. I've had my lapses. I don't deny them.'

'You've had your troubles, sir, and most unjust they were. I've often thought, if only I could lift this curse – for that's what it seemed – from off poor Mr Bevan . . .'

The woman was a marvel. If it had not been for her, Charles would have supposed such creatures extinct. They were certainly an endangered species. He must keep close to Mrs Plumber and no mistake.

'I've been aware of your sympathy, Mrs Plumber, and I've been touched by it. But there's nothing to be done. I sometimes wonder if I haven't become what is known as an ageing hippie.'

'You! Oh Mr Bevan, no!'

'I have gone to the dogs, Mrs Plumber.'

'Never!' she cried indignantly. Not even Mr Bevan might slander Mr Bevan.

'Well, perhaps not quite.' He was rather enjoying himself. 'Not yet. But I'm on a downward spiral and gathering momentum by the minute. I've descended into the maelstrom.'

'I don't know anything about maelstroms, Mr Bevan. It seems to me you simply want saving and that's that.'

'Ah, Mrs Plumber, who will save me? And you will kindly not propose divine intervention.'

'My husband and I are agnostics, Mr Bevan. And so are our three children.'

'Really? Mrs Plumber, I had no idea.'

'In Good we trust,' she announced.

'Yes. Of course you do. You're a sterling example of um – '

'But we're rather getting off the subject, Mr Bevan. The question remains, what is to be done about Miss Englefield? The money is now hers and she must be informed. It is your – our – duty to inform her and to transfer to her a considerable sum.'

'Dear me yes, and how am I – never fear, Mrs Plumber. I shall commence detective work immediately. Be assured I'll not rest until the young lady is found.'

Mrs Plumber sighed. 'That's what I knew you'd say. Can I help at all?'

'You can, Mrs Plumber. Bring me a telephone and a book of dialling codes.'

'Right away, sir.' Mrs Plumber's equanimity was completely restored.

The old number in Sussex put Charles in contact with a South Ken inflection, female, who informed him that she and her husband had purchased the house as a weekend retreat. Previous to their occupancy, the place had stood empty for 'simply ages'. She assumed it must have belonged to some sort of artist since what would have been the sitting-room was covered in paint, had been utterly neglected, and was 'filthy, *filthy*'. The decorators were costing them a fortune. She knew of no Mr Englefield, but if he cared to hold a moment, she would get him the name and number of the estate agent who might know something. Charles waited. Through the receiver he heard the Sussex wind as it attacked the old cottage, rattling the windows and throttling the rose bushes. He heard it as it had blown on the night of Clover's birthday when she was safe, secure, tucked up in bed and surrounded by love. He heard it blow as it had blown on all the long winter evenings when she and Jason were alone and uncommunicative, hidden from the world. He heard it blow as it had blown for the past three years, finding its accustomed way through every crack in the weakening walls, into every vacant room littered with Englefield debris. He heard it beat the dead rushes into cracking submission. Once again a chill ran down his spine. He felt as he had that day when he tried to ring Eleanor Linnane in the absurd hope of luring her to the Blacks' dinner party. He experienced the same sense of futility. Everything was ghosts, ashes, dust, dreams. Everything and everyone was gone.

'It's a Mr Hawkins you want. He's in Hailsham.' She gave him the number.

'You've been very kind and helpful.'

'Nothing at all. Goodbye.'

In five minutes the woman would have forgotten his existence. Of Clover's existence she was not even aware, unless she had come across a castaway dolly, a pink hair-grip, an old *Puzzler*. The image led Charles to the brink of deep and unmixed melancholy. Life was cold. Cold and empty. Above all, cold. He very much wanted a drink. He checked the time. Not open yet. Stoically he dialled Mr Hawkins of Hailsham.

At Hawkins and Appleby confusion reigned. No one seemed to have any idea what Charles was talking about. Mr Hawkins was out and had been out since ten that morning. From what he could gather, Mr Appleby had not put in an appearance in two weeks. Charles began to be amused. The southern slowness was suddenly endearing. The Two had lived in its midst, liked it, laughed at it, complained about it. It cushioned, no doubt, their impatience. He remembered what Eleanor had said about them – the farmers with their yarns, their drawl, their forecasts of doom, the shopgirls taking ten minutes to make change; the stalwart Protestantism that merged with a vagueness and a sweetness that seemed to come out of the ground itself. He thanked the girl and rang back in three minutes.

Mr Hawkins answered. Mr Hawkins had been in his office all along, but how was anyone to know that? Mr Hawkins was helpful to a point. Yes, yes, the Englefields. Father and daughter. Most peculiar. Unpleasantness about the rent. Finally, to everyone's relief, quit the premises. Place an absolute shambles. In fact Mr Hawkins too would be interested in knowing their whereabouts, as the cats had, ahem, done some damage to the carpet and Mr Englefield owed £173.57 for repairs. Well, to be accurate it was poor Mrs Draine who was out of pocket. She had previously owned the house and rented it to the Englefields when they were three. Everyone wondered what became of that red-haired woman. Fancy a mother deserting her child like that. One had to admire Mr Englefield in a way, even though he was an artist. At any rate, Mr Hawkins had acted as agent for Mrs Draine who had suffered no end of anxiety at the hands of Jason Englefield. What with the arrears in the rent, the broken crockery, the stolen – yes, stolen – bedlinen, the paint stains, the stench of cat, the missing ironing board . . .

Charles was growing depressed again. Where had the Englefields gone? Mr Hawkins had no idea. It was over two years since he had spied them in the Hailsham launderette or passed on the road the little girl with the odd name riding her bicycle, usually alone.

Would Mrs Draine be likely to know? Possibly. Mrs Draine had sold up and moved to Alderney a year ago. If she didn't know, Mr Hawkins expected she would like to know – she and a few Hailsham tradesmen. Perhaps Mr Englefield had paid at last, but somehow he doubted it. He'd find the number. Again Charles waited. Again he was given a row of digits and a cheerful goodbye. Mr Hawkins assumed that he too was a creditor.

It was not yet five-thirty. He dialled Mrs Draine in Alderney but there was no reply. Mrs Draine was, Charles felt certain, a keen walker and sure to be out in all weathers. Perhaps she had even gone to Cherbourg. His flare of interest in the Englefield case began to die down and was shortly on the verge of being extinguished completely. He could not continue making cross-Channel calls from home (there was only a pay phone in the corridor) and reversing the charges was out of the question. He might use Anthea's phone but she was bound to be inquisitive and that would irritate him beyond endurance. Perhaps when she was at the hairdresser – oh, but the whole affair made him tired, tired, tired. He hadn't the heart for it or for anything much with the exception of a little Tacitus, a little Seneca, a little whisky. He had been going about in the certainty that he was to be left in an indefinite peace, once he had got the Inland Revenue off his back. Now this, and naturally this. That he had forgotten was too absurd, it being his duty and all. Moreover, he would have given much, even a good deal of peace and Tacitus, for the sight of Clover Englefield as she must now be. But to launch himself into detective work which might involve endless troubles (he could sense it doing just that and his instincts were still bloody good), trips to remote areas of the United Kingdom, even foreign excursions. The ramifications of the quest spread themselves broad and deep before him. With a despicable cowardice and a profound lethargy, he imagined it all. Oh no, oh no. He couldn't do it. He had spent too long being the tree.

He cursed himself for a malingerer and headed for the pub. By the time he had extricated himself from Mrs Plumber's solicitations and skirted whoever else might be lurking hard by with intentions of wishing him well, it would be after five-thirty.

eighteen

Rain splashed against the steamy windows of the Goat. It beat the pavement in a fierce dance. Nature was merciless, Charles observed, as he downed his second whisky and regarded his fellow mortals who were beginning to trickle in from nearby offices and shops. They were proof, if proof were needed, that he was not alone in his desire to forget.

Money was the chief external obstacle to the enterprise, he assured himself, unable to keep off the subject of Englefields. Money, money and always money. Money for phone calls, travel, all kinds of assistance and expenses. Even bribes, for it might come to that given Jason's passion for obscurity. (Charles was allowed to borrow money from the trust in the case of such eventualities, but the thought was distasteful to him. Besides, he would appear to be using the funds to float his dissolute life-style, and what would they all say *then?*) Well, Jason appeared to have achieved his end this time, damn him. But after three years as a tree, how was Charles to know anything of trends in art? A search would mean taking up where he had left off with the big, bad world. Above all, it would mean enquiries, and enquiries would mean seeing people he did not want to see. Reopening not one but several Pandora's boxes. Dear God, better have another whisky, double this time, although he could ill afford it. There were, of course, Jason's parents. But what might they know of their estranged son and more estranged granddaughter? He made a list of People Most Likely: George Facer, Dillon Butterworth, Monica Black.

Oh no, oh no. They had feasted on him once. He had no wish to offer himself again for their delectation. To their polite scorn he had no intention of submitting.

They had ostracized him and the cause was still a mystery. Why must he be forced to seek them out, after all these years, and ask their help, especially when he was not at liberty to explain the reasons? (A client might be ashes in his wardrobe, but she was still a client.) Oh no. By the time he had reached the Perth Hotel, he had made up his mind or what he told himself was left of it. With what remained of his mind he had decided to be sensible.

'Sensible. Sensible Charles,' he muttered as he turned the key in the lock. He felt the pay phone reproach him. He ignored it and switched on the overhead light.

'Sensible, sensible. For once in ten years, sensible. I am Charles

Bevan, sensible tree.' He turned on his crucified kilim and all the goadings of his noble maternal lineage. 'And you will please not forget it,' he said out loud.

In the morning he would pay a visit to the Public Trustee. He would file his petition. They had to say yes. They had to see that he was not the man for this job. Yet he knew their seeing that was unlikely. Such requests were seldom granted. He hung up his overcoat. In the wardrobe stood the urn with Eleanor's ashes. He supposed he must deliver it some day. But how could he part with it now? Anthea must be right. He had grown morbid. He picked up the urn, sat on the bed and held to his heart all that remained of Eleanor. Part with her? And what would life be like then, cold, empty vessel that it already was? He rocked the urn in his arms, swaying gently as the tears rolled down his cheeks.

('Charles, I trust you . . . You're a worthy man. Something in my soul couldn't help knowing your worthiness . . . ')

'No I'm not,' Charles bleated. He was not a worthy man. He had a rotten spot. And the rot was spreading. He even enjoyed watching it spread. *That* was how rotten he was.

Determined to affirm his rottenness, Charles set out the next morning for the office of the Public Trustee. The visit would mark the first time in his life that he had formally handed over a professional responsibility. He would explain his difficulties. He would ask the Trustee to administer the fund and trace the girl. It was a base act and he knew it. But Eleanor must understand.

At the Trustee's office he passed several familiar faces who did not recognize him or chose not to acknowledge him. Fine. He had no need of sturdy handshakes. In time he located the room, the desk, the secretary, the form, the chair, the pen. He answered the questions honestly and succinctly as he had, at long last, those of the Inland Revenue. He hoped for the best on both fronts. He reread what he had written, particularly the appended note. His style was still persuasive. He would win. Eleanor would win. Clover would win. God knew, even Jason might win. Charles hesitated, biting the end of his biro. Then he put his hasty signature to the document.

He took a bus back to his room and poured a glass of whisky to which, at three in the afternoon, he had the decency to add water. He thought he might draw, but ideas seemed to come best at night, and so he lay down on his bed instead. Immediately he was prone he began to wonder where Jason and Clover might be. Eleanor's ashes faced him squarely from the bureau. Dear God it was all too much for a poor, rotting tree, all these secrets, all this silence so pregnant. No, no, no, Miss Linnane, I am too tired to care any more about putting pieces together – even your pieces. But I am never too tired to care for you.

He was certain Mrs Draine was a keen walker; something in his bones told him she was. At three in the afternoon, the intrepid lady would be scaling rocks above a pounding surf or striding across a gale-swept moorland, bless her heart. He pictured her grey hair flying in the wind, for she would be sure to scorn a cap or scarf. He saw her hacking jacket, her gumboots. Oh she was quite complete He had begun to like Mrs Draine and didn't even blame her for being piqued about the ironing board. Perhaps she listened to Haydn quartets. But there would be no point in ringing at three on a Wednesday afternoon. No point at all.

Where *could* they have gone? Were they in London, right under his nose, around the corner, down the road? Perhaps Clover was married, living under another name. Like her mother, she seemed keen on the idea of children. But somehow he doubted she had done it quite yet. As for Jason, he had heard nothing of him since Eleanor's cremation. Anthea read all the reviews and she would certainly have told him if Jason had had a recent exhibition. Still, it might not be a bad idea to thumb through some of her art magazines. He would be going to Halford Road tonight. He might have a surreptitious look while Anthea was watching *News at Ten*.

'Oh stop it, you old fool.' It was the first time he had referred to himself as old.

'But I'm forty-six. I'm not old, dammit.' He ran one of his small hands through his curls. Still intact, scarcely a hair had deserted him, although he was decidedly greyer. Anthea even complained that he could do with a visit to the barber. Well. And his mid-section – he looked down at his tummy which was absolutely flat, the paunch having ebbed away during those first three years in Fulham. Why dear Mrs Draine would regard him as a boy. Perhaps Mrs Draine had a companion. No, she was too staunchly independent. A housekeeper, perhaps. And Wednesday was just the sort of afternoon a housekeeper would be likely to come. No, no, Friday. Wasn't Friday the day they always came? Moreover were there any housekeepers on Alderney? It was not quite the tax haven of Jersey or Guernsey.

Charles continued to reflect on Mrs Draine and upon her imagined entourage of housekeepers, visitors, relations, neighbours, cats and dogs. His instincts had stepped in. His instincts told him Mrs Draine did not live alone, the glaringly obvious reason being that there was a *Mr* Draine. This gentleman was too infirm for brisk walks and was in fact something of a scholar in the dear old Victorian amateur style and with a library safe from cats and housekeepers and the irritating crash of waves. He knew it.

In three minutes Charles had rifled every pocket for change. The pay phone seemed to brighten at his approach. He dialled Alderney.

'92416. Beryl Draine here.'

The shock was so great, he had so geared himself for the ailing, academic, although not unkind, voice of Mr Draine that for a moment he could not speak.

'Um. I'm so sorry to disturb you. My name is Charles Bevan. I'm a lawyer. Um – how is the weather in Alderney?'

'Foul as usual. Food shortage, didn't you know? Ferries can't cross from Weymouth. Planes can't land. Happens all the time. I beg your pardon, but who and what did you say you were?'

'Charles Bevan, lawyer. I wasn't aware that Alderney had a landing strip.'

'Mr Bevan, please excuse my abruptness. I have an invalid husband and – '

Ah-ha! His instincts *were* still infallible.

'Of course. I'll be brief. I'm enquiring after the whereabouts of a Mr Jason Englefield and daughter. I was told by Mr Hawkins that they were tenants of yours, and I hoped you might be able to give me some information – '

'Oh!' the lady gasped, 'them!' Then with a note of suspicion in her voice, 'Are you Mr Englefield's lawyer?'

'Not exactly. No.'

'Someone wishes to file suit against him, no doubt.'

'Not quite.'

'Well, I'm unable to tell you Mr Englefield's current address, although, excuse my saying this, have you tried Brixton or Dartmoor? No? Well, he was the most difficult tenant I ever – well, it was because of him that I decided never to let that house again and finally sold it. Mr Bevan, that man treated me shabbily.'

'I'm sorry. I heard about the carpet.'

'The carpet was only the beginning.' Mrs Draine proceeded with a long list of crimes that ended with the disappearance of the ironing board. Charles experienced an old glimmer of affection for Jason.

'Could you tell me, dear Mrs Draine,' he was forced to interrupt on account of his dwindling pile of change, 'just when the Englefields quit the premises?'

'Too late.'

'Could you be a bit more specific?'

'August 1981, the week of my husband's aneurysm. In my mind Mr Englefield is permanently linked with unpleasant experiences.'

'Where did they go?'

'He never said. Not surprising since he owed me two months' rent. I had driven over to negotiate with him, reasonably, of course. But reason had no effect on Mr Englefield. He was an artist, you know.'

'Have you any idea who might help me?'

'No. I tried ringing the girl's school, but she had simply been snatched away. They had expected her back in September, but she didn't appear. The truancy officer went in search of her but I never did learn what he found out. She was rather a sweet girl, pretty too, if she'd had a mother to give a thought to her appearance. I felt quite sorry for her.'

Ah. He had not entirely fallen out of love with Mrs Draine.

'I'm particularly fond of her.' Charles could not hold back. It was the first time in three years he had voiced his feelings for Clover. 'She has deserved better.'

'I daresay she probably has, Mr Bevan.'

'You see it's for her that I – ' Pips interrupted him. And no more money. The line went dead. Charles replaced the receiver.

'Goodbye, Mrs Draine. It was too brief.' And he had so wanted to ask after her husband's health. Nor had she mentioned anything about her passion for the great outdoors.

Charles realized there would not be enough money for the shopping. He would be forced to arrive early and to borrow again from Anthea who would accuse him of drinking away her livelihood. If she knew, if she knew. But she would never know, and he was a fool for allowing his feelings for Beryl Draine to run away with him. Women. They treated him as shabbily as Jason had treated his landlady. But didn't they always behave thus to the men whose overriding passion they knew themselves to be? He stared at the coin box. He was not only a fool. He was outmoded, undistinguished, unrequired. Anthea's requiring him hardly counted. He was indispensable only as a fixture. She would have felt the loss of the television much more.

Why oh why wouldn't someone marry Anthea? Was he the only noble man extant in Great Britain? But he was forgetting. He could hardly think of himself as noble now. He had been noble in the days when he kept confidences and took responsibilities and was bored to death. He returned to his room, locked the door and poured another whisky. This time he did not add water.

All the way to Halford Road Charles wondered about the truancy officer and what he had discovered. He tried to remember the name of

Clover's school. She had mentioned it that afternoon in Paris. If he were to consult the local directory the name certainly would come back to him. He asked Anthea for her stash of international art journals, but she announced that she had jettisoned the lot.

'The evidence of so many people making so much money from so much crap was just too depressing to live with.'

'You could have used them to make fires, my love.'

'Don't be fatuous, Charles.'

'You never came across anything about Jason Englefield, did you?'

'Can't recall. But I should think not. Who on earth would want one of those dull paintings, except you, that is?'

'Me?'

'Charles, you've got Alzheimer's Disease or it's the whisky. Anyway,' she marched to the corridor and returned with a framed drawing, 'surely you remember this.'

It was *The Three Virtues*, the drawing which had adorned his old office. Charles took it from her almost tenderly.

'Well?'

'Of course. I bought it from him the day after Clover's ninth birthday. You know, it's not too bad.'

'Not sure about that.' She peered at it. 'More interesting than some, I guess. If he is doing well, for God's sake sell the bugger.'

Charles said nothing.

'Don't tell me you have a sentimental attachment to it! I know – it's Eleanor. Reminds you of Eleanor. Well, much good may it do you, Charles, I'm not a jealous woman. But take it,' she urged him, 'take it, Charles. It may be worth something and I certainly won't miss it. Ask George. After all, it's not the Braque.'

The thought of 'asking George' was repellent. But Charles did want the drawing very much. He had always liked it. And even though it might prove a painful reminder of better days, he was tired of looking at his own works. They threw him back on himself, and he was more tired of himself than anything.

'Very well, darling.' He tucked the picture under his arm and kissed her forehead. 'I'll try.'

The past was gaining ground. In just a few days it had made considerable advances into Charles's serenely blank present. His capitulation was only a matter of time. Well. He turned into the Feathers for a last drink. (The bottle in his room was empty, and he had money for only one double whisky. Anthea had been severe.) He took a seat at a table next to some ghoulishly splendid punks. He quite liked punks.

Anthea said they made her think of piles of vomit, but he had grown fond of the trumped-up drama of their pose. His taste for eccentricity was evolving rapidly. He respected their going to the dogs straightaway – and celebrating it – instead of lolling about for forty years pretending to be responsible. Normally, he would have attempted an exchange with them. They amused him, and excited his curiosity. It was impossible for him not to take an interest in his ambiance, however bizarre or seedy. But tonight he was silent. He propped up *The Three Virtues* before him, resting it on some Guinness bottles, and studied it while he nursed his drink.

Mrs Draine, the truancy officer, George Facer. Mentally, he struck a line through the name of the lady. Cul de sac number one. But other names rushed in and flooded his consciousness. Why was he allowing the past to pose threats to the deepening roots and spreading branches of his tree? It was interference, that's what it was, interference with his quiet evolution into a quiet eccentric in quest of his inner paganism. It was the world. The world lures us back, we cannot leave it alone. It is too damned interesting. Only one in five million of us is cut out to be a hermit, one in ten million to be, as Jason supposed himself to be, the voice crying in the wilderness. The truancy officer, George Facer, Dillon Butterworth, Monica Black, Monica, Monica. His brain bumped against the image of his cousin, lodged and remained stranded there for five whole minutes before drifting away towards the Public Trustee. Could he really pass the rest of his life, years or even weeks of it, without learning the *dénouement* of this engrossing little melodrama? It was a bad novel he could not put down, a telly programme he could not switch off. Duty, responsibility, trust. Did the impulses now growing great within him spring from his old humanism, or was he simply stuck into the plot of the thing? And there was Eleanor whom he loved and whom he owed. And there was Clover, the sweet and pungent unknown quantity. And there was blood, too. He was a relative. And a lawyer. And a considerable busybody.

He wanted to solve equations again, to put pieces together. Whatever the reasons, he couldn't help it. He wanted to use his wits and his instincts both for his own satisfaction and for the benefit of another person who might, in fact, really require him. Above all, he couldn't help it.

Charles gulped the whisky, nodded goodnight to the punks, and walked briskly back to his room. It was nearly midnight and he was tired. But by a quarter to one he had written three letters – one to the Public Trustee withdrawing his petition, one to Clover's old school, the name of which he discovered in a letter from Eleanor dated April 1980, and one to Monica Black. Even in the heat of his sleuthing something in him drew back and he postponed the meeting with George Facer.

He rose at nine the next morning, intending to go immediately to the post office and imagining those he would pass in the street commenting to themselves on the air of decent resolution he was sure to be exuding. There was a long, brown, official envelope on the hall table. It was addressed to him. Good grief, he thought, more flack from the Inland Revenue. But the letter came from the Public Trustee. He tore it open, read it and laughed out loud. His petition regarding the Englefield trust had been denied.

nineteen

The Brompton Oratory? Of all places for a tryst – and at the altar of Our Lady of Sorrows. Charles pictured the black and grey paintwork, newly restored. She was going a bit far, it was unlike her. What, he wondered, had his little cousin been up to over these last three years? Either she had embraced Rome or she had been reading too much Henry James. Both alternatives suggested a plethora of time on her hands. Nevertheless, Monica was sweet, sweet; and in a way, he felt sure, that external circumstances, however compromising, could not change. He suddenly looked forward to seeing her again.

He had been surprised when she answered his letter. The reply had come within two days and had been flung at the bottom of the stairs along with the rest of the motley post. He almost didn't notice it. He had not anticipated any eagerness on her part to communicate with him, and he was preoccupied with a visit to Chancery which he had arranged for that morning. There was nothing for it but to proceed, now that he and the Public Trustee had arrived at their irrevocable decisions. He was without funds. To track down the Englefields, he must ask the court to sanction further expenditure of trust money. He hoped that a large amount would not be necessary. But he must issue an Originating Summons. He could take no further steps without it.

Having accomplished his task in the Division of Directors, he paid a visit of reassurance to Mrs Plumber, then made for the Goat. There had been no word from the truancy officer, and so further investigations were out of the question until the other brown envelope, the nice brown envelope, arrived with his supplementary benefit cheque. Now he had Monica, or rather would have her on 8 December at three o'clock. He removed some paper and an envelope from his old briefcase which he had begun to carry about with him once more, and composed a note to Jason's parents, or rather two notes, because there were two Englefields in that area of the Midlands which had spawned the irascible painter. He begged both parties' indulgence, hoped they would not mistake his interest for impertinence, and so on.

He went early to Anthea's. He planned to scan the personal columns in her very complete selection of daily newspapers. He wished to investigate costs, consider the way the thing might be phrased, what tone would be best to adopt. 'Would Ms Clover Englefield be so kind as to contact . . . Anyone knowing the whereabouts of J and C Englefield may apply to . . . Come back Cloverfield, Blue Eyes is Blue . . . C B calling Pretty Baby. Urgent.' The personal columns might be a last resort.

'Have you sold that awful picture?' Anthea enquired in the break between *Nationwide* and *Tomorrow's World*.

'Um – not yet.'

'Well, you'd best get a move on because I happen to know George Facer is in London and you might squeeze a few extra pounds out of the transaction by dealing directly with him. Then again, you might not. He's hardly been a regular visitor since our deportation to the Fulham Gulag.'

'You're right, I might not.'

'Might not what?'

'Um, George – as you said.'

'Charles, you're positively incoherent. I think your ears want syringing. And what's your drinking been like?'

'Insufficient. How do you know George is in London?'

'There was a notice in *The Times*. Dillon Butterworth is having a show – important new whojiwhatsits. George wouldn't miss an opportunity to fleece any itinerant millionaires with vague prospects and malleable tastes, would he?'

'Doubt it.'

Hmmmm. Looked as if postponing George was rapidly becoming an impossibility. Why *did* he so want to postpone him?

At two o'clock on 8 December Charles donned the suit, shirt, shoes and overcoat he normally wore only to the office. They fooled Mrs Plumber, but they probably would not fool Monica. The nice brown envelope had arrived and he had been to the barber. He inspected what he could of himself in the small mirror. Even his grandmother might not have been too disappointed with him. As for Auntie Di – well, nothing and no one could measure up to standards of polish and deportment that challenged those of Mr Turveydrop. Charles sighed. Monica could not have weathered the last three years without alteration either.

He was right. He found her kneeling before the altar which was softly ablaze with flickering tapers. Like the woodwork, like the suffering mother of Christ in the painting above the altar, she was also dressed in black and grey. Her wardrobe had always tended to Lenten tones, but they were now, ironically, the fashion. In every way she matched the season. Even her hair, which when they were growing up had reminded him of the feathers of the blackbird, was streaked with white. She was making no effort to conceal it. She was so sombre she might have passed for a very chic nun. Had they lived a hundred years earlier, Charles thought, she would have taken the veil by now. Soror Melancholia. Well.

He approached her from behind and on tiptoe, not wishing to disturb what might turn out to be real prayers, nor to contribute to the voluptuous echoes floating about the place. He thought it must be the noisiest quiet retreat in London.

Unnoticed, he passed Monica whose head rested on her folded hands. He hesitated, reluctant to barge into her meditations. He fumbled in his pocket, found three twopenny pieces and dropped them, very deliberately, into the iron box marked 'For the Poor'. Monica looked up.

'You appear to have cornered the market, Monica.' He pointed towards the candles. 'Are all these for you?'

She gave him an effortless, unmotivated smile. The smile of fortune and habit. From where he stood, she was still pretty. She slipped from her knees back on to the low chair and patted with her bird hand the empty one beside her. Charles took the seat and her hand which pressed his slightly.

'I'd have thought Our Lady of Sorrows would have attracted a larger following, times being what they are.' He studied his cousin kindly, the webs of lines around her eyes, the down on her upper lip. They must be nearly the same age. She seemed smaller than ever, a slowly withering child.

'The Sacred Heart is having a resurgence of popularity.' She pointed to an open door leading to the adjacent altar which was thronged with supplicants. He noticed that she wore no diamonds. Nothing but her wedding ring.

'So I see. Was it out of vogue for long? I seem to associate it with the mid-Fifties.'

She looked at him without much comprehension and smiled again.

'Sorry,' he hastened to say. 'I'm being fatuous. You're a regular here?'

'At this altar, yes.'

'I didn't realize you felt strongly about such things.'

'I'm trying to simplify my life.'

Charles took in once more the opulent surroundings. They accorded perfectly with Monica's idea of simplification.

'But we were all C of E.'

'Daddy was very High.'

'Of course. I'd forgotten.'

'I'm being confirmed in the spring.'

'They still do that?'

'Here.'

An elderly lady with a cane came in and sat behind them. Monica looked at him, scarcely blinking. He saw Clover beside a fire, drying her hair. It *was* the mouth.

'Shall we go somewhere? Would you mind?'

'I didn't plan on our staying, Charles. It's only that meeting here was – easier – and – '

'Safer.'

'That too.' She rose. 'You must light a candle, Charles. Our Lady will grant your wish.'

'Promise?' He chuckled and did as she advised, even quite liking the ritual. He wished only that his cousin might tell him what he wanted to know.

He offered his arm and she took it. She wore flat shoes and a long woollen coat and came just to his shoulder. She was silent as they walked from the church which she seemed to regard with great satisfaction. When they reached the gate she looked up at him.

'You used to make us all laugh so – when we were children. You said things no one else dared to say. You amused the grown-ups. You got away with everything.'

'So I did. But not now.'

She avoided his eyes.

'What about Bendicks?' she asked.

'Too many Americans.'

'Richoux?'

'Too many mirrors. Upstairs at Gloriette would suit me better. I rather like the roar of the Brompton Road again.'

'Don't you ever come back?'

'The social anthropology of Earls Court is most diverting. Monica, I intend to be serious. I'm sorry.'

'I'm quite prepared for your seriousness.'

They pushed their way up the crowded, narrow staircase and secured the window table. Charles sat facing the mirror on the opposite wall. He wanted Monica's eyes all to himself.

'It's a Holy Day, I see.'

'I lost my virginity on the feast of the Immaculate Conception.'

The confession was more like Eleanor, only she would have been making it up.

'Do you think that accounts for certain peculiar twists of fate?'

'Yes and no. Just tea for me. But have a sandwich, Charles, and some scones.'

'Yes. The works please. Why not?' He closed the menu.

'And now you mean to start on me.' She looked nervous.

'Gently,' he patted her hand, 'very gently.'

'I couldn't think otherwise. Only my guilt makes me uncomfortable.'

'Dearest Monica, you must please not be guilty. You have no cause for guilt.'

'Don't be kind, Charles. It only makes me feel worse than I already do.'

'I see you're unhappy. Why?'

'For reasons you know. For what you've come to cross-examine me about.'

'There will be no cross-examination.'

'But it's your right. Once you were too delicate to assert that right. I'm glad you want to now.'

'My dear, what *do* you mean?'

'That I'm ready to tell you, and that my only wish is that you will not hate me for eternity. Knowing you as I do, I hope and trust you'll eventually forgive me.'

'If you're alluding to that Teniers business, well, love is love is love.'

She took his hand. There were tears in her eyes.

'You're a little boy,' she said. 'A clever child who can please the grown-ups. But you don't understand how perfidious grown-ups can be.'

'I think I've witnessed sufficient examples.'

'Professionally, not personally. You don't understand.'

'All right. What don't I understand?'

'Why you should blame me.'

Charles felt as though he had stepped into what seemed a wading pool only to be swept by a powerful current into a vast uncharted ocean. This was not what they were meant to be discussing.

'Monica, I think we're talking at cross-purposes.'

'Let me finish. I may never be able to say this again.' She was surprisingly strong. He saw he must yield the floor.

'Why should I blame you then?'

'For letting you drown.'

He looked at her, baffled.

'They did it – Jeremy and George.'

Good Lord. George again.

'But I let them. I said nothing. At first I knew nothing, although I suspected. Later I knew. It was almost too late but I could have told you. You saved me. I knew you'd never betray me. I was obliged by every sense of honour to help you. But I'm a cowardly person. I will lie to protect liars. I will lie to keep myself safe.'

He was beginning to see.

'You *are* afraid of Jeremy.'

'Terribly. Charles Bevan, my cousin, once upon a time my friend, you were punished. You were punished for helping me, whom you wanted to help, and for helping Felix, whom you did not want to help.'

'I suspected Jeremy was – um – displeased.'

'Jeremy was furious. The withdrawal of our account was only one of a series of blows aimed directly at you. For over a year he worked against you. He implied things. He influenced people.'

'People like George Facer.'

'And Mr van Zupten. And others. Poor Charles, how could you know? They did it all.'

'I made a mistake or two.'

'Which would have meant nothing if your reputation hadn't already been undermined. Jeremy insisted you could have used other methods to get me off. Felix needn't have escaped. He suspected collusion. Later he accused you of pandering in my affair with Felix. He thought you thought Anthea was in love with Felix and that I was a good way of keeping him occupied elsewhere.'

'My God!'

'Of course they would never confront you. Never say it openly. Jeremy told George that you had protected a criminal, he wouldn't say who, that you were responsible for the loss of his money, that you were not to be trusted and that he was withdrawing his account. He urged George to protect his artists and the integrity of his fellow dealers and do likewise. They sent an anonymous letter to the Inland Revenue.'

'Well!' Charles leaned back in his chair to allow the waitress to place a plate of sandwiches, along with some scones and jam, before him. He commenced eating very slowly.

'It was George who, at Jeremy's instigation, persuaded Dillon and all his other artists to switch to Grievson, Gruber and Gruber.'

'Mmmmm.'

'Jeremy then put a word in Marion Enderby's ear.'

'I see.'

'He got wind of the investment and told everyone he knew who would be influenced by such a trifle. There's more. Little things. But the cumulative effect was – '

'Devastating. Lovely scones.'

'I didn't dare protest. I was deeply involved with Felix again and dreaded Jeremy finding out. When he did find out, my silence was procured for good.'

'Why hasn't Felix suffered a fate like mine?'

'You ought to know. You arranged matters in such a way that to incriminate Felix would be to incriminate us all. Besides, Felix is useful. He's proved himself so. Perhaps you don't know about America – '

'Clearly he's prospering. And in the full light of day.'

'Felix is wicked.'

'Tut tut. He's very clever. Good old-fashioned bounder. Thackeray rake.'

'A man like that is no joke, Charles. He feeds on others. He's a vampire, an incubus. I believe God will punish him. Something will happen, if not in this world then in the next. It will be his turn to ask for mercy. I'll be glad.'

'This is unlike you, Monica. Such sentiments don't become you.'

'I know.'

'Remember what Picasso said about people who deal in art: they're mostly impostors. Still, I'm not exactly fond of Felix.'

'You should hate him. He let you drown – and me.'

'For the last I dislike him intensely. But my dear, nothing can be done. We must not brood on the past but trust in the future, hmmmm?'

'That's a very Christian attitude. One I'm struggling to acquire. With difficulty. You see I'm bitter. My life has been bought and sold and bartered away like an *objet d'art*.'

'That is the price one pays for being exquisite – and a little foolish. The latter runs in the family.'

'You've been good to Anthea. You're a good man.'

'If I hear that adjective applied once more to myself I shall do something really quite violent. I almost prefer slander.'

'You don't mean that.'

'Of course I don't. And now that you've imparted to me this information over which I shall brood later, may I put my infinitely tamer case to you?'

'Oh Charles, how can you treat it in this way?'

'Because I am a little foolish.'

'I wonder. Perhaps you are. You treasure some Greek ideal of goodness giving pleasure. You still don't understand how people get pleasure from evil and cause cruelty for fun. It's a terrible thing to have to admit to oneself. I know. But you won't see it, or you can't. Why can't you see that? It's a flaw in your character.'

'One of many.'

He asked if she knew where Jason and Clover might be. He was very simple and direct with her and did his best to keep her on an even keel. He considered her more unhappy than himself. It seemed suddenly easier to be the injured party.

'You mean it was about Clover you wanted to see me?'

'I'm sorry. I thought you understood that.'

Monica started to laugh. She ran a hand across her forehead and shook herself slightly.

'Oh cousin Charles, isn't it mad?'

Charles did not offer his opinion that it might very well get madder.

Monica changed her tone, very interested. 'You're searching for Jason and Clover. Why?'

'I'm not at liberty to say. There's some money – '

She stopped him. 'I understand. I'm acquainted with the "privileges" of the client. To my eternal chagrin.'

'Don't go on.'

'But there's money. Oh that's good, that's good.'

'And it's my duty to see that it's handed over to her. Being out of society for so long, I really don't know where to begin the search. I'd hoped you might give me a clue.'

'I've seen about as much of society as you, Charles. For a while I was very ill. I hid myself and clung to Jeremy and the children, and at the same time – can you imagine? – I kept hoping that Felix would come and take me away. Absurd, isn't it?'

'And you haven't seen or contacted your – um, Clover – during that time.'

'I sent Jason a few hundred pounds. I've done so often. But I wouldn't be surprised if he returned the money to Jeremy. A bargain is a bargain, you know. Now I've given up. The last time I rang I was told that the telephone had been disconnected. You think it monstrous of me not to see my own child. But I cannot. I gave my word. It was another bargain, another deal, another secret, another trap.'

'Sweet Monica, I sympathize completely. But you've heard nothing, all this time, about either of them?'

'No. Haven't you tried his family?'

'I've written. No reply as yet.'

She was quiet for a moment, looking into her tepid tea. Then she said, 'There was something a few months after Eleanor's funeral. What was it, what . . . I think George told Jeremy – oh I really was very muddled then – that Jason had gone to America.'

Charles's heart sank. 'Where in America?'

'Was it New York? New York would make sense. But I can't imagine his staying there. He would long for the country. And he would hate the competition.'

'He always seemed to me to expect to win the prize without entering the contest. Did he take Clover with him?'

'I don't know. She was never mentioned and I didn't dare ask. The subject didn't come up again in my presence, but that may have been Jeremy's censorship.'

'Then Jeremy might know.'

'If he does he'll tell you nothing besides what I've told you. Especially since he knows you know about me and Clover. He's wary of you. He finds it difficult to believe you've said nothing about the relationship since the day of the funeral.'

'I've said nothing at all. To anyone.'

'You're the soul of discretion. It's what he counts on. Otherwise he'd have tried to buy you back.'

'Only you have the right to make that revelation.'

'I have no rights. I've bartered my rights for safety.' She hesitated. 'Ask George Facer,' she suddenly said.

'What do you mean? Why George?'

'Technically he's still Jason's dealer.'

'Is he?'

'Yes. We don't see him much now. We've lost touch with the art world. But ask him, Charles. Make him give us something to pay for his treachery.'

'George is an excellent dealer. He did what he did to please a good client. Jeremy was a good client.'

'You're wrong. Like the rest of them, George pleases himself.'

'No doubt. Are you referring to a specific instance of self-pleasing?'

Monica's eyes gleamed. She smiled. She was thinking something over.

'I have a particular dislike for George.'

'My dear, is there anyone left of the male sex that you do care for?'

'None but you – the one to whom I've done irreparable damage. Life is grotesque.'

'Monica, you must not waste time over *mea culpas*. You may beat your breast to your heart's content at the Brompton Oratory. For now, please tell me what I ought to know and what I should do.' Charles was floundering once more in that uncharted ocean.

'Make him tell you. Imply that you know it was he.'

'He. He who what?'

177

'You really don't know. You can't guess.'

'Don't be deep, Monica. It's another of those things that doesn't suit you.'

'Use it, Charles. For once use what you know.'

'But I *don't* know. Will you please enlighten me?'

She leaned across the table and whispered, 'The Teniers.'

'Oh Lord, not that again!'

'Shhhh. I wasn't going to mention this, being such a cowardly person. I thought I might save it until later. But now – '

'What? What?'

'Haven't you ever wondered who informed the police?'

'Often, but – ' Charles broke off, staring at his cousin's unaccustomed smile of triumph. They were so close that their noses were practically touching.

'But,' he whispered, returning her smile, 'now I know.'

Both sat abruptly back in their chairs, relishing in silence the moment of comprehension. Even when it is grotesque, life can be amusing.

Finally Monica spoke. 'If George thinks that you know he told the van Zuptens and that you might tell Jeremy, he'll be your slave.'

How melodramatic she was. Must have been the father's side of the family. The High side.

'But why is he not yours?'

'It would only endanger me further. If Jeremy divorced me . . . he's threatened twice. He'd ask why I hadn't told him sooner about George's treachery. He'd want to know how I found out. I daren't further my own ends. It's too late. But I could further your ends – and Clover's.'

'How can you be sure I won't let everything slip? I could tell Jeremy and exonerate myself a little. Curry favour.'

'Base acts aren't your style. Besides, you don't want Jeremy's favour. Anyway I trust you.'

Charles sighed and pushed his plate away. 'You haven't finished your tea, cousin.'

'I don't want it. I want you to see George. He's the weakest link. If anyone knows about Jason, he does. I'm sure of it, don't ask me why. And you might make him extremely uncomfortable.'

'Not half as uncomfortable as I'd be. But I'll certainly see him.'

'Good.'

'And I've gotten a great deal more than I bargained for.'

'Also good, I hope.'

'Not sure. I've been trained to postpone the leap to conclusions.'

'But you are good at guessing.'

He laughed. 'Apparently not quite good enough.'

'Then are you able to guess how I found out about George? Remember the police kept the identity a secret.'

'Yes, I remember. But it wasn't my primary concern at the time.'

He thought for a moment. He saw a white card pass from one hand to another.

'Guess, Charles.' She was definitely enjoying this.

'Felix Koning.'

'Brilliant. How I admire you, Charles.'

'Do I pass Go?'

'Absolutely. How did you know?'

'I didn't. It was a shot in the dark, and I wasn't aware until now that *you* so liked these little games.'

'Like everyone, I'm devious.'

'So you are. It has helped you a little but not enough.'

'I shall be a bitter old woman. I won't go to heaven.'

'What rubbish. Don't you want to know how I guessed?'

'Of course.'

'You had an affair with Felix. George was unaware of the liaison. I knew of it because Eleanor saw you together and told me. She was not too bad at guessing either, certainly where Felix was concerned. I saw Felix and George chatting amicably the day of the funeral. Either they've patched up their differences or George doesn't know that Felix was the fence. Perhaps they have dealings together.'

'Deals! They're positively thick. You see Jeremy didn't tell George that Felix was the fence. He didn't want anyone to know about Felix and me. He was frightened of any talk about our business arrangements or – the other. And Felix didn't tell George of his earlier career. Somehow, *somehow* he found out about George and told me. He has a wonderful way of finding out. George would never have confessed. So Felix knows, but George doesn't know he knows. Isn't that amusing?'

'Very. As for George's motives – well, you yourself said it. He wished to please his clients. And van Zupten had a good deal more money than old Jeremy who was not exactly a pauper either.'

'Mr van Zupten bought a Dillon Butterworth – a big one – three months after the Teniers was returned.'

'There you are! George is an excellent dealer. But he failed to take into account the intimacies of the boudoir.'

'Or good guessers.'

'Maybe. But what I still can't guess is why, really, you didn't tell Jeremy about George.'

'Why?' She made an uncharacteristically cynical gesture. 'Why, for the secret, darling Charles, for the waiting and seeing, for the *fun*. A bit of fun for poor Monica.'

'I see.'

'Mmmmm – no you don't but never mind.'

'And what about the Felix and George alliance? Jeremy must be stung by the irony of that – though not the full irony, thanks to you.'

'He's stung all right. But what can he do? He can't tell one tale without telling lots of tales. The three of them are checkmated. And all because of you.'

'Well . . . '

Monica glanced at her watch. The animation of pleasure drained from her face. She was a tiny, timid woman again. A withering child.

'Charles, I must go. I said I'd be home by four-thirty.'

'I'll walk you to the square.'

She blanched.

'Don't worry. Only to the corner. And I trust we won't meet any ghosts – dead or alive.'

She was silent most of the way up the Brompton Road. Christmas shoppers already pushed and shoved their way through the doors at Harrods: English, Americans, Germans, Italians, Arabs. Charles imagined the thronged food halls – miles of glass display cases featuring dairy products in various stages of acclaimed decay. He saw plump hands, white and brown, grasping at sugar and blood.

He and Monica turned the corner by Harvey Nichols and stopped in front of Sloane Pearls. She stood looking at a double rope of grey-black gems.

'Some day,' she said dreamily, 'I shall make Clover a present of one of those. Perhaps when she's twenty-one.'

'But you won't see her.'

She gave him the sweetest smile. 'Jeremy may always die.'

'My dear, and you may very well *not* go to heaven.'

It was cold and a fog was settling. Traffic was at a standstill. The square was beautiful in the mist and gathering twilight. The smoke of bonfires was pungent in the air.

'It's very mysterious,' said Charles.

'Not when all the sinister motives have been unearthed.'

'I meant the square.'

Monica shrugged. 'Yes, it's beautiful. A beautiful prison. I hope you're not distressed by what I told you.'

'I'm satisfied. It was a human equation after all.'

'Everyone who helps is punished. You, me, Eleanor. Punished for helping.'

'So it seems.' He yielded temporarily to her negativity.

'If you find her, tell me. You needn't say anything beyond what concerns her health and welfare.'

'I'll certainly tell you about Clover if I can find her.'

'And Felix – but perhaps you can't – '

He took her hand and raised it to his lips.

'I don't deserve your affection, Charles.'

He kissed the tiny claw.

'Wish me luck,' he said.

'With all my heart. Goodbye, dear Charles.'

'Goodbye.'

He watched her cross the road, pass the hotel and turn right into the square. He caught a glimpse of her small figure as she mounted the steps of number thirty-seven. The lights went off in Sloane Pearls as he turned towards the Underground. He could not leave his cousin to heaven, where she might not go, so he left her to the square, the Brompton Oratory and her terrible safety.

twenty

The Facer Gallery had changed completely. Over the last three years extensive renovations had been made in the Cork Street building. The floor above had been annexed, as had the next-door gallery, and substantial sums laid out for architects, builders, lighting and decor. Substantial sums were readily available. George Facer was prospering. He had recently wooed three important painters, two important sculptors and a conceptual artist away from competing dealers with promises of New York and Cologne shows, and even, in one case, a Lichtenstein account.

The floors were highly polished, the furniture hard, understated, dark and very expensive, the lighting impeccable. It was an ambiance both sumptuous and frigid, calculated to intimidate rather than invite. Charles found it difficult to imagine it as the cosy concern which had abortively launched Jason Englefield into the world of high art more than ten years ago. Was this where he had stood bemused while Eleanor and Jason swayed in each other's arms and where he had first encountered the moppet who was now, unknown to herself, forcing him out of his cocoon and back into the big, bad world in quest of her? On that night, on these walls, or their less well-appointed equivalent, had hung the drawing, now hastily wrapped in brown paper and string, that he carried under his left arm. Charles's sense of occasion was strong. He never left home without it.

He had wandered a while through the Mayfair galleries, putting off facing George Facer. It had been five years since he had passed an idle visual morning like that. And what novelties, what mutations he had seen! Every establishment (and there were several newcomers) overflowed with proliferating alternative styles, offered for sale in a manner haughty, chic or iconoclastic. Charles had found figuration behind one door, installations behind the next. His walking tour embraced symbolism, fantasy and anti-naturalism, social relevance, neo-romanticism, quasi-mysticism, documenta, neo-expressionism, American comic book graffiti, whimsical British literariness, Italian anachronisms. The whole circus of post-Modern eclecticism was running rings around his tired eyes. It amused and mildly alarmed him. He could only summarize what he had seen as a morbid retreat from rational thought.

He took up a gallery leaflet and read that Facer Fine Arts had opened branches in New York and Houston and that another was planned for Rome. Well, well. He pocketed the leaflet and began to study the paintings which comprised a selection of new works by a German artist he did not know but who Anthea later assured him was fashionable. He read the accompanying cards and saw that two of the pictures were on loan from museums. George had been dealing high. He had acquired some very grand connections. Charles found the paintings trivial despite their dimensions, their fastidious blues and greys a bore. Still, they would suit the right office or the right sitting-room. And clearly it was at FFA that the right picture might become engaged to the right sitting-room. FFA was a *bon ton* marriage bureau.

Next door, Dillon Butterworth's composite photographs were spread in glory. Charles was tempted but restrained himself from yet another postponement. It really was time to march into George's second-floor office and put his case.

As he moved towards the lift, the doors opened with barely a sound to admit half a dozen well-heeled people, all middle-aged but the last. This was a dark, young woman who spoke with an Italian accent that was probably Roman. She carried several documents, one of which she waved at the retreating back of the man she was following. The man was tall, slender, fair, tastefully rather than fashionably dressed, quite distinguished; arresting not handsome, and not at all English. His movements gave him an air of being simultaneously distracted and engrossed, as though he were looking for something that wasn't there and he knew couldn't possibly be found. (Not this, not that. Above all, not you.) Yet he looked, not seeing because he was looking, not hearing because he was listening.

Charles, rehearsing his speech to George Facer, accidentally brushed the man's arm with his package. The man's reactions were immediate, betraying a nervous sensitivity his surface concealed. He turned to Charles who murmured an apology then stopped short when he recognized the bright eyes of Felix Koning. Prepared for the deep blue sea, he had found the devil himself.

Mixed amusement and distaste crossed the faces of both men, then were efficiently masked. Felix extended a hand which Charles took without hesitation. In the age of social enlightenment they played the same games they had always played and played them expertly.

'Well,' Felix opened, 'that you were dead was clearly a salacious rumour.'

Charles drew back a little. He was unprepared for such a first bid. 'Perhaps it is a true rumour. Perhaps I am dead.'

'In which case we are having a combined hallucination. Gina, do you see this man?'

'Of course I see him,' she snapped. Charles recognized her as the woman who had driven Felix's car on the day of the funeral.

'Darling, don't get in a huff.'

Gina scowled at him and marched off, her heels clicking on the parquet floor. Felix shrugged. He placed his hand on Charles's shoulder.

'How can I repay you, Charles, for providing an opportunity to rid myself of her for twenty minutes?'

The question was so brazen it almost took Charles's breath away.

'Perhaps you can help me to postpone something. Detain me, Felix.'

'Gladly, but how?'

'Oh, I don't know – tell me what you're doing here.'

Felix smiled. 'But that's too easy. I work here.'

'Really. And so you are also employed in – ' he consulted his leaflet, 'New York, Houston, and – '

'Rome. Yes. Gina is Rome unhappily.'

'You don't care for her?'

'I don't care for Italians. Like the Irish, they care too much. One must go to absurd lengths to arrive at the simplest little compromise.'

Felix was certainly bold. Charles hung on with his very toes.

'Tell me more.'

'You find this interesting?'

'Oh very.'

'All right. I supposed all the world knew, but apparently you haven't been much in the world.' He glanced at Charles's frayed cuffs. 'I have for the past eighteen months been a director of Facer Fine Arts. I travel a lot although I keep my flat in London. But you like paintings, Charles. Come and see my little collection. It has much improved.'

'I'm sure. Any Old Masters?' There! thought Charles.

'Not any more.' Felix fell silent. It had gone far enough.

'No doubt you're *en route* to some other capital?'

'Next week. New York. But now it's my turn. I can just as effectively detain you by putting questions, no? What are *you* doing here?'

'Come to see George.'

'Reluctantly.'

'With hesitation.'

'But why? George is so amiable. He'll be delighted to see you. Is it business?'

'Yes.'

'That?'

'Uh-huh.'

'I understand. May I see it? But let's sit down. You're right, this *is* interesting.'

'You think so?'

They moved towards a rather forbidding couch, the graphite-coloured upholstery of which was suspended from shiny steel girders. Charles produced *The Three Virtues* for Felix's inspection. Alarm flashed in his face. Charles saw Felix hand Jason a card. He bristled. Perhaps he could avoid George Facer after all. And Felix was nowhere near as dull a conversationalist as his employer.

'Recognize it?'

'A Jason Englefield. Quite early. It is not too bad. A bit soft . . . too . . . perhaps a little . . . And you came by it? – '

'Via the artist.'

Felix stared at it, not noticing Charles staring at him.

'Why are you selling it? Excuse my asking – you are short of funds?'

'I'm selling it for my wife,' said Charles adroitly.

'Aaaahhhhh. Aaaanthea. Yeeessss.'

Charles pressed his small advantage. 'Have you heard anything of Jason?'

'Nothing. And you?'

'Not a peep. Actually,' he waded in, 'I'd like to find them.'

'Would you?'

'Very much. The daughter in particular.'

Felix continued to stare at the drawing. 'He always thought he could think. Why, I wonder?'

'The thing is, I'm Clover's legal representative. There is a matter of some – '

'Money.' Felix was unmoved.

'When is it not?'

He looked up. 'Eleanor Linnane.'

'I'm not at liberty – '

'Of course, of course.' Felix waved a dismissive hand. 'You've had lunch?'

Charles said he had not.

'Then join me. I invite you. But first I must rearrange a little. I'm coming back shortly.'

So. Felix was eager enough to talk to him that he was hastening to disappoint Gina or some other young lady. There must have been quite a few young ladies since they had last met. Dozens. Well, perhaps not dozens. Felix's distinguished air seemed bred of an even more profound weariness. If his eyes were quicker, his limbs were slower. Then there was the voice, so devoid of edge or harshness that it made one suddenly wonder if one might be shouting. Charles had noted with satisfaction that Felix's hair had continued to thin. And 2007 years had mellowed his once dramatic face. But it remained as enigmatic as ever. The man might be thirty-five or sixty. Who knew?

As to Felix's motives, it did not take much acumen to detect the lurking of a vested interest. The forthcoming lunch involved more than business and curiosity. Felix wanted Charles to tell him something without Charles realizing how much Felix wanted to know it. He might also wish to prevent a meeting between Charles and George. Perhaps there was something about the Englefields he would rather George didn't know. One thing was certain. The two men intended to sound each other, with the object of what Felix would call a little compromise. At any rate, Charles welcomed the diversion and the lunch.

'Charles, you are deep in musing.' Felix still made the occasional but always charming syntactical slip. Perhaps on purpose. Who knew?

On the way to the restaurant they talked only of art. Charles was eager to be brought up to date and Felix keen to oblige. He was not only well-informed, but knew everyone who mattered, had mattered or was about to matter. About his connections he was very enthusiastic. Charles caught the rare betrayal of a weakness. Felix was a snob. Worse than George and Anthea combined, he'd wager.

Charles had not eaten in the Caprice since 1978 and said as much to Felix whose response was to raise an eyebrow and call for the Carte des Vins. Charles was positively salivating. And to think he used to live like this all the time and could not do so anymore, probably never again, and mainly because of the creature seated opposite him who now lived like this all the time. Felix abruptly handed him the list.

'You choose. I drink very little at lunch.' Implying that Charles, being without affairs, might get as tanked up as he liked as well as loosen his tongue as much as Felix might require.

'With pleasure.' He hit immediately on a Pommard 1973.

'Hmmmm,' said Felix.

Charles allowed himself the luxury of a silent tasting before firing his first question straight at his host.

'Delicious. Try it. Then tell me, where are Jason and Clover Englefield?'

'Haven't a clue.'

'More of a clue than I.'

'I do?'

(Indeed you do, Snake. And you are worried I might know something you'd rather I didn't. Still, you're jolly well going to go first.)

'Do not fence with me, Herr Koning. An innocent girl's future is not meat for the jaded repartee of two middle-aged men, as delicious as they might find it.'

'Always gallant.' He made the slightest indication of a bow. 'Of course you're right. I'm just cautious.'

'With good reason, no doubt. But you're not being asked to incriminate yourself. Only help me please to find her.' Charles hesitated. 'It's the least you can do.'

'You've tried, naturally, other sources – parents, friends. But of course he has no friends. Ah, there is Dillon.'

'All dead ends,' Charles lied for his noble cause and to speed things along. Felix did not include Monica. Had she never told him? Had Eleanor never told him? Well, for the present he would not refer to Monica either. It was unchivalrous and might complicate matters unnecessarily. 'I'm stumped, you see. I need your help, Felix.'

Felix filled Charles's empty glass. 'I'm glad to help. But what I say is in your confidence – for the benefit of them, you understand. You will repeat only what assists you in discovering the young woman.'

More secrets.

'Please begin.'

Felix addressed him over his gravadlax.

'I first visited the Englefields in Sussex just after that ghastly funeral. Jason's technique had improved. His paintings interested me in a way they had before not. But his financial problems had compounded. The place was in chaos, the phone disconnected, he had several outstanding debts. And he was about to lose his position at the art college. Cutbacks. You know. I offered to relieve his desperate state. I offered to try, to *try* to sell his work in America. His back was, as one says, to the wall. He accepted my offer and a loan of £300. I told him it would be necessary to photograph the paintings, for which I myself would pay. To do this I would return in a week with a photographer who would make and number two sets of slides. One of these I would take to America plus two small paintings on consignment. He agreed, seemed even pleased and relieved. I don't think he trusted me, but then he trusts no one. As I said, his back was to the wall.'

'And were you representing yourself or George in this transaction?'

'Learned friend, I'm not in your witness box. My business arrangements are not being, I think, germane to the case. I'm not obliged, despite past misunderstandings, to render you an account of them. You asked me about the Englefields – '

'Yes, yes. Go on.'

'Allow me to complete first my statement. I did not invite you to interfere in the mess of the Teniers. You must know that I was, I am, very capable of saving myself.'

'You weren't the only one who wanted saving.'

'Ach! Monica simply panicked and the rest of you were infected by her hysteria.'

Charles could not deny it. Dear God, there just weren't any rules.

'Felix, I did not come to accuse you. I didn't even come to *see* you.'

Felix smiled. 'Sorry to be sharp. But your solicitude on my behalf still puzzles me.'

(Of course you're puzzled, Snake. What would you know of love's extremities, except from the receiving end?)

'On that score I'm not prepared to enlighten *you*.'

Felix shrugged. 'Another bottle?'

'Why not? But go on.'

'Yes. His back to the wall. I his only hope. His life disintegrating around him. The girl practically in rags.'

'You saw her?'

'Once or twice.' Felix took a longer sip of wine. 'She went in and out, said little.' He paused. 'You will not misinterpret if I tell you I saved them.'

'Then you were successful?'

'In one month I had sold the two small paintings and obtained promises for the sale of three more. Some inconsequential people in Seattle. But they have money and they listen to me.'

They are also women, thought Charles.

'Jason was stunned. Within three months I had doubled his income. I paid him immediately and took only a small commission for myself. He began to be sensible about America. He saw that he could not play the reclusive genius for ever and that I was the only person upon whom he could rely.'

(God help him!)

'Sometimes,' Felix went on, 'it is a great advantage to imagine oneself a genius. Normally, the delusion is a serious impediment to progress.'

'On that we agree.'

'I tried to persuade him to relinquish his beloved sty and emigrate. He opposed. I went away and returned in a month, another painting disposed of and another cheque for him. No opposing this time. I arranged for their passage, along with the packing, shipping and insuring of all the paintings. We left in August.'

'We?'

'Jason, the girl, myself. I was anyway required in New York. I found them temporary quarters in a loft off Hudson Street, very well appointed. I arranged for the girl a good school. Her father's fortunes were improving rapidly. Still, he was a very resisting person – suspecting, grumbling, always disagreeable. He could never have managed prospective buyers without me. About that time George opened the New York gallery. I persuaded them both to renegotiate. They did, with the result that George promised him a show the following autumn. To everyone's surprise, my own included, it was a success. A *succès fou*. The reviews were not discouraging. He was made much of. All was, as you say, before him. But he was, as usual, self-destructing. Leopards are not changing their spots.'

(Nor snakes, although they may shed their skins.)

'I think he's mad – ' Felix broke off with a twitch of the mouth.

'Possibly. What did he do?'

'Turned on George and myself. Turned on the whole art world. His typical behaviour pattern – treating shabbily anyone who helps him. Eleanor suffered a similar fate. He fears to be in what he interprets as someone's debt. His tactic is to accuse of exploitation. In short, he is an ingrate. And his work is overrated. His vogue was brief and his ensuing oblivion will be permanent. For a second-rate artist he could have gone far. Americans liked his pretentions. I knew they would. They found in his work what is not there and what he did not intend to be there. His personality invited a kind of transient celebration. The art market still demands heroes, provided they do not hang too long around. If he chooses to shut himself again away, that's not my fault. I made him a great deal of money. He behaved as though I had tried to take his life.'

'How so?'

'Threatened me, threatened George. Accusing us both of very libellous things, packing up, leaving New York. Legions of lawyers. (Perhaps *you* should move to America.) Then arrived the abusive letters. Then the abusive letters stop. No lawyers, no telephone calls, no address, no Jason. One can't do business with a man like that.'

'You mean he disappeared?'

'Yes.'

'When did he leave New York?'

'November 1983.'

'And the girl with him?'

'I suppose.'

'But if there was a correspondence with FFA, there must have been a return address.'

'There was.'

'What?'

Felix hesitated. His eyes were full of fine, sharp points.

'I'll tell you on condition that, for reasons of my own, you inform me and not George if you discover the Englefields. We have unfinished business. Money, et cetera. Contested paintings. You can imagine.'

'Of course. You have my word.' (Why not?) 'Besides, I have no wish to see George, as you guessed.' He reached for his pen.

'Don't bother to write it down. The address is unforgettable.'

'Yes?'

'Jason Englefield. Box 100. Hurricane, Utah.'

'Amazing. And that's all the information you have?'

'All that will do you any good, except that he's not now there.'

Felix looked him in the eye, serious, probing, malicious. Then a smile gathered up the fine lines above his cheekbones.

'I leave them with you, Charles. The bottle of wine and the Englefields. I must return to Kunst. Contact me when you have run the vixen to ground. Give her my best and advise her to leave her father to his ruination pursuits. She deserves better, I think.'

'So does Mrs Draine.'

'Who?'

'Friend of the family. Goodbye, Felix. Thanks for lunch.'

Felix nodded.

He walked out, stopping on the way at two other tables. Charles began ruminatively to finish off the bottle. In a moment Felix was back.

'But Charles, where are you?'

'In Limbo.'

He laughed. 'Does Limbo have a telephone? You must not be quite as unobtainable as the dead.'

'No telephone. An address of sorts.'

Felix removed his Filofax and entered Perth Hotel in a broad, balanced hand.

'I'll give you £1,000 for the drawing,' he said. 'I'll give you cash. That will be useful.'

Yet again Charles could feel Felix wanting to snatch everything from him. He was damned if he'd let him get the drawing, especially when he hadn't wanted to sell it in the first place.

'Yes, but no. I mean no thank you. Or rather, not now.'

'£1,200 then. But next week it will be again £1,000.' He smiled. Charles shook his head. Felix laid a hand on his shoulder.

'I'll write. Regards to Anthea.'

Charles returned to his glass. Already he was putting pieces together. Felix, as usual, had skimmed off all the cream.

IV

. . . .

C L O V E R

twenty-one

He had come back. She saw at once the Mercedes, the registration number of which she had memorized on his first visit. She jumped off her bicycle and dragged it to the beautiful automobile. Shading her face from the April sun's reflections, she peered through the window at the immaculate interior. He had said he didn't care for driving. Clover, who longed to drive, was puzzled by his disinclination. But then he was a person who did many things he did not seem to care for, at least not very much. She didn't understand Felix Koning. But his eyes were kind and he had a beautiful car. She had wondered for weeks what his life was like and where he came from. She wanted to ask Jason about him, but she was too shy. Her shyness worried her. She could not explain it to herself, and there was no one in the world whom she might ask for an explanation.

Instead of bursting in on her father as usual, she parked her bicycle under the oak tree, went discreetly round to the studio window, and dropped beneath the rose bushes which were sprouting leaves of deep new red. Cautiously, she peeped over the edge of the sill. They were taking pictures of the paintings – Jason, Felix and the woman photographer Felix had brought with him. All three looked very serious. Jason was smoking intently. Felix stood furthest from the window, leaning against the table, one hand in his pocket. Clover raised herself to shoulder level. He saw her immediately, as though he had been expecting her. He made no move, held his languid pose, gave her a slight smile. But his eyes locked into hers like missing pieces of a jig-saw puzzle. The excitement in those eyes both frightened and pleased her, because she knew the source of it to be herself. He had never told her that, never said anything, really, since the day of Eleanor's funeral. But she recognized the excitement. She was sure of it as she had never been sure of anything before. It was so important, so mysterious.

She wanted to smile. To smile was always her first reaction. But the awful shyness had taken hold of her and she could only stare at him, thinking how glad she was that he could not see her wrinkled, grubby uniform, too small for the exuberant growth of her fifteenth year, and the hole in her tights which would have shown him a knee cross-hatched with scars. She was painfully conscious of her pinned-up hair slipping down the back of her neck and flapping in the breeze. Suddenly, she disappeared into the shelter of the rose bushes. Jason had turned round to fetch another painting and she had anticipated his movement. She crept on her hands and knees to the corner of the house, stood up, brushed herself off and ran round to the back door, the one nearest her bedroom, her only thought being to alter her appearance as completely as possible.

She flung the uniform into a corner. She ravaged the bottom of her wardrobe – the repository of dirty laundry which might or might not be collected every two weeks – and pulled out a pair of striped calf-length trousers which she had pleaded with Jason to buy for her and to the purchase of which he had consented with reluctance. Impatiently she wriggled into them, barely able to close the zip and wondering if her bottom were getting too big. She pulled on two black legwarmers, the elastic of which was nearly spent so that they drooped annoyingly after five minutes' wear. She unfastened the detested brassière the headmistress had pressed her to buy and kicked it contemptuously under the bed. She saw no point in constraining a bosom which was quite able to hold itself up without assistance, thank you. She looked at her pale, prominent nipples in the glass, then did her hair in an arrangement of plaits, mauve and orange clips, and bows of pink and yellow wool. The whole was more or less controlled by a ragged Indian scarf that still sported a few of its original gold threads and which had been a present from Dolly Four. From her desk drawer she took her precious, secret, blue mascara and drew it over her lashes again and again, being especially careful despite the time she felt flying so fast away. 'Oh wait for me,' she prayed, 'wait for me, see me, look at me, but please, please don't speak to me. If you speak to me, oh God, if you speak . . .' She opened her summer drawer and selected a pink T-shirt which Emma had given her and which Jason disapproved of her wearing because it had words on it. The words said Number One Daughter. This she covered with an old, tartan jacket, too small. She looked again in the mirror. It was all horrible. But what could she do?

She tugged at her wellies and, with difficulty, managed to pull them over the legwarmers. Any moment Jason would come to look for her thinking she was late home from school. As she opened the back door, she heard his footsteps along the hall.

Keeping close to the house and running on tiptoe, she arrived again at the studio window before Jason had opened the door to her bedroom. This time she stood in full view of Felix who was conferring with the photographer. She rapped on the window. He turned to her. She did not understand herself, her behaviour, Felix, anything. She only knew she couldn't not do this. Felix came to the window and opened it.

'Hello,' he said.

She could see how he took her in, his eyes moving and glinting, fastening upon nothing but her. She did not reply, and held out her hand to him like a French girl.

Amused, he took it and put it to his lips, kissing the back, then the palm. She snatched it away and, without thinking, wiped it on her trousers.

Felix was unoffended. 'Will you come out with me?' he asked softly. 'Clover, will you show me something lovely?'

She stared at him in confusion. There was nothing to refer to, no one to grasp. Only him and he was terrifying. Yet she ran round to the French windows and opened them, facing him frontally, giving him an unimpeded view of all her five feet and eight inches, done up in concoctions he would have called rags. For the first time in his life Felix liked rags. Then she turned and, without looking back, ran towards the dyke. He followed her, despite the effects of the damp ground on his Italian shoes.

When Jason returned to the studio, he found the photographer hard at work. He saw the bicycle under the tree and assumed Clover had gone off into the fields with Emma. She'll come later, he thought, and asked Gina for a cigarette.

Felix found Clover beside the dyke whose banks were a combination of new, green reeds and the fragile, spiky corpses of dead ones, relics of seasons gone for ever. Ghosts among children. She stood with her back to him, delineated against the far beginnings of the Downs. She had removed her jacket. He stood behind her and she could feel him staring at her bare skin, her freckles, her loosening strands of hair. She knew he wanted to touch her. Yet he kept perfectly still.

'I'm looking for the heron's nest,' she said.

He asked if she saw the heron often.

'Oh yes,' she replied. 'He flies over every day.'

'To see you.'

'Me?' She faced him, smiling, embarrassed.

'Of course. Aren't you the most interesting creature in this wilderness? Who wouldn't want to spy on you?'

'It's not a wilderness, exactly.'

'You're right. I've altered my opinion of it.'

'Look, you can see the hotel over there. My friend's father is the chef, you know.'

'I'd much rather see the heron's nest.'

Clover eyed his shoes. 'Can you make it down to the water? It's not too terribly steep.' She was in her own element now, relaxed and wanting to take control.

'Must we really go down that bank?'

She feigned impatience. 'Just give me your hand.' He seized hers and pressed it. 'Now step where I step.'

They went down the bank, treading carefully, he letting her lead.

'This is much too easy,' said Felix.

'Shhhh! Be absolutely quiet.'

'All right.'

She thumped him on the arm. 'Get down,' she hissed and yanked him into a squatting position from which they might both, unless they clutched at the grassy tufts along the edge, have slipped into the water. She realized this was not quite what Felix had in mind. Nevertheless she continued to hold his hand while he studied at leisure her back and shoulders.

'There,' she whispered, letting go of his hand to point to a spot directly opposite them. 'See?' She forgot flirtation in the excitement of finding the occupier of the nest at home.

'Why yes,' Felix whispered too. 'She's wonderful.'

'He.'

'He.'

She leaned forward for a better view. As she did so, the soft bank gave way and she slid into the dyke with a splash as the heron took majestically to the air.

Clover stood in muddy water to the top of her knees. In silence they took in her state. Then they both laughed, loudly, almost without control. She had never heard Felix laugh.

'This always happens,' she gasped. 'I've been coming to this damned dyke for eight years and I still fall in about once a week. I can't tell you – how Jason and Eleanor used to scold me.' She laughed again. 'I was always getting my school shoes wet.'

Felix wiped his eyes. 'It was a magnificent landing.'

He took her extended hand and helped her to the top of the bank. She sat down and removed her wellies and soggy socks and legwarmers.

'I'm expecting Jeremy Fisher to jump out of one of these.'

Clover smiled. Felix took off his jacket and laid it on a patch of sheep-nibbled grass.

'Beauty, sit here,' he said, gazing at her ankles.

Clover hesitated then stood up. 'Watch,' she said and began walking about on her hands.

'Well. You've certainly mastered *that*.'

'It's taken me,' she landed lightly on her feet, 'years. I can do back-flips too and – '

'But it does make your face so red. Come here, why don't you.'

She shrugged and sat down next to him. He took her hand again. She felt unsure of both herself and whatever it was she wanted.

'Shall I show you the swans?' She couldn't bear the way he was looking at her.

'Not now. Kiss me instead.'

'Why?'

'Because I want you to.'

If she kissed him he couldn't look at her. 'All right.'

They kissed each other quickly on the mouth. He did not clutch her and grapple with her as Emma's brother did. He simply kissed her, keeping his eyes open, then touched the wisps of hair around her temples, then let her go. It was when he let her go that she wanted to kiss him again.

'Clover, what do you like best?'

'Oh dancing, reading, laughing. Things everybody likes. Music, talking. I like The Police.'

Felix made a face.

'I like Mozart.'

'Very good.'

'And Mahler.'

'He's excessive.'

'Sometimes I listen to pop music on the radio but Jason doesn't like me to. I listen at Emma's and sometimes at night when Jay's asleep. I even watch television, which he really hates. But I tell him when I do.'

'Do you tell him everything?'

'Everything I can say. Some things can't be said.'

'Clover, let me look at you.'

'Why? – no, don't tell me. *Because you want to.*'

'Some things can't be said.' He tugged at the hem of her T-shirt. 'I'm shy.'

'But I like that.' He tugged again. 'Come.'

She hesitated then pulled off the T-shirt, taking the Indian scarf with it and destructuring her hair.

'You're every minute more disarranged.' His fingers touched her nipples and she watched while he brought them to hard little points.

'Isn't it mysterious?' he whispered. 'Why do they do that I wonder?'

She waited for what he would do next. He stopped.

'Do you like that, Clover?'

'Not your stopping, I don't.'

'Why?'

'I don't know,' she answered a little petulantly.

'But I want to please you. That's why I ask.'

'How can I know what pleases me? I don't even – I don't – ' She felt the threat of mortifying tears.

'Ah, that's what I thought. Now don't cry.'

'I'm *not* crying.'

'Of course you're not. Kiss me. And really this time.'

She put her arms around Felix's neck. She let him press her gently backwards on to his jacket. Instinctively, she slid her thigh between his legs while her back obeyed the insistence of his hands that she come close to him, as close as close could be. He touched her everywhere. She felt faint, sick, blind with happiness.

'Felix,' she whispered.

'Yes.'

'Are you going to take my virginity?'

'I haven't made up my mind.'

'*Will* you take my virginity?'

'Why?'

'Because I want you to.'

Abruptly he held her to him, harder than before, so that she gasped in surprise.

'Yes,' he said, through the tangles of her hair and the bits of wool. 'Yes, but not now.'

'Why not?'

'Because your father is not a fool and I am not a madman.'

'I suppose you're right. Jason wouldn't like it.'

'He would like it less than the television.'

'Anyway,' she jumped up and began turning cartwheels. 'Anyway – anyway – you will – won't you?'

Felix was stretched on the grass, leaning on his elbow, watching her. She stopped and stood over him, panting. They looked at each other. Felix's face had changed completely. The eyes were not sparkling, they were not teasing, they were not merry, they were not kind. They seemed to have turned inwards, dragging the image of her back into themselves.

'Now,' she thought. 'He is thinking Now.'

She lifted her naked foot and made a movement to place it on his exposed neck. The foot hovered for a second above the neck. Felix's breathing was rapid and shallow. Lightly, barely touching, she pressed her foot against a little throbbing vein.

'*Erbarmen*,' he whispered and closed his eyes.

She started to giggle.

'*Erbarmen*.'

The word was barely audible. It seemed terrible. What did it mean?

She snatched her foot away and stepped back, as if she had found something startling under a stone or brushed an unexpected presence in the dark. Felix opened his eyes. Holding his gaze, she stooped and picked up her T-shirt. He held out his hand to her, but she turned and ran, leaving her wet socks and wellingtons all over the grass.

An hour later Jason found her, mascara removed, absorbed in *Madame Bovary*.

Clover did not see Felix again until June. She understood that he had gone to America, that he was helping Jason and that he was also being careful about Jason. That he would come again she did not doubt. Not so much – not at all – because he was a man of his word, but because he would never stop until he got what he wanted. She knew that about him and she knew he wanted her. She pined for him a little and fantasized about him non-stop. As to looks, she told herself, he is not the greatest. But he can pull you to him – with his eyes, his voice, the way he moves. In these respects he was not unlike a woman.

Felix seemed always to be giving an inward No. No, not good enough, no, not quite; no, not to my elevated and very specialized taste; no, not beautiful enough, not peculiar enough, not ugly enough. Clover understood how this inner no might make some people very nervous. One might easily live one's life in preparation for the abrupt and irreversible exit, wondering if one were satisfactory and if not why not, forever under the shadow of the reject stamp. But that was precisely why, when he turned on you the full force of his approval, the resultant happiness was total and unique. He had turned his approval on her. She was engulfed by his rare yes. She with her torn tights and dirty nails could not see why, but she imagined it had something to do with an aspect of his specialized taste. She was an acquisition to be made at all costs. He had never sampled anything quite like her.

So she went ahead with her life, certain of being acquired. She felt not at all passive, for she too was on the verge of obtaining her prize. Felix was not the only one with standards. She too was capable of knowing exactly what she wanted. Felix was very fine. He was like platinum; clichés could not touch him. Other men seemed suddenly like louts. She discouraged then repelled the advances of a baffled Stuart Tozer. Her grades slumped, and she gave no thought to the fact that she was about to deceive her father.

twenty-two

One afternoon in June Clover returned from school to find the Mercedes at the entrance to the lane, now degenerated into a condition even worse than on the day of her ninth birthday. Felix sat in the car, alone. He had driven, alone, to see her. No chauffeuse. She saw him watch her approach through the rear-view mirror. He opened the door and got out. Clover drew to a halt, straddling the bicycle, her heart racing and no idea what to say. It occurred to her that she might have been fantasizing too much. There he stood in all the radiance of his freshly laundered shirt, as clean and smooth and polished as his automobile, with the difference that his sheen was permanent and his surface undentable.

'Beauty, hello. Are you going to open the gate for me?'

'All right.' She was absolutely serious, unable to return his smile. And she had been feeling so wonderfully brave. She opened the gate and the Mercedes bumped through. She closed the gate and went round to the driver's window, wishing with all her heart that Felix Koning would go away.

He looked her up and down. 'You've grown.'

'I haven't. I'm the same.'

'Intact,' he smiled.

She shook her head. 'I don't understand.'

'Yes you do. Anyway, I've brought something for Jason. Something he pretends not to like, but which he'll be very glad to get.'

'What's that?'

'Money.'

'Oh.' She laughed a little. 'I know what you mean about his pretending. It's a bore sometimes. He's ill today.'

'How interesting. What's wrong?'

'His teeth. They're rotten and he won't go to the dentist. He takes codeine until the pain stops. Stupid. I said he ought to have them seen to.'

'Well, I shan't take much of his time.'

'Aren't you staying?' Clover could not conceal her distress.

'I thought we might – meet. Later.' His eyes swept over the scene. A flock of sheep strolled across the paddock. No one else was about. Felix reached through the open window and touched her cheeks, her hair, her breasts.

'Darling little one. I've missed you so much.'

She stopped his hand and held it in both of hers, pressing with all her might.

'Oh,' she said, her face strained and urgent. 'What shall we do?'

'I think we'd better make a plan.'

A plan? Until now everything had just *happened.* Suddenly, she thought of Jason and was miserable. She gripped Felix's hand even harder. She must risk what she couldn't risk. It was Now and she knew it.

'When you've finished with my father, drive half-way up the lane and I'll meet you,' she said and pedalled off towards the house as fast as she could.

Even Felix's cheque and Felix's cash were insufficient distraction from the torment into which Jason had been plunged by the activity in his lower left molar. He could only nod over the encouraging news delivered in the dealer's subdued tones. He could hardly believe the prompt payment and solid projects, the plans for shows in Minneapolis and Fort Worth. Pain precluded his passing judgement. He couldn't carp with this particular gift-horse. Pain took precedent over the moral issues. Jason took the money. He said he would consider Felix's suggestions for his future. Felix offered to drive him to a chemist, a dentist, whomever he might require. Although not sympathetic, he had no objections to being of use. But Jason preferred suffering to assistance and loped away to his room, asking Felix to tell Clover, if he saw her, that he would want no supper and wished to be left alone. Felix promised to contact him the following week and, with a minimum of solicitousness, wished Clover's father better.

It was nearly six but the sun was still high among the purple-white clouds that hung over the Downs. Clover crouched by the hedge next to the road. She had brought her novel, not knowing how long Felix would be with her father. The book lay on the grass, unopened. Beside it was a bunch of campion she had gathered for Felix. They were looking sadder by the moment. She had picked them too soon. Did that mean everything was going to go wrong? She felt afraid of both Jason and Felix and wished she had Molly to hug.

She looked down at herself, at her white skirt of fake broderie anglaise, a plaid shirt of Jason's tied at the waist and a pair of dirty white plimsolls. All wrong as usual. In exasperation she began undoing the knots and plaits and ribbons she had woven into her hair. One side had fallen to her shoulders when she heard the sound of the engine. Forgetting everything but the first love affair of her life (groping with

Stuart Tozer and those other nanas didn't count at all), she stood up and waved at the approaching automobile.

Felix smiled at her dishevellment. Clover rushed at him with the bunch of flowers and thrust them through the window right into his smiling, shining, undentable face.

'There!' she said, as though she had just performed a back-flip. 'Do you like them?' She rested her hands on the window-ledge and lifted herself up and down, unable to control her agitation.

Felix brushed away what he must have thought was pollen.

'You are the most irregular girl,' he said. 'You are the sweet of the earth. Thank you.'

'They won't last.'

'Well, nothing does. Why don't you get in?'

'No. Come with me. Back to the house.'

'The house?'

'Why not? Jason thinks you've left, doesn't he?'

'But darling Clover, the – um – noise . . . '

'What noise? We'll be ever so quiet and Jason will be asleep.'

'That is absurdly optimistic. You will scream.'

'Will I?'

'Of course, unless you're more spartan than I supposed.'

'Stuff something in my mouth, then.'

'Really, my dear, I'm not a brute. Besides, it would be nice if you screamed. I don't think you'd care to miss it. I know I wouldn't. Believe me, the house is out of the question.'

How strange, she thought, to be negotiating so openly.

'I know a place!' She clapped her hands to her temples. 'Why didn't I think of it before? But we'll need sheets and blankets and pillows and things, otherwise we'll get kidney infections. I did once, you know.'

'The eminently practical Miss Englefield. Then it's to be *sur l'herbe*.'

'If that's what I think you mean, yes.'

Felix sighed. 'No doubt the appropriateness will compensate for the discomfort.' He got out of the car and locked the doors.

'Oh Felix, Felix!' Clover jumped on him, wrapping her arms around his neck and her bare legs around his waist. He stood holding her bottom in both hands, kissing her.

'Please, darling girl,' he gasped. 'Please let's go.'

She laughed and bumped to the ground. 'By the back way.' She took his hand and kissed it and kept it fast in hers. He followed her through a copse of beeches, then quickly across a field of Friesians to an earthen bridge leading to the opposite side of the dyke where their progress would be hidden by the reeds.

'Here.' She stopped, suddenly subdued. She pointed to a deep curve in the bank, surrounded by grass and reeds, not far from the water's edge, almost a cave.

'It's charming,' he said. 'It's a little bed.'

'It's my secret place. Wait here.'

Felix took her in his arms. 'Clover, I can't wait.' He was so serious.

'Please. I'll come quickly, I promise. I don't want you to get a kidney infection.'

'Most girls would be worried about something else.'

'What do I care what they worry about?'

In a few minutes she was back, carrying a pillow, two blankets and a sheet that trailed along the ground.

'Jason's snoring,' she announced and laid out their impromptu bed. Felix watched and said nothing. The water lapped around the reeds. High overhead swifts circled and dived. The Downs were distant waves, arrested, forever breaking. Slowly, slowly they engulfed the sun as Clover arranged the crumpled pillow on her hands and knees. Felix knelt behind her, lifted her white skirt and gently placed his hands on her hips.

'Clover,' he said, 'I love your secret place.'

Gently, he laid her down and undid the other side of her hair, removed her clothes and put them a little way off. She lay looking at everything he did, her eyes very wide, trusting him. Not that she wasn't afraid. She simply knew he wouldn't make a mess of things.

'Will you do it straightaway?' she asked.

'Of course not. I'll do other things first. Sit up and unbutton my shirt.'

'Really?'

'Yes. Then my belt and zip.'

'It's like dolls,' she laughed, diligently unfastening each of Felix's white buttons.

'This far.'

'You're so clean!' She marvelled at the shirt, the socks, the underwear, all of which she carefully folded for him, knowing instinctively what he would want. Without his clothes, she thought he was even better: legs long, bottom neat, no fat, even the spectre of some muscles, fair hair nicely distributed, one or two scars of interest. Only the sight of the erect penis made her quake a little.

They lay down together. He kissed her nipples, her belly, her thighs, her legs, her feet, her ears, her underarms, her vagina. At the last she jumped. She liked his other caresses better. He held fast to her hips and buried his face between her legs. It was so queer. Everything had stopped being romantic. She watched it all from outside. She could tell he was exerting great self-control to be gentle with her. When he kissed her again on the mouth, she tasted herself for the first time. Like her first sip of wine, she was unsure of the taste because it was new. But she was sure she would come to savour it and, like wine, taste quite a lot some day.

He took her face between his hands. She was surprised by his expression. She imagined it was how women looked when they were about to give birth. She felt afraid of him, sorry for him. He was both awesome and ridiculous.

'Clover,' he said, 'you're very beautiful. It's against my nature to damage anything so beautiful. But I cannot promise not to hurt you. And I cannot wait any longer.'

She bit her lip. 'But I don't want you to wait. It's all right. Really. I understand. Oh Felix,' she hugged him, 'I'd never have asked you to do this if I thought you'd – I mean, I just had this feeling that you'd be good to me.'

'Ha!'

The cynical outburst unnerved her, but she went on. 'I want to know everything. I want you to show me. I don't want to be a stupid little girl.' Hesitantly, she stroked his thinning hair. She knew she wasn't doing it properly.

'Darling girl,' he raised his head. 'I promise to show you. I'll just do it. Fast and hard, it's best. Hurt me if you need to.'

'Oh no, Felix, no.' She was not sure whether she meant no Felix I couldn't hurt you, or no don't do this to me. But she knew that flirting was over, that romance was over. This was serious business and there was no stopping it now. Some terrible engine had been switched on, impossible to switch off until it blew itself entirely out. He was so strong and he would not wait. Clover lay frozen in her appalling weakness. He forced open the legs that had suddenly clamped shut, his tenderness turned to steel. His weight, his urgency, the noises he made, the mad things he said filled her with panic. They had ceased to know each other, ceased to be human. She fought him, silently, her lips tight together, with all her strength and will, as though he were her murderer, as though her life were at stake. But he went on and on, allowing her not one second's respite from the pain which made her as blind and brutal as his pleasure made him.

'Don't,' she cried, 'don't.' Her whole being was concentrated on a single point of pain from which there was no escape until the point became a hot, sharp knife that ripped her through, simultaneously destroying and delivering her.

She lay panting as he panted beside her. She was dumb, ruined, wrecked. She would never walk or speak again. She had no name, no hope, no desire. She had no hate. How could she hate him when she didn't even know who he was? Besides, they were both dead anyway.

Clover awoke in Felix's arms. She became conscious of the warm evening and of the light that faded as it lingered, of a splash in the water, the first star, the breeze on her damp body, the blood between her legs. Her hand gripped Felix's shoulder.

'Well.' He was calm and smiling.

She kissed his cheek, aware for the first time of a trace of beard.

'Are you glad we did that, Clover?'

She smiled too. There was nothing to say. All the world seemed to reflect the two of them: the sky, the land, the air were one giant mirror. Wherever they looked they saw only themselves, delirious yet absolutely steady.

They went hand in hand to the water's edge. She saw there was blood on them both. She touched it, smelt it, tasted it. She was not at all shy. She put her hand on Felix's chest, pressing her palm against the soft hair, stroking slowly, a bit awkwardly, up and down. Then she let go of his hand and leaned slowly, slowly towards the water. He watched as she surrendered to gravity and sank beneath the surface. She lay on her back, washing herself and kicking high arches of sparkling drops into the insect-riddled air. He said he couldn't swim. So she came to him and knelt before him in the soft mud. She emptied handfuls of water over him, watching the blood as it ran in little rivulets down his long legs. He stood passively as she rubbed him with her hands until all the blood was washed away.

'Clover,' he touched her shining shoulders. 'Clover, shall I show you something?'

'Yes, please.'

He pressed her head towards him.

'Like that?' she asked.

'You're awfully quick.'

He stroked her wet hair, telling her where to put her hands, what to do with her tongue. She said he tasted salty and strange but good. He lifted her up.

'Would it hurt you, do you think, if I came inside you?'

She shook her head. They wrapped themselves in the blankets and threw the bloody sheet aside. All her spoiling self-consciousness had vanished like snow in the sun. She did not wait for Felix to show her how it must be done. She tried out her own feelings. She knew that what she did might not be right for critical Felix who only liked what he liked, but that didn't worry her. It was precisely her wanting to show him herself that pleased him. This was as new for him as for her, and he told her so.

'Have you never taken a girl's virginity before?'

'Yes. But never in such an exotic setting. Never with such interest and such pleasure. With more than pleasure.'

She tensed in his arms. Way, way off, someone was calling her name.

'Oh God,' she whispered, gripping Felix's arm, 'it's Jason.'

'Clover! Clover! Clov*er*!' Jason's voice was full of the old anxiety. How many times had he called her like that and how many times had she playfully or angrily hidden from him. All of a sudden she regretted her little trick for tormenting him. She felt so sorry for her father that she burst into tears.

'He's looking for me,' she sobbed into Felix's neck. 'It's getting dark. He's afraid I'll drown. Oh dear.'

'Shhhh, angel. Be practical. Can he find your secret place?'

'Of course not,' she sniffed, embarrassed that she had behaved like a stupid little girl.

'How far off is he?'

'By the copse, I think.'

'How do I get out of here? You will please instruct me.'

'Oh Felix, my head is scrambled eggs. Wait.' She sat up. 'I'll get dressed and go to him. Stay here ten minutes then go back to the car.' She began to dress. 'Just turn right at the top of the bank and follow the dyke until you come to the bridge. Then cross the field. It will be too dark to see you by then. Here's my torch.'

'Clever Clover. You are so prepared. For a moment I doubted you.'

'Don't doubt me, Felix. I'll leave the paddock gate open for you. Go around the back of the house and cut through the gap in the hedge which you'll see because the studio light will be on. You'll find the lane immediately.'

As she was about to go he caught her hand. 'Goodbye, my Clover. I can't remember when I last sat alone in a field. Perhaps I never did. But it has been a day for the new.'

'Oh Felix . . .'

'Better run.' He kissed her hand.

'Goodbye,' she whispered.

'Goodbye.'

In the near darkness Clover quickly spotted the questing point of Jason's torch. She skirted the copse so that she might run round behind him.

'Boo!' She leapt from out of the hedgerow, nearly knocking him down.

'Great Christ!' Jason gasped. 'Clover, will you *not* do that!'

She laughed nervously and backed away, suddenly aware of the way she smelled.

'You'll give me a cardiac arrest one day. Where have you been?'

'Walking.' She went towards the house. 'Reading.'

'Reading? Where's your book?' He turned the torch on her.

'I must have left it by the dyke.'

'Your hair's wet.'

'I had a swim, it was hot. How's your tooth?'

'Six on the agony scale. This afternoon it was ten.'

'Poor Jason. Shall I make you a cheese omelette and a cup of tea?'

'If you put whisky in it – the tea, that is.' She could hear the smile in his voice.

They stopped by the back door. The light was on and Jason saw the full extent of Clover's dishevellment.

'You look peculiar. Are you all right?'

'Of course,' she said, pretending to be impatient.

'Clover, don't frighten me again.'

'I won't. I'm sorry.'

'You always say that and you always break your word.'

'I'm sorry. I do keep it about other things.'

'That's true.' He took something from his pocket.

'Look, honey,' he began, 'I've had some good news today. I realize you need clothes and – oh, other things I don't understand or notice sometimes. Anyway, take this and do whatever you like with it.' He thrust something into her hand. It was a twenty-pound note.

'Thank you,' she murmured. As she followed him into the house, she heard the distant revving of a car engine. She stood on the steps until it had died away.

After supper, Jason retired to his room with a sci-fi novel. Clover did three days' worth of washing-up, her battered portable radio beside her at lowest volume. When she was certain Jason was asleep she took his torch and went back to the secret place to collect her bedding. She sat for a long time under the stars, turning her light on the bloody sheet and wondering what to do with it. There was no washing machine and she could hardly ask Jason to take it to the laundry.

On the way back to the house she saw the bright windows of the hotel across the fields. She thought of Emma and how she would react when she heard about Felix. Emma was still a virgin.

The next afternoon Clover buried the sheet in the copse.

twenty-three

'Whatever happens,' Emma said, 'don't tell your father.'

Clover covered her face with hands. 'God, I should hope not.'

Emma regarded her sceptically. 'I never know with you. You're capable of all sorts of nonsense. Just remember – Jason will murder you, and you'll never see your nice, smart boy-friend again. Do you want to see him again?'

'I want to see him like anything, but I don't know when that will be. He's a very careful person. He might not come for a while. Or,' she added with pride, 'he might turn up tomorrow. He's also very daring.'

Emma withheld judgement. 'You still haven't told me what it was like.'

'I learned a lot.'

'I hope you learned *something*.' When Emma was cynical or envious she looked like her mother. But her intense interest in the event and her genuine love for Clover could not be restrained. 'Was it painful?'

'Awfully. But not for long. With anyone else it would have been disaster.'

'What makes you so sure?'

'Intuition.'

'Wasn't Eleanor in love with Felix?'

'I think she was.'

'So what would she think about you and him together?'

Clover frowned. 'I hope she doesn't mind too much.'

Emma patted her arm. 'You're a weird person, Clover. You're some sort of alien. No one can understand you. No one but me.' Just then Emma looked very much like her mother.

On 25 August, three months before Clover's sixteenth birthday, the Englefields boarded a plane at Gatwick for New York. Clover's cello was in the hold, along with three small paintings by Jason. Fifteen other paintings had been sent on ahead. George Facer, persuaded by Felix to renew his business association with Jason, had agreed to foot the bill for their passage as well as the shipping and insuring of the paintings. FFA made many investments, the majority of them lucrative. They could afford to float an impecunious artist and his messy daughter – for a while.

Felix had pressed Jason to make the move to America and what appeared to be its very real prospects of artistic and financial success.

Encouraged by Felix's Fort Worth profits, George offered Jason a New York show the following autumn. Jason was tired and, in his tiredness and against his better judgement, had allowed himself to be helped. Besides, he could not entirely dislike or dismiss Felix, although he would have been loath to admit to this weakness. What did he care if Eleanor had gone to bed with him?

During the weeks of preparation for the trip, Felix and Clover seldom met. He found her once alone in the studio where she had been awaiting a happy accident.

'Beauty, hello,' he said.

Her dark-blue eyes were puzzled. Just at that moment they saw Jason ambling across the lawn towards the house. Clover ran out, slamming the studio door behind her and immediately regretting she had done so. What on earth was happening, to her, to Jason, to all of them? Emma insisted it was careful plotting on the part of Felix.

Emma was right. A few days before their departure, Felix returned with the photographer. To take more pictures, he said, and to take the Englefields to dinner. Clover was anxious. They had hardly spoken since the night in the secret place. She sat outside on a kitchen chair, a little distance from the house. The afternoon passed. Her novel lay open, face down on her bare legs. She had been crying. Someone stroked her hair.

'Why are you crying, Clover?' Felix asked.

'I miss the cats,' she wailed without shame.

Clover had pleaded successfully with Mrs Tozer, and Molly had been adopted. But adamant Jason had insisted that the others could fend for themselves and would find new and better accommodations within a week, by which time they would have completely forgotten her existence. Clover only knew they were being abandoned. She came as close as she ever had done to regarding Jason as a vile brute.

'Cats are very capable,' Felix took her in his arms. 'They never mind too much.'

'I want Molly,' she sobbed into his pink shirt.

'But I am assuring you, Molly will thrive.'

'No, no. She thinks I've abandoned her. I can't bear it.'

'You cannot bear it, but she is bearing it perfectly well. Profit by her example and don't cry. Your nose is a silly red.'

'Stop it,' she pushed him away. 'You can't trick me into believing anything is funny.'

He shrugged. 'Perhaps I can persuade you then. You may sit here in dreariness or you may come and let me be very, very nice to you.'

She hung her head, wiped her nose on the back of her sleeve, pushed a delinquent strand of hair from her face, said nothing.

'Do you want to make love to me again?' she finally muttered, not looking up.

'Ach, you silly girl. What do you think all this is for?' He gestured towards the house, the sky, New York.

Clover grasped the plot. She also grasped the hand with which Felix raised her chin.

'I hope some day Molly will forgive me,' she said. 'Where's Jason?'

'With the photographer. She likes artists and she's young – well, reasonably young. Be sweet to her at dinner.' He kissed her. 'But you are sweet to everyone.'

'I'm not.'

'Then be at least sweet to me.'

She put her arms around his waist and he gently removed them. 'Sweet. And discreet.' He pressed into her hand a packet of birth-control pills and kissed her on the forehead.

When Jason and Clover arrived in New York, Felix delivered them to a hotel in the East Thirties saying that he must go back to the gallery to attend to some business. They were to meet him for lunch tomorrow. Clover understood that he wished her to know where he lived and how to find him. He had explained nothing of this to her, nor had he referred to any plans for the future, but that was his way. She felt a moment of panic as he handed her her cello from the back of the taxi. His eyes met hers in the alien light. She stood on the pavement, holding her cello and watching his taxi disappear into the traffic on Lexington Avenue.

She took in the view of Manhattan from the windows of their suite, feeling as though she had been teleported to Jupiter or Neptune. She thought of Molly and the marsh and her poor, empty, lonely, abandoned, secret place. She was as distant from them as though she had died. She had expected to be thrilled by what she saw sprawling before her, to be unrestrainable in her efforts to rush out and meet it, to explore it and come to know it the way a smart young woman would know it. But the city, the future, her whole life seemed a prospect which offered nothing but arid novelty.

That evening Clover and Jason walked down Fifth Avenue, hand in hand, not speaking, their proximity of minimal aid their mutual loneliness.

'I'm starving,' she suddenly said, pulling Jason to a halt before the Miami Deli.

'So am I.'

Clover devoured a Reuben, asked for an extra kosher pickle, and briefly thought New York a very good place.

'Get the recipe for the Russian dressing, Jason,' she whispered, sampling his turkey club.

She watched him over the top of her chocolate milkshake. Without the presence of Felix to blur the boundaries of her perception, the full dimensions of her betrayal came suddenly and sharply into focus. She pushed the drink aside.

'I'm sick,' she said dully. 'Could we go now?'

'No more milkshakes for you, my lass.'

The table made a space between them larger than any Sussex swamp. If it had been six months ago, if they had not been marooned in New York, she could have looked him straight in the eye, said something mildly defiant at which he would pretend to take offence, then asked him point-blank what on earth was going on and why were they both feeling the way they felt. Even if it meant two days' ensuing silence, they could have defined their emotions or at least given vent to them. Such luxuries were now out of the question. Both were in pain and they could not admit to it. They were uprooted, unknown, ciphers on the streets. Once they might have been lulled by the sense of each other simply being there. But now their positions had become so intricate, so in conflict with their original intents, that nothing might ever be clear again. Clover gagged on the thought: nothing clear, nothing open, nothing explained ever, ever again – and all because she had been the object of the scrupulously unvulgar lust of a man three times her age. The former distances between her and her father seemed full of intimacy and safety by comparison. The chance of her immediate desolation ever being blown away like the grubby bits of paper that skidded along lower Fifth Avenue did not occur to her. She was still, in spite of Felix, a stupid little girl. She understood nothing, least of all her own behaviour. She let go of Jason's hand and thrust both her own into the deep pockets of her jacket. She was alone, even with the person she knew best. She was a figure, barely discernible, in an alien landscape. She was fifteen years old.

The awful blank which was, that night, their future, was sketched in by Felix when they went to lunch the following day. They were joined by three men, one young and trim who worked for Facer Fine Arts New York, the second a slug-like creature with little eyes and thick spectacles who Felix said was an important art critic, and the third a tall, skinny Frenchman with a large nose who reminded Clover of a chicken and to whom she and her father always referred as the Capon. There was talk of his writing the text of Jason's catalogue. When Jason later took exception to his persona, Felix chided him goodnaturedly.

'Never mind,' he said. 'He'll cluck for you.'

Clover sat in the plush, busy restaurant, watching them all, feeling at once under- and overdressed, unable to speak. The food was wonderful. She had never tasted anything like it. Was this how it would be from now on, she wondered: listening to other people talk about art and Jason's career while she stuffed herself out of depression and boredom, feeling nothing but the weight of her own presence? Schuyler, the trim young man, made strenuous efforts to be kind to her and, just as it was time to leave, she began to tell him about Molly and the cello and Emma and wanting to be a biologist. He stared at her incredulously.

Lunch was followed by a visit to the gallery. In the taxi they kept on talking. She thought how art just seemed to generate words. More and more, not less and less, had to be said and explained about contemporary painting. Everyone appeared to want to turn Jason's paintings into words.

Felix despatched Jason and Schuyler to the office where Jason's signature was required on a number of forms. It was as though he were being admitted to hospital. He stepped into the lift and cast a nervous glance at his daughter who was looking at a painting and standing next to Felix. He made a move to step out again but as he did so the doors suddenly closed.

Clover was edgy. What would happen now, oh what? Felix remained unperturbed as a boa constrictor. Once Jason was safely upstairs he pulled Clover into a small room, switched on the light and locked the door.

'Clover,' he said, stroking her under her jumper, 'it's been too long.'

She was sick at heart and not sure whether she wanted to run away from him or with him.

'Felix – ' She started to speak but he placed an envelope in her hand. Inside were five twenty-dollar bills wrapped in a piece of paper on which were printed Felix's address and telephone number both in New York and London.

'Call me at any time,' he said. 'Come to me when you can. The money is for taxis. I'd have given you more for clothes but Jason would suspect. It will be difficult. We must be for a while careful but even he cannot keep you always under lock and key. As soon as he begins painting, as soon as you're in school – '

A hundred windows opened showing her nothing but freedom. Once again, Felix had amazed her.

'This is the first present you've ever given me.'

'Really, did you think I would try to buy you with trinkets as though you were a pygmy?'

'It will be difficult . . . '

'Especially since I must go very often to London. But then,' he smiled, 'I must very often come back.'

'Still,' was all she could say, looking from the money to Felix, 'it will be difficult.'

'The difficulty will make it interesting. Surely you've learned that.'

'Yes,' she agreed. 'Where are we?'

'I think it's called the paper closet,' he answered and switched off the light.

On the way home in the taxi Jason's nostrils twitched in a way that made her very nervous.

'Time you had a bath,' he said.

'Oh Jason,' she wanted to snap as she normally would, 'you're such a creep.' Instead she said, 'I can't help it, you know. It's my period.'

'Oh. Sorry, love.'

God he was ignorant. He was so wrapped up in himself he could work nothing out, not even the scandal that was taking place under his very nose. There he sat, trusting her like a great big fool. The dreadful thought occurred to her that she might lose all respect for her father.

Jason was satisfied, in his grudging way, with Felix's social engineering. They were to stay another week at the hotel then move into a loft on Harrison Street which would be vacant for the eighteen months the occupants intended to spend in Sri Lanka. Jason would be able to start work immediately on his autumn show. Clover's schooling was also arranged. It amazed her that they had allowed the management of their lives to slip entirely into the hands of someone who, until six months ago, had been a perfect stranger.

She soon found her way to the perfect stranger's flat and went there as often as she could. She was partially aware of muting her conscience. Her budding internal mechanism for determining motives had been turned down, like a radio, so low as to be inaudible. It had not been switched off completely. She simply couldn't hear it and chose not to turn the volume up. She was fifteen and what was happening to her would never happen again. Consequences, she suspected, would come later. Right now she was having fun with the volume down. Felix was having fun. Even Jason was having fun. And no one seemed to be having to pay for anything. Past that and what she was learning during her afternoons with Felix, she refused to think. She wondered if it were love

216

that was so efficiently smothering one part of her nature so that another might emerge and flourish.

She went to Felix's apartment after school and did not come out until six. He insisted she have a bath before leaving since the combination of their smells was particularly pungent. And although he liked it very much – she was learning to like it too – Jason most certainly would not.

They sat in the large tub together, finishing off the wine he sometimes gave her because it was good for her, chatting and laughing and forgetting the time. Felix washed her tenderly like a baby, insisting she pay greater attention to her toenails, fingernails and ears, she was nearly sixteen, wasn't she? At first she found these attentions embarrassing – he was meant to be the man, after all, and she had only Jason to set the example of masculinity. Then she began to enjoy them as a manifestation of Felix's high sensuality. He extended pleasure in every direction, found it where one would not expect. She was feeling much less a stupid little girl.

And she pleased him hugely, she knew. What she had not yet mastered was a method of using him as she knew he used her, to take himself as far as he could go without leaving her too far behind. She guessed such a method must be arrived at unaided. Not even Felix could teach her *that*.

Once she asked him if he had had many stupid little girls, wanting very much a report on her progress.

'Contrary to popular belief, I have ravaged few maidens. Besides, I'm not a vulgar lecher. I like what's interesting. Maidens are seldom interesting for more than twenty minutes.'

'But *I'm* interesting.'

He kissed her between the legs. 'Extremely.'

'Why?'

'You have a style. Quite a rare one. But you're wanting to be flattered.'

'A little,' she admitted. 'By popular belief, do you mean people think you're wicked?'

'Yes.' He lay down beside her and covered their lazy bodies with the sheet. Afternoon light squeezed through the cracked curtains, making a lemon-coloured streak on the opposite wall.

'I don't think you're wicked.' She considered it gravely. 'You're only yourself. I mean people say sheep are stupid but they're not. They're just sheep.'

'The analogy is not exactly complimenting.'

'Then do you enjoy being thought of as wicked?'

'Mmmmm – yes.'

'I see. Well, I don't blame you. Only don't blame me if I don't think of you that way.'

'I promise I won't blame you.'

'You needn't promise me anything.'

'Well, for now just remember that the pupil must love the teacher. Lie on top of me and put your hand where I showed you.'

At school Clover made acquaintances but no friends. All her classmates were the sons and daughters of painters, sculptors, journalists, authors, film-makers or teachers of related subjects. Many of them did not wish to be there and some dropped out. They lived at home, roamed the streets of Manhattan, took drugs. Few were attractive. She found them overweight and a bit loutish, despite their cultural advantages. They seemed to have little or no ambition. Their parents had done it all. Their parents were the special ones. She regarded this laxity with some contempt. Still, their sophistication was undeniable and they seemed to like her foreign manner and accent. They enquired into her past and suggested alterations in her style of dress. (Her bizarre hair was universally approved.) But they could not make her out. She wasn't a punk or a bumpkin or an aristocrat, nor was she middle-class, bohemian, old-fashioned or modern. Shy until she warmed to a person, then communicative to the point of garrulousness. They asked her, to her face, where her off-switch was. She was strange, they all said. She was definitely up to something, but what? Clover smiled at their curiosity. She *was* up to something but precisely what was none of their business.

Her classmates invited her to films, discos – she loved dancing and did it whenever she could – parties and concerts, but she was seldom allowed to attend. Jason suspected all American teenagers of criminal activities. She was aware that she often was sought as a social oddity but she didn't mind too much. She simply wanted to see it all, watch, learn, express her carefully thought-out opinions and indulge her natural inclination to explore. She was taught the streets of New York and, unknown to Jason or Felix, she travelled uptown, downtown, East and West side, mastering the buses and unafraid of the subway which Jason had forbidden her to enter. She hated his restrictions, resented his suspicions, yet, apart from the subway, she obeyed him. Perhaps to compensate for that other unnamed and ultimate disobedience. While sitting on the BMT reading her novel, surrounded by blacks, Puerto Ricans, Algerians, Chicanos, Ukrainians, Italians, white delinquents, frayed businessmen, junkies and whores, she would think of Molly and the marsh and the Downs and Emma and the river and would want to cry. But she could not go back. There was no way to get back.

Almost every girl she knew was sleeping with someone. She was approached by a few boys but kept them off in a friendly way. Felix, of course, was the main obstacle to further intimacies. Compared to him other males were like blunt instruments. She felt sure they would do something clumsy and she would be forced to feel embarrassed for them. Besides, she was so torn and confused by the deception of her father that a third man in her life was a complication not to be dreamed of. Divided as she was, nothing remained of her to be cut up and shared.

Clover turned sixteen. When Felix was in New York, she took the bus to his apartment in the East Seventies. She did not know what to do about him and understood her own feelings no better than on that afternoon when she had shown him the heron's nest and fallen into the dyke. Nor could she understand his attachment to her. That there were many women in his ambiance, some rich, some beautiful, some both, she had known almost from the beginning. When his telephone rang, she could tell if the callers were women by his manner of address. She heard the conscious controlled hypocrisy. Yet he was not a hypocrite to her. She'd have known if he were. He treated her unlike anyone else. Why was this distinguished, difficult, gracefully ageing man so damned taken with her? She was so rough and he so smooth. She was so stupid and he so clever. Why did he wish to hold her to him more and more, closer and closer? It frightened and flattered her.

Felix began to invite the Englefields to the opera, the ballet, openings and dinners. Jason was touched that so sophisticated a man never failed to include a sixteen-year-old girl in his social life. Often Jason declined, especially the openings, for he was no more fond of his fellow artists and those who lived off them than he had ever been. Then Felix would call for Clover and they would go off alone, supposedly to meet the rest of the party, friends of Felix. Jason was not entirely without misgivings as to these 'dates', but felt more at ease than when Clover was in the company of school friends. Of course, Felix and Clover simply went to bed.

Felix had become bolder about swooping down and carrying her off at will. When she returned from one of these fabricated evenings of culture, Jason would be hard at work at the back of the loft. He scarcely spoke to her, noting only that she was safely home and always at a decent hour. He carried on with his painting long after she was asleep, far into the night, often until dawn. Sometimes she would meet him as she was leaving for school, they would exchange a few words outside her room, then, without thinking, he would fall into the bed she had just vacated and sleep until three. As the opening drew nearer he did nothing but paint, working brutally on in a brutal silence.

What her father's real thoughts might be eluded Clover. When she asked him what would happen when the owners of the loft returned, he said he had no idea. When she asked how long they would be in New York, he said he had no idea. He talked less and less. He hardly talked at all. She had been used to his Sussex silences, but then it was only a matter of time until he broke them with a deluge of thoughts which were not always coherent but which brought her relief. Now she waited in vain for the silence to end. It did not. She wanted to know what he thought of their arrangements. She wanted to ask him why he had espoused or at least not refused everything he had formerly despised: money, help, probably even success. Most compellingly and most perversely, she wanted to ask him what he knew about Felix, about her and Felix. Was his work absorbing him to the point of blindness or was he simply too innocent to see? As she knew very well innocence could blind. But this – and for so long. She had been carrying on with Felix for over a year.

She remembered Eleanor's funeral. She saw, as in a photograph, Felix handing his card to Jason and Jason accepting it. She felt Felix's fingers brush her own. She wept and wished for Molly to hug. She tried to read her novel, but it was no use. She could not avoid the question: *had there been a tacit swap?* If everyone, even she, could betray, why not Jason? She could not free herself from the obsessing possibility. She might ask Felix, but his answer, true or false, would be delivered in the same manner. There would be absolutely no way of telling the difference.

The New York summer was horrible and all her classmates were away. The city was deserted. The air-conditioning didn't work and no one would come to fix it. Clover walked by the river, beside the docks and the West Side gay bars with their black façades. She looked across at Hoboken and the light made her feel empty and sad. She thought of her sweet, lazy river. She thought of Eleanor and Charles Bevan and wondered what had happened to him. He was a kind man who liked her. Not because she was his daughter or his mistress or even his friend, but because he simply liked her. Then she wished Felix, who was abroad, would come and rescue her. Her wish was granted. Felix arrived back from Italy and chastised Jason for shutting Clover up in the broiling loft. He had friends in the Berkshires where she might go for two weeks, Jason owed it to her, Felix would arrange everything. Jason protested then acquiesced. He took Clover on the train to Hillsdale, stayed three moody days himself, then, to everyone's relief, left her with the Merriweathers. Felix arrived the next day and the Merriweathers disappeared. Clover's time in the mountains was divided between expensive restaurants and bed. They went to Tanglewood once. Clover rang Jason in New York to say she was fine and having a lovely time and hoped his painting was going well and was it too terribly hot? She wanted to say that Felix was paying a visit but stopped herself and put the phone down.

In the mornings she would leave the converted barn (why did Americans insist on moving into spaces not intended for human habitation: cattle barns, factories, church towers, chicken coops?) to swim in the pond or walk up the mountain. She longed to go further – further and further, on and on. She realized how much she missed the country and how restless she was in New York. But always she felt Felix's presence pulling at her. Something about his being in the house kept her from walking over the next green hill and the next and the next. So she wandered back and appeared in time for lunch. And after lunch came bed and after bed supper and after supper bed. And the following morning she would make for the next hill and not get there and come back in time for lunch, bed, supper and bed. She was almost glad when Felix said he must leave for London.

In September when he called to invite her and her father to Lincoln Center, she told Jason she had too much homework. The following day she received a letter from Felix. It was the first time he had written to her and she regarded the move as foolish.

'Little schoolgirl,' the note read, 'let me help you with your French.' She tore it up and threw it in a litter bin. Nevertheless, she rang him at FFA from a phone booth on Canal Street and fixed a time for the next afternoon. He asked her why she had refused the opera. After all, it was *Don Giovanni*.

'I told you. I had too much homework. Don't you believe me?'

'Perhaps you have been to the Mud Club,' he teased, but she could hear no humour in his voice.

'I wouldn't lie to you,' she said. 'Besides, Jason won't let me go to the Mud Club.'

'Hmmmm. Well, you don't tell Jason everything, do you?'

Clover put down the receiver and burst into tears. She walked home via Hudson Street, watching the taxis race uptown, a frenzied yellow streak, pursuers and pursued. When she turned the corner into her own block a chill wind was blowing off the river. It whipped her hair into wild entanglements.

'I can't bear it,' she muttered, staring at the stained pavement. 'I can't bear it.'

She walked the two flights to their loft. Every door along the stairwell was sealed tight as the entrance to an Egyptian tomb. The stairs were concrete and without adornment. The walls, recently painted diamond white, already bore salacious graffiti. Her school books seemed to weigh a hundred pounds. She inserted the three keys in the locks and went to her room. As she expected, Jason was still asleep, fully clothed, on her crumpled bed. She deliberately dropped the books at his feet. He didn't move. Then she spied the bottle of Jack Daniel's beside the bed. Humph! And this was *her* room, the only room with a view of something pretty (a Dutch-style gable with 1865 in green bricks). It was the last straw.

'Jason,' she yelled in his ear. 'Wake up, will you.'

He opened his eyes. 'Christ, what's the time?'

'Four-thirty and you're still asleep in *my* bed. It's disgusting. Please get up. And get sober. I have to talk to you.'

'All right, baby bear. I had a hard night. Painting's finished. Want to see?'

She thought, do I have a choice?

'*The Virtues*,' she said in spite of herself. It had been so long since they had talked about paintings – talked at all.

'Yes. Come along.'

'Jason. I want to tell you something.'

He took her hand and walked her to the studio. 'There!' He placed her before the canvas. 'Isn't that a great painting?'

'Yes,' she replied dully, restraining her observation that it would look just lovely in a vault being someone's hedge against inflation.

Jason delivered one of his lengthy exegeses. He was clearly pleased with himself and very jumped-up about the show, which would open in three weeks. Clover's courage oozed away. She listened to him, immobile. Something enormous was just within his grasp and she felt she had no right to spoil it for him. But what about her? What was she supposed to do? Live through the next three weeks, she guessed.

The next day she took the bus from school to Felix's flat.

'Darling,' he exclaimed when he saw her face, 'have you failed your maths exam?'

'Oh Felix, listen to me,' she put her arms around his waist and hugged him. 'I like you so much, only – '

He lifted her jumper, 'And I adore you.'

'Felix, I don't feel well. Lately, I mean. Most of the time.'

'Then come and lie down with me. Bed is the best place to discuss these little problems.'

He threw back the white counterpane and drew her down next to him on the freshly laundered sheets. He took her hand. His was so warm and familiar that she pressed it, not intending to.

'Now. Nothing serious, I trust. You're taking the little blue pills?'

'Oh yes.'

'Then what could it be? You're having rather a nice life. Is it money?'

'No.'

'You are in love?'

'Felix, please – ' He had never cross-examined her before. He picked up one of her school books.

'Darling, what are you reading?' He took an interest in her education, it was true. 'Hmmmm. *Adolphe*. It's not too difficult for you?'

'I got an A in French, remember?'

'Please don't snarl, darling. It's so unattractive. But it doesn't make me want you less. If you won't discuss what is troubling you, perhaps we can resolve the difficulties in another way.' He pushed her shoulders back on to the pillows.

She wanted to ask if they couldn't go for a pizza instead. But she had no desire to offend him, only to explain. And explanation seemed impossible. Moreover, she had desires of her own, desires Felix could rouse in a flash and against which she had no interest in struggling. She was learning to use him as he used her, but differently. He had helped her to do that and she was grateful to him. They were not ungenerous with each other. For the next hour she forgot everything and was very happy. But when she went out on to Madison Avenue in the cold twilight all her anxiety returned and was compounded by the realization of how much she was dependent on, not to say addicted to, the happiness Felix gave her. She knew what she would lose if she lost him.

She wanted her father to be happy. She wanted Felix to be happy and to make herself happy with Felix. But generous impulses seemed to produce as much misery and entanglement as did malice aforethought. She hated the complexities she had engendered. She called herself liar, coward, stupid little girl. She returned to the loft where she lived surrounded by other people's belongings in the midst of an alien city with a father she could not talk to and whose love and authority she questioned. She was his prisoner. She was Felix's prisoner. At the same time she was a prisoner of her own desires. She was playing all ends against the middle and the middle was herself. Clover had never been so alone.

twenty-four

Jason's show opened on 31 October. He was nervous, working too hard and drinking too much. The structure of his solid face looked in danger of imminent collapse. His dark hair was matted and greasy because he hadn't washed it in ten days and he had gained too much weight.

It's wrecking him, thought Clover, just as he said it would.

Nevertheless, he was talking again, or rather expounding to his captive audience of one (there had been no New York Dollies). He was excited, and by the thirtieth Clover was excited too. They agreed that she must have a dress 'or something' for the occasion. Jason gave her fifty dollars, and she had not the heart to tell him that the sum was ludicrously insufficient. Perhaps he hadn't given her more for fear she would spend it on drugs. Oh Jason, she thought, you poor bloody fool. In consequence, she was forced to dip into her secret fund. This had been amassed from the money Felix gave her for taxis. A year of not taking taxis – and not buying clothes, although she had very much wanted to – amounted to $875. The sum had been accumulating in a bank on Canal Street and the interest came to fifty-eight dollars. The day before the opening, Clover withdrew $150 and took the IND uptown to Seventh Avenue and Fourteenth Street. Instead of going to school she went to Barney's.

'Ah,' she breathed as she stepped out of the lift into the women's department, 'free at last!' The reprieve, although brief, was intoxicating. That morning, Clover made the thrilling discovery that something besides sex and novels was capable of making one forget the bitterness of life – shopping. She called for one garment after another to be brought her by exasperated salesladies who looked askance at the peculiar young woman in plimsolls, a boy's overcoat and a deranged hairdo. She chose the best mix she could for the money she had, her imagination running riot all the while, and left the changing room a chaotic *mélange* of contemporary fashion. She never had learned to pick up after herself.

When she left Barney's she thought for the first time in four hours of Felix. A month ago she would have seized the opportunity to call him or go round to his apartment. Instead she went home, intending to perform a private dress-rehearsal for the opening. Jason had been hanging paintings all day and half of the past two nights. She might have seen Felix whenever she chose. (George was in town and Felix could have

224

absented himself from FFA for an indefinite period of time.) But she had stayed in the loft, having supper alone, doing her homework, reading her novel, eating an apple and going to sleep. When the telephone rang she had let it ring. It had rung twenty-nine times. She stared at it, munching her apple. Poor Felix, she thought. Poor me.

That night the phone rang thirty-three times, then twenty-five times. She let it ring. She stood before a large, frameless mirror which leaned against the bathroom wall, trying various combinations of skirt, jumper, belts, tights, shoes, earrings, necklaces and make-up. When Jason staggered in after midnight she was still at it. He opened the bathroom door and gaped at her. She had just achieved the desired effect with some blusher and was poised on a fulcrum of vanity and self-loathing. Before a mirror she was absolutely merciless with herself.

'Well,' drawled Jason, 'Shindrella *will* goddaball.'

She made a face at him and he went away chuckling.

'I wonder,' she thought, returning to the mirror and recalling a certain conversation on the day of Eleanor's funeral, 'is this the way Charles would like to see me?' She had been a mess then. This was at least some sort of improvement.

'Huh!' Jason was back, surveying her through squinted eyes that could barely focus. 'Y'lookike uh Shoho tart.'

Clover slammed the door in his face, sat down on the lavatory and wept away her mascara.

On the morning of the thirty-first at seven am she wandered into the kitchen wrapped in an old, tartan dressing-gown, her eyes half-open, her hair dishevelled, her spirits abysmal, and was yanked into consciousness by the sight of Jason, wide awake and sober, standing at the cooker frying bacon.

'Thought we might have breakfast together for a change,' he said sheepishly. 'No, don't do anything. Sit down, brush your teeth or something. It'll be ready in a minute.'

They ate in silence. On her way out he handed her a ten-dollar bill.

'I'm going to the gallery this afternoon, so you'll have to meet me there. This is for a taxi – a *taxi*, mind.'

'It's not enough,' she said coldly. 'I have to go all the way to Madison and Sixty-third, you know.'

He produced another fiver. Clover opened the door and turned to him.

'Besides, no self-respecting tart would accept less than fifty dollars.' She half-smiled. 'See you there.'

Jason heard the lift doors open and close. He went to the window and watched her cross the street: long legs in flat shoes under a boy's overcoat, yellow scarf, black beret, unmatched gloves, satchel full of books. He nearly doubled over with the pain of his love. He wanted to go after her, to slap her, to kiss her, to fall at her feet and beg her to forgive him, for what he didn't know. For Eleanor, he guessed, for Monica, for their poverty, for her loneliness. Above all, for her loneliness. He wanted to take her over his knee and spank her. He wanted to murder her, to worship her, to simply talk to her. When she reached the corner of Hudson Street she turned and looked back at the window where he was standing. She saw him, he was sure, although neither made a sign to the other. Her face was very serious. He had never seen her so beautiful.

That afternoon she rang him at the gallery. He was still sober.

'Daddy, it's Clover. Good luck.'

'Thanks,' he hesitated. 'Thank you, sweetheart.'

Advance publicity for Jason Englefield's exhibition of important new paintings had been alluring, ubiquitous and effective. Proof if proof were needed of Facer Fine Arts's devoted concern for its artists. Even at seven-fifteen when Clover arrived the gallery was crowded. She hesitated at the door, clutching her small handbag and looking simultaneously for Jason and Felix. George noticed her and came forward, intent on gallantries.

'Clover, my dear,' he kissed her on both cheeks, neither of which inclined to receive his attentions, 'you look wonderful. Marvellous. Really. Turn around and let me have a look at you.'

Despite his unwelcome fuss, the recognition of her efforts plus the English accent consoled her and she did as he asked.

'Marvellous,' he said again and laughed. 'You're the most beautiful woman here, but that must be between us.'

She smiled weakly. Whatever could she say to him? Probably anything since he wouldn't listen.

'How do you like the show? I want your opinion. You've followed the paintings from their inception to their installation. We're all very excited about them. What do you think?'

The room was so crowded and smoky that she could only make out a familiar patch of colour here and there. To obtain either a close or a long view of any Englefields would have been impossible.

'Very nice,' she said.

'Do you think so? I am pleased. Felix says you have a wonderful eye.'

'May I leave my coat somewhere?'

'Everyone is in the back room. We've been waiting for you.' He took her arm and led her through the chattering, smoking, drinking, gesticulating mob. Her wonderful eye was caught first by a necklace of black metal bats, then by a hammer and sickle rhinestone brooch, a pair of earrings that flashed like belisha beacons, a mass of purple-streaked hair, a studded belt, a handbag in the shape of a snoozing cat, occasionally a painting. There was a lot of heavy plastic. There was fake gold, fake silver, fake fur, fake pearls, fake skins for which they had all paid exorbitant sums at Bendel's and Bloomingdale's. She had always thought it was for the real thing that real money was to be spent. She supposed there was a joke lurking somewhere, a joke in which they felt safe in their collusion but which was really on them. Those ersatz splendours spoke for decor not art, fashion not style, effect not feeling. She supposed she must have an aberrant mentality. They were only clothes, after all.

'There's champagne,' George whispered as though they were fellow conspirators.

Slimy bastard, she thought. She reminded herself that George was her father's dealer and she had better be nice to him. (What was it Jason had said about George and his kind? 'You have to deal with them or they'll kill you.') Tonight she had better be nice to everyone. So when he turned to her she smiled.

'Charming.' He sighed.

When Clover entered the back room she thought for a moment she might part company with her reason. In the centre stood a table on which were placed several buckets jammed with ice and Moët & Chandon. Over one of the buckets leaned Jason, deep in discussion with Felix whom Clover could tell was not taking in one word. Clustered around the table was a large, noisy, overdressed group of people including George's wife Vivienne, Schuyler, the Slug, the Capon, several artists, collectors and, of all people, Gina the chauffeuse. Everyone but Felix was completely drunk.

If only you knew how you look, thought Clover. Only Felix has any dignity.

George presented her with a glass of champagne and to his beaming wife who looked like a Mary Astor clone.

'You are a dreeeem,' Gina gushed. 'And how you have grown so. You were leeeetle girl. Now . . . '

Clover waved at Jason. He squinted, smiled then resumed his one-sided conversation with Felix who watched her over Jason's shoulder. His expression did not alter but his eyes locked into hers, enquiring, indeed demanding. Where have you been, why, what have you been doing, with whom?

She knew she must speak to him and was glad of the impossibility of doing so. It was not her fault if fifty creatures stood between them like a troupe of chimpanzees dressed as humans. She refilled her glass, aware of several pairs of eyes following her movements, and of one pair in particular. As she made for the door she spied a school-friend who had just arrived with her mother, also a painter. As Clover moved gratefully towards Dana, a bronzed woman with prominent teeth stepped directly in her path and took her picture. Clover gave a small scream as the flash-bulb popped.

She drew close to Dana. 'This is terrible,' she said.

'What do you mean? Your Dad's going to be famous. Look there's someone from *Art News*.'

The delirious coterie from the back room had spilled out into the gallery and were in the process of seizing and being seized. It was like the BMT at rush hour only no one was going anywhere. Clover saw Felix obviously attempting to reach her.

'Can we go for a pizza?' she shouted at Dana who was goggle-eyed at the spectacle. 'I haven't eaten since lunch.'

'A *what*?'

'We could come straight back.'

'Clover, you must be nuts.'

Felix was halted in his progress towards Clover by Gina, who took his arm in a familiar way. His mouth twitched as he listened to her breathless Italian. Clover stepped backwards, spilling champagne over herself and everyone she touched. She tried to catch Jason's eye, but he was standing in front of *The Three Virtues* talking non-stop to some men in suits who were exchanging amused looks. He was telling them how he had been working on the painting for years.

'He's believing it,' she said to herself. 'He's believing it all. Oh Jason.'

She elbowed through to his side and tugged at his sleeve. Without a greeting, he put an arm around her shoulders. Felix extricated himself from Gina and started to follow Clover's trail. Seeing who stood beside her, he turned to the Slug. He smiled, but whenever his eyes met Clover's she could see that they were not smiling.

The men in suits laughed at some comment of Jason's upon his *magnum opus*. Silently, Clover took them in. There they were, hoping for instant art history, questing for the unacceptable which they would turn immediately into the acceptable.

'Fabulous, Jay.' One of them laughed again.

They don't understand, she thought. He must know they don't understand.

'Reagan is in and religion is back.'

'My painting isn't political.'

He had wanted his art to stick in the cultural gullet. Now it was being swallowed whole and barely tasted. They could assimilate anything, even Jason.

'When do we see the Seven Deadly Sins? That's what I'm waiting for. I could guarantee an immediate sale on that. Woman I know's obsessed with hell. Collects paintings of hell, nothing but hell. Old tapestries too, things like that. Spooky, very spooky. They say she murdered her husband.'

'My painting isn't religious ... my painting is structural ... my painting is pure ... '

'Don't worry, Jay. It's all right to be referential again.'

'It's never been all right.'

'Linguistic mechanisms are making a comeback.'

'Yeah, like weak women.'

'A painting is not a picture.'

Jason was patted on the back. 'We all know that.'

'The content is in the painting.' Clover's father was definitely swaying. 'There are no codes to be deciphered, no secret messages. The content isn't somewhere else. It's what the lines and colours and spaces do.'

They nodded amiably.

'Jason, Jason.' Clover hugged him tighter. 'They don't understand.' She must protect him. He must protect her.

'Huh?'

'They don't understand.'

Jason was looking hungrily elsewhere and began to move away from his pure painting towards some fixed and desired point. Clover clung to the sleeve of his new leather jacket. They were waylaid by trim, young Schuyler with a trim, not-so-young woman. Jason showed signs of frustration but listened politely enough. Gina was again at Felix's side, a beautiful petulant sourpuss insistently whispering in his ear. He turned away with what was for him an abrupt movement. Clover propped up her father who was giving incoherent answers to the trim woman. Oh dear, and she was important. She even looked as if she might be nice. In fact she was Muppie van Zupten. Jason's gaze wandered. What *was* he looking for? The noise was deafening. The smoke made Clover long to rub her eyes, but she bore up for the sake of her mascara.

'Clover,' Jason turned to her. 'Refill my glash, thereshgoodguhl.'

'Oh Jason, don't leave me.' But he was already moving away from Muppie van Zupten – in mid-sentence – towards what could only be Felix, the Slug and Gina.

'Don't be thilly!' He thrust his glass at her. Gina! The champagne had ignited some memory of a Sussex afternoon in the studio – intimate chats about Ascetic Aesthetics, no doubt – and he was looking for Gina. He shook off Clover's grip and left her holding two empty glasses. Felix was backing away from the Slug. Gina's eyes were flashing dangerously. Jason bumped into a woman who spilled a glass of red wine down the front of her pink suede skirt. As Clover pushed towards the back room, someone grabbed her arm.

'Psssst! Honey!'

She mustered maximum hauteur and faced a man in his thirties who was not bad-looking but headlong drunk.

'I am not honey, I am Clover Englefield.' Who was also drunk.

'You're buddiful.'

'Please let go of my arm.'

'Only if you give me ya telephone numbah. Imma sculptah.'

'I don't care. Let go of me.'

'Then I'll give you mine. What's that mattah, dontcha believe in art?'

'Let go or I'll kick you.'

'Oh please, honey, I'd be so grateful. Ouch! Oh that was wundaful. Now kick the other one.'

'George,' she called in desperation to the only back she recognized. He didn't hear her.

'You're terrific, terrific . . . '

Jason leaned over Gina who inclined steadily away from him, her black eyes fixed on Felix who was extricating himself from the Slug. Clover headed for the champagne. She gulped two glasses and filled one for Jason.

'Clover, darling, I'd like you to meet – ' Oh no, it was that dumb Vivienne Facer. Clover nodded and smiled and moved her mouth like a string puppet.

'Mizzzz Englefield, honey.' The sculptor had found her.

'I see you know Frank,' Vivienne smiled. 'That's nice.'

'I must take this drink to my father.'

'Of course you must, dear. So attentive.' She even pitched her voice like Mary Astor's.

The gallery made Clover think of a wreck at sea: hundreds of dazed survivors clinging to life-rafts and bits of wood: their last show, their article, their book, their husband, their wallet, their address, their holiday. Anything tangible and preferably in five digits. Each grasped at their little claim to recognition, to knowledge, to a future. Clover drew a long breath. Only she could swim. She saw the exit sign and struck out for it, unconsciously clutching the glass of champagne.

'Pssst! Honey!'

'Oh no, not you again.' Frank steered her towards the back room. With a sinking heart she watched the exit sign disappear. And here came Felix and behind him Gina and behind her Jason, each impeded in their progress by victims of the wreck who grabbed at their identities.

'Izzatfameee? Oh you're sho sweet. Now listen ta me, Clovah – thatza funny name.' He pushed her against the wall, rested one arm above her head and peered at her, the tip of his nose nearly touching hers. She was cornered. The room went round and round.

'789 – 4063. Goddit?'

'Wh – what's that?'

'My telephone numbah. 789 – 4063. Now say it.'

'You're cuck-oo.'

'789 – 4063. 789 – 4063. Dontcha like me?'

'Frank, do behave.' Vivienne patted her Mary Astor bob.

'Repeat after me, Clovah, 976-4063 . . .'

'Jason, Jason!'

Jason had caught up with Gina and was holding her by the arm.

'Now say it back to me and promise you'll call. Repeat.'

'789 –' Clover was exhausted, '4063.'

'See? 'Seasy. Now one more time.'

Frank's legs were spread apart. Clover slid to the floor, smashing the glass as she did so, and crawled between. She made on all fours for the shelter of the table and sat down under a bucket which was dripping through on to the floor. She tried to bring the whirling room to a halt by focusing determinedly on her right thumb. Slowly, she realized she was sitting in a puddle. Moving to a dry spot she saw in despair that she had torn her tights and that blood was dripping from her nose on to her new skirt.

'Goddamnsonofabitch!' She lay flat on her back fumbling in her bag for some kleenex. She applied the hopelessly inadequate wad to her face and watched the meaningless shifting of trousers, stockings and shoes on every side. She was two years old and she was having a nosebleed, and the world was a jungle of legs. Suddenly Frank was leaning over her on his hands and knees, panting like a Yorkie.

'Found ya, buddiful, ha ha!'

'Oh God,' she moaned and turned her face away into the gory kleenex. 'How can one say politely to somebody that it is all all, absolutely all out of the question? Can't you get me some tissues?'

'Aw you talk so nice. Whereya from, Australia?'

'I'm British!'

'Awww, you're terrific anyway. Wanna fuck?'

She kicked him as best she could in her compromising position, trying to decide whether to swallow the clots or spit them out on Frank the sculptah.

'. . . so terrific.' He clutched his leg.

Clover dragged herself to the far end of the table, holding the kleenex to her nose and travelling so fast in her panic that she collided with a pair of grey flannel trousers beneath which were a pair of very long legs. The legs belonged to Felix who was holding her coat.

'Well,' he yanked her smartly to her feet. 'Seems we can't take her anywhere.'

Frank lifted the tablecloth to peer up at the disarranged and bloody object of his admiration and the middle-aged man who gripped her by the wrist.

'Uh-oh. You her father?'

'Yes.' Felix turned on his heel and ground it, as he did so, into the sculptor's very important left hand.

'I could shue you for that,' he wailed at Felix's disappearing and utterly straight back.

'Frank,' said Vivienne, 'do behave.'

'Where are we going?' Clover asked, trying to hold her head back and keep pace with Felix.

'For a cup of tea.'

'But where?'

'My apartment.'

Felix dragged her through the mob who parted like the Red Sea before the rod of Moses. Clover had never known him move so quickly.

'Felix . . . Jason . . . oh bloody hell . . .'

He turned to her. 'Clover, you are drunk and, I suspect, intent on irresponsible action. You will now shut up. You will come with me. We will have a cup of tea and we will talk.'

She waved frantically to Jason who waved back, a foolish grin on his face as he followed Gina towards the champagne. Half an hour later he began asking if anyone had seen his little girl.

twenty-five

Felix hailed a taxi on Madison Avenue. Clover preceded him into the back seat, too tired to resist. He took her in his arms and she clung to him, sobbing blood and mascara all over his new shirt.

'Please tell me why you're crying.'

'They don't understand Jason's paintings.'

'Of course they don't. They have no capacity for understanding and there is nothing to be understood. Jason will be a success.' He produced another handkerchief. 'I've told you before. Art comes from only one thing and that is need. The need to make it and the need to have it.'

'Human beings are revolting.'

'So long as we are not.' He kissed her hair. 'You've been a very bad girl. Haven't you?'

'Very, oh very. So, so bad.' She nodded vehemently and sobbed again with disastrous consequences for Felix's overcoat.

'And now, Clover,' he said when they had returned to his apartment and he had set before her a cup of Lapsang Souchong, 'I will tell you what is the matter with you.'

She was inspecting her ruined condition in a pocket mirror and clearing away the remaining mascara with a piece of cottonwool. The bleeding had been staunched by Felix and he had disposed of the bloody towels and kitchen paper.

'I thought I was meant to do the explaining,' she said.

'One can't explain what one doesn't understand. Fortunately for us both, I do understand. Drink your tea, darling, and don't look at me like that. I'm not angry with you. You know I've always shown you the best way to get what you want – don't say you didn't know what you wanted because you did. When I met you you did not behave at all like a stupid little girl. Now you are behaving so.'

Clover sipped her tea in moody silence.

'I don't wish you to be unhappy or uncomfortable,' he continued. 'I wish you to enjoy your life. But you cannot enjoy it if you are all the time guilty. Guilt makes confusion and confusion makes irrational behaviour. It is obvious. You do feel guilty. I'm right.'

She nodded.

'You shrink from having deceived your father. Well, there are times when one has no choice but to behave despicably. You will feel easier if

233

you accept the fact. As the Americans say, so what? You've done him no harm.'

'It's me too,' she murmured. 'I've harmed myself.'

He sighed. 'So now you wish to compound the misery by harming me.'

He knew everything, anticipated everything.

'I'd never want to harm you, Felix,' she said, sounding absurdly feeble and false to herself.

'Nonsense,' he smiled. 'You are plotting my overthrow.'

She started to speak but he stopped her.

'But you are incapable of plotting it – or anything – without my assistance. I could never teach you to plot. You are not equipped. Pity. So because you cannot plot you let telephones ring and hide under tables and pretend to yourself to worry because the Ostrogoths don't understand Jason's silly paintings. It's all very childish.'

Clover wanted to cry some more but she forced herself to talk to him. 'Felix, the worst thing for me is not to be able to speak openly. I've been in prison, I've been bound and gagged. My growth has been stunted. I'm five foot eight and I feel like a dwarf. I can't live feeling the way I feel. I can't make-believe to myself that everything is fine and that I'm a nice person.'

He shrugged. 'You must cease to nurture your guilt, that's all. Because you will not give me up.'

'What makes you so sure?'

'You're unable to give me up.'

'What makes you so sure?' This time there was an edge to her voice.

'I'll prove it to you.'

Felix stood up, snatched away her tea cup and lifted her bodily from the chair.

'Felix, please ... '

He laid her on the bed, lifted her blood-stained skirt, removed her ruined tights.

'Tell me to stop,' he commanded, getting on to his knees.

'Felix ... ' she was crying like an idiot.

He whisked off her knickers.

'Say no.'

She stiffened. He pried apart her knees.

'Oh God,' she whispered and wiped her eyes and nose.

They lay holding each other, his eyes exploring her face like fingers. 'Felix,' she said, 'I've never been with anyone else. I haven't liked anyone else.'

'I'm glad.' He smiled and kissed her. 'But that's not the point. The point is what I have just proven to you. I've made you forget your guilt. I've made you forget your father. I've made you forget your nice new clothes, now in such an unprepossessing state. Your pleasure is more important to you than your guilt. So it should be. You're healthy. What we do is all there is to do. We are very good at it. It would be mad to – well, excuse me, angel, but life is short, especially mine. You understand.'

'Yes,' she said solemnly.

'You know what you need.'

'Yes.'

'And you know that anyone who does not get what they need and go on getting it as long as they need it is a fool.'

'Yes.'

'Who only makes herself and everyone else unhappy.'

'Yes.'

'And now, since we are not fools, we must return to that sewer of art.'

'Oh God.' She sat straight up. 'What's the time?'

Felix stroked her legs and looked pleased. 'You see? I've also made you forget the time.'

She began dressing. She brushed her hair and left it to hang, desire gone, drunkenness gone, panic uppermost. She could imagine Jason's condition only too well. She must get back to him. Felix went on talking in his soothing voice with its indefinable accent while donning new underwear and a fresh white shirt.

'I'll go first,' said Clover snatching up her coat.

'We'll go together. You appear. Say you went for a pizza. I'll arrive ten minutes later.'

'No, no, I'll go alone. I must see Jason. I can't just – don't you understand? – you and him – just like that – as though it were so easy for me.'

'Darling, please not to begin again this nonsense.' He was very annoyed.

'I'm going. Goodbye.' She ran for the door. He followed her, minus his trousers.

'Clover!' He had never raised his voice to her before.

She looked at him from inside the lift. Felix stood helplessly in his shorts and still unbuttoned shirt.

'Come back,' he ordered like a drill sergeant. He was ludicrous, terrifying.

In the lift, Clover trembled as she tried to make herself push the button. He looked in desperation to the right and left and crossed the empty hall, the fair hair on his legs glistening in the light.

'Clover,' he said quietly, 'don't force me to lose my dignity. I love you.'

'I love you, Felix,' she cried, 'I love you, I love you,' and pushed the Down button.

It was going to come out, she couldn't stop it: the truth and all its consequences. She could think of nothing but the truth as she sat in the back of the taxi, as she entered the building on Sixty-third Street, as she rode up in the lift, as she opened the door to Facer Fine Arts and saw the still delirious art lovers. The words she had held down and smothered for so long were now lodged at the back of her throat, straining at the gates of her larynx like a revolutionary mob about to storm the fortress.

If Jason isn't here I'll die, she thought, scanning the array of faces. She spied Gina and went straight to her.

'Where's Jason?' she asked, interrupting the cluck-cluck of the Capon.

Gina's irritation was plain. 'In the Gentlemen's. He's drunk.'

Clover went to the men's room, not hearing Vivienne Facer's enquiries about all being well she hoped. She burst in on Schuyler and the Slug in animated conversation.

'Jason,' she shouted, 'Jason.'

A low moan issued from the cubicle at the far end of the room. She marched to the door and opened it. Jason was sitting on the tiled floor, his knees drawn up to his chest, recovering from some internal upheaval.

'Shoald four paintings,' he said.

'Jason, get up.'

'Why? Like it here. Superior accommodations. Think I'll stay.'

She tugged at his arm. 'Get up now.'

'Nope. Can't make me. Where's Ginabrigit?'

If she didn't get him away to some quiet corner, it would come out, right here, in the presence of Schuyler and the Slug. The door banged. She looked out. They had gone. Clover checked the other cubicles. She and her father were alone.

'Shweetheart, ask George for a brandy. For *me*.'

'You'd better wait until I say what I've come to say.'

Clover told him. Everything. Even things that couldn't be said. When Jason vomited into the toilet, she tried to hold his head but he pushed her away with his elbow, so hard that she gasped, leaned against the wall of the cubicle and clutched her side. Someone came in.

'Jason!' It was Schuyler. 'George wants to know if you're all right. He's very concerned.'

'Tell him I'm coming.'

'Yes. OK. *Are* you all right?'

Jason did not answer. He went to the sink, turned the cold tap full on and stuck his head under it. Clover emerged from the cubicle, her eyes enormous, twisting a glove. Schuyler gave a nervous laugh. Jason and Clover looked like the sole survivors of an airplane hijack, or an embassy siege.

Jason rinsed his mouth and spat. He rubbed his head with a towel, not enough to dry it but to make it stand up in greying spikes. Under his jacket, his wet shirt was stained with vomit, wine and sweat. He pushed past Schuyler without saying anything.

'Please don't let him – ' Clover began.

'Excuse me, Miss Englefield, let him what?'

'Nothing. It's all right. I don't know.'

'I'm sorry. I don't understand. Can I help you?'

'Call a taxi. Straightaway please. That will be best, I think.'

'Yes. Of course. Yes. Right now.'

He opened the door for her and she preceded him into the gallery.

Vivienne Facer's jaw dropped and remained hanging for several seconds. She tapped her husband's shoulder and whispered something. She pointed towards the open doorway which was suddenly full of Jason Englefield, looking like a cross between a Hell's Angel and Ludwig van Beethoven. Without swaying, he walked to a table, picked up an empty champagne bottle and smashed it against the steel arm of a chair. Vivienne gave a short scream. Gina, no coward, approached and faced him squarely.

'Jason, put that away. You are behaving very badly.'

'In a minute.'

Jason walked towards the opposite end of the gallery. The others followed at a safe distance. They wanted to see what he would do while ensuring that he would not do it to them. Clover stood in the middle of the room, her hands in her pockets. Everyone except Frank drew back, leaving them to confront each other. Jason raised the broken bottle. Clover cringed but would have stood her ground if Frank had not pulled her aside. Jason was not aiming for his daughter though. He was looking past her at *The Three Virtues*. He steadied himself before the painting. The others stood like figures in a tableau, paralysed by the sight of his pain. He raised the bottle again, and with its jagged edge made a slash through each of the three panels.

Clover covered her face with her hands as a flash-bulb popped. Jason dropped the bottle.

George approached with caution, afraid of Jason, but aware of his responsibility as captain of an endangered ship.

'Jason, I must inform you that the painting is no longer yours to dispose of. It was sold twenty minutes ago to Mr and Mrs van Zupten. The painting belongs to them, Jason. It is their painting. You have inflicted deliberate damage on private property. For this act of vandalism you will make restitution or face litigation.'

Jason seized George by the lapels.

'You obscenity. *You* will make restitution to *me* for *everything*. You and he, the two of you – impostors, thieves. Nothing can repair the damage you do.'

'Jason, clearly you're distressed. Think, Jason. I'm certain you're confusing me with someone else. Jason, you have the wrong man.'

The door opened and Felix Koning walked in. He looked from Jason to George to Clover to the mutilated painting. He was very, very white.

Shaken from their stupor, two men came to George's assistance. But Jason had already released George. He let out a roar like a wounded tiger and, with all that remained of his strength, flung himself at Felix, who stepped neatly aside, leaving a space just wide enough and long enough for Jason to fall flat on his face as into an open grave.

Clover clutched her unconscious father amid the general uproar, resisting all efforts to prise her away.

'Is he dead?'

'Is he bleeding?'

'How much did they pay?'

'Sick mind, know what I mean?'

'Really.'

'Muppie, what can I say, what can I say?'

'$18,000.'

'Call an ambulance.'

'Ambulance, my ass. Send for the police.'

'No. Please. He's an artist.'

'Myth of the Individual.'

'Death of Modernism.'

'Irrelevance of the object.'

'$20,000.'

'Get me a taxi please.'

'Ambulance.'

'Police.'

'Bellevue.'

'The raffish art crowd ... '

'Thank God the man from *Art Forum* – '

' – left.'

'Thank God.'

'Thank God.'

'Clover.' Felix tried to take her hand.

'Don't touch me, Felix, please. A taxi, a taxi!'

'Summons.'

'Writ.'

'Clover.' Again she heard the only gentle voice in the room.

'Go, Felix,' she whispered. 'For God's sake go before he wakes up.'

'Felix come with me. I drive you. The girl is right.'

Felix shook off Gina's hand. He knelt beside Clover and the man who was feeling Jason's pulse. He looked at the artist's blue-white, striken face.

'What happened?' He lowered his voice.

'I told him.'

'You *told* him ... '

'Everything.'

'*Everything?*'

'Everything.'

'He must be got out of here. He can't stay here, you know.'

'Psychiatric ward.'

'Valium injections.'

'Get me a taxi,' Clover screamed.

Silence.

'You cannot be left alone with him,' Felix said.

'Chertainly not. He's a dangeroush – '

'You,' said Felix, 'shut up.'

'Don't you care about your daughter's safety? Whatkinda fatha're you?'

'*Will* you behave, Frank.' Vivienne led him away as Schuyler rushed in.

'Miss Englefield,' he panted, 'your taxi.'

'Thank you.' She pressed the hand that helped her to her feet. Jason moaned. He was coming to and Gina was trying to give him a glass of water. Clover looked round at the circle of hostile faces.

'Will someone help me to get my father downstairs?'

Felix took her arm. 'You can't go with him. You can't be alone with him.'

Gina stood up. 'Felix, let her go. It's for your good. He wants to hurt you.'

George appeared confused. 'He must do something. Something must be done with him. My paintings, Vivi, my paintings . . . '

Jason opened his eyes. They rolled around like pinballs then closed again. In her panic Clover began agreeing to everything.

'Yes, the hospital. Yes, of course. Yes, you come and you. Yes, yes.'

Schuyler, George and the Capon got Jason to his feet. Along with Felix and Gina they all descended to the street where the taxi was waiting. Clover went on saying yes and allowing Felix to keep his hand in hers. Jason was poured into the back seat.

'Please,' she said. 'Let me sit beside him.'

'Yes, of course.'

Felix helped her in. She held tight to the door handle. The moment he released her hand she slammed the door behind her.

'Lock it,' she screamed through the partition. 'They're all sex offenders.' There was a metallic klunk. The taxi was impregnable. Hands pressed against the window. Features were barely discernible through her tears.

'Drive, drive,' she shouted.

'OK, OK. Where to?'

'Around. I mean anywhere. Just step on it.'

'OK, honey.'

The taxi pulled away leaving behind two black streaks of rubber and five pale, shocked faces that hung in the night like waning moons.

'Franz Kline,' muttered Jason, 'Ad Rheinhardt, Jackson Pollock.'

'Downtown,' Clover called to the driver. 'Canal Street. Fast fast, please.'

'Kandinsky, Braque, Matisse, Mondrian, Malevich . . . '

'Oh shut up, Jason,' she pleaded. She opened her purse. There was not enough money to pay the driver. She should have returned to the gallery with Felix. What could she do? She rifled Jason's pockets and found nearly two dollars in change. He'd lost his wallet or not taken it. There must be money in the loft. There had to be. All that mattered now was that she get both of them home and lock them safely behind that Egyptian tomb door before anyone appeared with writs. She must save Jason and then she must face Jason. Beyond that it was impossible to think.

'Look,' she said to the driver when they stopped at Harrison Street, 'you've been fantastic – '

'You English, baby?'

'Yes and golly I need help.'

He glanced at Jason. 'Yeah, I can see dat. Boy-friend?'

'Father.'

'Sure. Drunk?'

'Exhausted.'

'Uh-huh.'

'As you see he's immovable. I must get him to the second floor. There's a lift. I'll pay you extra, I promise. There's money in the loft.'

'Yeah, yeah, I geddit. You seem in a pretty bad fix, kid. Lucky you can trust me. Lucky I ain't no sex offender. Come on.'

With an arm around each of their necks, Jason made it as far as the lift. On the way up, he looked at the driver then at his daughter.

'Clover, who is this person? He's not the one from *Art in America* is he?'

'Oh, ya faddah's English too, huh?'

'Yes.' She tried to smile at the lean, grizzled and utterly sceptical face. He was a small man, wiry but strong. He bolstered up Jason, who was easily two stone heavier than himself, while Clover fumbled with the keys.

'Who *is* this person?' Jason asked again as they let him collapse on to his bed. 'Whoever he says he is, don't believe him. The man's an impostor.' He passed out.

Clover dropped into a chair by the kitchen table.

'Thank God,' she breathed. 'Thank you, Mr – ' She looked up at him. The telephone rang.

'Romeo Dellajoia. It's OK, honey. You gonna get dat?'

'Oh Mr Dellajoia, could you answer it please and tell whoever it is that they have the wrong number.'

'Can I be rude?' He winked at her.

She smiled weakly. 'Why not?'

'Dere ain't no such poisen . . . you got da wrong numbah, Mac . . . ain't nobody here by dat name . . . no Clovah, no alfalfa, no buddacup, nuttin' . . . Say, buddy, you talk nice, hear? . . . Hey, yous foreign or somethin'? Yeah, dat's what I thought. Well, I'm an American citizen, geddit, and Americans don't like bein' bugged by motor-mouthin' foreign pansies who phone after midnight and invade the privacy which is guaranteed 'em by da Bill of Rights. And if yous invade my privacy again, I'll call the police. Goddit? Now fuck off.' Mr Dellajoia slammed down the receiver.

'Pardon my French, Miss Englefield. Dat's what he called you so I guess dat's who ya are.'

She couldn't help giggling at the thought of Felix's or George's consternation. She must be hysterical. 'That's me. Although a little while ago I wasn't too sure.'

'Hey, kid,' he sat down beside her, 'somebody giving you trouble? Somebody gonna show up here and bodda you?'

The telephone rang. Mr Dellajoia picked it up again. Clover listened to the driver's volley of verbal abuse.

'How old are you, sweetheart?' he asked when it had stopped.

'I'll be seventeen on 25 November.'

He looked her up and down. 'Jeeeeze! Hey, you know you got a big hole in your pantyhose?'

Clover flushed. 'Oh no,' she thought, 'oh no.'

'Maybe I bedda stay. You need protection, honey. Dere's somethin' fishy goin' on here, I can tell.'

'I'm all right, really. You've been awfully kind. But I can look after myself. No one wants to bother me.' (Would to God that were true.)

'Well,' he glanced at the tear, 'you are soitenly a nice big girl – uh, for ya age. Know what I mean?'

'I'm five feet eight inches,' she said absurdly. 'What do I owe you?'

'Weeeellll,' he flicked his splayed palm back and forth, 'dat all depends ... '

'No no,' she rose quickly. 'Just tell me, please. I'll get the money. Wait, wait. I'll be right back.'

She rifled Jason's drawers and found four dollars and fifty-seven cents. Her own small stash yielded another two dollars. She held out the crumpled notes to Mr Dellajoia.

'Dat ain't enough, sweetheart.'

'It's all I have. I'm so sorry. Please. It's been a terrible night.'

'It don't have to stay dat way.' He came closer. Clover stifled a scream and backed away from him.

'Look, sweetheart,' he went on, 'I come up here, you know, and we're alone and you say you ain't got no money, and already said somethin' about sex offenders. It's pretty clear dere's a lotta guys after you for somethin' or other and it's pretty clear dat comatose poisen in da bedroom ain't no relation of yours. And dere you are smiling at me and sitting with those bitchin' legs of yours spread all over. I mean, what am I supposed to think? You ain't playin' no deception games with me are ya?'

'Mr Dellajoia, I'm sorry if I gave you the wrong impression. I promise you the person in the bedroom is my father, Jason Englefield, and I am his daughter. I can prove it. I have our passports if you'd like to see them. Anyway, he's my father and he's been upset enough for one evening and as a matter of fact so have I. And I'm the cause of all this distress and it's my fault that we don't have the money to pay you, not his. But if you'd care to return tomorrow, I swear – '

'OK, OK. I ain't no male chauvinist. But you gotta give me a kiss in exchange for the rest of the fare.'

Clover shut off all her senses and gave Mr Dellajoia the most beautiful kiss he'd ever had.

'Sheeeet,' he breathed as she pushed him gently away.

'Now please,' she said, putting the money in his hand, 'please go and let me look after my father. Please. And thank you from my heart, Mr Dellajoia.'

'Yeah. Dat's all right, sweetheart.'

She led him to the door, her heart pounding. He stood on the threshold and stared at her.

'You know somethin', kid. You ain't no hooker, you're – I dunno what you are. Weird. I dunno. Somethin' special like I don't know what. Maybe you're from outer space.' He handed her the money. 'You don't owe me nuttin'.' He turned and ran down the stairs. Clover slammed the door and fastened all three locks.

Jason moaned. The telephone rang and she let it ring. Cold compresses, she thought, aspirin, coffee, *nux vomica*. She filled a basin with water and floated a flannel in it. Then she assembled her nursing requisites on the bedside table. When she looked at the clock, she was surprised to see it was only twelve-thirty. Years seemed to have elapsed since she had tried on her new clothes. Now the clothes were torn, stained, ruined. She went to her room and changed into her tartan dressing-gown.

'Oh Molly,' she whispered, pressing her head against the bureau.

She returned to Jason's room, switched the flannel on his forehead, turned off all but one of the lights and sat down to keep her vigil. The loft was in darkness. She hoped against hope that visitors would assume the Englefields had not come home. The telephone was off the hook. She sat still and waited. She remembered part of Eleanor's poem and said it aloud to herself.

> *Never leave that distance to surrender*
> *should he seek the woman in the maid;*
> *his mind can only read or render*
> *you as maids; the feeling in your tender*
> *wrists would snap beneath brocade.*

Once she had asked Jason who 'he' was. He hadn't answered. He didn't want her to know or probably he himself didn't know. The poem now seemed a warning not heeded, a message not understood. But how could Eleanor have known what would happen with Felix? Had she been thinking of Felix when she sent the poem to Clover? Or had she been thinking of Jason? In the poem there was more than one 'he', or rather 'they' turned into 'he'. Were 'he' and 'they' the same? Were Jason and Felix the same? They had both 'suddenly beheld her bloom'. But they were not the only ones to have done so; not the only 'he's'. There were other 'he's'. Not all of them need be so contradictory.

'What am I thinking?' She spoke out loud to clear her head. 'It's me who's mixed everything up. I'm the one who's contradictory. Why have I done this? Why have I ruined everything? To lie was bad but to tell the truth seems to be worse. Clearly, if one lies it's best to go on lying. Anyway, it's too late. It's no good saying well I did it and there we are so let's get on with life. I must understand and try to make it better.

'Perhaps the poem is referring to "he's" who can't be your friend. "He's" who keep you at a distance and keep you a prisoner because they love you or need you or desire you or are afraid of you. They seem to want you to cause them pain and then they hate you for causing it. You're a fantasy they can't afford to make too real. You can't afford it either. Eleanor was always doing that and letting them do it too. Her wrists snapped. What she needed was a friend. And so do I. Poor Eleanor. Poor me.'

She rinsed out Jason's flannel. Before replacing it on his forehead she leaned over and kissed him. He groaned and shifted position. She held the light to his face. His colour had improved. He would be all right. He just needed to sleep. Then he would wake up – a tiger.

Clover replaced the telephone receiver, waited a moment then picked it up again. She asked the operator for Sussex, England. It was two am. Emma would be eating her breakfast before cycling to school in the dark.

Mrs Tozer answered. 'Clover, shouldn't you be in bed?'

'Yes. Something's happened. May I speak to Emma?'

She waited.

'Clover!'

'Oh Emma, Emma, how are you? Is Molly all right? I want to speak to her.'

'Molly's stupendously well. But she's having her breakfast and can't come to the phone.'

Clover laughed. 'Hug her for me. Tell her I love her so much I could die. Oh Em, I'm in such a muddle. I've done something mad, Jason's done something mad, and I really don't know what's going to happen to us.'

'Get Felix to help you.'

Clover groaned. She told Emma all that had happened from the day she left England to her encounter with Mr Dellajoia. She imagined Emma looking exactly like her mother.

'Why didn't you call me sooner?'

'One of them was always around.'

'Well,' Emma sighed. 'This is very bad, Clover. The only thing I can recommend is that you marry Felix.'

'I'm too young to get married. And Felix is too old to get married. Oh it's impossible.'

'Make him marry you. Get pregnant. Still works you know.'

'Oh that's so corny.'

'I agree. But you have *very few options*. You don't understand that once people are turned into families things have a way of sorting themselves out, at least temporarily. I know. I have three older sisters. And my mother had nothing but sisters. Think about it. Once you were married and had a baby, Jason would calm down and make it up with the gallery, Felix would get bored and go off and you'd have enough money to hire a nanny and do as you pleased.'

'It's a horrible idea. It's not at all what I want.'

'Then what do you want, Clover?'

'I want to come back. I want to pass my A-levels and go to Oxford and be a biologist and have children and play first cello in an amateur orchestra.'

'That's very English. I'd have thought you'd have learned something over there. I mean you could live in Florida, you could write a screenplay or your autobiography or you could be Mrs Koning and wear diamond earrings and go out to restaurants every night and have affairs. You could be the daughter of a famous father and the wife of a successful husband. Isn't that better than an amateur orchestra? Isn't that enough?'

'No.'

'Well, Clover, no one can understand you, not even me any more. Still, I like you better than anyone and you've been nicer to me than anyone. I'm your best friend. And I have the advantage of a year's more experience of life and three older sisters. So think about what I said. By the way, Stuart is still crazy about you.'

Clover laughed. 'I love you, Em. If all else fails I can come to you, can't I?'

'Of course. But why you'd want to I don't know. My mother says we'd better stop. Think about what I said and for God's sake call me – before you get into more trouble.'

'I will. Oh Em – '

'Yes?'

'Do you still have that box I left with you?'

'The one with all your treasures? Of course.'

'Em – '

'Yes.'

'Are you still a virgin?'

Emma sighed. 'Yes. But after what's happened to you I suddenly think I'm better off this way. Anyway, it'll come right, Clover. You'll make it come right. Bye.'

'Bye, Em.'

Immediately Clover put the phone down it rang. At the thirteenth ring she dried her tears and answered it.

'Darling, are you all right?'

'Emma says I will be.'

'You will please not be facetious. Tell me exactly what is going on.'

'Jason's sleeping it off. Don't know what will happen when he wakes up.'

'Let me send someone to be with you.'

'No.'

'You have jeopardized our position. Perhaps irreparably. You realize that?'

'Yes.'

'Why did you do it?'

'Because I wanted to. I couldn't go on as I was. Not for one minute.'

'Ah, so your condition of one minute was more important than all the time we've been together as well as the time before us and your father's career and all I have done for you and your father, not to mention what he has also done for himself. Your one minute was more important.'

'Yes.'

'Clover, it is not my habit to pass moral judgements, but what you did was selfish in the extreme.'

'I know. I'm sorry. I had to do it.'

'You may indeed be sorry, but you don't *know* anything. You have compromised me, it is all very awkward. I tried to help Jason. I did a great deal for him, that is not deniable. Because I was – fond of you. Now you are so ungrateful as to damage my reputation and threaten my security . . . '

'What's wrong with you, Felix? You never talk like this. You're not yourself.'

'I'm grieved. I'm attached to you. As you are to me, you will not contradict. The perversity of your action is the ruin of my reason. Everything I have accomplished has been based on trust. I've made a great web of trust. That may now be in shreds. I trusted you – '

She was moved by his distress but vexed by his logic.

'Felix, you're a very clever man. You get what you want. You manoeuvre everyone. You're master of the way the world works. I'm only an adolescent girl. How can what I did threaten your brilliant career? I'm fond of you. I love you. But we must have ended sooner or later. You seem to know everything so you must know that. Please will you not blackmail me and try to put on me the guilt you yourself persuaded me to shake off.'

Felix hung up.

There were no more calls. Whatever his motives, Felix was the only witness to the evening's drama who, at two-thirty in the morning, cared what had become of her and Jason.

Clover returned to her father's room and sat with him snoring beside her. She thought of Felix and cried. She thought of what Emma had said. Emma was not stupid. But neither was Felix. Emma's suggestion was a way of making it all come right. But the operation would involve yet more deception. It would be founded on a trick. Something told her she had it in her power to accomplish that trick. In her power, maybe. In her nature, no. She couldn't do it.

At six o'clock the phone rang and she answered it.

'Darling, can I see you?'

'Not now. Jason's still – '

'When?'

'I don't know.'

Felix sounded tired. More tired than she had ever heard him.

'Felix, haven't you slept?'

'What do you suppose? You are alone with a madman.'

'He's not a madman, he's my father.'

'As in "they are not stupid, they're just sheep". Ach! When can I see you?'

'I don't know. I really don't.'

He hung up. She sighed and hung up too.

'Clover, what's the time?'

She whirled round in her seat. Jason stood there. Awake. A tiger.

'Are you – are you – ' she stammered.

247

Jason slapped her face. He slapped her so hard that she fell on to the floor.

'Don't . . . ' she whispered.

He yanked her to her feet and struck her again. Then again. 'No,' she said, 'no, no, no.'

He grabbed her shoulders and shook her so that her head wobbled back and forth like an old doll's. Taking hold of a handful of her hair, he used it to drag her to her bedroom where he flung her on to the bed.

'You're not going to telephone your boy-friend anymore.' He left her alone and locked her in. She ran to the door, pressed her throbbing, red cheek against it and pounded it with the palm of her hand.

'Jason,' she screamed, 'Jason, talk to me. Don't lock me in please. Talk to me, Jason. Oh talk to me.'

She listened as he picked up the telephone and dialled. There was a pause during which she heard nothing but her own heart. Then the slamming of the receiver. Footsteps away from the telephone and back. The click of the receiver, dialling, heartbeats. Then Jason's voice, quiet and awful.

'George Facer, you imposturing coward, I know you're there. You put on your coward's answering machine, but I know you're there. I will leave you to consider my message as you cling to the skirts of your frigid, frivolous wife. Sexless beings, both of you, incapable of creation, sucking my blood and the blood of others. Sucking the blood of my child, arranging for her corruption, swapping art for innocence. Traders in flesh, traders in hearts. If I ever see you again I'll kill you. I'll take a gun and shoot you. Meanwhile, I sever all connections with your polluted institution. I demand the return of all paintings by me held on consignment by you. You will forfeit your commission on all paintings sold, for which, by the way, I demand immediate payment. Immediate meaning by six o'clock today. I also demand the resignation of Felix Koning from the board of FFA. Otherwise I shall sue FFA and I shall win.'

'Oh Jason,' Clover moaned, 'you're so corny.'

More dialling.

'I want to speak to Sam. I know it isn't even eight. What do I care about time? What does time matter? I'm his goddamn client and I need to speak to him . . . About what is none of your business . . . all right, all right. I want to know about the Mann Act . . . I want to know how one goes about getting a warrant for someone's arrest in this country . . . America, of course, you silly bitch . . . hey, you can't hang up like that – '

Click, click, click. Receiver slammed. Heartbeats. More dialling.

'Ha! I knew you'd answer the phone. You were expecting, no doubt, my daughter. My daughter who you raped and corrupted and encouraged to betray her own father. Well this *is* her father. Who is going to personally kill you. Remember that and start grovelling now, you posturing vermin.'

Slam. More pacing. Dialling.

'Hello Slug's answering machine. This is Jason Englefield. I am informing you that I am no longer affiliated with Facer Fine Arts and that I will sue anyone who prints anything to the contrary. Goodbye.'

Dialling.

'Hello, Sam. Sam, look . . . what do you mean? Oh don't be daft, I didn't call your wife a silly bitch . . . Was that your wife? . . . Sam? . . .'

Silence. Click.

Clover listened, her eyes growing slowly blacker, as her father tore down, one by one, the supports that upheld the fragile structure of their life. A-levels and Oxford were a fading dream.

The telephone rang.

'You! You conspiratorial slut. You co-operated with the enemy. Don't lie to me, Gina, and don't for God's sake defend him. I believe nothing you say. I believe nothing anyone says. I'll never believe anyone again.'

He replaced the receiver, quietly this time. Clover heard a sob.

'Jason,' she pleaded, banging on the door. 'Jason, let me out. Please, please. No one's to blame but me, I swear it.'

'I repeat,' he shouted through the door, 'I'll never believe anyone again. Not even myself.'

'Jason,' she said softly. 'Please let me out. I'm so sorry for you.'

'God, I could – ' Suddenly he opened the door, looking as though he had reached the outermost ring of his reason and was about to launch himself into orbiting lunacy. He saw her face, swollen, blue-black, tear-stained, fearfully comprehending. He dropped to the floor and hugged her knees and cried.

'Look what you've forced me to do to you,' he sobbed into her dressing-gown. 'Why didn't you all leave me as I was? Why did we have to come here?'

'Coming here was not my decision. The other thing – that was my decision – *mine*.'

'I don't believe you.'

'All right don't, but it's the truth.'

Clover was so tired her legs gave way and she collapsed over Jason's back. She could not remember when she had last eaten or slept. There was a loud knock.

'Police!'

'Oh Christ!' Jason carried Clover to a chair and opened the door. 'I demand to see your warrant.'

'We ain't gonna search. Just checking a report.'

Clover grabbed a towel, put it over her head and began rubbing vigorously.

'A Mr Koning. Something about noises. Suspicious activities.'

'I never heard of Mr Koning. Besides, what the fuck does he know? He lives on Seventy-third Street.'

'Said something about your daughter and watch your language, pal.'

Clover stood up, her legs very wobbly.

'I am this man's daughter. I am Miss Englefield. As you can see, I'm perfectly all right. I have just now taken a shower and I am drying my hair. So if you don't mind I'll return to the bathroom. I know of no Mr Koning. There must be some mistake. Excuse me.'

She went to her bed and lay down. The police left. Jason appeared with some ice and a flannel.

'Here. Hold this on your face. I'm going out to Safeway to get a beefsteak. While I'm gone think whether you can forgive me.'

As soon as she heard the door bang Clover made for the telephone. Her legs were so weak and her head so light that she was forced to support her progress with worktops, tables and chairs. A pain had sprung up her right side and she touched the area gingerly. Perhaps she had cracked a rib. She sat down with a moan. Please, she prayed, don't let me throw up.

She rang Felix. It was the first time she had ever called him from the loft.

'Clover, my angel, are you all right?'

She wanted to weep like a little girl, to say she was battered, bruised, deformed, to point an accusing finger at Jason and say it was he who was responsible, he, he, he. She wanted Felix, overcome with love and indignation, to rescue her, to hold her in his arms and console her and tell her in his soft voice that she was safe for ever.

'I'll be OK,' she said. 'As far as I'm concerned the worst is over. You know he wants to kill you.'

'Of this proposed murder I'm very bored. Oh, I do *hate* melodrama!'

'I should leave town if I were you,' she said dully. She was doing her duty. She was behaving conscientiously.

'Do you think I'm being motivated by threats?'

'He means it. Felix, for the sake of all three of us, go.'

'I will not go. I don't want to go. I want to see you.'

250

She felt how, in spite of everything, her being incarcerated in the loft intensified his ardour.

'Felix, would you have wanted me as much if Jason hadn't been in the way?'

'I want what I want. There are no extenuating circumstances. So spare me your teeny-bopper, Freudian maunderings. When can I see you?'

'Felix, I'm trying to save you.'

'Oh save! I can save myself. I don't require you to save me, only to be with me. Obviously Jason is not there. Get in a taxi immediately.'

'I have no money. I'm in my dressing-gown.'

'No idiotic excuses. Come at once.'

'I can't leave Jason,' she said quietly. 'I must make everything right.'

'Don't you see, you stupid little girl, nothing can ever be again *right*?'

'No, I don't see. Please leave, Felix. Only for a week. While you're gone I'll – I'll do something.'

'You've done quite enough.'

'Jason is planning to tell George that you raped me. At the same time he's so mixed up he thinks George was involved. It will be very bad for you if he tells George. But it will be worse if he kills you. I can stop him doing both. Only you must be physically out of range.'

'He'll never tell George. The two of them are alike in one respect. They don't want their names besmirched. Your quaint honour is Jason's quaint honour. He does not want George – or anyone – to know what's happened to you. It would make him look a fool and that he cannot bear. He won't want the world to hear he was hoodwinked by his daughter and his dealer. All this is not very pure, you know. No, he will turn it all into money, into scandal. He will make himself raped by FFA. He will be the outraged virgin, you see?'

'I do. You're right. And you're talking like Felix again. But these ideas will take a few days to come into his mind. That's why you must leave town. You mustn't see me ... '

'Yes I must.'

'Felix,' she shouted, 'be sensible.'

'It is hardly you who should offer this advice.'

'I never thought you'd stay,' she suddenly said.

'What?'

'I thought you'd take my virginity and that would be that. Eleanor said you didn't hang about much. I never expected we'd go on. Honestly. I thought after the second or third time – '

'I'd conveniently disappear for ever. So you were making use of me.'

'No, no. I had no plans, no uses. It was as though there was a secret between us and I had to find it out. You seemed never to want anything for very long. I just didn't see why I should be an exception.'

'And so by the peculiar mental processes of a fifteen year old I was the fortunate fool designated to be your first lover.'

'My only lover, Felix. I don't think that makes you either fortunate or a fool. It's all too strange for name-calling. I think we loved each other.'

'We do now.'

'Yes.'

'Hopelessly. Without hope.'

'Yes.' She watched the tears drip on to her hand.

'I wonder what I shall do with this passion I have for you.'

'I don't know.'

'Clover, will you come to me? Right now?'

'No. Jason is – '

He didn't listen. He was taking a very long breath.

'Goodbye, beauty,' he said in his sweetest voice.

Clover hesitated. Jason's key was in the lock.

'Goodbye.'

Clover laid her head on her arms. Jason watched her breathing slowly and deeply. Timidly, he touched her hair. She was fast asleep.

twenty-six

'Jason is a mad person, you know, although he's a good man. He *is*. But I've never seen him as mad as he was those last days in New York. He wouldn't let me leave the loft. I wasn't allowed to go to school or make phone calls or answer the phone. If I stood next to the window or looked as if I might be going to he'd pull me away. He wanted to hide me, to hide us both. He thought there were spies in the street – George Facer spies, I suppose. He was even paranoid about the neighbours and imagined them conspiring with FFA. He didn't want anyone to see me the way I was. I looked pretty terrible with a black eye and a split lip and a lump on my forehead. Then there was the pain in my side. He was very guilty about what he'd done and frightened that he could have been so violent towards me. At the same time he was still angry. He felt betrayed – more by me than by either George or Felix. So he would nurse me and cosset me like a precious baby, then shout at me and call me a whore and storm about and smash things. Then he'd cry and treat me like a baby again.

'I was afraid of him. But I felt more sorry than afraid. I didn't try to explain or excuse what I'd done. It would only have made matters worse, so I hardly said anything. I had nothing to say. It was as though my brain had gone numb and my tongue dried up, and sometimes I wondered whether I'd ever speak again. I just watched Jason. I watched him behave like a madman.

'He spent half the day on the telephone. He'd ring the gallery five or six times and yell at the receptionist and bellow at Schuyler and demand to speak to George and be refused and rant and make threats and call everyone thieves and impostors and much worse. When he got really obscene they'd hang up. Then he'd call Felix, but Felix never answered. Felix was out of town or out of the country. Anyway, he was one hundred per cent unavailable. (He did send me a letter which Jason intercepted and tore to pieces.) Then he'd ring his lawyer who wasn't happy with him but agreed to help him. Jason wanted money for the sold paintings and the unsold paintings returned. At first Sam said that the gallery had agreed to pay him. Jason asked for a cheque to be sent round by messenger. The messenger never arrived. Then Sam told him that a cheque had just been posted but of course the next morning it didn't come. It never came. Then FFA said they would return the unsold paintings in six months. Then they said all the paintings had been sold and he would be paid in two months, provided he did restoration work on *The Three Virtues*. When Jason again demanded immediate payment, he was informed via Sam that he owed FFA $18,000 for the damaged painting. When Jason asked Sam why he hadn't filed a writ against the gallery, Sam said that it was an inappropriate moment in time for writs. Jason had a tantrum and called Sam all the usual names and implied that he was conspiring with FFA. The next day Sam's secretary rang to say that George had filed suit against Jason for wilful destruction of private property. Jason fired Sam.

'Meanwhile he was ringing critics and editors or they were ringing him. Each time he gave them his version of the opening the story became more distorted. I had the feeling they were all enjoying Jason's misery and rage. He tried the van Zuptens but they had left for Amsterdam. No one knew or no one would say what had happened to *The Three Virtues*. Then George's lawyer rang and warned that if Jason didn't calm down and keep quiet, George would sue him for libel as well as vandalism. Jason found a new lawyer who filed a writ against FFA and then went on holiday to the Bahamas.

'Felix had been right, though. Jason may have wanted to kill him, but he did not want to expose him. To expose Felix would have meant exposing me and exposing himself. In the end he stopped mentioning Felix completely. Felix seemed to have merged with George who merged with FFA which merged with the whole art business and probably half the world. He was waging the old campaign all over again, only this time it was not a preoccupation. It was an obsession. He was giving his life to it, the poor bloody fool. I sat and held my aching ribs and watched him.

'Finally he learned that George and Vivienne had returned to London and that Schuyler was in Toronto, his place being temporarily taken by Gina. Gina seemed to be the last straw. Even when she returned his call, he wouldn't speak to her. His frustration was like an ulcer that had suddenly burst. He saw how the mess would go on and on with the gallery and the lawyers doing nothing and everyone lying, including himself.

'He rang Peter Caccia, an artist on Broome Street, and got the telephone number of a warehouse in Brooklyn. Then he swore Peter to secrecy. When the van arrived two days later, I couldn't believe what I was seeing.

' "Jason, what's going on?" I asked. Four men were packing up the paintings and carrying them downstairs. Jason was watching the street for spies.

' "No concern of yours," he answered. Then, "Clover, you'd better start collecting your things." We were running away.

'What does it matter, I thought, and took down my suitcase from the top shelf of the cupboard. A man arrived that same afternoon. Someone I had met before named Zubik who liked Jason's work and had been introduced to him by Felix. Everyone had been introduced to him by Felix. Jason made me stay in my room while Mr Zubik wrote out a cheque for $5,000. The next day the painting was taken away.

'I read seven books in five days. It stopped me thinking about my face and the pain in my side and what was going to happen to us. Jason went to the bank. While he was out the telephone rang several times, but I didn't answer it. I wanted to desperately. I imagined Felix calling from London or Rome. But I couldn't pick it up. I'd promised not to answer the phone and I was really trying to keep my promise this time. When Jason returned he called Avis and rented a car for the next morning. I asked if I might withdraw my money from the Canal Street bank. I told him about the taxi fares, everything. He said over his dead body would I withdraw Felix Koning's dirty dollars. I protested it wasn't fair. The money was mine and I was doing everything he wanted to try to make up for hurting him so much and couldn't I keep it. He looked at me as he had the morning after the opening, so I let the matter drop. Later I asked very gently if I might take my cello and he agreed. When we left Harrison Street it looked as though we had never lived there. At least it wasn't as bad as leaving Sussex. There was no Molly and no secret place.

'It was while we were driving across Kansas that I realized why I'd done it. How can I explain it to you? I have difficulty with the words. They seem false. But listen. I wanted to be with Felix, and I knew Jason wouldn't want me to be with Felix. But my wanting was stronger than my wish to be a good daughter. At least it was then. So first of all I deceived my father for the obvious reason: to be with Felix and to go on being with Felix because there was a secret between us and I had to find it out. But there was another reason. I deceived him to defend myself – as a protection against Jason's personality which was too strong to bear. Deception doesn't suit me. It's not in my nature and so it makes me unhappy because I'm all the time fighting myself. But it was something I had to do to grow up. Do you understand? It was a way I could separate myself from Jason and still be with him. Because I wasn't ready to run away. Yet I couldn't be his baby anymore. I used deception to get free of him. Felix and deceit: they seemed to be the only way to grow up. But the strain of the lie began to hurt. It was always there, like the ache in my side. Felix and deception were not me. So I told Jason about Felix and deception. It's all my fault, but it had to be. Perhaps you think I just substituted one older man for another. That's what Emma said and Emma isn't stupid. Maybe it's true, but it had to be.

'Driving across Kansas in a great big Mercury, I suddenly felt sad but not sorry. I knew I was responsible but that I didn't have to be guilty. I asked Jason to stop the car so I could get out and walk a bit. I crawled through a barbed wire fence and went to the top of one of those little hills that rise up and roll all around one like waves. I could see sixty miles in every direction. I'd never been anywhere so open and soft, even the marshes and the Downs. I laughed and cried. I loved it. Although I knew I'd never come back to the place or see it again in my life. It was a moment and I was me, Clover, and I could do anything I wanted. Because I could do anything I wanted, I chose to remain with my father. I might not be happy and everything might be crazy, but I would never be again in the complicated misery of the past few months. Of course I wouldn't have Felix either.

'I called Jason and he came to me, all grumpy as usual, and stood beside me on the little hill, not really wanting to. (He'd rather look at nature than be in it.) I took his hand and he didn't snatch it away. I asked him if he thought we could ever make peace. He wouldn't answer, so I said I meant to stay with him until we did make peace because that was what I wanted most in the world, and that everything else, the rest of my life, must come later. That was what I wanted.

'Well, we began to talk again. Even when we argued I didn't mind too much because at least we were talking. I tried to be calm and patient with him and to hold my tongue and my temper, but he did annoy me so, constantly reminding me of my promise never to contact Felix and asking me over and over if my period had come. I admitted I may have been stupid in lots of ways but not in that way. Once, somewhere in northern Missouri, I was so fed up with his nagging that I told him he ought to be grateful to Felix for being responsible enough to have seen straightaway to my welfare in the maternity department. Tactless of me, but you can't imagine what a nuisance Jason was.'

'I think I can.'

'We drove and drove. For more than two weeks. Jason would decide we were bound for St Louis then change his mind and opt for Denver. *En route* to Denver, he announced that we must see the Grand Canyon. After those beautiful little Kansas hills, I couldn't think of anything more boring or more vulgar than a lot of big, coloured rocks and I told him so. An hour later he said I was probably right. We were going to

Brice Canyon instead. We drove north. I don't know how Jason kept it up. He seemed never to want to stop driving. Oh we were running away all right. He didn't even want to take a break for meals and when I reminded him that I was a growing girl and occasionally needed to eat, he said he thought I'd grown quite enough and that he'd prefer not to have any more growing, thank you.

'Some of the motels were all right. They even had swimming pools – enormous ones, although of course it was too cold to swim. I did manage to watch television – something Jason almost never allowed, and I don't know why he suffered it during that journey. Maybe he simply wanted to forget everything too in films and quiz programmes and endless, endless news. Sometimes we'd just pull over to a rest stop and sleep in the car. Whenever we did this I felt terribly nervous and would wake up at the slightest sound. I don't like America much. Even the countryside is menacing.

'Once we stopped for pancakes at a big diner just outside Cheyenne. I could see the city lights from the window. They looked glittering and cold and the air was so clear. It was three in the morning but the place was packed. There must have been fifty articulated lorries in the parking lot. I could hear the creaking of the brakes and the revving of the engines. It was bitterly cold and all the trucks were filthy with frozen mud. The diner was very warm. Besides the waitresses I was the only woman in the place. I asked Jason if I might play something on the juke-box. They have these little ones at every table, you see. It's really sweet. He said yes, so I played three songs. You get three songs for fifty cents. We listened to Sam Cook while we ate our pancakes with blueberries. Jason looked very sad. The song seemed to remind him of something. Suddenly, out of his usual eating silence, out of nowhere, he asked me the question he'd never asked.

' "Do you love Felix?"

'I blushed. I can still be quite embarrassed at times although I hate it like anything. It's difficult for me to think of Felix and my father simultaneously. I want to squirm away. I said I did love Felix but that it had taken me a long while to realize I loved him and now it was too late and I wasn't sure what my feelings were, everything being so crazy and driving around like this. I said I was unhappy because I knew Felix was upset.

' "Oh upset! And what about me? Don't give a damn if I'm upset. Perfectly all right if your father's upset, let's wring our hands over Herr Koning's delicate sensibilities."

' "I just like him. I can't hate him simply because you want me to."

257

' "Wonderful! My daughter is in love with a thief, a swindler, an impostor, a lecher and an ageing ponce into the bargain. It's like saying you *like* a green mamba."

'It didn't seem the right moment to list what I considered to be Felix's better qualities. So I said I'd sort it out with myself and probably get over it in time as I've been told by grown-ups that one does, but what did it matter anyway since I was never going to see Felix again. And yet at that very moment I was watching the door to the diner, expecting Felix somehow to walk through it. Imagine, in the middle of Wyoming. I said, speaking of driving around, didn't he think it was time we stopped somewhere. The sadness in his eyes became the Jason glare. He muttered something about the eminently practical Miss Englefield and whipped out a road map. He spread it on the table.

' "Choose," he commanded.

'I know Jason, and I know when to call his bluff and I was very tired just then, and it was hurting me to think of never seeing Felix, so I closed my eyes and made circles with my finger and stabbed at the map and said, "Here!" We both leaned forward to have a look. When I lifted my finger we read the word Hurricane. Jason gave a horrible grin and said that my instincts were perversely infallible and that I deserved everything I got, including him for a father. Then he drew radiating patterns around Hurricane while he drank his coffee.

'Well, we went. We had to go somewhere and somewhere turned out to be Utah. The scenery was very beautiful, although for me too big and dramatic. The little town was all new and ugly, but the air was wonderful. That night we stayed in a motel where we were the only guests, which seemed a bit ominous for our social life in Hurricane. I asked if we could go to a Mexican restaurant because I had developed this passion for chilli and tacos and also because it was Thanksgiving and the next day would be 25 November and I would be seventeen years old. Jason had completely forgotten.

'We rented a funny little stucco house that reminded me of the sort of place where the outlaw's mother always lives in Western movies. The immediate vicinity was pretty spare, but the backdrop of earth and mountains and sky was tremendous. I felt as I did that first night in New York. We sat at the table, our suitcases by the door and my cello lying on the couch like a patient recovering from an attack. We both felt how exhausted we were. We had been like dazed people for three weeks – sleepwalkers, I mean sleepdrivers. I burst into tears. Jason lay down on the bed and fell asleep.

'I lived in the house in Hurricane for over a year. I didn't go to school and Jason didn't want me to go. Educate yourself, he said, you'll be better off. Degrees and credentials are traps set by the academic establishment to ensnare good minds and impress bad ones. Jason is self-taught. But that's not the same as being self-educated. He went to public school. It was all very well for him to tell me to reject everything because he did. He wanted me to be a savage – a *pure* savage, of course.

'The nearest High School was thirty-five miles away and seemed a pretty dismal place. What could I do? I borrowed books from the travelling library and tried to find out as much as I could about my A-level subjects. A-levels were awfully chimerical just then and as for Oxford – well. I'd have to count myself lucky to get into Macalester. Anyway, I read a lot. A *lot*. Natural History, Ancient Greece, novels. And I practised the cello and drew and walked miles collecting plant specimens, and made a flower press and got hold of an old radio and so on. What could I do? I was so lonely. Lonely again. No one wanted to know us.

'I didn't hear from Felix. I realized I'd been wrong and that obstacles didn't necessarily sharpen his interest. Who could say what did sharpen it or blunt it or bring it into being in the first place? Even I, who had done so in the biggest possible way, couldn't tell. Every night I dreamt of him. Once I dreamt that he was a baby, a beautiful baby with bright-blue eyes, as he must have been long ago in Vienna or Prague or Munich, wherever he was born, if he was born. I dreamt he was mine and that I was breast-feeding him. I woke up terribly embarrassed.

'I would cry so hard I'd nearly choke to death.

'Meanwhile, Jason began another attack on FFA. Now there were four lawyers involved: two for George and two for Jason. All in New York and here we were in Utah with the money running out. We were in a worse position than we had been two years ago, except that now we had a washing machine.

'Then Jason met Annie, thank God. Annie was the waitress in the Mexican restaurant. At first I thought she was Mexican herself, but in fact she was a quarter Red Indian. She was small and dark and, I thought, by nature sad, or she'd had a sad life. But she liked Jason straightaway, I could tell. There's a type of woman who does like Jason straightaway. The Dollies of this world, I suppose. But Annie wasn't a Dolly. She was an Annie as I was a Clover and Jason was a Jason. Only she didn't make such a fuss about being herself as we make about being ourselves. She never went on about rights and reasons like we do. She was very patient and very tolerant and she needed to be because she moved in with Jason and me that spring and is living with him still.

About a month after she arrived, she told Jason she was pregnant but that she couldn't say whether the baby was his. It might be, it might not. There had been somebody else before Jason, you see, and she had broken with him when she met Jason. She's like me, I guess. A one-man woman. Not awfully modern. Jason just looked up from what must have been his sixtieth letter to George Facer and told her he couldn't give a damn one way or another. If she were worried about staying on, stop worrying. A baby was a baby.

'He kept at it for another month, writing letters, telephoning New York, talking about art and impostors and running out of money. I didn't even have a bicycle. Annie was practically supporting us. It wasn't fair and I told Jason so. He got angry and smashed something and wrote another letter. Then one day it just stopped. Stopped. Like a howling wind drops at sunset. You could hear the silence. We were all conscious of it. He took out his old red notebooks and began leafing through them. Annie and I exchanged looks. We liked each other, although I did most of the talking. We tried to make him eat, but he refused. He seemed to be satisfying some other craving. He read all night.

'The next day he drove in to town in our old banger of a Ford and cancelled our post office box. He returned with pads of paper, pens, pencils and a few acrylic paints. I knew what he meant to do. He was going to work out his theory of aesthetics. It was already running to five hundred incomprehensible pages and what he might still have to add I couldn't imagine. He certainly didn't intend to subtract anything.

' "Jason," I said, "why don't you paint? You're a painter."

' "I can't afford to paint. Besides, I'm in mourning."

' "For what?"

' "For the *Virtues*."

'I told him he couldn't mourn for ever. Why was he not thinking of the responsibility to his art that he was always running on about? It was still there, waiting for him, missing him. Besides, one didn't have to paint on canvas. Indians painted on the sand, cavemen painted on the rocks. Why didn't he paint the rocks? If a baby is a baby, then a painting must be a painting.

'Of course he snorted at me and grumbled something about standing too close to the scorching heat of my intellect. But you know the following week my watercolours went missing. And my wax crayons. I went for a walk, searching for plants for my press. I headed out towards the mountains and what do you think I found? Jason! With my watercolours and crayons and poster paints in the midst of all that glorious nature which he had always and only admired from a distance and which was beginning to bore me to death. He was crouched next to a boulder – painting rocks! He was moaning about how it just wouldn't do and he needed bigger brushes and the whole idea was ridiculous, and I could see what a wonderful time he was having. Jason was having fun! It was as though he had been the prisoner of the square and the rectangle and had suddenly been given a reprieve and was behaving like a child on his birthday.

'He painted little rocks, big rocks, everything he liked the shape of, slapping on the colour with an abandon I'd never seen in him before. Not being at all careful or considered, not agonizing for weeks over the placement of a line. The little ones he brought home and worked on in the evenings. They were all over the windowsills, the shelves, the floor. They began popping up in the barren front yard. First he grouped them in clumps. Then the clumps merged and became a rock garden. Annie and I applauded. Really, it was very fine. Then one day it rained.

'I stood with Jason by the painted boulder, the two of us under a big, black umbrella, watching the colours slip and slide from the surface and slowly merge like the ingredients in a batter. Jason didn't say anything. He seemed pleased. We stopped by another boulder next to the road. A great streak of red was running between the crevasses of the rock and into the ground where it was making a puddle which in turn would be absorbed by the parched earth. It reminded me of blood – no, blood and water; water washing away blood and running in rivulets down a body and leaving the body clean and shining. I felt a little sad, but I understood what Jason was doing. No one could take these paintings away. Only God could take them. He didn't seem to mind God too much. I told him I thought this was a good sort of mourning. He rested his arms on my shoulders and kissed me three times as fathers do in Russian novels.

'In the summer Jason took a job with a building contractor. Three or four times a week he would do carpentry and the rest of the time paint rocks and write in his notebooks. Annie couldn't work any longer so she was at home, but I still did all the cooking. I'm a very good cook, you know. I asked Annie to teach me to drive and she said yes. We bumped around the back roads, laughing all the time, nearly hysterical at my incompetence. Anyway, I improved and finally learned to do it. But I wonder Annie didn't have a miscarriage. She's a very healthy, absorbing woman, I guess. She could go bumping around and having babies for ever. She and Jason seemed happy enough. But I knew he would be very unhappy when the time came for me to leave.

'The time was coming. I told you before how alien America makes me feel. It's just too big and lonely and everyone is so afraid of loneliness. Americans seek each other out and flock together in dismal places where they make a lot of noise and get very excited. The crowded English are always having too much of each other and are clever at finding methods of slipping away and keeping their distance, even in proximity. I prefer the little distance to the great big spaces. Do you know what I mean? And the dryness didn't suit me. I missed the lushness of England, the way nature is never really dead. I was depressed, and I wanted company and to go to school and to begin making my life away from rocks, even beautiful painted ones, and away from Jason.

'On my eighteenth birthday I said, "Jason I have to go now." Of course I didn't have any idea where or how. "I wouldn't leave you, only I can't bear it here and you have Annie and quite soon the baby – I'm sure it's yours – and anyway, I'll come and see you. I promise I will."

'He raised all the anticipated objections: Felix, money, my age, very boring. He went on raising them for days. I kept quiet until he couldn't think of any more. Annie said that she had left home at seventeen and that I wanted and needed to go to school and somehow a way ought to be found for me to do so. I kissed her when she said that. Timidly, I suggested that if I were to pass my A-levels I might get a scholarship. Then Jason went sullen and brooded for a week. Finally, he announced, with great reluctance, that he had thought of a way I might begin. He could give me enough money for a bus ticket to New York and a bit more. I reminded him of my savings account at the Canal Street bank and he winced. Then I had to make all over again those promises about Felix. But even Jason could not escape the fact that I now needed Herr Koning's taxi fares.

'The bargain – I knew it would be a bargain – was that I go to the Brooklyn warehouse and check on the paintings in storage, then contact the Zubiks and try to sell them one or more Englefields. Jason would write to them first. They would probably say yes in advance. Anyway, I could stay with them and Jason and I could split the money for the painting. I might even be able to repeat the process if I were lucky. I might get some money and really make my start in life. A-levels and Oxford seemed suddenly more visible.

'Couldn't I go to school here, Jason asked for the hundredth time. I answered that I would be too unhappy. I didn't like the feeling that came out of the ground. I was very surprised when he said sadly that he understood. He even said he admired my spirit and that he supposed, in the end, that he was proud of me, which is a lot for Jason to say. I was sorry to miss the baby, which was due in February but, as you know, when I must do something I must do it. Everything else in the world seems to shrink.

'The day after New Year's I got on a Greyhound with one suitcase. It was snowing. I watched Jason shivering in the cold as he waited for the bus to pull away. I remembered taking Eleanor to the train station in Sussex and leaving her on the platform to wait for the Victoria train. I realized how desolate her waitings must have been. I never knew at the time. Now I know. I was desolate and I, supposedly, wanted to leave. Why, I thought, must we all always be saying goodbye? I opened the window and held out my hand in the freezing wind. Jason came and took it and kissed it, first the back then the palm.

' "Peace, father," I said.

' "Peace, daughter."

'That was the last time I saw him.

'Then came the long journey, during which I read and cried and ate a great many cheeseburgers. I was panting for a steak but was determined to save my money for New York.

'New York! There was so much to hide from, so many people to avoid. I felt afraid of the streets. One meets people on the streets in New York. First of all I must avoid Felix, although a very dark and powerful part of me wanted to see him and knew I could in a minute if I made even a little indication. Then I had to avoid George and everyone connected with FFA, even the artists and the artists' families. I must avoid my old school-friends, I must avoid the places where any of these people went. It seemed I was allowed only the Brooklyn warehouse and Marion Zubik's foldaway bed.

'When I arrived at Port Authority I rang Harry Zubik who said he would be away for a week but that I should come over immediately, stay with Marion and the children, and we would discuss the paintings when he got back. The next morning I went from Eighty-fifth Street to the Canal Street bank, feeling very peculiar to be back in our old neighbourhood. I dreaded meeting anyone. In fact I saw a painter from our building in the queue but I turned away and he left without noticing me. Outside I hailed a cab and gave the driver the address of the Brooklyn warehouse. I wanted to see the paintings myself before Harry Zubik set eyes on them. I couldn't help laughing at the way Felix's taxi money was finally being put to use. And after all my fantasies about Bendel's. Unfortunately, the outcome was not funny at all. Nothing has been funny since that day.

'The vicinity of the warehouse was so desolate and frightening that I was very extravagant and asked the driver to wait. I pressed the buzzer but there was no answer. I rang again, constantly looking over my shoulder to make certain the taxi hadn't abandoned me. Finally, a man came, big and surly with an accent I could hardly understand. I explained what I wanted but he just looked me up and down. I might as well have been talking to an orang-utan. I held out the duplicate papers Jason had given me and which the warehouse manager originally had given to him. The orang-utan said he would fetch the manager and started to walk off with my papers, but I snatched them back. I was terrified of him and of the whole place. I ran to the door to see if the taxi still waited. Eventually, the manager came. I introduced myself and showed him the papers. He checked them with a painful carefulness. Outside, the meter ticked away, gobbling up my little stash. When I think of all the freezing walks up Madison Avenue and Hudson Street, all the tights and jumpers I didn't buy in order to keep that taxi waiting.

'The manager looked at me through horn-rimmed glasses and said I must be mistaken. There were no paintings in the warehouse, none at all. I said *he* must be mistaken and begged him to check again. He said they'd never had any such paintings, ever. I said what about the receipts, what about Jason's cheque? He shrugged and said clearly someone had made a mistake. I became very angry. Being angry, I lost all my fear and demanded to inspect the entire warehouse. How could twenty-five paintings have gone missing? The manager bristled and said that if I wished to inspect the building I might do so. Well, I forgot about the taxi and followed him through room after echoing room. I saw fur coats, chaise-longues, pianos, garden urns, old radios, but no paintings. None. I was so desperate I begged him to tell me the truth. There was another room, wasn't there, a secret room with all the paintings safe inside? He assured me there was not. I was in tears, and I think he was beginning to feel a bit sorry for me because he went to great lengths to persuade me that there were not and never had been any paintings by Jason Englefield or any other artist. The answer was simply, he concluded, that there had been a mistake. I returned to the taxi in despair. The charge on the meter was seventy-three dollars and ninety-five cents. All the way back to Manhattan I kept thinking a painting is like a person. It can disappear. It can die.'

'That's why paintings are potentially so valuable. Like us they're mortal – irreplaceable as a life. A book can be reprinted, a song is sung many times. But a painting is different. A photograph of it or a reproduction can never pretend to be the real thing. To give a painting away or sell it can seem like abandoning one's child.'

'Exactly. It was as though a murder had been committed, or a massacre, although a kidnapping was probably more likely. I knew it in my bones, my heart, my capillaries, my fingernails, the roots of my hair. I knew it: Facer Fine Arts had doubled their collection of Englefields by adding to those of the October show and those on consignment the twenty-five Jason had hidden in the warehouse. Not one Englefield was left.

'I sat in the back seat, rattling over the Williamsburg Bridge, trying to contain my fear and my bafflement and not allow them to boil over into hysteria. I tried, with all my might, to think. I knew I must wait and not tell Jason straightaway. He'd been a good deal saner lately, but he was still capable of self-destructive actions. Perhaps there was a clue I was missing. Perhaps I might be able to do something, although I had no idea what. If all else failed I would buy gelignite with the rest of Felix's taxi money and blow up Facer Fine Arts before poor Jason did.

'There was no one in the Zubik apartment when I returned. I wanted to lie down and cry like a tired child. I wanted to tell someone what a terrible thing had happened and complain and cry and complain. But I kept saying to myself you must go forward, you must go forward. Like a robot I took out Marion's New York telephone directory. I phoned Peter Caccia, the artist who had given Jason the name of the warehouse, and asked him if he still remembered it. He said he did, and it was not the one I had just been to. Then which was it, I asked. He gave me the number of a place in Queens and asked if I would like to meet him for a drink at One Fifth Avenue? I said no thanks, I had another engagement. I rang the warehouse in Queens. They had never heard of Peter Caccia, Jason Englefield or Facer Fine Arts. With a feeling of awful certainty, I began looking through the Zubiks' collection of art magazines and exhibition catalogues – they hardly read anything else – and found the catalogue for a group show in September 1983 at FFA. In it were two large paintings by Peter Caccia. He had always been with Kozinsky.

'The hair rose on the back of my neck. I felt cold and started to shake. I thought I was going to be sick. Everything was suddenly sinister, even the Zubiks' cosy, splashy apartment. I was in a snake pit, a nest of scorpions. I was in New York and Peter Caccia knew it. The Zubiks knew it. Warning signals were all around me, and golly I was reading them.'

'You're a good guesser too.'

'Yes, but too late. I raced to the telephone and switched on the answering machine. Marion didn't return. I sat on her fat, persimmon sofa, holding myself in my own arms, listening to the telephone ring and thinking I must get out of here. I must go home, but I have no home. I calculated my chances of support from Jason's parents. Not much. They had been affronted by Jason, had never met me and wouldn't be happy to see me under the best of circumstances. If I had been five years younger, maybe. I'm always the wrong age. From Monica: if I were to turn up, Jeremy would send me away whatever my mother might think. After all, a bargain's a bargain, isn't it? From Jason's sister: I had no idea where she was.

'The telephone rang. This time I couldn't bear it. I let it stop then switched on the machine. There was a message from Marion's daughter, one for Harry, Peter Caccia again, and then a voice like platinum but soft as a cat.

' "Marion darling, could I leave a message for Clover Englefield . . ."

'I switched off the machine. I was shaking so badly my teeth began to chatter. He could appear, just appear at any moment, and here I was, a bird in a nest. I wouldn't be able to keep him out. I couldn't sit and listen to the doorbell ring. And if I let him in it would all be over. There would be no hope. Emma would have said use him. Use him to get the paintings back, but I couldn't do it. I would have to ask him what had happened to them and he would say it was all George, nothing to do with me, angel, and he could prove it. And I would have to believe him – or not. Then he'd want me to come back to his apartment.

'I went to the window and looked down at the street. It was snowing; New York was icy and beautiful. I could see into the apartments across the way, all of them warm, all of them, it seemed, full of paintings. Families and paintings. Acquisitions. I never wanted to get back to England so much. Here everyone turned to scorpions and slugs and orang-utans and green mambas. There were two people in England I knew I could trust. I thought of Emma and I thought of you.'

'I'm glad.'

'I sent a telegram to Jason to say I'd arrived safely and would contact him in a few days. I counted my remaining money. There was enough for a stand-by, if I were lucky. I telephoned Emma and told her my plan. I packed, got a taxi, terrified of meeting Felix on the street, got to the airport and made the flight. Emma met me at Gatwick.'

'And while you were travelling on Greyhounds across Indiana and Ohio, searching Brooklyn warehouses and fleeing the North American continent, I was wracking my brain for as yet untried ways of finding you.

'I now see that Felix was telling his own kind of truth. After lunch with him, I tried to contact Hurricane. As he predicted, no success. When I was informed that the box number no longer belonged to Jason Englefield, it was as though you had both ceased to exist. How could I know you were thirty miles down the freeway? But Jason is brutal. When he decides to cut, he cuts.

'I did locate his sister. She lives in Esher, married to a doctor. Now don't make a face. She's most concerned about you and wants very much to see you. There. You have an aunt, my dear, and this is her address. Cousins too as far as I can make out. The rest I leave to you. Monica I didn't see again. I wrote her a note expressing my frustrations at being unable to locate you. She replied that she was very sorry. After that, no more messages. I wrote to several New York galleries. Unanimously, they referred me to Facer Fine Arts. Then one evening at supper Anthea handed me your letter.

'I was surprised, as I never receive mail at Halford Road anymore. I opened the envelope as Anthea went on talking. A moment later I went into modified hysterics. There you were before me in the form of a firm little hand, the person I wanted most in the world to see, entreating me for an assignation, the whole letter brimming with mysterious import. There was your address, your telephone number – there they were. I burst out laughing, much to Anthea's consternation. I laughed until I nearly cried. When she asked me what the trouble was, I replied that it *was* a comedy after all. And it was. I was watching it from the orchestra stalls like the climax of some Restoration piece with all its stock characters, twists of plot, intercepted messages, lost children, missing relatives, mouldy contracts and secret lovers popping out of armoires to compound and resolve the chaos. I was forced to make quite a little fuss over Anthea after that and sat twitching through some dreary product of the Hungarian cinema. Consequently, I didn't have a chance to reread your letter until I returned to my room.

'When I rang you yesterday and told you about everything that's happened during these nine years, I felt in a kind of dream. I was delighted at the prospect of seeing you and yet, I confess, a little sad. You'll understand, won't you, when I say that I began to fear the emptiness now that there was no detective work to lift me out of my Limbo, no motive force to provide me with decent resolution. Don't worry, I'm not going to turn maudlin.

'Finding you compensates for everything. And so, dear Clover, here you are looking as I imagined you'd look when one day I had the very great pleasure of handing you this cheque as I'm handing it to you now.'

'Thank you, Charles. Really, thank you.'

'Don't go on.'

She lifted her eyes to him, troubled. 'Why did she love me so much? I was just a stupid little girl. What did I ever do to – '

'Please don't say deserve it. You were yourself. She loved you for yourself. The former is the best we can be and the latter is the most we can hope for. I know, know, I'd better shut up. Forgive me. Forgive also my insatiable curiosity. What will you do?'

'Hmmmm?'

'You're preoccupied. Of course you are. *Do*. With the money.'

'Why – um – pay your fee!' She gave him a celestial smile.

'Quite unnecessary.'

'Don't be daft, Charles. I know you're broke. You've had a lot of trouble. What happened?'

'One day I'll tell you. But for now let my fee be the answer to my question. What will you do?'

'Buy a flat for me and Em and Molly and live with them and go to a sixth-form college and pass my A-levels and get into Oxford. Buy a new cello and never throw the old one away.'

'Bravo.'

'Send something to Jason and Annie for the baby.'

'He'll send it back.'

'So will I. Eventually I'll win. Jason will be glad for me. He'll behave like a grump, but he'll be glad. Anyway, those are the first things I'll do. Oh Charles, where's the drawing? *The Three Virtues*.'

'It's here. I've been keeping it for you since your ninth birthday.'

He handed Clover the drawing, still wrapped in brown paper and string. She opened the package.

'I remember, sort of. It's been so long. Thank you for saving it, Charles and not selling it to Felix even though you needed the money. I'll send it to Jason. Oh, when he sees how this has been saved . . . '

'Everything is retrievable. I hope.'

'He'll be so happy. Charles, this is the best of all.'

'You do love your father. In spite of everything he's a man to be envied.'

'Charles,' she held out her hand to him. He prepared to say goodbye, possibly for ever.

'There's one more thing I want to do with the money. But I need you to help me. You're the only one I trust. Promise me you'll help me.'

'Of course I promise. To do what?'

'Sue Facer Fine Arts.'

Suddenly the idea of seeing George Facer was an idea Charles didn't mind too much.

twenty-seven

As Charles was making his way from the Perth Hotel, Clover was frowning over her pastry. The furrows between her pale eyebrows were not symptomatic of concentration on her cooking – she carried that off without thought, instinctively – but on the news, probably bad, definitely frustrating, which Charles would bring concerning the case of Englefield v. Facer Fine Arts.

Proceedings had begun in April and it was now September. The law is slow, said Charles over and over. It grindeth exceedingly small. Meanwhile she ground her teeth in her impatience. The law and justice were disparate entities, it turned out. She knew the generalization, but she had never experienced its maddening particulars. She had said from the beginning that she wanted no one to be hurt, 'no one' meaning not only Felix but George as well. There was no point in fines, jail sentences, ruined reputations – whatever she innocently supposed to be the certain and immediate outcome of such litigation. All she wanted was the paintings. Jason's paintings returned to Jason. It was so simple: the gallery had them, Jason wanted them, the gallery must return them to their rightful owner, Jason. Wasn't that simple? No. It was and remained endlessly complex. Charles's carefully worded requests met with silence, denial, counter-accusations, and demands both fresh and dredged up from the murky Englefield past. Above all, they met with delay. Delay in the form of lengthy documents which, no matter how well Charles explained them, only verified Clover's growing conviction that the Law was no beautiful humanist system designed to protect and defend, but the product of a diabolical imagination which had contrived that its end should be to defeat itself amidst labyrinths of ambiguity, excess verbiage and downright bad will. Charles would take her point then define her view of the proceedings as naïve. She would read to him heavily underscored passages from *Bleak House*.

The duplicity of FFA had raised serious doubts as to the possibility of all being well and all manner of things being well in this world. No one would be hurt because nothing would never happen. Matters could go on stagnating like this for weeks or months.

It was not at all to her liking. Especially since money had liberated her once restrained precipitance. On with it, on with it. Money was to make things *go*. She arranged the fruit in concentric circles in the flan tin and supposed she must not mope too much about paintings since everything else was so beautifully progressing. She was busy, she was free. She had Molly to love and Emma to quibble with and Charles for games and talking. There had even been two boys at college, both of whom she had liked dancing and flirting with. They had not been too unintelligent and were kind to animals. They didn't understand painting, but arguments with them proved stimulating enough, and she could win and they didn't seem to resent her winning. Meeting for tea and going to the cinema and talking about their courses was enjoyable. Going to bed was not. She was philosophical. What could one do in the world where even the nicest of boys seemed a bit of a lout? They were short on perception. Perhaps when they had read more, perhaps when they were simply older they would learn to be both more serious and more frivolous. They might turn out all right. But now . . . but after Felix . . . besides, studying and reading and passing her A-levels and suing FFA were more important than flirtations.

Meanwhile she loved the flat in Cornwall Gardens. It was still a bit spare, but it had lovely large windows which overlooked the garden; three bedrooms; a Conran sofa; a working fireplace; and her budding collection of paintings. There were those inherited from Eleanor, a couple of her own not too terrible efforts and three Charles Bevans – two sketches of Clover Englefield and one of Queen Molly, enthroned in wicker and velvet before the television which flickered away continuously for her amusement. (Westerns were the royal favourite.)

Emma understood neither paintings nor Clover's passion for them. Otherwise she maintained that she still knew Clover best and that, without her superintending presence, Jason Englefield's daughter would go the mad way of her mad father. Emma believed in heredity and continued unconsciously to verify her theory by looking exactly like her mother when occasion demanded. She was grateful to Clover for rescuing her from the bondslavery of the Manor House Hotel (Clover had adored rescuing Em) and considered it her duty to protect her friend from the effects of Englefield genes. She continued to insist that the only way out of that disastrous DNA mix-up would be a merger of those genes with Felix Koning's.

Alternatively, she pressed her other favoured design for Clover's future: the screenplay or the memoirs. They went on bickering goodnaturedly. They installed an aquarium, housed stray kittens, resuscitated missel thrushes, acquired a rabbit, and rescued an orphaned mongrel of fantastical temperament from the Battersea Dogs' Home. Molly observed the assembled riff-raff from her serene heights, was unmoved, and turned her attention to Randolph Scott. Clover paid for Emma to take a course in computer programming. Money meant you could save friends. Money also meant grand donations to the World Wildlife Fund, Friends of the Earth, Save the Whale, the Seal and the Tiger, CND, anti-vivisection, the RHS, the Cats' Protection League, as well as long-postponed visits to some shops on South Molton Street. She even made financial restitution to an astonished Mrs Draine. Clover and Emma agreed that all this was excellent. Emma cleaned, Clover cooked. The unlikely friendship flourished. It was still so important, so mysterious.

Money was nice. She sent Jason and Annie something for the baby which had arrived in February and for another which was due the following June. She also sent their air fares to London, but Jason persistently refused to come back. She could tell he was secretly pleased about the suit although he protested she ought to get a better lawyer. 'What you need,' he kept saying, 'is a real killer.'

She advanced Charles money for the litigation. Most of the retainer he gave to Anthea for a mortgage on the Brighton flat. But, like Englefield v. FFA, legal impediments precluded a quick and satisfactory settlement. Anthea continued to abide in the Fulham basement where Charles's presence was still required three nights a week. Nice money had induced her to relinquish the obligatory fourth. The obligatory fourth and sometimes fifth were spent at Cornwall Gardens where Charles initiated Clover into the mysteries of the table and the wine cellar. He also instructed her in virtually every game playable by two people. Emma knitted, watched television and went to bed while they carried on laughing, bidding, groaning, accusing and dragging out the OED until the small hours when Charles walked back to the Perth Hotel. Friday nights became an institution. Anthea got wind of them and raised objections. After three gins too many she accused him of philandering and he was forced, for the first time in months, to raise his courtroom voice to prevent her uttering the dread words she was only too ready to utter: Dirty Old Man.

Tonight was not a Friday, but Charles was coming to dinner anyway. He wanted to talk to Clover. He would not explain why on the telephone, but she knew it was about the suit. She put her tart in the oven. She had a paper to write and a lab report, but still – this was more important. Making everything right must come first. And she would be glad to see Charles. He would make her laugh, correct her first draft and lose at backgammon, whatever George Facer in his deep cupidity might be up to.

The doorbell rang. Emma answered and Charles appeared, a bottle of

St Estephe extended to his hostess, who kissed his cheek and told him that he must not squander his money on wine for her.

'But it's for us,' he protested as usual. 'For your dear burgeoning wine cellar. Your cellar is a great consolation to me.'

'Charles, please tell me what's happened.' She poured him a glass and pulled out the wicker chair on which he liked to sit and watch her cook, making suggestions about the meal until she accused him of kibbutzing. She was a cool cook, if an impatient client, and went smoothly ahead with her preparations. Her hair was cropped, the current fashion allowing her to capitalize on the wisps, now not so golden. The rest of her was a modified version of the old, anarchic Clover couture – a pink jumpsuit and a pair of Dr Martens dyed Gorgeous Guava. She regarded the ensemble as her hardworking-girl uniform. Well, she was a hardworking girl and she wanted to know what was going on.

Charles took a long swallow. 'Precisely nothing.'

She stopped for a moment, giving herself space for a sigh.

'What can we *do*?' She turned to him, her outstretched hands encased in oven gloves that were two alligator heads. Impatient. Always impatient.

'I've come with a proposition,' replied the soul of patience. 'But first you might refill a poor man's glass.'

She did as he asked and smiled. 'You're a bit of a tease, Charles. What's up?'

'More verbose and highly ungrammatical letters.'

'Something new and different.'

'They might keep us at bay for months. Shall I elaborate?'

'No.' She clutched her head. 'Oh God, poor Jason. He's got to have the paintings back. He'll die without them. Painting rocks is good therapy, but . . . '

'Shhhh. They will also, as you know, cost us a good deal of money. That's what I've been thinking about morning and night for the past week. It's true that we might eventually defeat them. There have been a few similar cases. But they went on for years. They also turned very nasty.'

'I know. I know. People *died*.'

'Well, yes. I know what you're thinking of. Very ugly. There's not so much at stake here, but there is enough. If FFA should ever be able to release those paintings – '

'They'd make a lot of money.'

'The most we can hope for over the next few months is an injunction to prevent them selling any more Englefields.'

'According to them there are no more Englefields.'

'That's their story this week, yes.'

'They could have been selling them secretly for the past year. Oh we've discussed this a million times.'

'Therefore my proposal. The money involved. Your money, Eleanor's money – '

'Please Charles, we know that paintings are more important than money. Besides you're implying that Eleanor wouldn't like my using the trust to save Jason.'

'I implied no such thing.'

She ignored him. 'You know Eleanor. This money is attached to absolutely no invisible strings. She made me a present, not a puppet. I can do as I please with the money, just as she did as she pleased. Besides, even if she did want to make a sort of point to Jason, she believes in art more than she likes revenge.'

'Quite right. I'm sorry. And your priorities are absolutely in order. Nevertheless you are keen to expedite matters.'

'Very.' She jabbed the roast and watched it run a medium rare.

'Then may I offer my proposal?'

'Propose.' The oven door closed with a bang and she leaned against it, arms folded, warming her bottom, all attention.

'I suggest we regroup. That we go underground. My preference for the valour of open combat has yielded to the tactics of the *résistance*.'

'You mean be sneaky.'

'Yes.'

'That's rather out of character.'

'For you too, although we've both accomplished subterfuge with some success, if not inherent flair.'

'Come to the point.'

'I propose that we behave in a manner contrary to our natures, that we fight fire with fire, that we smile to bare our fangs and so settle out of court.'

'How could we do that?'

'Blackmail. It might work, it might not. If it does, this mess could be resolved with alacrity, even amiability – or the pretence of it.'

'But if we settle out of court how will you become a famous lawyer again?'

'You really are quite wonderful. Who says I want to be a lawyer again, let alone a famous one? I took this case for the pleasure of it. It's no longer amusing me. It's ceased to be redolent of poetic justice. It threatens the security of a deserving young woman and subverts the career of a major artist.' Charles was very impressive. When he did come to the point, Clover stood slightly in awe of him. 'The destruction or dispersal of a man's life's work is no laughing matter, however provocative his behaviour. Do I have your permission to try my new plan?'

'Naturally. What is it?' She was so intrigued she nearly burned the potatoes Anna.

'I'll have to backtrack a bit, so you'd better refill my glass. Thank you. Several years ago I subverted a scandal and by so doing brought disaster on myself and my family. The affair involved a painting. It also involved George Facer and Felix Koning.' He hesitated.

'And?'

'Well, others, but those two are the relevant scoundrels.'

'You are close, Charles, even with me.'

'Old habits, my dear.'

He rendered Clover an abbreviated account of the Teniers and its aftermath. She went on with her preparations, aware that he was omitting some cogent particulars.

'So George doesn't know Felix was the fence. Felix does know that George was the informer, but George doesn't know Felix knows.'

'Only we know. And by our knowing we may pull the rabbit out of the hat.'

'But how do *we* know?'

'We have been informed.'

'That means you refuse to name your source.'

'Not indefinitely.'

'Oh Charles, you know there's no better way to exasperate me than by offering a hint and then withdrawing it. I won't let you off. Who told you?'

'If I tell you, will you promise not to question me any further for the moment?'

'Yes.'

'Well, it was my cousin and your mother, Monica Black.'

'But how did she – '

'Uh-uh, you promised. We must get on with this and not linger making soap.'

'All right.' She pouted. She would get it out of him later.

'So Felix would not care for George knowing about his former profession.'

'Not the full iniquity of it, no.'

'And George would certainly not like Felix knowing – although he does know – that his current partner in crime was the stool-pigeon who nearly, without meaning to, put the finger on him.'

'Precisely. One is forced to give Felix his due, though. Few men would so coolly join forces with someone as near a potential threat as George. But then, Felix may have hoped to use his own information against George some day. It would certainly give him a leverage and no doubt a good deal of pleasure. However, I intend to deprive him of that pleasure.'

'Well,' Clover sighed, 'he does adore to plot.'

'He should have lived at the court of Louis Phillipe. He'd have made the ministers jump through hoops. And the rest of us would have been spared a good deal of unpleasantness. Oh I am sorry.'

Clover winced under the sting of Felix's unpalatable past.

'So the plan is to pay each of them a visit?'

'And to inform each of them with a politeness exceeded only by the expenditure of effort necessary to mask my glee, that I am possessed of information which might considerably alter each's opinion of the other and affect their unholy alliance. If it were known that George were partner to a former fence his reputation would certainly suffer. Felix might wriggle away. He's one up on George, but I'm counting on his position being too lucrative to risk or to relinquish without pangs. Then, too, George needs Felix. Felix might set up on his own, but I don't think he'd care for that. He prefers to have someone around to betray for fun and to desert if necessary. The murderer requires a victim. The exploiter cannot exist without the exploited.'

'Don't Charles, please. Felix wouldn't physically hurt anyone. He loathes violence.'

'Maybe so. Anyway, I'm prepared for once in my life to use what I know. They'll understand that I am also prepared, on condition that the paintings are returned within sixty days either to Clover or Jason Englefield, to consign said information to the great and beneficient paper-shredder of my mind. That part they'll have to take on trust.'

'Charles,' she examined the leg of lamb.

'Yes.'

'Dinner is ready.' She turned to him with a huge smile.

'It might not work. It simply might not scare them enough. They know their own strength.'

'It will work. I know it will. Everything will come right. And no one will be hurt.'

'Like your mother, and like me, you have a penchant for protecting those who want no protection. It's a family failing. But yes, hopefully.'

He began to lay the table, making an extra place for Fausta. (Queen Molly preferred dining *tout seul*.) 'Goodness,' he bounced himself up and down a little, 'this really may turn out to be fun.'

'It's too clever.' Clover clapped her hands and brought an hysterical Fausta racing for her supper. 'Imagine them both pretending to have changed their minds about Jason's paintings. I wonder who'll make the first move.'

She quieted the dog whose joy was driving her frenziedly between Clover and Charles. Violet, the rabbit who had the run of the flat, hopped into the kitchen followed by Emma redolent of hairspray and Disco-Gel. Emma had a date. When Fausta had stopped barking and they were all seated, Charles rose to carve.

'If it comes to cracking,' he said, not bothering to conceal his pleasure, 'it'll be George.'

For three weeks they waited, twitching, nailbiting, unable to concentrate, accused by Anthea and Emma of not listening. They speculated, grumbled and swore, but they waited. They played game after game of Scrabble. Clover got a C on her lab report but considered it the price of their gamble. She asserted over and over that she was learning patience at last. Charles could not bring himself to say that this was nothing. He had known waits . . . well, at least this one was costing them neither money nor love. It was a positive delay. He imagined the two culprits conferring, circling each other with cat-like tread. They were at it. The waiting meant they were at it. (If only he could *see* them at it.) They had bitten, he knew, and said as much to Clover and Mrs Plumber, both of whom backed his infallible instincts.

Charles went frequently to his office, having left instructions with both Felix and George that he might be contacted there. He had confronted George Facer at last, and he confided to Clover that he had not minded, not minded at all. In fact he had unashamedly enjoyed himself. He was glad he had not used Monica's information when she had wanted him to, glad he'd saved it, unconsciously, for the critical moment. When he asked Clover if she wished for an account of his meeting with Felix she said no, then yes, then no. A week later she asked him to tell her about it. Charles replied that Felix had listened, unlike George not visibly moved, said he was surprised that a man as intelligent as Charles would bid with such a worthless hand, offered him a drink which Charles refused, then said he was leaving for Rome the next day and had a great deal to do.

'Did he say anything else?' Clover asked.

'He sent you his love.'

It was a Wednesday morning at the end of October. Clover answered the knock at the door, still in her dressing-gown, rubbing her eyes after a late night with a lab report. Leaning against the corridor wall were two broad, flat crates for which she was being asked to sign. She scribbled her name and called for Emma. Together they attacked the crates with hammers, screwdrivers, pliers and kitchen knives, having to contain their excitement to avoid damaging what they knew the contents of the crates to be: two Jason Englefields, both painted before his emigration to America and both listed by FFA as sold. One was now described as 'Recovered', the other simply as 'Found' in a letter received the same morning by Mrs Plumber who rang Charles who rang Clover.

'We've won,' he said, 'but not quite. The paintings are tokens of FFA's willingness to negotiate.' The two works had been surrendered, he had no doubt, because they were to hand, that is, somewhere in London. Perhaps they had never been sent to America at all. The rest, those 'Sold' or stashed in Canadian or European warehouses and sitting-rooms, would take longer to retrieve, to make mysteriously reappear.

'We must give them the chance to rationalize this legerdemain.'

Felix and George were making stipulations to gain time. They were also attempting to save face before the world, Charles Bevan, the Englefields and each other. What they wanted, of course, was a compromise.

Charles stuck by his sixty-day ultimatum, but on the crux of their compromise he procrastinated. He wanted first to speak to Clover. The compromise was a touchy business, one with which he thought they must eventually comply, but which would require the utmost tact since it involved Jason himself.

'They want restoration or re-creation of the van Zuptens' *Three Virtues*.'

'Oh eek. Jason will spit.'

'He'll also chafe when he learns that they are demanding he return the rights to five Englefields – of their choosing.'

'Absolutely no.'

'Dear Clover, the recovery of twenty paintings is hardly a pyrrhic victory. My advice is that we allow them to capitulate with grace.'

'Well, I'll ring Jason.'

As she expected, his first response was a ferocious negative decked out in the sort of abuses which only high moral natures can muster. She gave up but rang again.

'Another flea in my ear,' she reported to Charles. But she knew Jason would eventually co-operate because a compromise meant that Eleanor's money would no longer be involved. Of course he was angrier with her than he had ever been. He sensed a conspiracy but with whom? With whom do the dead conspire?

Clover rang her father twice a day, every day for a week. On the eighth day, between clenched teeth, he gave himself up to compromise with *his* stipulation attached like a limpet to the pact.

'*Four* paintings, understand, *four*. And I will not start work on *The Three Virtues* until all twenty-one paintings are in our possession.'

FFA agreed upon condition that they not be liable for shipping costs in America. Clearly, arrangements for sending the paintings back to London were too far advanced for FFA to U-turn to Hurricane. Clover was to receive the lot, and there, hopefully, to the grudging satisfaction of all, the case of Englefield v. Facer Fine Arts would end.

twenty-eight

By Clover's nineteenth birthday ten paintings had been stored south of the river, three were promised for next year, and three were hanging in her sitting-room. The mutilated *Three Virtues* was *en route* to Utah. On the morning of her celebratory lunch with Charles, she went into the sitting-room to look at the paintings. Slowly she inspected each one.

'After all,' she said to herself, 'they are not too bad.'

She went to her bedroom, took something from a drawer and slipped it into her handbag. She put on her coat and scarf and a pair of yellow gloves with pink buttons at the wrist. The day was cold and the fog was threatening to freeze. She kissed Molly, admonished Fausta and looked in on Emma who was in bed with her boy-friend.

'Goodbye, darling Em,' she said. Emma didn't hear.

Clover closed the door softly, went down the two flights of stairs and walked to Gloucester Road. She took a tube to the restaurant which was not far from Lincoln's Inn Fields where Charles was spending the afternoon. He was reading the paper over his half-lenses as Clover arrived ten minutes late. He stood up in his nice new suit, wished her happy birthday, and kissed her.

'Thank you.' She sat down, her cheeks tingling from the cold, and unwrapped her scarf. 'I'm nineteen,' she said.

'So I hear. This is for you.' He handed her a piece of paper rolled up like a diploma and tied with brown string.

'A drawing?'

He nodded.

'Yours?'

'I wish it were a Matisse.'

'I'd rather have yours.'

He waved a dismissive hand and folded the paper. 'Well, let's hear it. The news, the gossip. Haven't seen you for ten days. Why aren't you giving a party?'

'I think I'd have had a party if I were lonely or dissatisfied and wanted to jump myself up. I'm neither of those things just now. Anyway, Fausta has been exceedingly naughty and Emma permed her hair, and I got an A minus on that paper thanks to you, and the woman upstairs *is* having an affair with the electrician and – what would you like for lunch besides lots of Côtes de Beaune?'

When they had finished she asked if she might return with him to his office.

'I've never been to your office.'

'Then why don't you come? It's not the grand affair it once was. And the coffee's foul. But Mrs Plumber will be thrilled.'

'Mrs Plumber is secretly fond of you.'

'All agnostics are. Shall we go?'

He gave her his arm beneath the dripping trees. They made their way carefully along the slippery pavement, shivering, supporting each other. In her flat shoes they were exactly the same height.

'Oh!' She stopped him suddenly and slapped her forehead. 'I forgot to tell you the funniest thing of all.'

'Well?'

'FFA approached Jason – with caution – and asked if he'd be interested in a London show next October.'

When he had stopped laughing and recovered himself they went on.

'Jason was so incensed he actually sprang for a telegram.'

'Saying?'

'NEVER.'

'Bravo.' He opened the door to Crouch and Fielding. 'But can't he be persuaded to join another gallery? The new genius is expected quite soon, isn't it? They'll need money.'

'Oh Charles,' she pushed him gently, 'babies aren't expensive. You get them for nothing. It's children who cost money. I expect he'll sell a couple of those paintings – ones he never cared too much about. Otherwise I don't know what he'll do. He won't teach and he won't have anything to do with dealers. I said to him you can't stay in Utah for ever, can you, and he said why not. I said what about London or New York and he said there was no going back. Absolutely. He said they were false centres and that now wherever *he* was was the centre. So I said then it doesn't matter where that centre is, does it.'

'The eminently practical Miss Englefield.'

'Well, one should be what one is and Jason is a painter. Hello, Mrs Plumber.'

She took the secretary's dry, veiny hand with its shiny, crinkled surface. She smiled into the eyes at once sharp and sympathetic, the thin, unwavering mouth, the hair with its aura of pink rinse, the silk scarf which matched the hair, the brooch which held in place the scarf.

'My warmest congratulations on your nineteenth birthday.'

'How did you know?'

'Some things one does not forget, my dear.'

'Any messages, Mrs Plumber? Anything I haven't done?'

'Nothing of any importance, Mr Bevan.'

'Then may I stay a bit?' Clover asked. 'Shall we have a game?' She knew the backgammon set was never far away.

He took her coat and scarf. She sat down opposite him and began arranging the pieces like the seasoned professional she was. She sent the die spinning against the wall of Charles's venerable board. 'My go.'

She took the first game in concentrated silence. Mrs Plumber brought coffee, frowned indulgently at their nursery pursuits and left. Clover held her mug in both hands, warming them in the heat of the metallic-tasting brew with its scummy rainbow surface.

'I want to show you something, Charles.' She was very solemn. 'What I want to show you – ' She opened her handbag and removed an envelope from which she took a coloured postcard of the Blue Mosque, its sunset backdrop rendered in improbable tints of pink, orange and cerise. Birds of indeterminate species hovered about its minarets while a purple Marmara wound round to the right. 'To show you – ' she hesitated, looking at the card, then thrust it across the desk at him, 'is *this*.'

She held the thing so near his half-lenses that he had to push her hand gently away in order to focus on it.

'This?' he said, almost stupidly.

'Take it,' she urged.

He stared at it, flipped it over, peered again at the Blue Mosque, then read in bewilderment the date, 1973, his Chester Street address, the salutation, the message and the signature, which was Simon Delamere's. He read something about a cruise, a private joke the arcane significance of which he could not now recall, then references to a secret restaurant and a lobster.

'Remember?' she pressed him. 'You're not at a loss for words are you?'

'Yes.'

She kept quiet while he continued to scrutinize the card.

'Remember?'

'But – didn't I give this to you?' How uncharacteristically dim he was being.

'I was nine years old. You came to my party. The lights went out and you gave me champagne and I got a bit drunk and you taught me to play backgammon and I wanted never, never to stop and Jason was angry at both of us because I wouldn't go to bed and you gave me this card and promised to take me to Constantinople and then I didn't see you for years but I kept the card because I loved it so much and I wanted to go to Constantinople. It was the first place I ever wanted to go. I thought about you taking me there and how jolly it would be eating at this secret place and all. And when we went to America I put the card in a box of special things from all my life and left it with Em along with Molly, and when I came back to England I asked her for the box, and there it was with your card still inside, only because of all the excitement and the money and the lawsuit and moving and whatever, I didn't open the box until last week. It was then I found the card and remembered why I'd kept it. Anyway, now I'm showing it to you.' Her mouth snapped shut as though it would never open again until he spoke to her.

He started to say something then changed his mind. 'You're proposing a trip to Constantinople?' he asked gently.

'Good guesser.' She began setting up the board again. 'What do you think, Charles?'

'I think it's a lovely idea.'

'But as a reality?'

'I'm almost frightened to say.'

'Oh you can't be frightened of me!'

'Well I am. You must – help me a little. I'm bounding very far ahead of myself. I'm guessing like mad and it's terrifying me.'

She stood up and came round to his side of the desk. She put both hands on his shoulders and stared at him. Abruptly, she sat on his lap.

'Will you come with me?' She took his hand.

He kissed hers. 'How could I not?'

'And when we come back to England will you stay with me? I want you to, Charles. I mean I'd like you to. Very much. Is that what you guessed?'

'In a mad moment.'

'It's not mad. It's a beautiful, sensible thing.'

'It is very beautiful, but – '

'Please don't address me as my dear girl and make fatuous, undermining advice.' She stood up.

'You felt wonderful,' he smiled ruefully. 'Won't you come back and sit on my knee?'

She walked away, her back to him.

'Not until you're sensible.'

'Forgive me. I'm very slow.'

'I know it.'

'I'm old, Clover.'

'You're not.' She turned round. 'Well, maybe you are, but only a bit. Anyway, what does it matter? You're what I want.'

'But not who.'

'What implies much more than who.'

'All right. But you're very young. You've had a difficult life. You've barely had a youth.'

'I haven't had *a* youth, I've had *my* youth.'

'You talk as if it were a *fait accompli*. There's still a good deal to come. Think of it, Clover. There are bound to be boys – excuse me, young men.'

'Oh how corny. I can't believe you'd ever say anything so corny. You know I don't care much for boys. It's not their fault but I can't help it. I suppose I might run off, in a fit of vanity or lust. But it couldn't last. I know myself. I'd miss you too much.'

'You look so appealing I'm beginning to feel like a brute.'

'You couldn't be a brute, but you are resisting, damn you. Resisting like a lawyer.'

'You're still my client. It's my duty to protect your interests.'

'Then I dismiss you. You are no longer in my employ. Now can we talk like humans?'

'Clover, I am something more than a half-wit. I understand you want and need the security of a family.'

'That's true.'

'Before you do anything rash, please consider that a family, indeed families, already exist for you. There's your mother and your two half-sisters.'

'But I don't need a mother, Charles, I have you. Besides, my mother didn't want me. And only silly people run after someone who doesn't want them.'

'She may want you now.'

'I don't make a secret of my address.'

Charles pushed stoically on against his own inner current.

'There's your aunt, Jason's sister, your grandparents, Jason himself.'

'You don't understand. I don't want to go back, I want to go forward. I don't want old families, I want new ones. The old ones are a mess.'

'All families are messes.'

'OK,' she shouted, 'I want a new mess!'

Charles stood up, walked around his desk, removed his spectacles, massaged the bridge of his nose, sat down again, put on his spectacles, took them off.

'Admit it, Charles, you're losing.'

'Perhaps.' Nevertheless he played his last card.

'I can't take your money.'

'It's not my money. It's *our* money. Which two other people in the world would Eleanor have wanted to share it? Why must you dig up these dead moralisms? Don't you know that they're extinct like smallpox and the dodo bird? Oh,' she clenched her fists in frustration, 'you're a dodo!'

'Better a dodo than a base self-seeker,' was his immediate response.

Suddenly she broke down, fell completely apart. He sat paralysed, watching her distress. Face in her hands, she stood rigid except for her heaving shoulders. She was pathetic, yet she was too strong to pity.

'Don't you like me, Charles?' she sobbed.

'I adore you. I've worshipped you since the night I gave you that postcard.'

'Oh postcard!' She rushed to the desk, tore the picture into tiny pieces and flung the fragments in his face.

'I don't want you to worship me,' she cried. 'What does worship mean except that you're afraid to come too near? I don't want to be a figure in your mental landscape. I want you to come close and like me. Why can't we simply like each other?'

'I thought that's what we did do.'

'Oh Charles,' she moaned, 'I tried to help you. Won't you help me? You're not trying at all. It's not fair!'

He was trying. He was exerting every effort to keep from crying too.

'Darling Clover,' he held the desk to steady himself, 'I like you better than I've liked any human creature except Eleanor.'

She stopped crying. 'I'm glad.'

Charles played absently with the pieces on the board and the bits of torn postcard. 'If this were the end of a nineteenth-century novel, you would now walk to the door, turn and look at me – your last look – walk through the door, close it and disappear from my life. And I would sit here, principles all intact.'

'But I won't leave. I felt like it a moment ago, but I won't.'

'I wouldn't let you,' Charles said.

Clover ran to his chair, fell on her knees and threw her arms around his waist, pressing her face against his heart.

'Why shouldn't we?' she said. 'Why shouldn't we have everything we want for a while? It'll be snatched away soon enough or we'll wreck it ourselves.'

'You *have* learned a lot.'

'Just take it all while it's going, Charles. Take me.' She looked up at him.

'But I feel unworthy. I can't possibly reciprocate the enormity of your gift. Besides, think what a blackguard I'd be depriving the World Wildlife Fund.'

'But you are worthy, you've only forgotten. I can make you remember. I'm Clover and I can. I'll look after you, Charles, and you'll look after me. We want looking after, we're only human. Why shouldn't we do these things for each other? What's to prevent anymore? Oh Charles, why shouldn't a good woman rescue a good man?'

He touched the wisps of hair around her face, making them stand straight up. 'Why not?' he said, 'why not?'

'Then you give over. You've lost.'

'My heart, my case, everything. Cloverfield, I can't resist you. Daughter takes all.'

She rubbed her head against his jacket, so that her hair became a lopsided cloud. She had, for the moment, nothing to say. He had, for the moment, nothing to think. He therefore took courage and asked if she would now consent to return her thighs and bottom to his aching lap. It had been missing them badly. She climbed up on him, her arms encircling him like an ivory necklace. She sat exhausted, recovering, letting herself be held. Winning a case was hard, the effort involved tremendous.

'I'm sorry I can't give you my virginity.'

He had an impulse to laugh at her old-fashioned notion but didn't.

'You don't mind too much, do you? I mean, it would be absurd anyway at my age. You wouldn't want a stupid little girl.'

'Certainly not. In fact, I'll benefit from the fruits of your experience. It's been a while for me I don't mind telling you. Darling Clover, I haven't had much fun.'

'Oh I'm very good about fun.'

'Yes. You can – um – instruct me.' He flushed under her kisses.

Suddenly, she drew back, worried, the corners of her mouth a little depressed.

'Have I said something tactless?' she asked him. 'Have I been blundering about in my happiness, not thinking? Charles, have I been a brute?'

'I don't know what you mean.'

'Are you sensitive about Felix?'

'I understand he's rather a hard act to follow.'

'I'll tell you whatever you want to know. Do you want to know?'

Charles confessed to feeling like someone alternately knocked out and revived ten times within the past hour.

'You never asked me about him.'

'It was none of my affair.'

'You are discreet. I'll bet there are a thousand things you'll just never tell me.'

'Because I will have forgotten them. Perhaps we should make a pact. For a while we won't speak of Felix, and after a while I'll tell you all the stories you wish to know.'

'Felix is in those stories, isn't he? Damn, I've broken the pact already. Oh dear, I'm so rash and you're so reasonable.'

'Anthea wouldn't agree.'

'Anthea!' she gasped. 'My God, I forgot all about Anthea. What shall we do with Anthea? Charles, you're about to be contended for by two women.'

'Isn't it extraordinary?'

'She'll never forgive you.'

'She won't.'

'I can't bear it. She'll suffer. She'll feel so injured, so rejected, so *old*.'

'She might not suffer too much. Divorce, though, is out of the question. Brighton would be an insufficient distraction.'

'But money wouldn't?'

'No.'

'Then why not just buy Anthea a lot of presents and hope for the best? She could go to Switzerland and have a face-lift and maybe marry a banker.'

'Now, now.' He chuckled and kissed her hand. 'You really are interesting, quite a spectacle. And I'll be able to watch it all.'

'You talk as if I were going to be alone on the stage.'

'You won't be alone, my Clover. I'll be there but a bit in the background. Not even you can uproot a tree like me.'

'But you can be whatever you want — a tree, a lawyer, an artist, a husband, a father, a brother, a mother, a scholar — God knows I'll need help at Oxford.'

'You're very grand sometimes.'

'It's because I'm simple really.'

Charles was beginning to feel more confident of not being knocked out and revived within the next few minutes. 'Now are there any further obstacles to be cleared from the road of life before we can travel it together?'

'Well, I was hoping you wouldn't mind Em being around for a while. She has no money and nowhere to live.'

'Of course. Em must be looked after. Good God, not only will I be contended for by two women. I shall be cohabiting with two women!'

'And Molly and Fausta and Violet and all the fish! Oh Charles, won't it be fun? Aren't you glad?'

He thought of what everyone would say – Anthea, Jason, the Bevans, the Blacks, the Facers, Felix, his old friends, his clients, his ex-clients, Mrs Plumber, even; what London, the whole, vile world would say. This would confirm it, every suspicion, every malicious rumour, every bit of ill-will floating loose and searching, like the cuckoo, for somewhere to nest. They'd fit every piece together: a motherless nineteen-year-old girl and a second cousin into the bargain, a dead client's money, an abandoned wife, a trove of paintings. He heard them say it all: jetting to Constantinople, drinking her money away, stealing from her father and then the inevitable – Charles Bevan in league all along with Facer Fine Arts. What further evidence need be summoned to corroborate his base self-seeking? None. Guilty as long ago charged. Then he thought of the room in the Perth Hotel, the brown envelopes, the dinners at Halford Road, the walks home past the cemetery and the coal yards, the colour of the light when he woke at eleven am, the steadiers, the afternoons stretched out on an empty, unmade bed. He thought of Clover's company, permanently available, Clover's presence, lingering even in her absence, Clover's kitchen, Clover's bed, the ivory necklace of Clover's arms. Glad? Glad?

' . . . and if our first child is a girl do you mind if we call her Eleanor? No, of course you don't. Do you mind if we have a child pretty much straightaway? I know it's a bit mad with my going to university, but we can do it. Why not? I suppose I want everything at once, don't I? I suppose we'll just squander the money. Oh well. Do you mind? Charles, you're not listening. Charles, you're upset. I haven't been a brute again, have I?'

'No, no. I'm just glad.'

'Really? I haven't bullied you too much?'

'So much that I'll need a holiday to recover.'

'Constantinople?'

'I refuse to go anywhere else. When do we leave?'

'When we've finished our game.'

She rearranged the board, picking out bits of the Blue Mosque, the birds and the Sea of Marmara.

'I wonder how many games of backgammon we'll play before we die,' she mused, tapping the sole of his foot with her toe.

There was a knock at the door. Mrs Plumber looked cautiously in.

'Still at it?' she asked.

'He's losing,' Clover reported.

'Very sportingly.'

'Mr Bevan was always a good sport,' said Mrs Plumber, collecting their mugs which were three-quarters full and stone-cold.

'Oh Mrs Plumber, my dear.' Charles stopped her before she reached the door. 'I shan't be in on Tuesday.'

'Oh?'

She was burning to know and he was burning to tell her.

'I'm running away.'

'Away?'

'Mmmmm. Very far.'

'For good?'

'Oh no, we have to be back in time for a French exam.'

'Ah, you're going to Paris.'

'No. Constantinople.'

'Excuse me, Mr Bevan. Isn't it now – Istanbul?'

'What's in a name, Mrs Plumber?'

'Not a lot.' She hesitated. 'You'll send me a postcard, won't you?'

twenty-nine

The grey automobile turned into the drive and stopped at the entrance to the museum. Clover noticed it immediately she stepped from the revolving doors. It was a lovely evening, a beautiful car. A dark-haired woman was in the driver's seat. From where Clover stood, waiting for the others, she could make out no particulars of the woman's appearance. But she discerned the aura of money and fuss – from the irritated tilt of the head and the dissatisfied curve of the arm to the hand that rested impatiently on the wheel. Unmistakable.

Clover had had quite enough of money and fuss for one day. One day of the year was enough, one evening enough of that day. Charles was loving it, of course, which was why she waited on the top step of the museum, shifting her weight from one foot to another to ease the pain in her back. He was talking to an old friend, someone he had not seen in years. She did not begrudge him his talk and his drink. Not that life in Oxford lacked opportunities for talk. Charles was simply a Londoner and he liked coming back. Moreover, they did not come back very often. Train fares were expensive. So was petrol. So were rents. They had had to give up the house in Boar's Hill.

Emma appeared, dragged by Fausta who had been entrusted to the guard and who had behaved very badly. Emma's other hand grasped that of a small child who, like Fausta, stretched excitedly, determinedly, unsteadily towards Clover. She held out her arms to the child, lifted it, said Mummy couldn't just now, oh she couldn't, Ellie was such a big girl and Mummy's back was hurting so. She put the child carefully down. The child began to cry and Fausta to bark in sympathy.

'Where *is* Charles?' Clover turned in exasperation to Emma. 'Go fetch him, Em, do you mind? I'll get the car.'

Clover went slowly down the steps, Fausta on one hand, Ellie on the other, each pulling in opposite directions and forcing her to take the steps like a child herself. She picked her way among the students who sat in groups eating ice-lollies, and watching the woman in the car and what appeared to be the argument she was having with the man beside her. Other automobiles arrived, people alighted, the automobiles pulled away. The opening of British Painting 1960–1980 had attracted a large crowd. The Bevans had come and left early, at Clover's request. She wanted to see her father's four paintings, particularly *The Three Virtues*, see them in peace, look at a few others and go away. She wanted to represent her father who had refused to come. To see the paintings was to see her father.

Her back hurt, her legs hurt, and Charles was still talking. She knew he wanted to stay. Perhaps Emma wanted to stay too. Emma was a great one for fuss and glamour. Perhaps she should have told them to stay. She could go back to Emma's flat with Ellie and Fausta. She decided she would tell them to stay. She would be quite happy to put her feet up and read her novel. Despite the demands of her daughter and her dog, she made her way to the bottom of the steps and nearer the car. It had not moved by the time she reached the drive. The woman continued to argue with the man who was in late middle age, quite bald and wore spectacles. Clover was very tired. So tired she didn't hear Charles and Emma calling her name until they were beside her.

'Sorry, my love, I ran into – ' He lifted Ellie in his arms and kissed her and said all the things she was accustomed to hear from her father who was the soul of patience and the soul of nonsense. Emma relieved Clover of the frenetic Fausta. The car door opened and the man got out. He was tall and well-dressed. His face was deeply lined. Unless one already knew him, one might hesitate to approach him.

'Why don't you stay?' Clover said abruptly, her eyes following the man as he closed the door and waited for the car to pull away before crossing to the steps.

'Don't be silly, darling, I've had quite enough. I'd much rather go back with you and Ellie. Emma might stay. Would you like to stay, Emma?' They discussed Emma's staying.

Clover moved away from them towards the man in spectacles who was moving towards her. She smiled at him, a smile that came naturally and that she could not stop if she had wanted to. Felix's eyes were bright and blue behind his thick lenses. They looked into hers and would not look away. Clover and Felix stopped within a yard of each other. Behind them, Charles and Emma continued to deliberate over Ellie and Fausta. Clover took a step forward. She held out her hand to him like a French girl.

'Well.' He took her hand but remained where he was, as though there were a narrow but infinitely deep and unbridgeable chasm between them. His hand felt dead. Warm but dead. His eyes were all of him that moved. They scanned her hair, now very much darker and tied simply back with a ribbon, the finer bits curling out around her face; her loose print dress with the smocking that concealed her breasts, and the sleeves pulled back to the elbows in the warm June evening; her white arms and hands with their flattened, calloused tips; her ring, her only piece of jewellery; her bare legs and her long, thin feet in pink shoes; her belly, perfectly round and just beginning to protrude under the loose dress she wore nearly every day.

'Felix,' she said, smiling her fixed but unforced smile. How could she not smile? Even at those eyes alternately kind and cold, even at the deep creases which gave away his 2013 years, even at the yellowed teeth, the definite twitch at the lips, the harsh vertical lines above those lips.

'You've come with your entourage,' he said.

'My family. You've come – '

'With my chauffeuse. But she has left.'

'She'll come back.'

'Probably. Will I like the show?'

'Not much.'

'No matter. I haven't come for the show.'

'Why have you come?'

'To show up.'

'Oh.'

His fingers rubbed hers lightly, a corpse revived. Silence was suddenly awkward.

'You are biologizing I hear.'

She hesitated. 'I got a first.'

'Of course you did.'

'Now I'm going on.'

He glanced at her belly. 'So I see.'

The light was fading. The rosy reflections in the river turned to grey like the buildings beyond. Still, there was a rare clarity in the air. She saw with heightened distinction the stationary clouds, the signs on the opposite side of the river, a train that slid noiselessly between the buildings.

The lamps came on along the Embankment. Felix raised her hand as though to kiss it. But to bring it all the way to his lips would have required taking another step towards her. It would have meant crossing that narrow and deep chasm which had so mysteriously opened by the steps of the museum. He lowered her hand, although he held it still, as if to take that one step were too difficult or too dangerous and demanded an energy he could not muster.

He frowned. From the frown sprang a hundred little creases that cross-hatched his high forehead.

'You're tired,' he said.

She saw him straining to study her face. The light was fading like the sight in his blue eyes.

291

'I am – a little.' She sensed Charles, Emma, Ellie and Fausta approaching from behind.

She let go of his hand. Perhaps he let go of hers, she couldn't tell. She was so tired. She couldn't tell really. Still she smiled, her eyes in his until the last moment when he looked away.

'You'd better go. Go,' he said. 'It's getting dark.'

A NOTE ON THE AUTHOR

Mary Flanagan was born and grew up in New Hampshire. She was educated by the Sisters of Mercy, attended the local High School and received a degree in History of Art from Brandeis University after which she spent three years in New York working for publishers. In 1969, following a year in Morocco, she emigrated to England where she has lived ever since, residing mainly in London but spending long periods in Sussex and Scotland, as well as making frequent returns to New York. She began writing fiction at the age of thirty-six, and in 1985 published a collection of short stories, *Bad Girls*, which has been translated into several languages. Mary Flanagan has also written screenplays and reviews. *Trust* is her first novel.

PANTHEON MODERN WRITERS ORIGINALS

THE VICE CONSUL

by Marguerite Duras, translated from the French by Eileen Ellenbogen

The first American edition ever of the "masterful novel" (*Chicago Tribune*) that Duras considers her best—a tale of passion and desperation set in India and Southeast Asia.
0-394-75026-8 paper, $6.95

MAPS

by Nuruddin Farah

The unforgettable story of one man's coming of age in the turmoil of modern Africa, by "one of the finest contemporary African writers" (Salman Rushdie).
0-394-75548-0 paper, $7.95

DREAMING JUNGLES

by Michel Rio, translated from the French by William Carlson

"A subtle philosophical excursion embodied in a story of travel and adventure...it succeeds extremely well."—*New York Times Book Review*
0-394-75035-7 paper, $6.95

BURNING PATIENCE

by Antonio Skármeta, translated from the Spanish by Katherine Silver

A charming story about the friendship that develops between Pablo Neruda, Latin America's greatest poet, and the postman who stops to receive his advice about love.

"The mix of the fictional and the real is masterful, and...gives the book its special appeal and brilliance."—*Christian Science Monitor*
0-394-75033-0 paper, $7.95

YOU CAN'T GET LOST IN CAPE TOWN

by Zoë Wicomb

A "superb first collection" (*New York Times Book Review*) of stories about a young black woman's upbringing in South Africa.
0-394-75309-7 paper, $6.95

THE SHOOTING GALLERY

by Yūko Tsushima, compiled and translated from the Japanese by Geraldine Harcourt

Eight stories about modern Japanese women by "a subtle, surprising, elegant writer who courageously tells unexpected truths."—Margaret Drabble
0-394-75743-2 paper, $7.95

NELLY'S VERSION

by Eva Figes

An ingenious thriller of identity by the author of *Waking* and *The Seven Ages*.

"A taunting, captivating novel."—*Times Literary Supplement*
0-679-72035-9 paper, $8.95

Ask at your local bookstore for other Pantheon Modern Writers titles